CAGED: LOVE AND TREACHERY ON THE HIGH SEAS

BAAL'S HEART
BOOK ONE

BEY DECKARD

BEY
BDB DECKARD
BOOKS

CONTENTS

A big thank you to M for helping to make this happen, to S for being so awesome, and to my muse for lighting my imagination on fire.

CONTENT WARNINGS

abuse, murder, dubcon, and a lot of rough sex and general pirate shenanigans.

SOUNDTRACK

https://geni.us/CagedOST

PORTSMOUTH

*The cure for anything is salt water: sweat, tears or
the sea.*

— ISAK DINESEN

J on stood in the shadow of the short wall, hands on hips,
looking down over the steeply piled rocks of the harbour to
the grey-green waters beyond. There weren't many boats
out there, just a few navy frigates near the mouth, some
fishing vessels, and what looked like a small corvette just entering
the harbour.

He frowned; squinting and shading his blue eyes with a pale
hand, Jon saw that the ship wasn't flying a flag.

That's weird.

The wind blew at his dark-brown hair, making the curls dance
around his head as he rubbed his eyes to take a better look. He
narrowed his gaze against the bright, late-afternoon sun; the
black and red corvette was a gorgeous, sleek, three-masted ship.
Jon could see the crew, like scurrying ants, running across the
deck preparing to anchor down. Jon wished again that he had

brought one of the long-sights with him today. He enjoyed watching the boats come in even though the thought of being on one horrified him.

So many people in such a confined space...

The crew of this ship looked to be no more than thirty men, but that was still more than Jon thought he would be able to stomach. As his eyes scanned the approaching vessel, he spotted a lone man standing on the quarterdeck. The tall figure had his arms crossed over his chest; the tails of his long, black coat flapped in the wind behind him as he stood stock-still, supervising the flurry of activity on the deck below.

The captain.

As Jon watched, the man slowly raised his head and looked up at the hill high above the harbour. Though Jon couldn't clearly see the captain's face, he suddenly had the uncomfortable feeling that the man was looking directly at him. Jon's skin prickled with the uneasy thought, and he rubbed his hands over his arms.

He stood with his back to the ancient, crumbling stone wall—dubbed the "first wall" for its dubious role as the first line of defence—and should have been hidden from sight at that distance; there was no way that the man on the ship below could see him.

It isn't possible. You're just imagining things again.

Jon ran a shaky hand through his hair and thought it best to get out of the sun; his head was already starting to pound, and he was beginning to get strange ideas. With a last look over his shoulder at the corvette and the tall, dark man, Jon made his way back up the hill towards the crumbling castle he called home.

T he door of the stable banged shut behind him. Jon leaned against one of the stalls with a hand on his head, his eyes closed. *The headaches are getting worse,* he thought desperately; the debilitating pain was becoming an almost daily thing.

Jon coughed into his hand, a sudden shiver taking him. Taking a few deep breaths and clenching his jaw, he forced himself to stand straight. He had to get back to his room before the brunt of the agony hit him or else his stepfather would find him collapsed in the hallway again; it was not an experience he wanted to repeat.

Just as he was taking an unsteady step, something came hurtling out of the darkness. With a great bound, the brown and black shape flew through the air and crashed into Jon, knocking him flat on his back to the dirty, straw-strewn floor. He yelled out in surprise and pain. Fending off sharp teeth, he struggled against the creature that was attacking him. A large, pink tongue left a wet trail along the side of his face, and he smiled slightly despite the pain in his head.

"All right, all right, Brutus. You got me. Now... enough. Stop it! Arggghh!" He grimaced and shoved at the giant mastiff's chest, trying to dislodge him.

The dog stopped trying to drown Jon in saliva and sat back on its haunches with an almost-human look of concern on its face and let out a low whine.

Jon groaned and rubbed his temple with a trembling hand; the dog's enthusiastic greeting had torn new holes in the decaying fabric of his composure. These surprise attacks were a habit of Brutus's that Jon had been trying to break him of, with little success, since the night he found the huge dog wandering loose on the high road. He sat up slowly and ran his hand over Brutus's coarse brown and black-spotted fur.

"Shh. You're hurting my head," he whispered, wincing.

The dog stopped whining, and its mouth hung open, pink tongue lolling as he stared lovingly at his master.

Jon sighed and shook his head as he used the dog's sturdy frame to help him to his feet. Standing at nearly four and a half feet tall when on all fours, Brutus was one of the largest mastiffs that Jon had ever seen. His colouring was incredibly unusual too; unlike the dark-brown or black mastiffs that were raised at the castle, Brutus was a light caramel brown with strange, dark patches. He was a gorgeous animal and Jon's closest companion.

After patting the stable dust from his fawn-coloured leather pants, man and dog walked slowly past the empty stalls to the small castle entrance used by the stable master and climbed the stairs to the apartment Jon shared with the head of the castle guard.

The rooms of the small apartment were sparsely furnished, and the walls were barren except for the family crest on an old, moth-eaten tapestry that hung over the small breakfast table.

He shuffled through the empty front room to his tiny bedroom in the back, which was barely bigger than the cot shoved against the wall. Just as he was finally laying his head down on the pillow, he heard the door open and the heavy footfalls of his step-father enter the room beyond.

"Jon?" The gruff voice was heavy with irritation. The old soldier's fuse was shorter than ever these days. Despite Jon having no control over his strange malady, he was constantly admonished for shirking his duties.

"I'm here, Reginald," he said, trying to raise his voice.

Brutus lifted his head from his great paws and turned his gaze towards the door just as the portly man crossed the threshold.

When he saw Jon lying on his bed, sickly pale and swallowing against his rising nausea, Reginald let out an exasperated sigh. His dark brows came down over his eyes, and he crossed his arms over his chest.

"You went out when you were supposed to be resting, didn't you? Goddammit, Jon, you're no good to me when you're like this," he said angrily.

Jon pressed his knuckles against his closed eyes, making strange, red and white shapes dance in his vision.

"I thought the sea air would help. It *used* to help. I'm sorry, Reginald. I'll be all right for tomorrow," he said softly, without an ounce of conviction. With a headache this bad, there was little sleep in store for Jon. Without sleeping powders, he would toss and turn, drenched in sweat, and be trapped in nightmares until morning. He wished that he'd thought to go to the old man who mixed medicines for the castle. There was no way he could send his stepfather on his behalf.

The old soldier stared hard at Jon a moment longer.

"What you do *saves lives*, Jon. Don't you ever forget that. I need you to be able to do this," Reginald's deep voice rasped. He frowned when the younger man made no move to answer. Spinning on his heel, the captain of the guard left Jon alone to suffer in misery.

Jon stood on the deck of a ship. The wood beneath his soles felt smooth from years of constantly being polished under leatherlike, bare feet. He looked up. It was night. The moon was almost full above his head, and the stars were a shimmering net across the sky. Jon could hear creaking and the soft splashing of water against the hull. He smiled to himself and stroked his hand over the beautiful wood railing in front of him. When he felt something sticky, Jon raised his hand to his face. His palm was marked with something dark. Something that spiked the cool nighttime air with a metallic tang. Jon recoiled in horror and took a step back as a pale hand came up over the railing. The face that emerged out of the gloom was misshapen... The eyes were milky and the jaw hung open unnaturally. Jon took another step back. He recognized the decaying figure as the man he had most recently interrogated: a dockworker accused of rape and murder. The dead man hissed at him as it climbed up onto the deck. Jon tripped on something behind him and landed with a hard thump on the wet wood. Looking down, he realized he was sitting in a large puddle of blood. The shambling figure came closer as Jon crawled backwards into the pool of cold, viscous liquid. The deck felt like it was at an angle. His terror and nausea came to a head when he realized that the blood was pouring thickly over the side and the ship was being dragged down into a stinking sea of red.

5

Jon woke up and gasped; his breath caught in his throat, and he began to cough loudly, pawing at the phantoms that still lurked in his vision. Brutus was nudging at his arm, whining softly, as Jon tried to clear the bloody images out of his brain. He sat up slowly, his head still screaming in agony. Jon was soaked through; the old linen shirt and shorts he wore to sleep were sodden with sweat. He grimaced, teeth clenched, as a shiver took him. Jon was beginning to fear that something was horribly wrong with him. Another shudder shook his slight frame, and he nearly gagged with a coughing fit that overtook him.

When it finally seemed that the worst had passed, Jon struggled to pull the wet shirt over his head and then threw it in the corner of the room. He lay down and dragged the worn quilt up over his shoulder with a trembling hand.

Brutus kept his chin on the edge of the bed, watching with liquid-dark eyes as Jon struggled through layers of fevered consciousness and tried desperately to reclaim sleep.

Morning came too early. The gulls that flew in circles over the harbour all day were screaming to each other. Though there was no window in Jon's tiny, cell-like room, he could hear them as loudly as if they were right above his head. He groaned and turned onto his back.

The sleep that had finally descended upon him had been fitful at best. Jon was sore in both mind and body as he lay in the murky gloom, trying to find the motivation to get out of bed. Thankfully, it seemed that the worst of the headache was over; maybe his words yesterday hadn't made a liar out of him. Jon thought that maybe after some strong coffee he would be able to make his way to the dungeons. Sighing, he slowly sat up and reached out to pat Brutus's bony head.

Another long day in the dark dungeons interrogating prisoners for all sorts of terrible crimes.

J on had been very young when his beautiful mother was claimed by the weeping plague. His father had died in a fall when he was still nothing but a squalling, pink thing at his mother's breast and as such had no memories of the man that everyone said he resembled. However, he remembered clearly how his mother had smelled of the mint-and-rosewater she bathed in. Her dark-brown hair, the same colour as his own, had been very long and so very soft, tickling his cheeks as they sat in the summer gardens singing childish songs together.

She had been his whole world; even when she was courted and had eventually married the gruff, heavy-set captain of the guards, she had spent all of her spare time with the strange, small, dark-haired boy. The other castle children shunned him for reasons Jon never comprehended, and his new stepfather understood nothing of sensitive souls; so, when she fell ill and quickly passed, Jon was left completely on his own. Out of loneliness, he had taken to standing silently in the corners of rooms just to watch people interact—a soft-fingered touch on an arm, a brow wrinkled in confusion—nothing escaped his eyes.

One time, the frail, pale-skinned boy had been locked in a room overnight because no one had seen him lurking in the shadows. Jon remembered how he had cried but kept from banging on the door for fear that Reginald would think it was all his fault.

The room soon grew pitch-black as night fell, and Jon, utterly terrified, had felt his way across the tiled floor in search of some sort of shelter in the big, echoing space. In the end, he had curled up like a puppy on a hard horsehair chair. He wrapped his thin arms around himself to ward off the cold. This was the only comfort he had. Quietly sobbing, Jon had played his "what if" game to try to lull himself to sleep. The game was simple; it consisted of running through scenarios in his mind and predicting all possible outcomes based on the people he placed in them.

Over the years the game had taken on a life of its own inside Jon's clever brain. It had turned into a keen empathy, and Jon gained a seemingly magical ability to both predict and recreate the behaviour of others; more and more Jon began to feel that he was having visions and not simply using his imagination.

Nearly five years ago, after it became evident that he didn't have the temperament to follow in his stepfather's footsteps, Reginald secured him a spot with the executioners' guild. The head of the guild had already heard of his strange talent, and when Jon arrived in the dungeons that first day, the man had him sit and interrogate each of the thirty-two prisoners that had been locked up that week.

It had been a gruelling exercise to stare into the hollow eyes of prisoners already broken by torture and decide who was guilty and who was simply unlucky. In the end, the head executioner had agreed with his analyses and had let a few souls free. Though Jon's almost uncanny ability to take the perspective of others served him well as an interrogator, he slowly began to feel like he was losing little parts of himself to the horrific task.

Then the nightmares started.

Jon poured a small amount of clean water from the chipped ewer to the mismatched basin and proceeded to splash the cold liquid on his face. He could hear his stepfather in the next room rummaging around; Jon would wait until Reginald had departed before making his way through the common space they shared.

Brutus, a veritable stomach on legs, bumped Jon's elbow with his nose. There would be coffee, bread, and cheese waiting for Jon in the castle kitchen as well as offal and scraps for the dog; if he was lucky, he might even be able to beg an apple from the cook.

Feeling surprisingly well, Jon took the steps down two at a time. Maybe if he finished his tasks early enough, he'd be able to steal away a bit early to take a closer look at that sleek warship and allow himself to daydream for just a little while about leaving all this dreariness behind.

As Jon walked down the steep, narrow steps to the dungeons, one hand sliding along the damp stone wall, he was dismayed to hear Reginald's voice rising up through the dank air from the large open room below. He sighed, straightened his shoulders, and swallowed down the last of the warm, nutty-tasting bread.

This didn't bode well for him.

Reginald usually shunned the dungeons although they (and the executioners' guild in general) were part of his jurisdiction. Jon thought that perhaps his stoic stepfather stayed away because he was a tiny bit afraid of the men who worked so far underground; he smiled to himself despite the apprehension he felt.

When Jon rounded the last bend, he was greeted by the sight of Reginald's broad back. His dark hands were clasped behind him, as he spoke brusquely to the fat torturer everyone called "Flayer." Jon stepped forward lightly and cleared his throat as his gaze darted to the side to avoid accidental eye contact.

"Reginald?" he said quietly.

The head of the castle guard turned towards him with a broad, gap-toothed smile on his round face.

"Son," he said.

Son? What in hells?

"I need you to follow me. I've told, uh… Flayer to advise the rest of your colleagues that you'll be working up top with me for the rest of the week," said Reginald with a smile.

Interesting.

It wasn't often that Reginald called in a favour. The old soldier was most likely stuck in a bind that only Jon's expertise and talent could get him out of.

Reginald patted Jon on the shoulder somewhat awkwardly before turning to the spiralling staircase. He looked back, his expression fading quickly from fatherly to annoyed, as he waited for his stepson to follow him.

Jon sighed.

. . .

T he sun was blinding him again. He held a hand up over his eyes and frowned at Reginald's words.

"You want me to what?" he asked, surprised.

"I want you to visit the *Rose Garden* and observe," the older man said gruffly, looking somewhere over Jon's left shoulder as he fidgeted with the cuff of his shirt.

"You want me to go to a brothel and observe? What am I observing, Reginald?" Jon's voice came out a little louder than he had aimed for.

The old soldier glanced at his stepson with a scowl on his face.

"There's always the odd murder of a working girl in that neighbourhood. Usually, they're badly bruised, cut up, and dumped in the river. However, this morning they found one with just her heart missing. She was... displayed in one of the rooms. I have a bad feeling about this. I want you to get a sense of the customers. Take a look around. I want to nip this in the bud. Do you understand?" Reginald growled his words.

Jon hitched his shoulders slightly.

Brothels were crowded. There were naked women. He groaned inwardly.

"Why can't you do this yourself?" he asked and looked down at his clenched fists.

"Because I am asking *you* to do it." The older man flared his nostrils and looked piercingly at Jon as if daring him to refuse. "Now get over there. Use your magic. Do whatever you do... but find *something*. I'm counting on you." With that, Reginald frowned, nodded once to dismiss Jon, and turned to leave.

Jon watched with dismay as Reginald walked heavily away. A slow, burning pit of anxiety was already churning in his stomach.

"How long do I stay?" he yelled out to the back of Reginald's head, but the wind grabbed his words and whipped them away. He stood there awkwardly for a few moments longer and then pulled his grey jacket close around him before slowly making his way down the narrow road to town.

J on stood looking up at the painted, wooden sign for nearly ten minutes. It featured a crudely drawn, naked woman on all fours with a rose growing out of her rear.

Charming.

He could see that the sign had been repainted a few times; the brothel was one of the oldest in the small town of Portsmouth. Steeling himself, he rehearsed the prepared words under his breath, "Hello, my name is Jon. I am here on behalf of the City Guard. I have come about a murder." He took a step up onto the dilapidated porch just as the front door burst open with a loud bang.

A giggling, half-naked woman ran out and crashed into Jon, knocking him into one of the beams that held up the second-floor balcony. She paused, round-eyed, and gasped.

"Oh, I am sorry!" she said, her voice high and girlish. It seemed like she would reach out to help steady Jon when a bearlike man wearing only a pair of stained shorts ran out the door and quickly smacked the girl loudly on her behind. She squealed in surprise and laughed. Running away swiftly on nimble feet, she went back in through the front door with the staggering, hairy man following close behind.

Jon was left alone on the porch again in a daze, a tiny pulse of pain starting right behind his eyes.

Great.

Jon took another deep breath of air redolent of fish, rotting vegetables, and salt, as he stepped through the threshold to the world of debauchery and vice beyond.

2

THE ROSE GARDEN

T he first thing Jon noticed was just how warm it was in the brothel. The air was moist like a hot, perfumed breath. Jon felt slightly ill from the sudden change in temperature and began sweating under his layers.

He looked up and blinked in alarm at the dimly lit scene before him; it seemed everywhere he rested his eyes, breasts peeped back at him. Women of various ages and states of undress leaned suggestively against walls, reclined in plush chairs, or sat on the knees of pawing patrons. From the room to his left, he could hear laughter punctuated by soft moans of pleasure.

Jon ducked his head and coughed into a fist, unsure of how he'd be able to put one foot in front of the other; he felt frozen in place by red-faced embarrassment. He hitched his shoulders and risked another look around; the decor was frilly and tawdry and *oh god what is he doing to her to make her make those sounds?* He was on the verge of panic and was about to retreat back out to the porch when a pair of large breasts, bound tightly in a red, satin bodice, appeared before him; a gentle hand grasped his arm.

"First time, son?" asked a voice roughened by age and vice.

He pulled his eyes away from the long line of the woman's

cleavage and looked up into the heavily painted face of the broth-el's madam. She was looking at him kindly, a motherly smile on her rouged mouth; the woman was so close that he could see where the stain was escaping the contours of her lips, little streaks of red in the fjords of her wrinkles.

He licked his own lips nervously and nodded.

"Yes. Wait... no. I'm not here for that. I'm here about murdering a girl," he spluttered, aghast at the words that were coming out of his mouth.

The madam frowned at him, her hand dropping to her side.

"No! Not that... sorry. What I meant was... I'm here about the murder. This morning. Of a girl," he sighed, shrugging his shoulders.

The madam smiled a little sadly.

"You're Reginald's boy, aren't you?" she asked softly.

Jon's brows came down over his storm-blue eyes.

"He's my stepfather," he said, sounding more defensive than he liked.

She reached out again and patted his shoulder.

"Well, I thank you for coming. Your name is Jon, isn't it? You can call me Madam Bellarta," she said kindly.

He smiled crookedly and stared at the tiny mole on the skin of her cheek.

"I would like to see where she was... found," he said, his voice sounding strangely high to his ears. "Was she found here?"

Madam Bellarta frowned slightly but nodded.

"You want to see the room? Why?" she asked.

Jon lifted his shoulders in a tiny shrug.

"To get a sense of what the killer saw. Or his intentions. I'm not sure. It just seems right to go there first. I'm sorry... I don't do this very often. I'm used to interrogating the living, not the dead, but Reginald finds my insight useful. Is that a problem?" he asked, making eye contact for the first time. Jon was instantly trans-ported back to a time when the lipstick she wore had no wrinkles to invade, when her hair was dark without dyes, when her limbs were lithe, before the loose-skinned heaviness of age and misuse. Her catlike eyes, sparkling like emeralds, held his for a moment. He smiled softly at her, and she shook her head.

"Not at all, dear Jon. Follow me," she said and led him towards the wide staircase.

Jon kept his head down, watching his boots and avoiding the curious eyes around him. He could feel the sweat dripping down his spine and wished he had taken off his jacket earlier. Now if he took it off, everyone would see how nervous he was. He trudged up the stairs behind the madam and tried to feel less conspicuous.

Madam Bellarta opened the door to a small bedroom at the back of the house. There was a young, blond woman crouched over a basin of water near the foot of the bed, scrubbing at her crotch with a grey rag.

Jon's head swivelled away, and he closed his eyes. His jaw worked convulsively as he swallowed back his unease, blood hot in his face. He could smell the scent of her sex in the air; the thought brought out a small reaction in the front of his pants. Jon shifted uncomfortably and held his breath while he tried to clear his mind.

"Dee… Can you please do that in another room?" asked Madam Bellarta quietly.

Jon heard shuffling sounds and felt the rush of air and warmth as someone passed him in the doorway. He waited a moment before opening his eyes. Looking around, Jon saw the madam standing a few paces inside the garishly decorated bedroom; he let go of the breath he'd been holding and took the few steps to join her.

"It's been cleaned," he said, turning around slowly, frowning.

Madam Bellarta nodded.

"Of course! We need all the space we can get. I can't afford to have a room not in use," she said simply.

Jon nodded once and rubbed the bridge of his nose; the headache was unfurling like a dark flower of pain inside his head.

"Who found her?" he asked after a moment. He couldn't help

but notice the giant wooden phallus on the night table; Jon averted his eyes and concentrated again on Madam Bellarta's mole.

"One of the girls did... But she came to get me right away. I saw it all," said the older woman, face thoughtful. "You know, Sofia wasn't even supposed to be working last night. There was no reason for her to be here... The girls don't sleep in these rooms. They sleep in the dormitory in the back of the house. I just... don't understand it. Why was she here?" The madam looked around, gesturing to the room with a large-knuckled hand.

Jon walked forwards a few steps and turned around. He pointed to the bed.

"She was found here?" he asked. When the madam nodded, he turned back and ran his eyes carefully over the chipped headboard and the coverlet.

"There was a lot of blood? Reginald said she was missing her heart. Was there anything else? Where is she now?" Jon asked, his questions coming more easily and his tone becoming more businesslike. Gleaning information was what he did for a living, after all.

"Yes... She was lying in a huge puddle of blood. There was so much... Those sheets will have to be dyed black to hide the stains," she replied. "And... She's where all the dead bodies wind up, love. She had no family or friends. She's probably already burned up."

Jon grimaced. He'd hoped to take a look at the body before it went to the crematorium.

"What else can you tell me? Was her heart cut out with a knife? Like, were the cuts straight?" he asked, making slicing motions over the palm of his hand.

The madam put a hand to her own breast, a subconscious gesture.

"Yes. It looked very... clean? Like the way a butcher would cut. Yes, just like that! Like she was butchered." She exhaled hard and then, surprisingly, let out a small laugh. "Although I don't know why anyone would want *that* girl's heart. It would be so hard and bitter." She walked to the side of the bed and smoothed the duvet with a wrinkled hand.

Jon frowned.

"She wasn't liked?" he asked.

Madam Bellarta laughed again and shook her head, her neck wattles swaying with the motion.

"No. Not since I bought her nearly a year ago. She was a foreigner... a mainlander. Never got along with any of the girls here. I had her beat, what... not two weeks ago, for being rude to a customer." She sighed. "A bad investment, though she did come cheap. But no one should ever have to die the way she did."

Jon's dark brows came together, a furrow creasing the skin above his nose.

"You think she was still alive when her heart was cut out?" he asked.

The older woman nodded slowly and twined her fingers together.

"She was on her back, not a mark on her except for the big hole in her chest. Her eyes were so wide... It looked like she was seeing the devil himself. Her hands were gripping the blankets so hard." Madam Bellarta suddenly looked pale underneath the mask of rouge she wore. "We had to... break her fingers to get her off the bed."

Jon felt nauseous. He looked up and saw that there were brownish-red dots on the ceiling.

Probably from the knife? The struggle?

The older woman followed his gaze up and made a harsh sound in the back of her throat.

"Now that's no good for a john to see while lying on his back, is it? One more thing to clean." She turned to Jon, her hands clasped in front of her. "I'm not sure how much help I've been, but I really do have to get back downstairs."

She pursed her lips and stared piercingly at Jon.

"Reginald said you would probably stay a while, and that's fine with me, but don't go bothering the customers. I do have a business to run here," she said, smiling.

Jon nodded quickly. With the pain mounting in his head, he doubted how much longer he'd be able to stay.

The older woman turned to leave but paused, hand on the doorknob. She turned back to Jon and looked appraisingly at him.

"For your troubles… Can I offer you a girl for a half hour?" she asked.

Jon felt his heart skip a beat, and he swallowed hard. He moved his hands, subtly he hoped, over the crotch of his worn, brown pants.

"No. No, thank you. That won't be necessary," he answered stiffly.

"How old are you, Jon?" she asked, her green eyes scrutinizing him.

"Twenty-two," he said and rubbed a hand through his dark curls. "Almost twenty-three."

Madam Bellarta chuckled softly.

"That's awfully old never to have dipped your wick before," she said, shaking her head. When she saw that her comment had frozen Jon to the spot, his eyes staring hard at nothing and his jaw clenched tight, she pressed her lips together and nodded. After a moment, Madam Bellarta patted his arm kindly again.

"Take your time, Jon. I'll be downstairs if you need me," she said quietly.

With a rustling of stiff chiffon and satin, the old madam exited the room, leaving him standing alone with his burning thoughts.

Nearly an hour later, Jon stood with his head against the tattered striped wallpaper of the hallway. He had questioned a few more girls, all with the same result: no one liked Sofia, no one cared that she was gone, and no one knew why she had been at the brothel after hours. His head was pounding in time to his heartbeat; it was time to give up, damn what Reginald would say.

He felt slightly dizzy as he pushed himself away from the wall and made his way to the staircase. From below he could hear the strange sibilant accent of the northern isles; it seemed that a new crop of clients had arrived. A few girls that were not already occupied pushed past Jon on the stairs, and he had to clutch at the railing to keep his balance.

Jon's vision swam for a moment as he hung limply against the worn wood; at this rate, he would be lucky if he made it back to his bed before collapsing. Shakily making his way down the stairs, Jon looked around for the madam. He was about to step into the hallway when suddenly his eyes were captured by the sight of a man sitting in a high wingback chair across the room.

The imposing stranger was wearing black leather pants and a crimson brocade vest over a white shirt, which was undone to the navel. A half-naked girl leaned over him, whispering in his ear while stroking the thatch of hair on his broad, deeply tanned chest. The man's booted feet were planted far apart as he reclined in the chair, staring intently at Jon with eyes hooded by a stark brow. Jon's heart thumped hard in his chest; he felt rooted to the spot by the man's brazen stare. The richly dressed stranger looked to be older than Jon and had an exotic handsomeness; he had high, razor-sharp cheekbones and a thin, well-shaped nose sitting above lips that curved like a gull's wings. His face seemed carved of sandalwood, all angles and stillness, as he held Jon locked in his gaze.

A sudden hand on Jon's shoulder startled him, and he turned, finally able to break eye contact with the intimidating stranger. Madam Bellarta stood next to him, a worried expression on her worn face as she peered into Jon's eyes.

"Are you all right, Jon? You don't look very well," she said with concern.

Jon glanced back at the man in the chair, but the spell had broken; a charming smile now bowed his lips, transforming the calculating look into one of amusement. As Jon watched, the man laughed throatily at something the girl said. His eyes, crinkling at the corners, looked at Jon a moment longer before completely dismissing him.

Jon shook his head and swallowed hard.

"I'm… I just need to lie down," he said weakly.

"Come with me. You can use my bed. You poor boy, you're shaking like a leaf!" said the older woman, gripping Jon by the arm.

He looked over his shoulder as he was led away by Madam Bellarta, but the chair across the room was now empty.

J on lifted his head and blinked sleepily. The room was blessedly dark and smelled like flowers. Jon felt groggy; it took a few panicked moments before he remembered where he was.

The brothel.

Jon's head still throbbed, but he no longer felt sick to his stomach.

How long have I been sleeping?

He sat up and rubbed his face, clearing away the remnants of a deep sleep unbroken by nightmares. Madam Bellarta had kindly mixed a tincture for him before he lay down, and Jon couldn't remember the last time he had slept so soundly. He stretched out his arms, and his shoulders groaned in protest; being so anxious all the time was wreaking further havoc on his health. He smiled sadly to himself and ran a hand through his unruly hair; loneliness and isolation made for terrible mistresses.

Jon could hear footsteps and muffled voices coming from outside the door, and he stood, grabbing his jacket from the foot of the bed. It was time to go; he would find Madam Bellarta and thank her before he left.

After opening the door and stepping into the hallway, Jon came face-to-face with a young man about his age. Naked to the waist, he had his muscular arms draped over the shoulders of a girl to each side of him. The stranger winked at the startled Jon; he was boyishly handsome with smiling eyes the colour of the sea and a sly grin on his full lips. Looking quickly down, Jon saw in shock that the man was rolling one girl's nipple between his finger and thumb; he swallowed and cleared his throat.

"I'm sorry, I was... I'm going this way," Jon stammered and glanced back up.

The young man's face had creased into a wide smile, and he chuckled; Jon frowned.

With his eyes focused on something over Jon's shoulder, the stranger nodded and said a few words in a strange language. Before Jon had a chance to turn, something dark and suffocating came down over his head. Strong arms came around him, and Jon felt his wrists being seized by huge, rough hands. The man holding him seemed a giant; Jon struggled against him, hoping to work himself free of the vicelike grip, but the bag over his head was robbing him of breath. His heart hammered against his ribs as he choked, dizzy with panic, and panted into the material.

A voice that could only belong to the grinning stranger spoke close to his ear, "Aye, mate, if ye stop wigglin', it'll go a lot easier." He spoke the common language accented with the broad vowels and glottal stops of a mainlander. "If ye don't, I'll have to knock ye about a bit. And lovey... We don't want that, do we?"

Jon sagged against the tree trunk that was holding him and nodded weakly. He was feeling lightheaded from the lack of oxygen.

"Please... I can't breathe," he rasped. He heard the man in front of him chuckle as the bag was adjusted at his neck. Cool air touched his lips, and he took in a gulping breath. The giant behind him took a step; Jon was being propelled forwards, his feet clumsy as he stepped awkwardly in the pitch dark.

"Where are you taking me?" he asked, the bag muffling his voice.

"Hush now, poppet. It ain't for me to answer questions," said the mainlander from a few steps ahead.

Jon heard him say something unintelligible, and the girls giggled; the sound of them faded in the distance as he was led around a corner and then down some hard steps. A door creaked, and Jon felt chilled with the sudden wind; they were outside.

As he tried to quell his mounting panic, Jon struggled to understand what was happening to him. His mind reeled, trying to find an answer. Was he being led to his death? Why would anyone want to kidnap him? Their island was a poor one; there was no treasure, no wealth. It just didn't make any sense. Their lord was constantly absent; Jon had seen him only a handful of times in his life, even though he lived in the castle. He had no connection to Lord Barton. Yes, Reginald was the head of the guards, that was true... but that meant nothing in such an insignificant corner of the kingdom.

I'm the son of no one, he thought miserably.

After a few more steps, he said, "I don't have any money!" but there was no response.

As they descended a hill, he tripped and stumbled over rocks in his path, twice nearly twisting his ankle. He could taste the briny, wet smell of the sea at the back of his throat, even through the heavy material. Soon they stopped, and Jon was lifted into what felt like a wooden boat. He was pushed down onto a hard seat and released. His hands flew up to the hood covering his head.

"I wouldn't do that," said the mainlander, sounding very close; though his words were spoken in the same friendly tone he'd been using all along, there was the promise of violence in them.

Jon froze. He then hunched his shoulders in despair and dropped his hands to his lap.

The other man laughed cheerfully.

"Good choice! Now sit pretty, my dove," said Jon's kidnapper.

Jon rocked forward as the boat was pushed off the rocky beach, and he clutched at the splintery bench beneath him. He could hear oars splashing; a gull cried out above them. Jon suddenly felt like he would hyperventilate; it was too much. The motion of the boat was making him nauseous; sour spit pooled in his mouth, and he felt himself suffocating again. In terror, his hands took on a life of their own and grabbed desperately at the bag over his head, pulling it off.

He sucked in the night air and coughed.

"Now why would ye go and do that, lovey?"

Jon whipped his head around. He caught a glimpse of the curved hull of the black and red corvette before something cracked against his skull, making the world flash bright as lightning before Jon felt nothing at all.

3

CAGED

When a sinister person means to be your enemy,
they always start by trying to become your
friend.

— WILLIAM BLAKE

It was dark. Jon felt himself jostled, his head hanging down. Were his eyes open? There was a sickening pain in his left temple. A taste of blood.

Where am I?

Jon tried to hold onto consciousness but slowly sank beneath black water.

[...]

It was still dark. There was something soft beneath Jon's cheek... Yes, he was lying on something soft. The pain in his head was making his stomach churn, and he felt as if he were swaying back and forth. Jon could hear voices.

"—hit him so hard in the head? I recall telling you that he is suffering from a brain ailment."

"Aye, ye did, but he wasn't mindin' me, Da."

Jon listened to the two men speak, one with the rounded accent of the mainlands, and the other with the strange shushing sounds of the islands to the far north. He lifted a hand to his head, and it came away sticky with what could only be blood. The pain was immense, and the swaying feeling was a mounting tide of nausea; when he tried to turn, his head the world spun in darkness.

Suddenly his guts clenched, and he felt the vomit leave his mouth in a burning splash. He coughed weakly and tried to sit up but felt hands on him, holding him in place.

"Shit," said a voice above him.

A wet cloth was roughly swiped across Jon's face. He felt his lips being pried open, and he tried to shake his head.

"Stop movin', silly duck. I'm goin' to get this into ye one way or another."

Callused, dirty fingers breached his mouth, and he gagged. A bitter liquid was poured over his tongue; Jon choked, gasping for breath. He realized that he could see now; he had indeed had his eyes closed. The winking mainlander that had accosted him in the brothel hallway was leaning over Jon with a look of exasperation on his youthful face.

Jon blinked, his vision fuzzy. The man holding him down curled his lip in annoyance and tilted the bottle of liquid to Jon's mouth again.

"Drink, ye bloody arse. I'm tryin' to help ye," said the rough young man.

Jon frowned, but something told him that the words rang with truth; there would be time later to struggle. He opened his mouth and meekly drank down the rest of the bitter potion.

"There ye go, lovey. Ol' Tom will make it all right."

Aren't you the one who hit me?

Jon blinked sleepily; a warm, tingly feeling was spreading

through his body. He felt a hand pat his chest. His eyes were closed again.

[...]

The next time he awoke, it wasn't as dark. He squinted across the room at the pinpoint of brightness with its yellow halo; a candle on a table was casting a flickering light. Jon's mouth was dry and sour, and his eyes felt gritty in their sockets.

When he reached up to touch his temple, his fingers encountered something that felt like a bandage wrapped around his head. He turned onto his back on the narrow cot, steeling himself against the pain, but he was surprised; though his head still hurt, it was a numbed, distant throbbing. Jon took a deep breath and sat up slowly, looking around at his surroundings.

It seemed that Jon was in a sort of cage that was bolted to the wall. It was about three long paces to each side and was made of flat, wide bars in black metal. Looking up, Jon saw that the bars bent over his head close enough that if he reached up when standing he could touch them. The only furnishings in the cage were the narrow cot he was sitting on, a closed chamber pot in the corner, and a small wooden barrel that served as a table; on the table was a big metal cup, beads of perspiration trickling down its sides.

Jon reached out with a hand and took the cold cup in a shaky grip. He saw that it was clear liquid and sniffed it, but it didn't have a scent. Hoping that it was what it seemed, he carefully brought it up to his lips and took a small sip.

Water.

He was thirsty, but since he didn't know whether he'd get more, Jon only took a few mouthfuls before setting it down again on the barrel. The cold water felt good in his mouth and on his lips, but a small fever-shiver took him.

Jon looked down at himself and saw that someone had stripped him of his pants, boots, vest, and jacket, leaving him only wearing his worn cotton shirt and the linen shorts he wore as underthings.

Slowly standing up, he stepped forward to hold onto the bars; he was amazed to see a large, richly decorated room beyond his small prison. The wooden walls shone golden brown in the wavering light of the candle. The floor was covered in beautiful rugs, the likes of which he had never seen before; they were a riot of dark colours and forms, abstract repeating shapes and flowers twining together to make strange patterns that made his head hurt. In the middle of the room, there was a heavy wooden table surrounded by chairs; they were all glossy and dark with gracefully curved legs, and the chair cushions were made of something dark red and velvety looking.

Jon's eyes rested curiously for a moment on the glass-doored shelves filled with more leather-bound books than he had ever seen; his gaze then swept the walls where heavy-framed paintings hung. He could see what looked like a large map covering most of the wall to the left of him; above the map was a large crest with the black silhouette of a roaring lion resting on a field of red.

Suddenly the floor rocked under his feet, startling him, and understanding dawned.

I'm on a ship.

Memories of the sleek black and red corvette came flooding back to him.

Only when Jon heard a small whispering sound, like paper sliding against something, did he realize he wasn't alone. He narrowed his eyes against the candlelight and saw that the dark shape on the other side of the table was a large, low bed; on it, a figure was reclined, reading a book.

Jon's heart faltered at the unexpected sight, and he tightened his grasp on the bars, unsure of what he should do. In numb panic, he moved quietly to sit back down on the cot; it creaked under his weight, and he anxiously held his breath. The figure on the bed turned another page in the book.

After a moment he heard a man's voice, which was flavoured with the softly sibilant accent of the north.

"Go back to sleep, Jon. We have much to converse about in the morning."

Jon sat still, his heart hammering in his chest. He heard another page turn across the room and pressed his lips in a hard line. There would be no answers tonight.

Frowning, he rubbed his head, mindful of the bandage. He doubted he would be able to sleep, but something in that low voice compelled him to try. He lay back down, noticing for the first time that the covers on his small cot were made of bright, rich fabrics. He pulled the sheet over his slight frame and stared hard at the bars in the dim light. The man beyond couldn't be anyone but the captain of the ship, judging by the size of the room and the sumptuous decor.

What does he want with me?

Surprisingly, Jon soon felt his lids grow heavy despite the nervousness and confusion he felt; as he slipped softly between the folds of slumber, his last thoughts were on the dark-eyed man from the brothel.

The forest was black and silver, the trees in it very narrow and tall. Jon looked about in confusion, unsure which way the path to home lay. There was the crackling, snapping sound of something moving towards him, and he turned around just as a massive, black shape emerged out of the woods. It stared at him impassively with glossy, dark eyes. From behind the great lion came a hot wind, ripe with the smell of carrion...

J on was hot, and the sunlight was very bright on his eyelids. With his eyes closed tight, he buried his head against the pillow; Reginald would be up by now. He reached out a hand to touch Brutus's head, never far from his bedside. When his fingers encountered nothing, he frowned to himself. The cot suddenly rocked under him, and there was a small splashing sound from beyond the wall; Jon's eyes snapped open.

The ship.

He lifted his head and narrowed his gaze against the sunlight pouring through the round window above him.

"Well, lookee! The sleepin' princess awakens at long last!" said someone in the room.

He recognized the voice as belonging to the aggressively cheerful youth that had knocked him unconscious the night before; Jon clenched his jaw and turned to look at him.

The muscular young man, stripped to the waist and barefoot, was lounging indolently in one of the dark wooden chairs and noisily eating a wedge of apple off the end of a sharp knife. When he saw Jon looking at him, he curled his pink lips into a smile.

"Yer a noisy sleeper aint'cha, lovey?" he said, carving another slice out of the red-cheeked fruit he held in his rough-knuckled hand.

Jon frowned at him and pulled himself into a sitting position; his shoulders came up as he sat hunched on the bed, staring at the stranger for a few moments.

"Where are my clothes?" he asked softly, his voice hoarse with sleep.

The shirtless man laughed.

"We burned 'em, mate. They couldn't be saved!" he said cheerfully and munched on his apple. "Ye know I was up half the night cleanin' the sick off ye? Bloody awful business."

Jon swallowed and opened his mouth to say something.

Why should I apologize?

"Jon, you should learn right now to take a grain of salt with anything Tom says," said another voice.

Jon turned his head as someone entered the room. His breath caught in his throat as the man who had so brazenly stared at him from across the brothel sitting room walked through the open doorway. He was still wearing the dark-crimson vest over a white shirt, but both were buttoned up and covered with a long black coat with bell cuffs and brass buttons. His light-brown hair was tied back out of his face; when the man turned to look at Tom, Jon saw that his ponytail was held in place with a black velvet ribbon.

"That's unkind, Da," said the shirtless man at the table, smiling up with sea-green eyes at the imposing stranger.

The older man's lips made a little moue of disgust as he shook his head. After turning back to Jon, he dipped his head a fraction of an inch and smiled charmingly.

"I am Captain Baltsaros. This absurdly brash young man is Tom, my first mate," he said in his exotic accent.

Jon realized his mouth was still open; he closed it quickly and felt blood heat up his cheeks.

Baltsaros's brow lifted, and he scrutinized Jon for a moment with dark-brown eyes. When Jon didn't respond, he finished the introductions for him.

"And you are Jon of Portsmouth. It is a pleasure to meet you, Jon," Baltsaros said lightly.

The older man's eyes crinkled at the corners, and he sketched a shallow bow with a large, tanned hand held to his chest. The man breathed elegance into the room with his words and manner, and Jon found himself sitting up a little straighter on the cot.

"We did not burn your clothes; ignore Tom. However, you might be more comfortable in something less... shabby," said the captain, smiling.

The corners of Jon's mouth turned down, his sudden shame swiftly followed by anger. He averted his gaze.

"I like my clothes just fine. I thank you to return them to me. And to release me." Jon's words were spoken through clenched teeth. He looked down to where his hands were clutching the bedsheet tightly; his heart was beating fast and the blood sang in his ears. In dismay, he realized that there was a pounding in his head that was quickly gaining momentum; he swallowed hard, fearing the pain that he knew would soon overpower him.

"You heard our friend, Tom. Please fetch his clothing. It is my desire for Jon to feel comfortable during his stay with us. Whatever he asks for, you shall provide. Do you understand?" asked Baltsaros.

There was a long pause. Jon looked back up and was alarmed to see that Tom was staring at him intently with a new emotion in his blue-green eyes.

Jealousy.

"Includin' lettin' the puppy out of his cage?" the muscular first mate asked as he stood, rubbing the side of his callused thumb on the stubble of his jaw.

Baltsaros shook his head slowly.

"No, I'm afraid our guest will have to stay in his cage for now," he responded, sitting down on the chair that Tom had vacated. He leaned forward and placed his forearms on his knees, hands clasped loosely in front of him. Baltsaros peered curiously at his prisoner and smiled.

Jon's eyes followed Tom's departure.

"Welcome to my ship, Jon. I was being genuine when I said that I would like you to be comfortable; please know that," the captain said, his tone both friendly and apologetic.

Jon turned his eyes to Baltsaros's and was surprised by the warmth he found there. Despite the outrageous situation, he nodded once.

"Why am I here?" he asked quietly.

Pondering the question, Baltsaros sat back in his chair and rubbed a hand on the black leather covering his knee.

Jon's temple throbbed in time to his heart, adding to the mounting discomfort in his head. He reached out unsteadily and grabbed the metal cup, the water in it now tepid. He took a small sip and tried to ignore the pain that shadowed his every move.

"I learned of your unique talent and had to see it for myself," said Baltsaros finally. "I like interesting things; and you, Jon, are interesting to me."

Jon frowned and coughed into his fist; his skin prickled with another fever-shiver. He drank down the rest of the water and started turning the cup around in his hands nervously.

"I'm to be kept in a cage? Like an animal on display? Are you going to make me perform?" asked Jon, his voice sounding harsh.

The handsome face of the captain creased into a wide grin, and he laughed, his eyes twinkling with merriment.

"No, no, no! You misunderstand. You're not to be a pet, Jon." Baltsaros stood and walked to a strange metal cupboard. He opened it and took out a pitcher; motioning to Jon to hold his cup through the bars, he then poured water from it.

Jon was amazed to feel that the water was so cold; the cup started sweating immediately in the heat that had settled in the captain's quarters.

"How... is this so cold?" Jon asked, taking a small sip.

Baltsaros smiled and went to replace the pitcher.

"Ice," he said simply, pointing to the large block of it at the top of the cabinet.

The captain's face became serious as he closed the door and turned back to the man in the cage.

"I can show you many more interesting things, Jon, if you decide to join us."

Jon laughed, though there was no humour in it.

"So if I'm not to be a pet, what will I be? Are you offering me employment? If so... Why all this? Why not just ask me?" he asked. His teeth were starting to chatter, and his words sounded strange to his ears.

"Because you are the son of an honourable man, a lawman, Jon. My ship and its crew... We kneel to no man, no laws. I couldn't be sure where your loyalties lie," said Baltsaros, one shoulder coming up in a small, graceful shrug.

Jon shivered; the pain and fever were starting to take over. He closed his eyes and licked his lips with a suddenly dry tongue.

"And what if I say no?" he asked quietly, lifting his gaze to the man who stood above him.

It could have been a trick of the eye, but the captain's face seemed momentarily to go blank of expression. It was as if something completely inhuman was looking at him through the older man's dark stare.

Jon felt a strange numbness in his body, and his vision seemed to pitch forward. He felt simultaneously hot and cold. All motion suddenly slowed. Before the world went black, his eyes saw a dark hand reach for him.

Then there was nothing.

Baltsaros knelt next to Jon's twitching body, a deep frown on his face. He smelled burnt tobacco and realized that Tom was back in the room. The handsome boy walked on cat's feet; without his keen sense of smell, Baltsaros would have had a hard time tracking his motions, and the lad was as dangerous as he was beautiful.

"What's the matter with him, Da?" Tom asked, leaning against the bars of the cage, Jon's clothing tucked under one muscular arm.

Baltsaros touched the stricken man's face; it was burning. He shook his head at the provincial nature of these small towns; without proper medical care, Jon would not have lasted the month.

"He has a brain infection. Your manhandling of him did not help matters, Tom." With a mildly reproachful frown, Baltsaros looked over at his first mate.

Tom chewed on the side of his thumb; he shrugged at Baltsaros. The boy was invariably unapologetic when it came to his violence.

"So he's broken, eh? Are ye goin' to fix him? What do we want with this broken puppy anyway? He's got hands like a girl," said the first mate, curling his lip in amusement. "Maybe I'll get him to use his girl hands on m—"

"You'll do no such thing, Tom. Obey me in this," Baltsaros hissed quietly.

The younger man's sea-green eyes widened, his pupils dilating, and he swallowed.

"Aye, aye, captain sir," he said, his tone only slightly mocking.

Baltsaros nodded once and turned his attention back to the man lying on the floor of the cage. Jon had stopped twitching, but his breath was uneven and a sheen of sweat covered his sickly pale face. Broken puppy, indeed. Baltsaros sighed; he could fix him, but what if Jon refused to join his crew? What point would there be to cure him of his ailment, only to kill him for turning down his generous offer? With a thoughtful expression on his rugged face, Baltsaros slid his strong arms underneath Jon's limp body and lifted him back onto the cot; he would simply wait for Jon's answer before mixing the medicines that would save the boy's life.

He picked the cup up off the floor and placed it back on the small rum barrel before exiting the cage and locking the door. Looking at Tom sternly, he pointed to Jon.

"You're to be the guard dog for this 'puppy,' Tom. I will be up on deck. If there is any change, you must come to me immediately."

He looked back at the stricken man on the narrow cot and frowned. After a moment, Baltsaros picked a shiny, red apple out of the bowl on the table and reached through the bars of Jon's cage to place it next to the empty cup. What was it about this boy that seemed to call to something long buried inside of him? He shook his head slightly.

After narrowing his dark eyes at the first mate again, Baltsaros turned and left the heavy heat of the stateroom for the crisp, blue world of sunshine above deck.

4

PIRATES

Jon woke up nearly an hour later, groggy and disoriented. The pain in his head was sharp, and he felt terribly weak. Completely miserable, Jon covered his face with his hands; he wanted nothing more than to be in his own bed, Brutus at his side. Hell, he would even welcome Reginald's temper if it meant an end to the raw fear and pain that hounded him. Overwhelmed, he felt shameful tears well up and started weeping quietly to himself.

"Hey, mate… Mate, don't go cryin' now! Shit," said Tom from somewhere close by. Jon heard movement but made no move to acknowledge him. "Now, when did cryin' do anyone a lick o' good? Pssh… cryin'… Listen, lovey: all the tears in the world ain't goin' to get'cha out of that cage, so stop that now."

With his hands hard against his eyes, Jon let out a shuddering breath.

"My head… The pain is like a lightning storm. I can't…" he said hoarsely. The words sounded ridiculous as soon as he had uttered them.

Tom chuckled softly; Jon rubbed his face and cracked his eyes open, shielding them from the light with his fingers. The muscular first mate had pulled a chair up to the bars and was sitting there staring down at Jon with a wry grin on his face.

"No worries! My da will give ye somethin' for that. Soon, soon, lovey," he said, smiling. Tom placed his hands on his knees and leaned forward to get a better look at Jon.

The first mate's chest was broad and tanned, the muscles well defined under his sun-darkened skin. Jon could see streaks of grime where Tom had obviously wiped his hand, the dirt and sweat having made stripes under the man's curling chest hair. Again Jon noticed that he was incredibly handsome; the scar above his eye, the coarse stubble, and the sardonic grin lent his otherwise cherubic face a roguish quality. Tom seemed so very full of good humour, though something told Jon that the handsome youth could murder him as cheerfully as he spoke.

Jon coughed into his hand, startled by how deep it sounded in his chest. Holding his head, he sat up stiffly on the bed and pulled a blanket around himself.

"So the captain is your father?" he asked after a moment. He could smell Tom from where he was sitting: tobacco smoke, sweat, sunshine, and liquor.

The big man nodded, a glint of something in his blue-green eyes.

"Aye, he is!" he said, smiling wide.

Was that pride?

Jon frowned.

"Why do you sound so different then?" he asked. They also looked nothing alike.

Tom laughed and shook his head.

"My mum raised me, ducky. A pirate's got no time for a wee babe. Yer a daft thing, aint'cha?"

Jon's heart pounded. *Pirates.* Despite everything, he felt a small thrill. A distant relative of his had been a pirate. When he was little, his mother had told him stories of this Captain Black, and Jon remembered hanging on every word; it had seemed like such a gloriously dangerous existence.

"So you're pirates, then?" he asked.

Nodding, Tom sat back in his chair.

"Aye. We're pirates. Does that scare ye, dear Jonny?" He pulled his long knife out from somewhere behind him and started cleaning his nails with it. "Or do ye have man-size balls in those shorts somewhere? Da said ye were some sort of torturer. What I think is if I yell 'boo' at'cha, ye'd die of fright."

Jon closed his eyes and pinched the bridge of his nose. Even though the first mate's tone was mocking, he *seemed* honestly friendly; something in his manner was steadily chipping away at Jon's defences. For the first time in a long while, he was completely unable to read someone's intentions. Jon opened his eyes and blinked.

Make that two someones.

The captain was as unreadable as his first mate. Maybe it was just his illness… He looked into Tom's smiling eyes.

"I was just an interrogator. My only tools were my words," he said, pulling his shoulders up closer to his ears. "And sometimes a teacher… I taught others how to read body language."

Tom's brows came down; he looked somewhat disappointed by Jon's words.

"So no torture then? Pah! No wonder yer like a snail without a shell," he said and started to flip the sharp knife into the air, catching it confidently in a rough hand. "I was supposed to get Da when ye woke up. Ye won't tell him I dawdled, aye?" Tom grinned wolfishly and winked. When Jon shook his head hesitantly, Tom stood up and turned to leave, his knife disappearing into a sheath behind him that was buckled into his belt. Jon noticed for the first time that the first mate's large back was a mass of scars under the sweat and tanned skin. He frowned.

"Tom?"

The big pirate turned back towards the cage. "Aye, lovey?" he asked.

Jon groped for his words.

"If I... don't want to join you... Will your father let me go? Alive, I mean?" he asked, his voice faltering.

Tom threw his head back and laughed, the sound booming out of his broad chest. After a moment he looked down at Jon, his face crinkling in amusement.

"Now I don't know why ye'd choose that shithole town over the open sea, mate. Could be I punched ye too hard, eh?" He stopped chuckling when he saw that Jon's face was drawn with worry. "Ahh, Jonny. Just look at those big blue eyes... Ye'll make the captain sad; we came an awful long way to poach yer scrawny arse. Ha ha... but my Da's a good man, heart o' gold, I swear! If ye say no, I'm sure he'll let ye off."

With those words, Tom winked again and disappeared through the open door. Dread descended on Jon like a sheet of cold water; he didn't believe a single word.

Baltsaros ducked his head and stepped into the stateroom, his sight momentarily impaired by the change in light. However, he could hear what his eyes could not have told him: Jon's infection had spread to his lungs.

Or maybe it had started there, hidden? Something to think about later.

He heard the crunch of teeth breaking the skin of the apple; the scent of the fresh fruit rose up through the air, mingling with the bitter tang of nervous sweat that emanated from the young man in the cage. Baltsaros walked farther into the room, his vision slowly adjusting to the darker space, and set a covered plate down on the large table. When he turned towards his prisoner, the captain saw that Jon was watching him warily, his grey-blue eyes filled with so much emotion that Baltsaros felt an unexpected tingle of sympathy. He curled his lip into a smile.

"Hello, Jon. I'm relieved to see you up," he said, approaching the cage. "I see you're indeed hungry?" He motioned to the half-eaten apple that Jon mutely clutched in one hand. Baltsaros saw with dismay that the hand was trembling slightly and the younger man's skin had taken on a greyish cast.

After he stepped up to the cage, Baltsaros undid the lock and opened the door. The tall man smoothly lowered himself to one knee in front of Jon and peered into his captive's face.

"How do you feel?" he asked, his stark brow wrinkling in concern.

Jon's eyes slid away from the captain's face.

"I've felt better," he replied softly and tugged the coverlet tighter around him. Baltsaros nodded.

"When did these headaches start, Jon?" he asked. This close, the captain could tell that the infection was progressing far faster than he had earlier thought. Jon's face was drawn and gaunt, sickness marring his graceful beauty. Not for the first time, Baltsaros felt curiously drawn to the sensitive young man. He watched closely as Jon swallowed, his Adam's apple bobbing in his thin neck.

"About a month ago, I think. Maybe less," came the reply; Jon's voice was rough and his breath whistled in his chest. Baltsaros reached out towards Jon's head but stopped short.

"May I?" he asked softly. The younger man stared hard at him a second before nodding once. Holding the back of Jon's head, he gently put a hand to the sick man's forehead; he felt the astonishing heat of the fever in him, as well as the tiny shudders that shook his slight frame. Baltsaros slid his large hand down the side of Jon's face, feeling his jaw clench, and down his throat, finally placing his palm over the sick man's chest; he didn't have to put an ear against him to know that he had fluid in his lungs.

As he looked into Jon's eyes, he was astonished to see that the dark-haired man appeared to be on the verge of tears and not, he believed, from pain. Baltsaros wondered to himself how long it had been since someone had touched Jon with anything resembling affection. He dropped his hands and stood, noting the sudden look of meek humiliation that flashed across Jon's fine-boned face before it settled back into fearful distrust.

"You're very sick, Jon," the captain said simply. "Here, I've brought you something a little more substantial to eat." He turned and exited the cage, leaving the door wide open behind him.

With his back to his captive, Baltsaros pulled the cover off the plate; he smiled to himself when he heard a shuffling step approach. Baltsaros walked across the room and opened the wooden box atop the teak dresser; he pulled out some beautiful, heavy silverware and turned back to Jon. He was wrapped in the sheet, one hand clutching the material to his chest, as he peered down curiously at the food on the fine white plate. Jon looked up at Baltsaros as he approached.

"What is it?" he asked, his storm-blue eyes narrow with distrust.

"An omelette," replied Baltsaros, smiling. "Some vegetables and meat covered with cheese and cooked in an egg. Roughly."

Jon turned back to the dish and licked his bottom lip. Baltsaros could see that the younger man was hungry.

"Sit."

He pulled out the chair and slid it behind Jon, bumping it against the back of his knees. Jon slowly sat, and Baltsaros pushed the chair a little farther before rounding the table to sit across from him.

"Eat," he said, pointing to the plate.

Jon frowned at Baltsaros and let go of the sheet to pick up the fork, turning it around in his hand. He glanced up at his captor, making no move to comply.

Baltsaros laughed in amusement, startling Jon whose eyes widened at the outburst.

"Jon, eat. Please. I would not poison your food. See?" He leaned over the table and plucked the fork from Jon's grasp; he cut a piece from the still-warm omelette and brought it to his mouth. He chewed and swallowed, smiling at Jon before placing the fork back on the plate.

The look of distrust lessened, replaced partially by naked hunger, as Jon picked up the fork again and took a bite of the egg for himself. His eyebrows lifted in surprise, and he took another mouthful, handling the fork awkwardly; it was obviously not an implement he was used to.

Baltsaros waited until the younger man had taken a few more bites before he broached the subject of Jon's future. He leaned back in his seat, elbows on the chair arms, and steepled his hands in front of him.

"Have you given any thought to my offer, Jon?"

Bolstered by the warm meal, Jon looked directly at the captain.

"I'm still not sure exactly what you're offering," he said, his voice stronger than before. "But I don't know that I'm willing to take up with pirates."

Baltsaros dipped his head thoughtfully, acknowledging Jon's words. It was true; the captain had not given Jon anything that would make him feel otherwise. So far this endeavour had been less than ideal; Tom would have to be taught another lesson in obedience.

Baltsaros lowered his hands to the table, palm up.

"Jon, I am offering you a place on my ship. I believe your talents would come in handy with our type of... work. You can see things that others do not, and I think that it would be an incredible boon to us, and to me. Your gifts were being squandered in that dank dungeon, Jon. Here, you will be a free man. Respected. An equal. My crew is varied and loyal, and everyone shares in the wealth. The choice is yours, and you're free to go if that's what you'd like, but... Was I wrong in thinking that you are a man who is extremely dissatisfied with the cards dealt to him by fate?"

Baltsaros widened his eyes at Jon, who had laughed sharply at the word "fate."

"Fate. What is fate, Captain? Is it my fate to be here, sitting at your table, wondering if I will ever get out of this alive? Is it my fate to have been so bereft of choices in my life that when faced with one all I feel is paralyzing confusion? *Fate*," Jon said with disgust and shook his head, taking the last mouthful of egg.

Baltsaros's eyes swept over the man's face; there was an interesting strength behind the high walls that Jon had erected to keep others at a distance. The captain felt that an important corner had been turned. As he leaned towards Jon, Baltsaros smiled grimly.

"How's this: you're dying. Does that change matters for you?"

Jon blinked slowly, and after a moment he nodded; the news didn't seem to shock him. After pushing the empty plate away with one hand, Jon turned his head, looking at the blue sky visible outside the porthole. After a long pause, he spoke in a strained voice.

"Sometimes, at night, I leave my room to stand on the hill over the harbour. It's dark, but I can see lights in the boats or hear a snippet of song, a laugh, and other... things." Jon reddened slightly. Baltsaros tilted his head, listening to the friendless, young man speak of things he had obviously never shared with anyone. "And I'd think to myself, *You could be out there!*" He laughed, the sound ugly, and turned his stormy eyes back to Baltsaros. "But the truth is that I can't. I... am not good in situations where there are people. I'm caged by my own pathetic fear. *Next year,* I think, *next year I will leave the dank dungeon,* as you so aptly put it, *I'll be free!* and now you tell me that I am dying?" Jon's mouth turned down at the corners, and his eyes shimmered. "What a sad, sad little life," he said angrily.

Baltsaros slowly reached out with one hand and placed it gently on the younger man's arm. He felt a twitch as Jon forced himself to accept the touch; a deep crease wrinkled his brow as he stared at the captain's large, sun-darkened hand on his forearm.

"Tomorrow," Jon said faintly. "Let me give you my answer tomorrow."

. . .

Baltsaros looked down at Jon, sleeping under the power of the heavy painkillers the captain had mixed for him. After twisting paper around a second dose, he placed it next to the cup of water. Perhaps Jon would find the answer in his dreams. Feeling strangely drained by his conversation with the deathly ill younger man, Baltsaros stripped off his shirt and vest and lay down on his own bed; the captain stared up at the wooden ceiling, thinking hard about the strangely entwined concepts of fate and loyalty.

A small whimper woke Jon up.

Sleepily opening his eyes, he saw that it was night. When Jon had woken up earlier in the afternoon and stood to piss in the chamber pot, it had appeared that he was, for once, alone in the room. When he had reached for the metal cup, Jon had found the twist of paper containing the pain-numbing powder the captain had given him. Gratefully pouring it into his water, he had swallowed it down quickly.

It wasn't that he had been in any real pain upon waking; he had simply wanted to be free of thoughts of his death. At least that's what he had tried to tell himself. It wasn't that Captain Baltsaros's touch had brought out an unexpected reaction in Jon that had eclipsed any fear he felt and that he'd wanted to hide from the truth in the dreamless sleep that the drug afforded him.

There was another whimper, a little louder this time. Jon slowly lifted his head and looked around, freezing when he saw movement on the bed across the room.

"Please... Da..." said a voice that was unmistakably Tom's; it was filled with pain. Jon was aghast when he heard Baltsaros's low laughter. There was a hiss of pain and then a groan of pleasure. In shock, Jon pressed the heel of his hand against his mouth; he quickly closed his eyes and put his head back to the pillow.

"You'll obey me, Tom," Jon heard the captain's voice say, rough with desire. There was a low moan that ended in a whimper; it was followed by a gasp.

"Yes… yes, Da. Please… Please fuck me. Fuck me and I'll ob—" Tom yelped as Baltsaros did… something to him.

Oh god… oh god.

Jon's face burned as Tom started murmuring terribly scandalous things, the sound of skin smacking against bare skin punctuating his words. In dismay, Jon felt himself growing hard in response, and he shifted on the bed, trying not to encourage his treasonous erection. Pressing the coverlet hard over his ear, Jon tried to slow his breathing as he prayed for an end to the wanton depravity across the room.

It was a long time before his prayers were answered, and an even longer time before he managed to convince himself the feeling he felt was disgust and not something closer to desire.

5

THE SHIP

Captain Baltsaros had his hand on Jon's head, feeling for a fever. He moved it down the side of Jon's face and neck, just like he had done the previous day; but, instead of stopping at his chest, it continued farther down. Jon gasped in shock and tensed as the captain's fingers slid warmly under the waist of his shorts, curling around the molten flesh below. His cock grew hard in the captain's firm grip, and Jon clenched his jaw, a tremor of desire running through him at Baltsaros's skilled touch. He was unable to move... or simply unwilling? He moaned softly as Baltsaros's long arm slid around him to pull him closer. He heard the sound of someone laughing. Jon reddened with embarrassment when he saw that Tom was standing there watching the captain fondle him. He watched, horrified, as Tom pulled out his knife. It flashed quickly through the air and slid through the skin of Jon's throat. A torrent of red arced out of him and ran down his chest. He didn't feel any pain, only incredible pleasure, as the captain smiled down at him, his hand spreading the gore over Jon's rigid cock.

When he woke, Jon was immediately and uncomfortably aware of his erection pressing hard into the thin mattress. He couldn't remember all the details of the dream, but what he could remember brought blood to his face.

A soft noise, as of something being moved, turned Jon's head; Tom was approaching from the far side of the room. Jon quickly closed his eyes and deepened his breathing to mimic sleep. He wasn't awake enough to deal with Tom's cheerfully menacing banter; besides, the stiffness between his legs had yet to go down, and the first mate was the last person in the world he wanted to see *that*.

As Tom muttered something about chambermaids under his breath, he replaced the chamber pot and refilled Jon's cup. Jon cracked one eye open a slit and saw that Tom was in his usual half-naked state. While wondering wryly whether the first mate actually owned a shirt, Jon noticed with dismay the bruised bite mark plain on Tom's muscular shoulder. The events of the previous night flooded through him, burning his mind anew.

He clenched his eyes shut and tried to still his breathing until he was sure Tom had left. After a few minutes of silence, he risked another look; the room appeared empty. Jon sat up, his head throbbing. Sick to his stomach from the pain and fever, he groaned out loud, tears gathering in the corners of his eyes.

On top of his sickness, Jon felt terrible shame over his body's reaction to the captain and his first mate... his son... being... (*the way he grunted like a beast when he finally came*) lovers. Jon gritted his teeth against the memory and clenched his fists tight in his lap, rocking forward, a tear running down his nose and falling from the tip.

Lovers? There was no love in that.

Jon heard the heels of the captain's boots on the wooden floor, and before he had a chance to resume his possum act on the cot, the older man had entered the stateroom. After wiping his eyes and crossing his arms across his chest to try to keep from shivering, Jon sat mutely on the narrow bed, staring down at the floor between his bare feet. He listened as Baltsaros stepped across the colourful rugs to the front of the cage.

"Good morning, Jon. Are you hungry?" asked the captain, a smile distinct in his voice. When Jon didn't look up or answer Baltsaros after a long silence, he heard the lock on his cage being released and the hinges of the door creak quietly. A hand reached for his shoulder, and Jon recoiled violently.

"Don't you fucking touch me!" he yelled, his throat raw. Jon's eyes were wide as he stared at the startled captain, his teeth bared in a grimace.

Baltsaros's expression went completely flat before confusion slowly etched lines across his brow.

"What happened, Jon?" asked the captain, his voice soft with concern.

The younger man stared at him, trying to find the words. After a moment he replied.

"Last night…" He had a deep pain in his chest that was getting worse with each breath.

Baltsaros frowned for a moment, but his rugged face quickly creased into a wry smile. He held his hands up as if trying not to startle a small, frightened animal and looked kindly down at Jon.

"I'm sorry if Tom and I woke you. This is the downside to keeping you in—"

"He is your *son*!" Jon hissed through clenched teeth and glared at the older man in disgust, though his fever was starting to dull his vision again.

Baltsaros started shaking his head; his lips curled into a subdued smile, and he dropped his hands.

"Tom is not my son, Jon. Did he tell you that?" he asked. When Jon nodded tightly, the captain sighed. "Ah, Tom, always in need of a game to play. Jon… Tom is an ex-slave that I bought a few years ago."

Jon let the words sink in. He frowned at Baltsaros in confusion.

The captain pressed his gracefully curved lips together as he looked down at the dark-haired man on the narrow cot.

"May I sit?" he asked, motioning to the space next to Jon. The younger man sagged back against the bars, and he dipped his chin, feeling utterly drained. Baltsaros sat down slowly on the bed, arranging his hands in his lap.

Jon ran his fingers through his dirty hair, suddenly aware of how long it had been since he'd washed himself or changed his clothing; he could smell his own stink. Embarrassed, he leaned further away from the older man.

The captain continued.

"Tom was a slave. He was slated for a horrendous fate... He had managed to escape from the mines where he was being worked to death. He then murdered his owner and the man's family in their home before he was caught."

Jon swallowed hard.

"He said his mother raised him..."

Baltsaros shook his head.

"He lied. He's never known a mother." The captain let out a low laugh with little humour in it. "Sometimes I believe that the hells simply opened up and a demon pushed Tom out. He's a ruthless killer, Jon, completely without remorse, smiling Death himself. In fact, he was the reason I built this to begin with," said the captain, motioning to the bars surrounding them. "Tom had been put in stocks in the town centre to be punished by the townspeople in whichever way they wanted... and punish him they did; Tom's owner had been well-liked, and his death was seen as a horrible tragedy. By the time I found Tom, he could barely walk. He had been brutally abused by the men in town... I will spare you the details, but it was a long time before he was completely healed."

"And you bought him *why*?" Jon asked, aghast.

"He's very useful in our line of work. I took an interest in his history and purchased him, though now he is as free as anyone in my crew. He spent the first five months locked in this cage... a wild animal. I still haven't *quite* tamed him, but at least my sleep is no longer as disrupted." Baltsaros smiled wide. "I am sorry for all the trouble he has caused, Jon. He calls me Father out of some misplaced affection. I... oblige him. I find him alluring." He chuckled softly. "I did attempt to break him of the habit, but as you might have gathered by now, beating him is largely counter-productive. He enjoys it far too much." The captain grinned; the lines on his face showed a man that smiled often and easily. "Besides... How old do you think I am to have fathered a son Tom's age?"

Jon looked down at his hands. It was true. Tom had to be close to his age, and the captain could be no more than ten or so years older; though the realization didn't alleviate his discomfort over the two men, or any men, sharing a bed, Jon felt suddenly sheep-ish. He raised his grey-blue eyes back up to Baltsaros and shrugged, forcing himself to smile.

The captain, narrowing his eyes at Jon, went darkly serious.

"If you join us, you will have to thicken your skin, Jon. You'll see far worse than what you assumed you saw, I can guarantee that." Baltsaros leaned towards Jon, a calculating look on his face. "I believe you are stronger than you let on and much more suited to this life than you think you are. I need your decision, Jon. I would like us to become friends. And"—he laughed, all sternness leaving his face—"I crave a little more privacy." His eyes crinkled at the corners.

Jon frowned at the non sequitur until he realized Baltsaros meant that with his enlistment, he would have to move into the crew quarters. The thought sent a sudden pang of anxiety through him, but it was strangely brief; he realized then that Captain Balt-saros had a strong calming effect on him.

Jon stared hard at the man sitting on the low cot, and some-thing inside him suddenly gave. Baltsaros's words came back to him... *free as anyone in my crew.* Jon wanted to believe the captain's words and that this near stranger had more faith in him than his own stepfather.

Freedom.

It was something he'd been wishing for his whole life, and it was right here in front of him. Jon looked searchingly into the captain's friendly brown eyes; taking a deep, shaky breath, and feeling like he was stepping off a high cliff, Jon spoke the words that already seemed written in the air between them.

"Yes. Yes, I will join you."

With Jon's words Baltsaros felt a strange sense of relief. He almost frowned, momentarily unbalanced by the sensation, but instead smiled into blue eyes wide with the need for his approval. He nodded and held out his hand; Jon looked confused for a moment before sliding his own hand into Baltsaros's grip. They shook on it, securing Jon's spot on the crew.

The younger man's hand was alarmingly hot; Baltsaros saw immediately that Jon's eyes were glassy, one pupil more dilated than the other. The sounds of his fluid-filled lungs were filling the cabin with a harsh wheezing.

As if reacting to the captain's scrutiny, Jon suddenly went still, his eyes rolling in his head as he fell back.

Baltsaros's hand shot out and caught Jon before he crashed into the hard metal bars; as he laid Jon down on the cot, he looked down at him, a thoughtful expression on his face. Something needed to be done, and quickly.

Baltsaros stood and walked to the teak dresser. After pulling out a few drawers, he selected the ingredients necessary to make the infection-fighting medicine. As he ground them with mortar and pestle, Baltsaros prodded at the surprising feelings he had towards the young man.

When he had brought his crew to Portsmouth looking for the boy with the gift of empathy, it had just been simple curiosity. He hadn't known what to expect. Besides, killing the girl to lure Jon had felt good. Killing always felt good to Baltsaros; it restored the peace in his mind and shored up his self-control. However, when he had seen the boy at the foot of the staircase, hunched as if afraid of being hit, pale and sickly with bright spots in his cheeks, something inside Baltsaros had whispered to him. Like a sculptor who could see the forms in marble just waiting to be released, Baltsaros had seen the potential in Jon.

He frowned as he expertly mixed the ingredients into a paste. Baltsaros had never felt relief at *not* having to kill someone before. It was… noteworthy. The captain pressed most of the paste into a small mould and heated it over a candle. In a few hours, he would be able to remove the tablets and coat them in oil so that Jon could swallow them down. For now, he could just mix the paste with some boiled water to get it down the younger man's throat.

Baltsaros turned with the cup in his hand and saw that Jon was once more awake, watching him with eyes that sparkled with fever. His dark hair was plastered to his forehead, and Baltsaros could see he was shivering. Idly, he wondered whether the brain-swell had caused any permanent damage as he walked back to the sick man on the cot, sitting down next to him.

"I won't be alive long enough to be any use to you," said Jon, his voice quiet. Baltsaros was surprised to hear neither bitterness nor sadness in it. He shook his head and smiled down at the young man on the bed. With one hand behind Jon's head to tilt it up, he placed the cup against his lips.

"Drink. It will taste terrible, but drink all the same," he said.

Jon took a sip and grimaced but drank all the bitter liquid down without complaint. Baltsaros lowered Jon's head back onto the pillow and sat back. The slight dark-haired young man on the bed brought a shaky hand up to wipe his lips. The medicine would work to fight the infection as well as make Jon sleep deeply while he healed.

Baltsaros stood to leave, and Jon's eyes opened a crack, a slight frown on his drawn face.

"You're healing me," he said simply. The captain nodded once, pleased that Jon had deduced as much. "Why didn't you tell me you could heal me before I made my decision?" Jon asked, confused.

Because I didn't want to waste my medicines on someone who was stupid enough to refuse my offer.

Suddenly, Baltsaros wondered if that was the truth. He curled his lips into a gentle smile.

"Because I didn't want you to base your decision on it," he answered. "I would have healed you regardless," Baltsaros added, lying.

Jon smiled softly and nodded against the pillow.

I wanted you to come with me because you chose to, not because I bought you.

The words barely touched Baltsaros's mind before he dismissed them, feeling almost angry. His dark eyes watched as Jon's eyes fluttered closed again before he finally left the cage.

Hours later, Jon woke up with a hollow pit in his stomach and bladder crying out for release. As he sat up shakily, he was surprised to see that the door to his cage had been left open.

So I am, indeed, free.

Jon lurched to the chamber pot and pissed into it, relief so great he almost moaned out loud. His clothes were still sitting in a neat pile on the floor of the cage where Tom had left them, but Jon just frowned; they were the clothes of a stable boy… not a pirate.

He grinned to himself, real excitement bubbling up inside him for the first time. His head still ached and his lungs hurt, but he trusted that the captain wouldn't lie to him; he would be made well. Jon shook his head a little and pulled a sheet off the bed. After wrapping himself up against the cool night air that came in through the open door of the stateroom, Jon took a step outside his cage.

The rugs were soft under his bare feet, and he smiled to himself. The captain's tastes were certainly refined. He saw that there was a covered plate next to a cup on the big mahogany table and hoped that there would be some more of that delicious egg dish for him.

He raised the cover and saw a simple meal of bread and cheese; Jon tried not to let the disappointment get to him. Next to the staples he'd eaten his whole life were things that looked like dried fruit, but nothing he recognized. He lifted the round, yellow shape to his mouth and bit down. The pink-brown meat of the fruit was surprisingly sweet and filled with little seeds that crunched in his teeth; Jon grinned and ate a few more in quick succession. He was delighted when the cheese turned out to be richer and sharper than any he'd ever eaten before, and the bread, darker brown than he was used to, was savoury and flavoured with exotic spices. The cup, he realized in surprise, contained sweet cider instead of plain water. His earlier disappointment extinguished, Jon dug into his meal with relish.

When there was nothing left on the plate but a few crumbs, Jon decided to look around. He could hear the occasional thump of someone walking overhead, and twice he thought he could make out Tom's voice calling to someone, but otherwise, the night was quiet and cool. It seemed like the sea was quiet too as the floor barely moved beneath his feet.

The captain's bed was empty. With a glance to the open door, Jon approached the scene of last night's debauchery with some curiosity. It was a low, wide bed that curved against the inside of the wall. At the head was a wooden board with something carved into it, but it was too dark to see in the candlelight. Jon reached out and touched the scarlet coverlet, running one finger against the soft, silky material. There were beads and embroidery sewn into it to make a strange circular pattern; Jon thought it was the most beautiful thing he had ever seen.

He heard a noise and snatched his hand away, looking over his shoulder in surprise, but there was nothing there. Jon's heart pounded in his chest, and he laughed to himself; what was he doing messing around with the captain's bedclothes in the dark?

Imagine it on your bare skin.

The unexpected thought made his heart leap in his chest, and he backed away, crashing into the corner of the table with his hip. Smarting both in body and mind, Jon stood in the near dark trying to decide whether he should go back to his cage when he heard the splash of water outside.

With breathless curiosity, Jon approached the door and peered out, remaining hidden in the shadows. He gasped as the scene before him rendered his situation finally, and completely, real.

He was standing at the rear of the ship (*the stern*, he reminded himself) looking down the polished wooden deck. There were men lounging on crates and talking softly as they fixed some netting not far from where he stood; the smoke from their pipes and rolled tobacco curled into the air, disappearing into low clouds backlit by a nearly full moon overhead. Jon spotted movement to his right and was amazed as he watched a lithe, dark shape climb up some rigging. The wind rustled Jon's hair, and he could hear the little chuckling sounds of water hitting the hull; there was a steady, soft creak as the ship slid over waves, and the cool night breeze was flavoured with salt. He heaved a long sigh: clean, fresh air. Jon felt his chest tighten.

A fresh start.

He suddenly thought his heart would burst in his chest.

Jon turned to go back inside and saw with a start that Tom was perched on the rail of the quarterdeck; the first mate was staring down at him with eyes glinting in the lantern hanging above Jon's head. He gasped; for a moment the muscular youth resembled nothing so much as the animal he was named for, a malevolent feline shape in the dark. There was a flash in Tom's hands, and Jon saw with disquiet that the man in the shadows had his knife out. Jon suddenly felt genuine fear as the first mate's face curled into a wicked grin.

As he passed through the doorway, he heard Tom's cheerful voice call after him.

"Nighty night, Jonny boy. Sweet dreams."

6

ALL AT SEA

all at sea • *naval slang (18th century)* in a state
of confusion and disorder.

altsaros studied Jon's face over breakfast. He was thin to
the point of gauntness with patchy, dark stubble covering
the fine lines of his jaw. The angle of his nose was slightly
crooked, and there were deep shadows beneath eyes that
constantly shifted from sky-blue to storm-grey. *His hair is a disaster,* thought Baltsaros with a small smile. It was seal brown, the
curls matted from being slept on, and Jon's nervous habit of
rubbing a hand through it when he was thinking had caused it to
stick up almost comically in whorls and cowlicks. Overall, he
made for a charming waif, all big eyes, messy hair, and bird bones.

After taking another bite of his food, Baltsaros sat back,
amused. At the speed with which Jon was devouring the meal of
egg scramble and sausage, it wouldn't be long before he filled out
some, and work on the ship would pile more weight in the form
of muscle onto that slight frame. Baltsaros frowned, his nostrils
flaring delicately; Jon was a work in progress with one unfortunate trait that could readily be fixed.

He caught the captain's eye and stopped midchew.

"What's wrong?" Jon asked, his voice tinged with a little nervousness.

"You need a bath," said Baltsaros with a wry grin.

Jon's face reddened, and chewing furiously, he stared down at his plate. Baltsaros laughed, adding to his discomfiture. After he took a sip of the strong black coffee, Jon surprised the captain by replying in a sardonic tone.

"*You* try smelling like a rose when you're sleeping and sweating your days away," he said, tearing off another hunk of sourdough from the loaf in the middle of the table.

Baltsaros nodded once, and his graceful lips parted in a wide smile to show sharp white teeth. Jon was obviously feeling better; there was strong metal buried within that frail shape.

The captain rose from his seat and walked to the open door. He put his fingers between lips and whistled a short, shrill blast. In a few moments, Tom came loping down the deck to see what Baltsaros wanted.

The burly young man was sporting a new large bruise across one cheek and a split lip; it had been days since they had last shared a bed, and it seemed Tom was relieving his tension in other ways. Baltsaros wondered who had been on the receiving end of Tom's hard fists and whether there was someone with torn skin in need of stitching.

The look on Tom's face as he approached Baltsaros was both hopeful and resentful at once; his first mate was not dealing well with being ousted from his usual spot in Baltsaros's bed. Jon would have time later to come to terms with the captain's proclivities, but for the moment Baltsaros didn't want to unduly stress him. The captain had decided that as long as Jon was recuperating, he himself would sleep alone. He thought a gentle hand would work best with Jon; it was a pleasant change from the strong touch that Tom constantly required to keep him in line.

"What is it, sir?" asked his first mate, blue-green eyes sliding away from the captain's scrutiny.

Sir...

Baltsaros sighed and reached out a large hand to cup the back of the first mate's neck. He drew Tom into a quick embrace, pressing his lips to the bruise on the man's cheek; Baltsaros hoped that was enough to mollify Tom for the time being.

"Start heating some water, and bring a tub to my quarters, Tom," he said, releasing him.

The muscles in Tom's strong jaw moved under his tanned skin a moment before he nodded somewhat curtly.

"Aye, Da," he said and turned to leave. As he ran down the deck, Tom began bellowing for ship hands to start hauling the nonpotable water out of the large tank at the front of the ship.

Baltsaros shook his head in amusement as the crew scrambled to obey Tom's orders. If nothing else, the ex-slave made for an effective taskmaster; half the crew was terrified of him.

After he stepped back through the door, the captain saw that Jon stood in front of the large map, the sheet he had taken to winding around himself discarded on the chair where he had been sitting a moment ago.

Baltsaros walked up to him.

"It's a map of the known world," he explained.

Jon's brow furrowed as he looked at the large drawing mounted on the wall.

"Where are we now?" he asked, turning his blue eyes to Baltsaros. The captain reached out with a sure hand to trace the curve of the islands they were currently sailing past and then tapped his finger on a spot near the mainland.

"Here. Roughly," said Baltsaros, smiling at Jon.

The younger man frowned again at the map.

"I'm not understanding the scale, I think. Where is Portsmouth? How far have we come?" he asked, curious.

Baltsaros slid his finger along the course they had taken, about three inches across the shaded waters.

Jon's eyes widened, and he stepped back.

"We've only gone that far in five days? Is the world so big?" he asked, his eyes darting over the whole map. Baltsaros chuckled.

"Well... We aren't going full speed; but, yes, the world is big. Bigger than this map shows, even. This is all that we have discovered. There may be far more." He crossed his arms over his broad chest and watched Jon as he absorbed the information. Jon nodded then looked back at Baltsaros.

"Where are you from?" he asked, somewhat shyly.

Baltsaros felt a small pang in his chest, strangely touched by the fact Jon wanted to know more about him. He reached out again and slid his finger far north, nearly to the top of the map.

"This is where I was born," he replied. "In my mother tongue it's called 'Heaven's Gate,' but it's really just a lot of snow and darkness." He smiled. "It's not such a terrible place, but I prefer the warmth in the south."

Jon smiled back at him.

Baltsaros leaned once more towards the map and pointed to a spot about three feet south-east of their position. His dark hand rested on the map a moment, his mind suddenly full of the smell of fresh figs and ripe oranges.

"This is where my home is," he said softly. "It's called Madierus." When he turned to look at Jon, the young man had a sad expression on his face; was he missing his own home? He was about to ask the question when a loud crash sounded behind them.

Startled, Baltsaros saw that Tom had dropped the metal tub on the wooden floor. In dismay, he saw that Jon and his first mate locked eyes for a tense moment before Tom turned to the captain with a broad grin on his face. Baltsaros was not happy with the hostility that Tom was showing towards their newest recruit.

"The water'll be here in a jiff, Da," said his first mate. Jon's shoulders came up in an awkward hunch; he was obviously made uncomfortable by Tom's presence. To make matters worse, the muscular youth winked sassily at Jon.

"Don't worry, love! Yer majesty will get her bath!" he said with a short bark of laughter. Tom, seeing the dark look on Baltsaros's face, just grinned wider and strolled out of the room, the handle of his knife peeping above the belt at his narrow waist.

Watching Tom walk away, the muscles moving fluidly under the scarred skin of his sun-darkened back and the saucy way his hips moved as he padded silently on bare feet, Baltsaros felt a sudden pulse of desire. The dangerous young man was indeed a beautiful specimen.

He turned his head back to Jon who was staring at him with an expression bordering on horror. Jon quickly settled his face back into a neutral expression, but Baltsaros felt uncomfortably like he had taken a peek inside his mind.

Interesting.

The discomfort gave way quickly to curiosity. He wondered what else Jon could see; was he just reading expressions or could he predict intentions? From what he had heard, Jon could read someone's future simply in the way they drank their coffee, but Baltsaros dismissed that as ignorant hyperbole. Regardless, the boy's talent was certainly intriguing. The captain couldn't wait to put it to the test.

They watched in silence as deckhands poured bucket after bucket of hot water into the large metal tub. When it was three-quarters of the way full, Baltsaros dismissed them.

Tom stepped lithely back into the stateroom and smiled; he crossed his arms over his tanned chest, his large forearms scarred and muscular, and leaned against the wall. Baltsaros frowned at Tom, who pulled the sliver of wood he was chewing on from between his teeth.

"What? I wanted to watch," said the first mate, shrugging; his sea-green eyes were narrow, challenging the captain.

Baltsaros closed the space between them in a few steps and stared down hard at the shorter man.

"Don't be cheeky, Tom. Leave us be," he growled.

Tom glared up at the captain for a few seconds, then, turned on his heel, slamming the door behind him. Baltsaros closed his eyes a moment, purging from his mind the image of his hands around Tom's throat and the sudden surge of lust it brought.

He turned back to Jon, who was just standing still, looking down at the water-filled tub. In amazement, he watched as Jon pulled the soiled shirt up over his head, dropping it to the ground next to him.

He had expected Jon to ask him to leave.

Baltsaros felt his pulse accelerate at the sight of Jon's pale skin, ribs clearly visible next to the starkly defined muscles of his sides.

Not so weak, then.

Baltsaros realized he was staring when Jon stopped moving, his hands at the waist of his shorts, and his eyes fixed on the captain's face. The older man smiled and dipped his head, turning around to give Jon some privacy while he undressed.

When Baltsaros heard Jon settling into the hot water with a gasp, he walked to the chest near the foot of his bed and pulled out a few things. After crossing the room to pull up a chair next to the metal tub, Baltsaros handed a small block of sandalwood-scented soap and a rough towel to Jon as he sat down.

Jon let out a pleased groan as he reclined in the tub. He looked up at the captain and smiled.

"I haven't had a bath like this in ages," he said. He brought the soap to his nose. "This smells great. Thank you, Captain."

Baltsaros watched in amusement as Jon began lathering himself, the dam that had held back his words suddenly broken.

"Reginald didn't believe in hot baths; he said it made a man weak. I took cold baths from the time I was four, when my mother died, until I was able to go to the baths in town on my days off. That was only a little over a year ago. I think I may have actually wept the first time I sank into a bathtub full of hot water. Such a luxury." He laughed and smelled the soap again. "And, never with soap that smelled this good. Can all your men afford these things, or is it only because you're captain?" he asked, looking up at Baltsaros.

The captain smiled and shook his head. "We can all afford these luxuries, Jon. My cut of our… earnings, if you'd like, is only marginally higher, and that is only to defray costs like maintaining the ship or docking in specific harbours. I may be captain, but we are all more-or-less equal on this ship," Baltsaros replied, skimming around the fact that he was the one who meted punishment and could veto all crew decisions.

Jon nodded thoughtfully.

"What will be my work here?" he asked after a moment.

Baltsaros's eyes watched as suds followed the curve of the young man's shoulder and rubbed his palm against his knee before closing his hand into a fist. Jon was definitely having an effect on Baltsaros. He shifted his gaze away from the man's naked skin.

"Not much at first, I'm afraid. Initially, you will work at learning your way around the ship; with that will be a lot of cleaning and putting up with mediocre or odious tasks, but that's because you are new. It's not glamorous, but it's necessary. If you accept it all with grace and patience, you'll earn the respect of the crew." He smiled kindly at the disappointment in Jon's face. "You'll also act as an advisor when I deal with other ships. That is where your unique talent will shine. I plan on using you tomorrow when we unload our current cargo," he added, and almost laughed at the excitement and terror that suddenly widened Jon's eyes.

His gaze narrowed thoughtfully for a moment, and Baltsaros started rolling up his sleeves. Suddenly on guard, Jon's dark brows came down. There was a new tack the captain wanted to try. Baltsaros leaned towards the tub.

"Here, I'll wash your back," he said, keeping his voice light. He had no idea whether Jon would let himself be touched. Jon had willingly put himself into Baltsaros's hands when it came to having his fever taken, but this was a different matter entirely.

Jon's cheeks, already rosy from the heat of the bath, darkened to a deeper shade of red, and he looked like he was about to refuse Baltsaros's help.

"Pass me the soap," said the captain, his tone commanding, and Jon moved to obey him, a strange expression in his stormy-blue eyes.

He really does not know what he wants.

Baltsaros was attempting to ease the young man's anxiety with a human touch, but he realized in dismay that his motives had little to do with how useful that would make him to the crew; the truth was that Baltsaros foolishly wanted to win Jon over, both mentally and physically, for himself.

To what end?

He rubbed the soap onto the cloth and reached out to scrub Jon's bent back. The cloth slid smoothly across his slippery ribs and bumped over the ridges of his spine. The angle was slightly awkward, and when Baltsaros shifted his grasp it brought his thumb into contact with Jon's supple skin, he felt his chest tighten with sudden longing. Baltsaros felt Jon tremble slightly under his touch as he stroked his thumb slowly across his back, following the path of his lithe muscles.

Baltsaros felt suddenly weak and strangely like he was losing control of the situation. Standing quickly, he dropped the towel into the tub, then turned to leave. He looked back over his shoulder at the startled Jon and made his excuse.

"I'm sorry, you'll have to finish bathing yourself. I have pressing things to attend to," Baltsaros said and left through the door, his mouth dry. Where a solid wall once stood in his mind, keeping the messy, howling beast of his humanity under strict control, there was a breach. It was tiny, but it was troubling.

J on watched in shock as the captain left the stateroom, an obvious lie on his lips. He lay back in the tub, a chorus of conflicting emotions in his mind. Over the past few days, he'd felt himself growing bolder in the captain's presence, gaining admiration for the elegantly handsome man. Baltsaros was intelligent and inquisitive; Jon never felt like he was boring the captain with his questions or annoying him with his insecurities. On the contrary, it seemed like he was genuinely interested in him. Jon began to notice the captain looking at him in a way no one else had: like he was worthy of attention. While Jon couldn't admit to himself yet that what he was feeling was attraction to the enigmatic captain, he found his confidence buoyed by it.

Earlier, when Baltsaros had shooed Tom from the room, he had expected the captain to follow him out. When he hadn't, a shocking recklessness had taken over Jon; he had stood there, amazed at himself, stripping his clothing off in front of the other man.

It was only a lifetime of insecurity that had finally stilled his hands as they were about to render him completely naked before the captain's eyes. Baltsaros had just stared, face sombre and eyes dark with something that pulled at Jon.

Then later, the ridiculousness of being washed by a pirate captain. Jon sighed to himself and soaped his shoulders again.

Was it really ridiculous?

He closed his eyes and leaned back. Why had the captain left so abruptly? Had Baltsaros seen something of Jon that displeased him? That small touch, the surprising sensation of skin sliding against wet skin... Jon moved his soapy hand down his chest.

Or had he seen something that pleased him too much?

The thought sent Jon's heart careening, and he laughed softly. The idea of wanting a man to... desire him. It was simply staggering. Jon frowned and thought of the shocking dreams he'd begun having nightly; his cock responded by moving again in the warm water to resume the stiffening that had started with the captain's touch.

The last dream in particular... Baltsaros had been moving over Jon, using him face-up like a man used a woman. Jon clenched his eyelids tighter, the images in his mind filling him with a hot sensation that made the bath feel cool in comparison. His hand slid below the water, down his belly to the dark hair curled around the base of the rigid staff that bobbed stiffly in the water. What was it about the dark-eyed man that made him feel like this?

With equal parts shame and desire, Jon finally closed his hand around his cock. He imagined that instead of his own slim fingers, Baltsaros's long, sun-darkened ones were stroking him. With a low whimper in his throat, Jon began to slide his fist over his shaft in the warm water.

Yes, it was Baltsaros's hand on him. Now his mouth, hot and wet, around his cock. Jon shuddered with pleasure, feeling a little wicked for even forming the word "cock" in his head. He slid further down in the water until his chin was immersed. He spread his knees, imagining the captain's head bobbing between his thighs. With all thoughts to shame out of mind, Jon stroked his shaft, pulling at the sensitive head with thumb and finger, imagining them to be Baltsaros's lips. Nearly panting with the force of his desire, Jon felt the climax start deep within himself. He groaned out loud and clamped the washcloth over the head of his cock as his lust finally crested in hot waves, spilling seed into his covered hand.

For a few moments, Jon could hear nothing but his breathing and the rushing blood in his ears. Thighs trembling, he eventually pulled the cloth out of the water and stared down at it with dismay.

Baltsaros had Tom up against the back wall of the galley. Tom's hands were clasped behind his head, tied there by the belt around his throat. The captain was thrusting himself into his first mate in a fury, driving his cock into Tom's ass so forcefully that Baltsaros heard the man's collarbones knock hard against the wooden slats.

Tom had stopped struggling and now whimpered or moaned as he pushed back into every thrust. Baltsaros didn't need to reach around to know that the first mate's cock would be rigid and wet with his own pleasure; the captain gritted his teeth and grunted as he ploughed faster into the younger man. When orgasm quickly burst out of him in a hot torrent, he wrapped his hand around Tom's shaft for the last few thrusts and felt the other's cum hot against his palm almost immediately.

Panting hard, Tom let out a sobbing cry and sagged in the captain's grasp.

Baltsaros, chest heaving, pressed his forehead against Tom's shoulder for a moment before stepping back and releasing him.

The first mate slid, almost bonelessly, down the wall. Baltsaros shoved his softening cock almost angrily back into his pants; he felt strangely unsatisfied and frustrated. Tom looked up at the captain with wet, red eyes as Baltsaros undid the belt that was looped around him.

What was it about Jon that had him so wound up?

He frowned into Tom's upturned face for a moment. Feeling only annoyance at the man on the floor, Baltsaros lashed out, backhanding his first mate as hard as he could. Tom let out a yell and collapsed on his side. Baltsaros crossed the room to the door, leaving Tom bleeding on the floor, and heard the man begin to laugh behind him.

7

CLOSE QUARTERS

When he heard footfalls behind him, Jon quickly closed the book he was holding. He turned and saw that the captain had entered the stateroom, a plate in each hand, just like he had the past three evenings.

Baltsaros raised his stark brows, looking at the younger man in curiosity.

"You can read?" he asked, sounding amazed.

Jon's guilt at having taken the book was replaced by embarrassment.

"Yes. Of course, I can read. I'm not stupid," he said, hating the fact that he sounded so defensive. Baltsaros placed the plates on the table and shook his head slightly.

"Jon, you'll have to stop assuming that everything I say is meant to wound you in some way," he said in a soft voice, smiling at him. Though Baltsaros had been terse when leaving so abruptly earlier that day, it seemed that he was once more his affable self.

Jon took a deep breath and nodded, his lips pressed into a hard line. He placed the book, a lexicon of mythical sea creatures, back on the shelf and closed the glass-fronted cabinet door. As he approached the table, the captain looked at him appraisingly.

"You look better, Jon," he said. "And the change of clothes suits you."

Jon looked down and smoothed the front of the shirt Tom had given him, feeling a little bit at a loss.

S hortly after his bath, Tom appeared with a bundle of clothing for Jon. The muscular first mate, sporting yet another bruise on his handsome face, seemed strangely passive as he set the pile down on the table. With a preoccupied expression, the unusually silent Tom just stood there sizing Jon up before picking out a light-brown, loose linen shirt and dark-grey trousers that could be rolled and tied at the knee. Then, after a thought, Tom also pulled a clean pair of unbleached, knee-length linen undershorts out of the pile.

Jon felt a little suspicious at Tom's placid nature as he took the clothing from him. When the first mate saw his distrust, he just shook his head and tutted.

"Lovey, just try these on, ok? Captain's orders." A hint of his usual brash cheerfulness faintly touched the smile on his face. "I'll even turn around so ye don't have to show me yer willy, Jonny," he added, his grin widening.

Jon frowned at Tom. Earlier, loath to put his soiled clothing back on over clean skin, he had opted instead for the marginally cleaner sheet; he had hoped the captain would come back to lend him some clothing.

Disconcerted, Jon stood holding the sheet around him as he watched Tom turn around, granting him some unexpected privacy.

What happened to you today, Tom? he wondered as he quickly pulled on the shirt and fastened the pants at his hips. To his chagrin, Jon saw that they were too big at the waist. He cleared his throat, and Tom turned around to look at him.

"Yer a skinny thing, aint'cha, lovey," he said, shaking his head.

He turned and walked out of the stateroom without another word, leaving Jon clutching miserably at the waistband of the ill-fitting trousers.

However, after only a few moments Tom strolled back into the room, a roll of narrow hemp rope looped over his shoulder. Jon watched as the first mate slid a few feet of the rope through his big, scarred hands, cutting it off with his knife when there were a few parallel lengths. He passed the ends of the pieces through a metal ring and doubled the rope up.

"Be a dove and hold this," he said to Jon, passing him the ring.

As Jon looked on in amazement, Tom's surprisingly nimble hands swiftly braided the lengths of rope together to make a corded belt. When he was done, and the ends were knotted off, he took the ring out of Jon's hand and leaned forward.

Jon flinched and felt his pulse start to race when Tom's muscular arms came around him. Tom's laugh rumbled deep in his broad chest.

"I ain't goin' to kiss ye, poppet. Just keep still like a good little lad," he said, his tone amused. Jon noticed that Tom had fresh abrasions down the side of his neck, and the skin around his right collarbone was mottled and bruised.

He had to close his eyes as Tom fiddled with the belt at his waist; the bigger man was so near that he was completely overwhelming Jon's senses. In dismay, he felt his body responding to Tom's proximity; Jon could feel the heat coming off the first mate, the other man's lusty masculinity making him feel incredibly flustered.

What am I becoming? he thought miserably.

Jon gasped when he suddenly felt Tom's hands stroke down his hips and grasp his buttocks as the first mate pressed him against his hard body for an instant before pulling away with a sly grin. Jon reeled in shock at Tom's temerity, and he tried to quash the steady pulse of desire the bigger man's actions had wrung out of him.

Tom stepped back a pace and cocked his head at Jon, his brash good-nature revived as he winked at the stunned man.

"There. That'll do ye until we dock somewhere's ye can buy yerself something in good leather," he said, his white teeth flashing in his tanned face.

Jon looked down at the belt knotted expertly at his waist, trying to hide the fact that he felt more than a little breathless. When he raised his head Tom had gone, silent as a cat. Jon closed his eyes.

Tom is dangerous, he reminded himself. *He means you no good.* Jon knew he had to keep that thought in mind; anything else was pure folly.

A s he stood looking down at his shirt, Jon thought he could still smell Tom on him: clean sweat and smoke, and something of the sea. Jon pulled back the chair and sat down across from the captain, forcing his face into what he hoped was a pleasant smile.

It felt uncomfortably like a lie not to tell the captain of Tom's brazen advances, made solely of mischief though they might be. On the other hand, if he did complain, Baltsaros might perceive him as someone who couldn't handle his own problems. So, in the end, he decided to say nothing at all.

The captain lifted the cover off the plate in front of Jon; the smell that wafted up from the meat dish was divine. He smiled as Baltsaros sat down and uncovered his own dish.

"What are we having tonight?" he asked.

"It's called *Cormarye.* Basically a pork roast with caraway, coriander, red wine, and loads of garlic," Baltsaros answered before pulling the meat off his fork with sharp teeth. Jon picked up his own utensils, handling them with increasing skill, and took a mouthful. It was, like everything else he'd eaten while on board the ship, delicious. The captain, seeing the appreciation plain on Jon's face, smiled wide.

Jon chewed happily, his problems momentarily forgotten.

"You have one hell of a cook, Captain," he said, cutting one of the tender, young potatoes in half and spearing it with his fork.

Baltsaros laughed, a glint in his dark eyes. "My cook is very good, yes. However, I make my own meals," he said, smiling at the stunned look on Jon's face. "Cooking is a hobby of mine."

"Well. It's amazing. As always," Jon stuttered, desperately wishing he had half the poise of the older man. The captain grinned and bowed his head, a graceful acknowledgment of Jon's compliment.

Jon watched as Baltsaros looked down at his plate, carving another bite from the juicy meat; his face was all planes and angles, eyes darkly shadowed by his alpine brow. Jon saw that the short stubble on the captain's jaw was lightly dusted with white hairs, but his skin remained smooth and unlined; he found himself wondering what it would be like to run his thumb along those sharp cheekbones down to the rough curve of his jaw.

Baltsaros looked up, his dark eyes widening slightly when he saw himself being observed so closely; Jon's cheeks burned, and he smiled awkwardly. When he reached for his cup, he was happy to see that it was filled with red wine, barely watered. He took a long swallow.

It seemed that the air was thick with a strange tension; the darkened room made a cocoon around the nimbus of candlelight, trapping the men in a warm, glowing space that was increasingly intimate with every glance they shared. Though the meal was one of the best in his life, Jon was beginning to have a hard time swallowing it down.

Desperate to break the long silence, he chose the only subject he could think of.

"Uh. So I can read, yes. Reginald thought it important that I know my letters," he said in a rush. The captain just nodded, the smile on his face now subdued and his brown eyes impassive. Jon longed to know what was going on in Baltsaros's head. Was he making a fool of himself? Was that desire he saw in the other man's eyes? He took another swallow of wine; he was a blind man feeling for pitfalls in a dangerous cave.

Alarmed, he realized the captain was now staring hard at him; Baltsaros tapped his finger lightly against the side of his cup, an oddly nervous gesture for the normally imperturbable man.

Jon was astonished; it was suddenly crystal clear to him that the man across the table was fighting to get himself under control, as though the captain were desperately closing storm windows against a howling tempest within. Only the slightest hint of the struggle showed on Baltsaros's enigmatic face, but Jon's strange talent had honed in on it. Before he had a chance to say anything, he saw the captain's brow crease for a moment, his large hands curling into fists on the table before sliding flat, palms down on the warm wood.

Captain Baltsaros looked at Jon, all expression wiped from his face.

"You'll be moving to the crew bunks tomorrow. Good night, Jon," he said and stood.

Jon watched in dismay as the captain turned his back and walked out into the darkness, the plate of food he left behind barely touched.

Jon felt terribly alone.

High up on the quarterdeck, Baltsaros was lost in thought. He knew that below his feet, Jon would most likely be trying to find sleep on the narrow cot in his cage.

Not his. Mine.

As he drank deeply from the bottle of wine he held in one large hand, the dark-eyed man stared off over waves glittering with the moon's reflection; the night sky was clear and cool, and the stars twinkled like cold embers in a field of deepest blue. However, the man in the long black coat saw none of the beauty as he stood there, the wind blowing against his face.

He took another swig of wine and frowned. Why was he acting this way? It should be nothing to take the boy to his bed— to kiss the dark shadows under his eyes, to bewitch him with pleasure, to show him the secrets of exquisite pain.

The captain gritted his teeth; Jon was like a poisoned well, and Baltsaros was dying of thirst. While something deep inside him reached out with grasping claws, desperate to pull the younger man tight against him, something else screamed *danger* every time he contemplated it... and for good reason: more small cracks were beginning to show in Baltsaros's composure.

He took another long pull from the bottle before whipping his arm out and launching it high into the air to fall unseen into black waters beyond. He closed his eyes and took a deep breath.

"Tom. You're not needed. Go away," he said to the man on the stairs below; Baltsaros had caught the scent of the first mate's cheroot in the breeze. Dismayed at the note of rough emotion in his voice, Baltsaros opened his eyes and turned. When he saw that Tom hadn't yet moved from his perch, he called out. "Bring me some more red. The one in the darker green bottles. Bring it to me, my tomcat, and then leave me be," he said wearily.

The captain watched as Tom's shadow moved stealthy away on silent feet before he turned back to the sea; as dangerous as the ex-slave was, Jon was turning out to be more so. He had seen desire in the young man's face, and it had *rattled him...* And earlier, Jon in the bath... He swallowed hard, and licked his lips; Baltsaros had to keep away from Jon until he regained his inner calm. That night would be the last time they shared a room; things would be better once Jon went to stay with the rest of the crew.

Better? Or worse?

Tom startled Baltsaros from his thoughts by handing him a bottle of the rich red wine he had brought from home. He dismissed the first mate and watched him slink back into the shadows with an expression of misplaced worry on his battered face. He realized then that Tom had never seen his captain drink alone in the dark like this. Baltsaros nearly laughed as he pulled the cork from the bottle with his teeth and spat it out overboard.

T he sky was starting to pinken when Jon heard the captain finally return to his quarters. Blearily opening his eyes, he watched as Baltsaros walked heavily to the other side of the room and lowered himself onto the bed. The older man pulled off his boots and threw them to the floor before lying back on top of the coverlet. After a moment, Jon thought he had gone to sleep; however, when he lifted his head he saw that Baltsaros's eyes were open, staring in Jon's direction. Their gazes locked for a moment, Baltsaros's expression nearly inscrutable, before he turned over. Disturbed, Jon laid his head back on the pillow; he had seen something in the other man's eyes he had never expected: a touch of fear.

8

NELSON'S FOLLY

Nelson's folly • *naval slang (19th century)* rum.

J on stood uneasily on the deck just outside the captain's quarters, blinking into the bright sun. Tom gave him another nudge from behind, and Jon took a second reluctant step forward. He heard the larger man laugh, and Jon winced; this was not going to be easy. Coming around to sit on a small crate near the stairs to the quarterdeck, Tom looked up at him, brows furrowed in confusion; in the morning light, the first mate's face was a mess of yellows, greens, and purples.

"If yer goin' to be part of this crew... yer goin' to have to, y'know, be part of the crew," he said to Jon, rubbing his thumb against the stubble on his chin. "Now what's the bloody problem, ducky?"

Jon stood barefoot on the wooden planks, staring in near panic at the men on deck who, for the most part, were completely ignoring him.

Stupid. Stupid, why did I think I could do this?

"I... have problems with people. I'm not good with them. I just sort of shut down," he stammered, bringing up his hands to clutch at his biceps. Tom let out a whoop of laughter and slapped his knees.

"Fuckin' hells!" he said, chortling. "Fuckin' bloody fuckin' hells." He shook his head and stood up, forcefully draping one of his muscular arms around Jon's shoulders. Because Tom wasn't much taller than him, Jon was stooped slightly under the larger man's weight as he tried to lean away from his bare side.

Tom started dragging Jon along as he pointed out parts of the ship with a callused, tobacco-stained finger.

"That's a mast. That's a crate... We're startin' real simple here, lovey. That's Old Ben, passed out like usual. Don't let him fool ye though... He's a good one once the hangover wears off," he said, kicking the sleeping man's boot. To one side of the ship, a man who must have been near seven feet tall was pulling a rope through a pulley. Jon suspected he was the giant who had held his wrists at the brothel.

"That's Beard. Well... His name ain't really *Beard;* he just has an unpronounceable name in his shitty northern language. Dont'cha, Beard?" he yelled up at the incongruously clean-shaven man. The huge, burly brute just frowned down at Tom before sending a jet of spit overboard. Tom laughed.

"Can't speak a word of anything else," he said, shaking his head. Jon gingerly put one hand against Tom's warm side to try to pull his head out of the bigger man's hold, but to no avail; Tom just shifted his grip and steered him in another direction. Jon could feel the hard muscles flexing over Tom's ribs and pulled his hand back; the contact had sent his heart racing.

"That is the capstan," Tom continued, pointing to a large spoked wheel. "Ye'll be helpin' to turn that later today if ye don't fall overboard and drown first." The first mate chuckled to himself and then stopped. "Ye *can* swim, right?" he asked, looking down, sea-green eyes crinkled in amusement. Jon nodded quickly, and Tom patted him hard on the head with his free hand. "Good, good," he said and then pointed up, resuming the above-deck portion of his tour.

"Yardarms, ratlines, quarterdeck, mizzen mast... and... uh, the captain." Tom's voice trailed off at the last, the wind blown out of his sails at the sight of the man in the long, dark coat. Jon used Tom's momentary distraction to extract himself from the heavy arm over his shoulders. He stood next to the first mate, looking up at the captain's back, high above them.

When Jon had awoken that morning, the older man was nowhere to be seen, even though it couldn't have been more than a few hours since he'd lain down.

Baltsaros seemed to be watching the wake behind them, standing eerily still, a black silhouette against the bright cerulean sky. The muscles worked in Tom's broad jaw as he watched the captain a moment longer. When he finally turned his head back to his newest recruit, Jon thought he could see apprehension in Tom's blue-green eyes.

What is going on?

The first mate's face swiftly creased into a broad grin, discarding the solemnness that had settled for only a moment; he curled his big hand around Jon's bicep, turning the shorter man around again. Jon had to keep his mouth from dropping open when he saw the woman who was approaching them.

There are women on the ship? he thought with alarm.

She was slim and walked with a confidence that nearly turned her long strides into a swagger. As she came closer, Jon could see that she had dark, almond-shaped eyes and ebony hair in a long braid over one shoulder. She was dressed in a sleeveless, dark-brown leather jerkin and black trousers that came down just past her knees with brown leather lacing down each side. In wonder, Jon saw that she wore two gun belts crossed and slung low over her hips, the beautiful, silver-chased, hardwood handles of the pistols resting against her thighs. Jon was happy to see that, unlike the captain and his first mate, she was an open book. Here was someone who was honestly friendly and, Jon realized, mildly concerned that he was in Tom's care.

The first mate laughed low in his chest.

"Jon, this exotic bit of skirt is Katherine. Don't piss her off or she'll make some new holes in that curly, black head of yers. Wont'cha, lovey?" he said, addressing the last to the woman.

Her lips slid into a wry smile, dismissing Tom completely as she turned her dark-brown eyes to Jon; he could easily feel the deep animosity that existed between the two pirates.

"Kat, if you'd like," she said, smiling. Jon swallowed and nodded, nearly choking when Tom clapped a large hand to his chest.

"Kat, my darlin', meet our new little Jonny. Isn't he a dove? Lived under a rock, so's I can tell from his complexion. Completely mute. Hung like a bloody mule," said the first mate loudly. Jon felt his face grow hot. Tom leaned in close to his ear.

"Ex-whore, this one. Sewed her cunny up tight, I hear to tell, when she took up with the crew. A total man-eater. She's got a string of cocks above her bunk that she stirs her coffee with," he said in a stage whisper.

Jon had to smile when Katherine rolled her eyes at him.

She turned and frowned at Tom.

"I see you fell down another flight of stairs, Tommy. You're so hard on that pretty face of yours," she said; her voice was girlish despite the cocksure way she held herself. Tom shook his head slowly; the smile on his face was almost menacing.

Jon took a deep breath.

"I'm not mute... I can talk," he said, somewhat lamely. Tom's big hand slid up his back and squeezed his shoulder.

"Course ye can, lovey. Course ye can," said Tom, his face filled with mock pity.

The air was suddenly split with a shrill whistle, and Tom's head jerked around quickly. He released Jon and pointed at Katherine.

"Show him the bunks; get him working on deck. He's needed this afternoon for the exchange," he said and took off at a jog towards the rear of the ship. Katherine shook her head.

"Off to see his master," she said, her smile crooked. "It's a pleasure to meet you, Jon. Welcome aboard." She crossed her arms across her midriff and gave him an appraising look. "First time at sea?" she asked.

Jon ducked his head and ran a hand through his dark curls.

"That obvious, huh?" he said. At her laugh, he looked up with a frown. However, there was no malice on her face, only gentle amusement; Jon found himself smiling back at her.

"So," said Katherine, her hands on her hips. "What do you want to know?"

Jon brought up one shoulder in a shrug.

"I suppose everything you're willing to tell me," he said truthfully. Tom's lessons, so far, had been largely unhelpful. He started and then, cringed as a big, black-bearded man pushed past them. Katherine's eyes widened at Jon's reaction.

"Not a fan of people?" asked the woman with the guns, looking at him curiously.

Jon shook his head.

"Not really."

Katherine nodded and pressed her lips together.

"Not to sound unkind, but are you sure you're in the right place?" she asked softly. Jon swallowed hard and shrugged again. Katherine nodded her head once in understanding and swiftly launched into the ship rules. Grateful for her tact, Jon found himself quickly absorbed by her words.

"And basically, we vote for anything that affects us. You really don't want to go to the eastern seas? We all vote. You're not happy with what Cook's been making? We all vote. Etcetera. It's pretty easy. We're really a skeleton crew on the ship… She could take twice our number, but we're all hard workers and it actually isn't so bad. It also makes us richer," she laughed. "The captain's got the final word on everything, but he's generally happy as long as we're happy."

Jon's eyes turned to the quarterdeck, but Baltsaros and Tom were nowhere to be seen.

"Don't steal. Don't fuck over your mates. Those are the two big ones. We're to be loyal to each other. If you've got a problem with someone, you can resolve it privately. However, if you want to make it the business of the whole crew, the usual punishment for the guilty party is time in the brig," Katherine said. "It might not sound like much, but ask Tom about it some day; he's done three long stretches down there just this year."

Jon felt the corners of his mouth turn down, his impression of the roguish first mate not improved by this news. Also, as the morning wore on, he was becoming increasingly aware of how ill-suited he was for this. Though Katherine was nice enough, he wished that the captain would... Would what? Talk to him? Let him stay locked away in his quarters? When Jon remembered the fear in Baltsaros's eyes he swiftly clamped down on the tumult rising up inside before he lost his nerve.

Just don't think about it. You don't know what it means.

At a touch on his arm, he looked up. Katherine was looking into his eyes, worry plain on her face.

"Are you ok?" she asked.

Everyone is always asking.

As he took a deep breath, Jon straightened his shoulders and stood a little taller.

"I... I can do this," he said, more to himself than to the woman who stood before him.

Katherine tilted her head slightly as she crossed her arms again. After a moment, a slow smile crept across her face.

"So, are you really hung like a mule?" she asked. Jon started to blush but then realized that she was only teasing him. Smiling crookedly, Jon blinked in amazement as he heard himself quip back.

"I'll show you if you get us out of this blasted sun."

B altsaros stood on deck, watching the other ship's approach with his binoculars. Behind him, he could hear Tom barking orders to the deckhands.

"C'mon, ye bunch of lounging fucking strumpets! Put yer backs into it. I want to see them all on deck before we heave to! Shake a leg... Oh, I *am* sorry, lovey! Did I wake the lady from her nap? I'll keelhaul the bloody lot of ye if ye don't put them kegs up smart-like!" The mainlander's rolling accent, amplified by his loud running commentary, brought a small smile to Baltsaros's face— the first of the day.

He sighed and pinched the bridge of his nose. As he turned his gaze up deck towards the bow, he saw that Jon was helping to lower the anchor; on the next spoke of the capstan was Katherine. Baltsaros nodded to himself. Jon would do well by befriending her. She was the best shot in his crew and a fair hand with a sword; their newest recruit could certainly learn a few things from her.

The fact that Jon was out dropping anchor in the hot sun, however, brought a frown to the captain's rugged face; he had explicitly told Tom not to put Jon to work just yet. The younger man was on the mend but in no state to be doing hard physical labour. Annoyed, he looked back to his burly first mate, but Tom had gone belowdecks again. Though the ex-slave was at most times desperately loyal, his interpretations of the captain's orders left something to be desired. With Jon aboard, the problem seemed only to have worsened.

Baltsaros lifted the binoculars to his eyes again and saw that Magrette's ship, the *Nelson's Folly*, had anchored; a jolly boat was slowly being lowered down her side. It was soon time to see whether their newest recruit would prove his worth.

If not...

The captain furrowed his brow and turned his gaze back to the dark-haired young man. After last night's drinking binge, Baltsaros felt less than stellar; however, it seemed to have brought some calm to the storm created by his attraction to Jon. Baltsaros knew they would be working side by side later, but since the captain had taken a step back, he felt that he was again in total control. Or at least he hoped he was. If Jon failed to dazzle, he would simply drop him off at the nearest port.

Why not just kill him?

Baltsaros passed his hand over his face and grimaced.

Why not, indeed... came the whisper from within.

"Two small barrels of pepper, and a crate of nutmeg," listed out the first mate. The scrawny, black-haired man then turned to his captain and nodded. "It's all there," he said.

Earlier, Baltsaros had explained that they had recently over-taken a huge merchant ship and were trading off the plundered foodstuff and spices. In return, the other captain, someone they dealt with occasionally, was giving them gold. Jon's job was to make sure that there was no swindle involved; Baltsaros had reason to believe that this Captain Magrette could no longer be trusted.

Trying his best to appear aloof and confident, Jon stood to the left of the captain. In reality, he was so nervous and distracted by Captain Baltsaros's presence that he feared his talents would prove to be useless.

Tom stood to the captain's other side, thick arms crossed over his broad chest, his bare feet planted wide apart on the wooden deck. The first mate slyly glanced over to where Jon stood and winked. After shaking his head at Tom, Jon turned back to the deal-ings. He watched carefully as the men pulled three small chests up from the boat below. When the third chest was hefted, Jon noticed that the pirates lifted it easier than the other two, and he frowned. Their movements were exaggerated, as if in a pantomime. The men shared a quick glance with their captain before setting the lighter chest down, and Jon's eyes slid from the gold to the pale-skinned man with the large hat. There was definitely something amiss. *Why would they want us to notice that one chest was light?*

The captain of the other ship was nothing like Baltsaros. Where the northerner was all planes and angles, Magrette was doughy lumps and curves. The man wasn't hugely fat; he was just not as slim as his straining clothes would have liked.

Jon narrowed his eyes at the other captain and caught something in the man's demeanour that reinforced his feeling of unease. Swinging his eyes back to the chests that now sat open on the wooden planks, Jon's clever mind presented to him a scenario where a lighter chest would somehow benefit someone trying to hustle them. It reminded him of the way merchants would present an item and "prove" its quality before selling identical-looking wares of an inferior worth. He smiled.

Baltsaros turned to him, his eyes dark and impassive.

"What do you see, Jon?" he asked. Jon felt himself blanch; no one had told him he would have to speak in front of everyone. Foolishly, he had imagined a private conversation with the captain. The silence stretched on, all eyes turning to him. Feeling like he was going to burn his way through the hull, Jon took a deep breath and finally spoke.

"They're short-changing us, Captain," he said in a voice that wavered. The other ship's skinny first mate looked askance at his own captain; Jon could tell that he had not been told of the deceit. When Captain Magrette opened his mouth to dismiss his pronouncement, Jon felt suddenly bold with indignation.

"The third chest, the one on the left, is lighter than the other two. Not by much, but enough. They gambled on you noticing it was slightly lighter and counting the gold in it right away to make sure the amount is right... and it will be. They're trying to make us think that we're coming out ahead of the deal; but, it's only when the other two were emptied that you'd notice that it was the chests *themselves* that were heavier. False bottoms with something heavy like lead inside, I think. Crude and stupid," he finished, looking up at the older man by his side.

Captain Magrette had started to sputter, but the sound of gold rolling across the deck, and Tom's long string of expletives, confirmed Jon's theory. Baltsaros turned to look down at Jon; he was astonished and reassured by the depth of amusement (*and... relief?*) in the captain's brown eyes. Jon smiled.

Baltsaros smiled back; with his eyes still on his newest recruit, he gave the command.

"Tom. Take them," he said, his voice deadly quiet. There was an incredibly short struggle as Tom and the gathered deckhands disarmed the would-be thieves. The scrawny first mate spoke up.

"I ain't never was a part o' this, Cap'n sir," he said, his voice nasal and sharp. Baltsaros raised an eyebrow at Jon and tilted his head slightly. Jon understood this as an invitation.

"He speaks the truth, Captain. He might be a complete worm, but he wasn't a part of this. If you let him go, he'll warn others about what happens when thieves cross us," he said, his breath short in his chest as the captain continued to hold his gaze.

"Katherine?" said the captain, his graceful lips curling further into a pleased grin. There was a splash and yelling from below; Jon gathered that the skinny first mate had been pushed overboard.

Baltsaros nodded once.

"Good job," he said simply and finally turned away. Jon nearly staggered, his heart careening in his chest; however, for the first time in his life, he felt incredibly in control... confident.

He looked on as the captain stalked slowly towards the doughy Magrette. The two men shared quiet words; Jon was unable to hear what they were saying, but it was clear that the fat captain was pleading for his life.

In strange detachment, the captain's new advisor watched as a river of red began to flow down the deck.

J on tripped and ended up sprawled on the floor. He rolled over onto his back and started laughing, his hands clutching his stomach as he fought for breath. Tom's face appeared above him; the first mate's ocean-green eyes were narrow with amusement, and his pink lips were stretched in a wide smile.

"Aye, lovey... Yer a bit of a lightweight, aint'cha?" said Tom, holding out a hand to help Jon back to his feet. The world spun a little, so Jon leaned against the bigger man's side. Tom chuckled as his arm came up behind Jon. Jon laughed again and held out his hand for the bottle of rum they were sharing.

The golden lights of the lanterns made streaks in his vision, and for some reason, that made him giddy with joy. He narrowed his eyes, head nodding, at the men who were dancing and shouting. It was a celebration. He was a pirate! Doing pirate things! Jon grinned wide and wiped at his mouth.

Tom's hand was warm against his side as the first mate took the brown bottle back from him. Jon felt fantastic. He could see Katherine standing on the capstan, a fiddle in her hands as she whipped the men into a frenzy with music birthed from wild emotions. For a moment, he thought he saw the captain's silhouette... Jon fell back against Tom's shoulder and looked up at the endless stars. Tom wasn't such a bad guy.

"You're not such a bad guy," he yelled. He felt Tom's hand squeeze him, and it sent a sudden thrill through his body.

No... this is wrong. Isn't it?

He laughed and shook his head, making himself a little dizzy in the process.

Jon had never been to a celebration before. Not really. There were the times when their lord came back to the castle, and Cook would make something nice for the occasion. Sometimes Reginald's men would gather in the courtyard, and there would be dancing with the maids. But... nothing like this.

The captain was pleased with him! It was because of him that they were drinking and dancing under the stars. On the sea. The calm sea. He was at sea!

He went to take the bottle from Tom's hand but the first mate held it out of reach. Jon grabbed at it, grinning like a fool. Tom pulled the slighter man against him. Only for a moment, Jon felt Tom's scratchy stubble against the bottom of his jaw, and then the muscular pirate poured rum into his mouth.

"I want to show ye something, lovey," said Tom, his handsome face serious... handsome!

Dangerous.

Jon realized that one of his hands had looped around the muscular back of the first mate. He was being led away from the music. They were in the captain's quarters. He managed to stumble over the edge of a rug, and he was down again. Giggling. When had he ever giggled before? Muffled voices. Oh, the captain was here.

Tom leaned down and scooped him up. The boy was so strong. Felt so smooth for being so rough. He shook his head, trying to clear it as he was held upright by the first mate. He smiled at the captain who was reclining on his bed, shirtless and with a book in one hand.

"Hi," he said, feeling suddenly shy. Tom's hands were wandering into strange territory, and Jon pushed at them half-heartedly.

Baltsaros put his book down beside him, his expression frustratingly unreadable. Tom pushed Jon down onto the bed and he rose up unsteadily on his knees on the soft mattress.

"He's drunk," said the captain, or so that's what it sounded like. Jon missed what Tom was saying because Baltsaros's hand came out to steady him. To pull him back. Jon was leaning back against the captain's bare chest. Large, steady, warm hands stroked down his arms, and he felt himself shiver. His mind was reeling; he was leaning against the captain... against him on his bed and *oh god, he's...* Jon groaned when Baltsaros slid a hand into the open collar of his shirt, moving slowly to tease his nipple; an incredible pulse of desire went through Jon.

"You did well today, lad," said the captain softly into his ear.

Baltsaros's other hand was doing something at Jon's waist. Jon watched wide-eyed as fingers not his own unfastened his pants.

Sudden panic began to well up inside him when the captain's hand started tugging down on the waistband of his undershorts. Jon's breath was coming fast, and he heard himself moan as Tom's nimble fingers quickly helped to divest him of cover.

Time felt sped up. He felt cool air on his exposed cock and gasped as Baltsaros's hands slid up to Jon's shoulders, holding him gently against his chest. This was too much. He shuddered as Tom stroked the skin of his stomach, of his hips. Just as the first mate's hand came into contact with Jon's growing erection, he heard the captain's voice.

"Use your mouth, Tom," said Baltsaros, his words an order.

Jon's breathless reaction to the shocking command forced blood to surge faster into his cock, making it throb. He felt as if balanced on the edge of a precipice. Was this really happening? His head was foggy from the rum, but when Tom's tongue slid wetly up the underside of his hardening shaft, Jon's senses came alive.

He whimpered, his cock bobbing of its own accord in reaction to the contact. He looked down into Tom's sea-green eyes and held his breath; the first mate's mouth curled into a wicked grin before his lips parted over the head of Jon's cock, completely engulfing the sensitive skin.

The foreign sensation was pleasure that was rendered so exquisitely raw that it pulled a cry from deep within Jon's chest. Tom's mouth was so wet and unbelievably hot. Jon strained against the captain, tilting his head up and back against Baltsaros's strong shoulder, his eyes closed tight.

Tom began swallowing him down, and Jon moved his hips up in response, astonished by his eagerness. Baltsaros's hands stroked the taut muscles of his stomach and chest through his shirt; whisper-light, tender touches that only worked to enhance the rougher treatment Tom was giving him in contrast. Nearly his entire length slid down the red, wet tunnel of the first mate's throat, and Jon groaned.

Tom's hard hands grabbed him around the hips as he forced himself down further, his wide-open lips making contact with the very base of Jon's shaft. Then Tom began to move, and Jon's cock began sliding in and out of the first mate's mouth. Baltsaros's large hand played at his throat, clasping it slowly in time to Tom's motions.

Jon bucked his hips in abandon, hot lust unfurling inside, opening him up. He felt Baltsaros's mouth against the side of his neck, and he let out a shuddering breath. Jon opened his eyes and turned his head, desperately seeking out those graceful, cruel lips with his own.

When their mouths met, Jon let out a soft sob, a fresh surge of desire searing through him. He opened his mouth to Baltsaros's tongue and wantonly quested out with his own; feeling the captain grow hard against the small of his back as their mouths moved together, Jon gasped and brought up his hand, Baltsaros's sharp stubble rasping against the skin of his palm. The tide of pleasure inside him was climbing steeply, and he moaned into the kiss.

Tom steadily increased his pace; Jon had to break away from the captain in alarm, pushing at the first mate's head.

"Don't! Oh god... don't... I'm going to..." he gasped. He couldn't say the words. *I'm going to cum.*

The thought of ejaculating into Tom's open mouth was what tipped the balance, and he tensed as his senses narrowed down to a white-hot spear of ecstasy, the cum rising through him and surging out of his throbbing, hard cock in thick pulses. Jon moaned as his body strained up with the force of his orgasm, his shaft completely engulfed by Tom's talented mouth.

When he finally went limp, shaken and almost weeping, Tom released him. The first mate's lips were red and shiny with spit and cum as he looked down at Jon.

"Ye going to survive?" he asked, wiping his mouth with a smile.

With his shirt soaked through with sweat, Jon lay panting against the captain; he nodded, closing his eyes. Baltsaros stroked a hand down Jon's side softly before gently pushing him off.

The young man curled up on his side on the red coverlet, helpless tears leaking from his eyes to darken the bright satin. He felt loose limbed and relaxed... though keenly emotional at the same time; finally catching his breath, Jon wondered drowsily how he would feel about this later.

Across the bed, the captain pulled his first mate into his arms, kissing him deeply. Jon watched, slightly confused. A little bit hurt.

I'm the interloper.

He closed his eyes.

Not so special.

Now that the rush of adrenaline had ebbed, the effects of his overindulgence came creeping back, making his body heavy.

He forced his eyes open again to see Tom working the fastenings loose on Baltsaros's pants. He blinked, and when his vision cleared, the captain was up on his knees, long fingers clasped behind Tom's head as he fucked the first mate's mouth.

Jon's lids were drooping shut as he felt himself being pulled away by sleep. He tried once more to keep them open and saw that the captain was looking down at him. The kiss came back, clear in his mind... and then Jon was gone.

Baltsaros watched Jon's eyes close, and he shut his own; Tom's skilled mouth had him skirting the edges of oblivion, but it brought with it none of the blazing, exquisite heat that had clenched like a fist inside Baltsaros at the touch of Jon's lips to his.

9

A FORTNIGHT

Stand upright, speak thy thoughts, declare The
truth thou hast, that all may share; Be bold,
proclaim it everywhere: They only live
who dare

— VOLTAIRE

J on rubbed a forearm across his forehead, wiping the sweat away. The sun was beating down on his back, but he was quickly getting used to that. He looked down at the brush he was holding and flexed the cramped fingers of the other hand; he was getting used to this too. After dipping the brush in the water, Jon leaned back down and scrubbed at the wooden planks. Even though the chore was unbelievably monotonous, it felt remarkably good to be useful.

Every night, Jon went to bed exhausted, barely able to keep his eyes open for the evening meal, and woke up stiff and sore in the morning. As he felt the muscles of his arms harden and the blisters on his hands turn to calluses, he also began to perceive other changes. Though he was never going to be completely comfortable in a crowd, being forced out in the open, surrounded by so many people, was teaching him to cope with his anxiety.

Jon smiled to himself as he wet the brush again and crawled slowly backwards to start scrubbing a new spot. The past couple of weeks had been eye-opening to say the least; he now knew how to braid rope and fix a net, gut a fish and clean crab, load and fire a pistol, oil and maintain a block and tackle, as well as the simplest of tasks that he'd never had to learn before, like how to peel a potato.

Jon looked up at the quarterdeck where the first mate was perched on the railing, staring down at him. He'd also learned very quickly to avoid dark corners when Tom was around.

J on woke up and groaned. The brutal pain in his head sent waves of nausea through him. Was his sickness returning? This felt awfully familiar. However, when he swallowed he realized that there was a horrible taste in his mouth, and his stomach roiled.

He could hear people talking.

Jon's eyes flew open at the sound, and he was immediately and completely disoriented. Above his head was the sagging, corded bottom of a bed with a stained mattress bulging through the supports. He closed his eyes for a moment, but when he reopened them, the scene was the same. As he turned his head, the pain rolling through him with the motion, Jon saw that he was in a bottom bunk in the larger of the two crew quarters. He closed his eyes tight against the light coming in through the small portholes, but his head spun. He groaned again and pressed his fingers to his eyelids.

"Here. You'll probably be sick," said a soft voice nearby. Jon blearily cracked open his eyes and saw Katherine walking towards the bed, holding a wooden bucket in one hand. The dark-haired woman smiled grimly at him as she placed it on the floor next to the bunk.

"What... happened?" asked Jon, his tongue dry and coated. He reached out for the cup of water she was holding.

Katherine laughed and shook her head as she rose to her feet.

"You don't remember getting blind drunk last night?" she asked.

Jon coughed on the tiny sip of water he took. *Drunk. The rum.*

"You got awfully chummy with Tom," she said, frowning. "I... it's none of my business what you do, Jon... but I didn't figure on you cozying up to the likes of him. You do realize that he's more than a little unhinged, right?"

Tom. Oh god... Tom's mouth.

Bits and pieces of last night's debacle were rising up in his mind like pieces of meat in a soup. Jon leaned over the bed and vomited a thin, burning stream into the bucket. He heard Katherine take a quick step back. Jon retched hard, his stomach hitching, and he puked again.

Tears ran down his face and off the end of his nose as he hung over the bucket for a long time, a string of saliva swinging from his upper lip. When it seemed that his stomach would stay put, he wiped his mouth on his sleeve and rolled onto his back.

Katherine picked up the cup he had dropped and walked to refill it from the barrel against the far wall. Jon swallowed, his throat raw. The shame and embarrassment that he felt was threatening to choke him, and not only from what he could remember; what he couldn't recall was what scared him the most.

"How did I get here?" he asked quietly.

Katherine handed the cup back to him and sat down on the edge of the bed. Jon moved his legs to make room for her, sitting up slowly against the back wall. Katherine shrugged.

"I don't know. Maybe you walked?" she said. "I was asleep."

"Tom carried 'im in like a sack o' potatoes," said a rough voice across the room with a dry, raspy laugh.

Jon squinted and saw a dark-skinned older man sitting on the edge of his bunk, rolling up the bottom of his pants. When he grinned at Jon, he could see that though his teeth were pearly white against his black skin, the man was missing a front tooth.

"Ye was loaded to the gunwalls, mate. Near dead," he said and stood. Jon felt like crying. Katherine patted his knee gently.

"Drink the water, Jon. It'll make you feel better... eventually, anyway. Next time, don't drink so much if you're not used to it," she said, smiling wryly. "I just hope you didn't get yourself into any trouble."

Trouble? More like disaster.

Jon took another small sip and grimaced. Katherine touched his knee again—the sister he never had.

"I have to go. Get some more sleep... The captain wants you to report to Cook later this afternoon, but that's hours from now. And here, take this," she said, handing him a small metal flask.

He took it and pulled the plug out. Jon nearly gagged from the smell.

Oh god, no more rum.

"No, thank you," he said, trying to hand it back to her.

Katherine shook her head.

"Trust me. When you feel a little better, drink some. It'll help," she stood, tugging down the bottom of her jerkin and adjusting the gun belts at her slim hips. "I'll come around later to check on you if I can," she said and left.

Jon looked around. The other man had departed too, leaving him alone in the bunkroom with his shame. He slid back down and pulled the thin blanket over his head. If only he could go back in time and refuse that first drink. Slow tears leaked out of his closed eyes from both the pain and the crushing humiliation he felt. That he'd let Tom... do... that to him was bad enough without remembering with horror how he had shamelessly kissed the captain. How was he ever going to face him again?

A short while later, waking up briefly from a dream of Baltsaros's warm mouth moving slowly over his, Jon thought he saw a muscular silhouette leaning against the door jamb.

When he blinked, the man had gone.

J on stared up at Tom for a moment longer and then bent his head to his task once more. It had felt like forever before Jon was able to get out of his bunk that morning, shaking and pale but desperate for something to distract his mind from the previous night.

Cook had turned out to be a tall, bald man covered in lewd tattoos. Jon's first job had been to peel what seemed like an endless pile of potatoes.

Jon smiled and scrubbed the deck harder; his hands had been so raw and full of small nicks by the end of the day that Cook had laughed at him and given him an extra helping of the fluffy, garlicky mashed potatoes with his supper.

The last to leave after the meal, Jon had been putting his dishes away in the back of the galley when strong hands had come up around his hips and slid up his chest; in shock, Jon had let his plate fall clattering to the floor.

Jon frowned, sitting back on his heels; his heart beat a little faster at the memory.

"W hat do we have here?" purred the voice in his ear.
Jon pulled out of Tom's grasp and turned to press his back against the wall. The first mate pushed himself up against Jon and looked down at him, his blue-green eyes half-lidded. Jon could smell the spirits on Tom's breath, and his heart lurched in his chest.

"Tom. Don't," he said and gasped as Tom leaned in to slide his lips against the underside of his jaw.

"And why not, love? Ye seemed happy enough to have me suck

yer cock last night," said Tom, his voice husky against the side of Jon's neck.

Through his fear, Jon was dismayed to feel himself stirring in response to the first mate's touch. In a panic, he pushed hard on Tom's shoulders.

"Please, Tom. I was drunk. I'm sorry, but please don't," he said and was amazed when the first mate released him after a moment, taking a step back.

There was a dark frown on Tom's rugged face, his eyes narrowed in confusion.

"Yer feelin' poorly. I get'cha, darlin'," he said, nodding. He reached out and touched Jon's bottom lip with a wide thumb. When the first mate swayed slightly, Jon realized just how drunk Tom really was.

Turning to leave, the burly young man said "I'll see ye, Jonny. When ye feel better."

Jon watched in relief as Tom staggered across the room and up the stairs.

That had been only the first of a half-dozen similar encounters. It seemed like almost every time Jon found himself alone in a secluded part of the ship, Tom was there with rough kisses and groping hands. Thankfully, Jon had thus far been able to free himself from the first mate's amorous advances; however, he was both terrified and shamefully excited to think of what would happen if Tom cornered him when the first mate was feeling less tractable.

Word around the ship was that the first mate had somewhat fallen out of the captain's good graces, and Jon suspected that the drunken night in the captain's quarters had something to do with it.

The first time Jon had spoken to the captain since that evening, he thought he would melt into the deck with shame.

However, the older man had been so businesslike and dispassionate towards him that Jon began doubting his memory. Only once in the last two weeks did Baltsaros give any hint of acknowledgment of what had happened between them.

They had been going over the plans for yet another exchange of goods when he realized that Baltsaros was staring hard at him as he talked, his dark eyes on Jon's mouth and the tip of his tongue against his own bottom lip. The younger man had felt heat in his cheeks and an incredible tightness in his chest.

Noticing Jon's reaction, Baltsaros had suddenly straightened his shoulders and walked away without another word. Jon stung with the memory. He wished he could do something to repair some of the damage his foolishness had done to the already crumbling relationship he had with the captain. While they had worked side by side on numerous occasions since, Baltsaros and Jon were never alone together.

Jon stood and swung the wooden bucket so that the water poured over the planks and sluiced through the drains that dotted the gunwales of the ship. He turned his head back to the quarterdeck, but Tom was nowhere to be seen. He frowned, wondering where the first mate had gone, when he noticed Captain Baltsaros standing in the doorway to his quarters, quietly watching him.

Baltsaros was pleased with the changes in Jon. Nearly gone were the stooped shoulders and the furtive glances; instead, the young man walked with a slight spring in his step, and he was often seen with an easy smile. The peeling sunburn that had plagued him for the entirety of his first week had given way to a light tan that made his blue eyes stand out attractively in his fine-boned, sun-kissed face.

The captain felt a strange pain in his chest as he watched Jon scrubbing the deck. The way that Jon had sought out his lips was burned into him. A fortnight had not been enough to diminish the feeling, and Baltsaros had finally admitted to himself that he did not want to see it diminish at all. He had felt keenly alive with Jon in his arms; the kiss, so fraught with inexperienced desire, had left him completely breathless. Feeling strangely hollow since, his mind had begun obsessively returning to the memory again and again, trying to recapture the feeling.

Baltsaros was furious; Jon's unexpected kiss had disarmed him completely, and he was fighting to get himself under control. It was as if there was a terrible, shattering cry echoing down a dark well as he pushed away the unexplainable feelings that Jon had wrenched out of him.

Lust. Bury it in lust.

With a grunt Baltsaros came hard, his cock bumping the back of Tom's throat as he thrust himself into his orgasm. He clenched his fist tight, a handful of Tom's dirty-blond hair tangled through his fingers as he held his first mate still until he was finished. Tom started choking, and Baltsaros pushed him away hard. The first mate fell back against the pillows, his fist moving fast over his own shaft.

"No!" said Baltsaros, his voice rough. "You do *not* get to enjoy this, Tom." His first mate's hand ceased its motions immediately at the command in his captain's voice; but, instead of the usual excitement that blazed in his eyes at being forced to submit to Baltsaros's will, his face was drawn with apprehension.

Tom raised himself up on his elbows, his rigid cock resting against the bulging, hard muscles of his stomach. He stared at the captain, panting slightly.

"What the fuck did I do, Da?" he asked; though his voice was coloured by resentment, Baltsaros heard guilt. He pointed to the young man passed out not far from them.

"You got him drunk, Tom. You shouldn't have brought him

here," he said, his voice quiet and stripped of the turmoil he felt roiling inside him.

Tom's eyes slid away from Baltsaros's for a moment; when he looked back his gaze was fierce.

"I didn't see ye complainin' a few minutes ago when ye bloody reached out and pulled him against ye... when... when ye kissed him..." Tom said, his voice breaking unexpectedly.

Baltsaros frowned as he watched the younger man's composure crumble. Tom was right, and the thought unnerved him. Baltsaros shook his head slowly.

"Then why, Tom? Why would you bring him to me if you didn't want me to touch him?" he asked, genuinely bewildered. This was beyond comprehension for the captain. Though he spent his life mimicking the emotions and reactions of others, there were things he could not account for. "Why, Tom?"

"I seen the way ye look at him, Da. Ye never, not once, looked at me the way ye look at that broken boy. Ye want him. I know ye do. I ain't stupid. I just thought..." he said, his voice raw with emotion. Tom's face was red with anger and grief.

As he spoke, Baltsaros finally thought he understood. Like a cat who traps a mouse and brings it to its owner, Tom had brought Jon to him as a gift... His first mate knew he couldn't compete with the effect that Jon had on Baltsaros and had tried instead to win his esteem by bringing him something he knew the man wanted.

Was it so blatant? the captain thought, alarmed.

Baltsaros swallowed hard and sat back on the bed, suddenly feeling terribly weary.

"Oh, my tomcat," he said; his voice was sad though he truthfully felt absolutely nothing for the handsome and brutal young man. Things would never be the same between them, and they both knew it. After a long silence, Baltsaros nodded to himself.

"Tom, please take Jon to the crew bunks. And... find yourself somewhere else to sleep tonight. I would like an evening to myself," he said softly. He watched as Tom paled slightly under his sun-darkened skin, but the muscular youth obeyed, quickly tying up his pants before sliding off the bed. With ease, he lifted Jon over one shoulder.

"Yes, Da," Tom said, his voice ragged and quiet as he turned to leave. The captain watched his first mate depart, closing the door behind him.

As he lay back against his pillows, Baltsaros frowned up at the ceiling. It was incredibly stupid and unwise of him to have let it all happen. He could have simply said no and sent the two away.

Could I have?

When Jon saw him staring, Baltsaros smiled. He took the few steps needed to close the distance between them. The younger man's eyes widened for a moment, looking apprehensive.

"Jon. I think we should talk," said the captain quietly. The dark-haired youth looked down at the scrub brush in his hands. In a small voice, he said, "I'm not done with—"

Baltsaros let out a sudden laugh.

"Boy, I am the captain. And when the captain says he wants to speak with you, you say 'yes, sir.' Do I make myself clear?" he said, his tone light and teasing.

Jon looked up, his brows furrowing slightly before a smile creased his face.

"Yes, sir," he said and dropped the brush into the bucket.

Baltsaros felt his breath come up a little short in his chest when he saw the bead of sweat run from the corner of Jon's strong jaw and follow the lines of his throat to the collarbone visible through the open neck of his linen shirt.

"Why don't you come out of the sun. Have a drink with me," he said and motioned to the open door of the stateroom. Jon's eyes flashed in suspicion when Baltsaros said the word "drink", but he turned to follow the captain anyway.

Jon ducked through the door of the stateroom feeling bizarrely like he was coming home. Without a word, he walked to the cage and looked in. The cot was bare now, no longer needed. As he touched the black bars with one finger, Jon smiled softly. He'd come far in two weeks.

All that fear and misery...

Jon laughed inwardly. There was still plenty of fear and misery, though now he was in a different sort of cage. It was one of his own design, and Jon was weary of the guilt, shame, and uncertainty he had locked himself into.

He turned and saw that Baltsaros was sitting at his usual spot at the heavy table, an earthenware mug in front of him. Jon slid into his old seat across from the captain and picked up his own mug. When he saw what was in it, Jon grinned and closed his eyes as he brought the mug to his lips, breathing deeply.

Bliss.

He took a sip of the hot, black liquid and sighed.

"Cook's coffee might be good, but yours is exceptional. I've really missed... this," he said and lifted his blue eyes to Baltsaros. He knew immediately that the captain had picked up on his meaning. Though the man's brown eyes were alive with curiosity, his handsome face was entirely devoid of emotion.

"Jon. I should have never let things go the way they did," he said quietly. It wasn't an apology, nor was it an admission of regret. It was something altogether different; it was an offer. Jon watched in amazement as the other man went through herculean efforts to appear calm and collected; to his strange talent, it was clear as day that something was different in the captain. A door had been opened.

"What do you see when you look at me?" asked Baltsaros

suddenly, sitting back in his chair, a small smile on his captivating lips.

Jon felt his heart beat hard once before it settled into a swift rhythm. He looked at Baltsaros and took a deep breath. Everything went still inside his head as he spoke the truth laid out before his eyes.

"What do I see? I see a man who has higher and thicker walls than I will ever have. I see a terrifying beast enveloped and hidden by a cleverly fashioned mask. I see tears that will never fall. I see blood and death. I see a heart that devours itself. I see the promise of pain and deceit. I see a lot of things, Baltsaros. Many of them frightening," Jon said, his voice low; the need for titles between them had passed.

Baltsaros showed no surprise over Jon's words. Instead, he leaned towards him, intrigued.

"And you're not afraid," he said. It was a statement.

Jon shook his head.

"I'm not afraid. I should be," he admitted. "But I'm not. I see a man who is so lonely that he's willing to sacrifice himself to the secrets holding him together. I see a man who fears me for what I can see, yet who asks me to look."

Baltsaros's head nodded slowly. He had the distinct impression that the older man felt relieved.

"But... Baltsaros, I'm not your puppet... I won't be your plaything," added Jon when the captain remained silent. "You already have my respect and my loyalty." He laughed timidly as he pushed a hand through his dark curls. "What I *am* scared of is what else you want from me."

The burst of confidence that had caused his words to flow so easily had left him, and Jon was at odds once more. Baltsaros started laughing; Jon saw that the captain was charmed by his words, and he couldn't help but grin despite how self-conscious he felt.

"We will do as you like, Jon," said Baltsaros. "But it would seem that you want the same things, no?"

Jon felt the heat in his face and took a sip of the rich, black coffee to hide his sudden awkwardness; the memory of Baltsaros breathing into the kiss and the man's blatant arousal was making him feel lightheaded. He looked down at the tabletop and tried to find words.

There was the sound of movement from across the table and almost-silent footfalls approaching on the thick carpet. Jon turned his head and leaned it against Baltsaros's shirt, the captain's hard stomach against his forehead. He felt Baltsaros's hand come down and stroke his hair, a simple comforting gesture that, nevertheless, gave Jon goosebumps.

After Jon got the tears that were threatening to fall under control, he leaned back and looked up into Baltsaros's sombre face.

"You have to do something about Tom," he said, his voice thick. He watched as Baltsaros's stark brows came down over eyes that glinted like black glass. Feeling the restrained fury that came boiling out of Baltsaros, Jon recoiled slightly.

"Tell me, Jon. What has Tom done?"

10

TO RIGHT A WRONG

Baltsaros was unprepared for the rage that had welled up inside him at Jon's words. His initial reaction had been a staggering, almost uncontrollable urge to find Tom and beat him to death with his bare hands, to dig into his flesh like a wild beast and tear him asunder.

When he realized in annoyance that he was pacing, he stopped at the side of his bed and made himself sit down. Baltsaros clenched his jaw as he forced open the tight fists his hands had curled into.

Where was this was coming from? What did he care if Tom was making advances at Jon? Jon was terribly inexperienced; a few rounds with Tom and his talents would do him some good... *wouldn't it?*

Baltsaros swallowed down hard on the anger that spiked hotly in his gut with that thought; looking up, he caught his reflection in the small mirror above the teak dresser and was startled to see the naked emotion on his face. Baltsaros smoothed out his features and groped inside himself for the well of calm that was always within reach.

Before Jon had left, promising to come back to dine with the captain later that evening, Baltsaros had sworn he would take care of Tom.

But... how?

What exactly was the threat? He lay back on the bed, brow once again furrowed. It was midday, and he should have been above on the quarterdeck by now, but his head was still somewhere strange.

Baltsaros's thoughts were again on the reeling, drunken boy that had been so warm against him in the dark cabin. Jon's eyes had been full of stars, and the rum had put colour in his wan cheeks. Baltsaros had been powerless not to touch him; he remembered how smooth Jon's chest was, and how the sensitive pink nipple had hardened alluringly under the captain's fingertips.

He groaned softly at the memory.

Baltsaros pressed his fingers against his eyelids, his other hand tugging at the loose white shirt he wore tucked into his pants. He worked his hand under the waistband and cupped the hardening mound there with his palm, bearing down on himself roughly in response to his tension.

It was only when Tom's mouth had closed over Jon that Baltsaros had realized *just how innocent* the boy really was. Having had his first mate milk the lust out of the beguiling young man now felt like an incredible blunder.

Baltsaros opened his eyes, keenly aware that he was lying on the very site of Jon's ravishment. The thought of anyone else touching him brought a hot, dull ache to the captain's chest.

Never again, he thought angrily. What was Tom even thinking, approaching Jon?

Why shouldn't he? We've shared our conquests so often in the past...

He knew the answer, however: Tom wanted Jon because Baltsaros wanted Jon. He gritted his teeth—those callused fingers running over Jon's soft skin, Tom's rough kisses bruising Jon's lips.

Growling deep in his chest, Baltsaros realized he was working himself into a rage. His cock was rock hard in his hand, responding treacherously to the thoughts of Jon's defilement that ran through his mind.

No. Never again. No one was to touch the dark-haired young man.

However, he couldn't just kill his first mate outright.

He threw open the door to his quarters and looked out; Tom was sitting nearby on an upturned keg sharpening his knife against a small whetstone. When the door banged against the wall, he looked up, blue-green eyes wide; there was that worry in Tom's rugged face again.

Baltsaros frowned at him and cocked his head before retreating back inside, leaving the door ajar behind him. Turning to watch Tom step through the doorway, he breathed deep.

"Close the door, Tom," he said quietly. The first mate moved to obey, darkening the room.

Taking the few steps to reach him, Baltsaros grabbed Tom by the throat and rammed him hard against the wall. Tom let out a grunt as his head cracked against the wood, his hands reaching up to grab the captain's wrist.

Baltsaros brought his face close to Tom's.

"You are not to go anywhere near Jon. *Do I make myself clear?*" he said through clenched teeth.

Tom's eyes went steely as he stared up into his captain's face.

"And why the fuck not, Da?" he asked, venom in his voice. "It's not as if yer fuckin' him yet, are ye? I just thought I'd break him in for ye since yer so keen on the fuckin' brat."

Baltsaros bared his teeth and tightened his hold on the first mate's neck, quickly dashing him again on the hard wood. Tom's face grew red, his fingers scrabbling at the captain's hand trying to loosen his hold.

Baltsaros frowned and eased up slightly.

"I mean it, Tom. Don't touch him. Not ever. And if I find out that you have, *I will take my whip to you.*"

The first mate stopped struggling, going completely still in

Baltsaros's grasp. The captain saw the deep hurt in Tom's eyes and pressed his lips together.

"Da… but… ye promised me. Ye promised that I'd never feel another bloody fuckin' lash… never again," said Tom, his breathing hoarse.

Baltsaros felt Tom's pulse racing against his fingers, and his face softened. It was true; the first thing the captain had said, over and over, to the wild, angry young man in the cage was that he would never again feel a whip tear into his flesh.

"Just… leave him alone, Tom," he said softly, memories washing over his anger and smoothing it out like an ocean wave over dimpled sand.

Tom stared hard at Baltsaros, his gorgeous sea-green eyes completely unreadable; after a moment, he closed them and dropped his hands to the captain's waist, deft fingers working quickly to unlace him.

Surprised, Baltsaros made a small noise in his throat. He frowned at Tom as he felt the first mate's rough, warm hands skilfully free his cock from his pants. When he pressed his thumb up into the sensitive nerve cluster under Tom's jaw, Baltsaros smiled at the grunt of pain that burst out of his first mate; however, Tom's hands had not paused for second.

This was Tom's greatest talent; Baltsaros could drown him in pain, and the beautifully muscled youth wouldn't back down. With a low groan, the captain felt his need completely grab hold of him. For the first time in a long time, his mind was completely on the boy in his grasp.

With his free hand, Baltsaros stroked the side of Tom's face. The young man opened his eyes, a silent plea trapped in them, and moved his head so that his lips could brush Baltsaros's palm.

The captain smiled softly, his body reacting to the guileless charm of the younger man. This was Tom, after all. They had done the same dance so many times that the boy's body felt like a second skin. He let go of Tom's throat, and the other immediately sank down to his knees in front of Baltsaros, quickly swallowing the captain's cock down to the root.

Baltsaros rested an arm against the wood panels and pressed his forehead to it, the other hand reaching down to stroke Tom's hair. The captain groaned loud and began rocking in time to his first mate's movements.

J on dipped his brush in the paint and moved to the next curving spindle of the railing running around the quarter-deck. The fumes were making him feel slightly ill, and his hands were covered in red splotches. This was his least favourite chore so far. It had never occurred to him just how much upkeep a vessel of this size required.

From a distance the black and red of the sleek corvette appeared pristine, but it was far from the truth. Damage from the sun and saltwater marred the paint, causing it to curl up and fade. To keep her looking her best, the old paint had to be scraped away and a new coat applied at least once a season. Jon, being the newest on board, was automatically put on the work crew this time around.

Jon leaned down to dab at his first coat, but his attention was caught by what he saw below; Tom suddenly stood up from his perch where he had been watching Jon paint and walked to the door of the captain's quarters.

Frowning, Jon concentrated on his work. The paint was drying strangely in the hot sun, causing it to bubble up when he applied it too thickly.

Baltsaros will be telling Tom not to come to me, he thought.

It would certainly not make the relationship between him and the first mate any easier, but Jon was tired of looking over his shoulder. Strangely, he felt a touch of regret and pushed it away in disgust. Tom was just trouble. A loose cannon. Never mind that his eyes were sly and his smile wicked, or that his tongue knew exactly where to—

Jon's mouth opened slowly in shock. From below him came an unmistakable groan of pleasure. He stood still for a moment, not believing his ears. When another sound of passion came up from the open porthole in the captain's room, he placed the brush down on the edge of the bucket of paint and sat down heavily on the deck; it hadn't even occurred to him that the captain would maintain his... *dalliances* with the first mate. He had foolishly assumed that he and the captain would... *would what?* he thought, feeling perturbed and strangely betrayed.

Staring down at the paint-spattered hands he had folded in his lap, Jon quickly tried to banish the emotions that were ricocheting through his head; he didn't hear the soft footsteps until they were right next to him.

When he looked up, Jon was relieved to see Katherine's concerned face gazing down at him. She gracefully lowered herself to the deck beside him; her hand, confident in a way that Jon's never seemed to be, came up and rested on his shoulder. He felt ridiculous tears rise up hot in his eyes and lifted a hand to wipe them away.

"Jon, what's the matter?" asked Katherine.

Jon shook his head, looking over her shoulder at the clear blue sky. He felt the heat in his face when there was a sharp cry from below.

"Ahh," he heard Katherine say, and he turned his eyes to hers. "This is what they do," Katherine said softly to him, motioning to the captain's quarters below them. "You shouldn't be hurt by it. It's just the way things are."

Nodding, Jon picked at the red on his hands, embarrassed by his reaction.

"It's so completely absurd," he admitted, even though his heart was beating hard, and his mouth was dry. "I just thought he and I..." he said, trailing off. The thought that kept echoing through Jon was simply: *how could he?*

Katherine leaned against his side, a warm pillar of strength. She played with the leather cord at her calf with long, slender fingers; Jon could sense that she was trying to find her words. Finally, she broke the long silence.

"He belongs to the captain, you know," she said, her brown eyes kind.

Jon frowned at her.

"Tom? You think I'm crying over *Tom?*" he asked, incredulous.

Katherine's eyes narrowed at him, and Jon chuckled low, shaking his head at her. Katherine pulled her hand away slowly and looked at him with an expression of disbelief on her pretty face.

"Oh Jon, please don't tell me you're pining for the captain? You know he's..." she began and stopped suddenly. She shook her head, and Jon felt his stomach knot.

"He's what?" he asked.

Katherine grimaced and shook her head again.

"He's... complicated, Jon," she said, "And... he's the captain." she ended lamely, lifting one shoulder up in a shrug.

Jon scowled at her for a moment and then sighed. He looked over the side of the railing and saw that Tom had emerged from the stateroom below; the first mate stood still, looking up at them with a dark expression on his face. Jon almost gasped at the amount of animosity that he saw in the other man's eyes... and then it was gone.

Tom's lips stretched into a wide smile, and he winked before turning away to swagger down the deck.

J on hadn't managed to get all the paint off his hands, the red having completely stained his skin in some places. He grimaced, feeling self-conscious as he rapped his knuckle against the wooden door.

"Come," was the reply from within.

When he pulled the door open, Jon was bombarded with an

incredible, mouth-watering smell. He closed his eyes and took a deep breath. At Baltsaros's chuckle from across the room, Jon smiled and looked at the captain. The older man was leaning over the table, putting down the heavy silverware to each side of the plates.

The sight of him loosened something in Jon; Baltsaros was wearing a long-sleeved, dark-red shirt tucked into his black leather pants. The laces at the neck were partially undone, and Jon could see the captain's broad, tanned chest, covered in curling dark hairs. The man's light-brown hair looked damp as if he had bathed recently; it was combed back and tied with a leather thong, falling in a messy tail over his shoulder.

He took a few steps forward, utterly captivated by the handsome captain as he straightened up at Jon's approach, smiling charmingly. Baltsaros's brown eyes crinkled at the corners.

"Hello, Jon," he said, his accent, as always, lending an exotic flavour to even these simple words.

"Hello, Baltsaros," he replied, grinning ruefully.

Jon had spent the afternoon wrestling with his demons and had come to the conclusion that he was being utterly foolish; he pushed the feelings of resentment and confusion aside, wishing only to be pleasant and not cast a dark shadow over the meal. He was also incredibly curious about what Katherine had refused to say.

Did I know that Baltsaros was what? Dangerous?

Jon sat down in his chair and glanced up at the captain who had turned to get something else. As he watched the older man, Jon noticed once again how fluid and precise his motions were. Baltsaros was indeed a dangerous animal, and that was a large part of what drew Jon to him.

He raked back his dark curls with one hand and lifted his eyebrows when the captain set a domed ceramic dish in the middle of the table.

"Lamb *tagine*," said Baltsaros, pulling off the cover and

revealing something that looked like a thick stew. "With couscous."

Jon took a sip of the chilled, dark beer and looked on as Baltsaros ladled some of the stew onto the strange yellowish mound on his plate.

It smelled absolutely wonderful.

He scooped some up with his fork and took a bite, acutely aware of Baltsaros's eyes on him. Smiling, he chewed the tender meat and carrot. It was savoury and strangely sweet at the same time, mildly spicy on his tongue. He nodded happily at the captain, who was sitting back in his chair watching the younger man eat, and took a bigger bite.

Baltsaros laughed out loud, the smile creasing his enigmatic face.

How strange is it that a man with such a darkness inside him can laugh so easily and so often? thought Jon as he swallowed.

"I have to admit, Jon… I derive extreme pleasure from feeding you. Every meal is an adventure. I will have to find new dishes to make once I've exhausted my repertoire, just to see that precise look on your face," said the captain, taking a bite of his own.

Jon felt a small thrill at the words. "Oh? You mean to keep me for so long?" he said, amazed at the easy, bantering tone he had taken.

Jon watched as Baltsaros's eyes darkened, and he suddenly sensed the depth of the man's strange isolation. He cleared his throat and looked down at his plate, concentrating on the food in front of him. The long silence made him uncomfortable, but the lump in his throat was preventing him from speaking.

"It's still going well with Calum?" asked Baltsaros, his voice light.

Jon frowned and nodded, glancing up briefly.

"He's a lot stronger than he looks. I still haven't managed to pin him," he replied, smiling slightly.

It was true; the much older man regularly threw Jon down to

the deck during his fighting lessons. He was nearly useless when it came to straight boxing, but there was something about learning holds that intrigued him. Jon knew he was fast, and his slight frame came in handy when trying to worm his way out of Calum's grasp, but he was nowhere close to being skilled at anything yet. He rubbed the bruise visible on his forearm and had to laugh.

"I'll get the hang of it eventually," he said, looking up again at the captain.

Baltsaros nodded, the corners of his lips lifted in a small smile.

"I do not doubt it," he said and paused for a moment, putting his fork down. "Jon, I don't know if you've already heard, but it's nearing the end of the season, and we must start our way south soon. We'll be stopping for supplies before we go; the journey is a long one and we need to stock up," he said, narrowing his eyes at Jon. "You will be able to go ashore with the men... if that is what you would like."

Though feeling a little giddy at the news, Jon held his tongue. There was something else the captain wasn't saying. Baltsaros stood and walked to the ice chest, pulling out a pitcher that Jon assumed contained more beer. Refilling the younger man's mug, the captain spoke.

"We'll be near Portsmouth," he said at last, sitting down.

Jon frowned.

"I don't want to go home, if that's what you're so worried about," he said.

Baltsaros took a sip of beer and smiled.

"No, I know that. I just want you to be careful. Your stepfather may be looking for you," he said, his eyes pensive.

Jon laughed, a small, ugly sound.

"Reginald? Looking for *me?* I doubt it very much. The man was most likely glad to be rid of me," he said.

The captain dipped his head slightly.

"It could be so. However... I just wanted to warn you. Sometimes men hide their affections in strange ways," he said, his face serious.

118

Jon nearly burst out laughing at the irony. Instead, he shook his head and scraped his fork against the plate, trapping the last morsels of the delicious meal between its tines.

"He couldn't fool me," Jon said, *and neither can you,* he added silently.

As he sat there thinking of his former home, Jon was suddenly struck with an idea. Since coming on board, he had been plagued by a reoccurring nightmare and the monstrous guilt that it caused him. He looked into Baltsaros's eyes, bolstered by the affection he saw there, and grinned.

"Something tells me you're not going to like this," Jon said softly.

The man slowly raised his stark brow and waited for Jon to speak.

This was his chance to right a wrong.

"I want to go get Brutus," he said, watching the captain's face.

"Brutus? Who is Brutus?" asked Baltsaros, his brow furrowed in confusion.

"My dog," said Jon.

11

SAFE HARBOUR

Love is whatever you can still betray. Betrayal can
only happen if you love.

— JOHN LE CARRÉ

Baltsaros stared at Jon for a moment, incredulous.

"You wish to bring a dog aboard my ship?" he asked, his eyes wide.

Jon grinned and slowly nodded his head, obviously excited to start piecing together the rescue plan.

The captain leaned back in his chair and just stared at the dark-haired young man. Baltsaros's initial reaction was to flat-out refuse Jon's request. However, as he watched the smile fade from the face of the handsome dark-haired man across the table, he realized just how much this might mean to Jon. There had never been a dog on board before. Some cats in the distant past, and once a monkey, but never a dog.

Baltsaros frowned; he didn't quite understand the allure of companion animals. While pets provided their owners with unconditional affection, it was a crude stand-in for human love.

At least that's what it seemed like to Baltsaros; he had no need for something to stare up at him with mindless, wordless devotion to make him feel better. Not when there were much more satisfying creatures to tame, like Tom and the slender, sensitive young man that was staring at him with eyes like a storm-heavy sky. Jon's words came back to him suddenly.

I won't be your plaything.

Baltsaros pressed his lips together.

"A ship is no place for a dog, Jon," he said, attempting to use reason to dissuade him. He was completely taken aback when Jon narrowed his eyes in anger at him.

"What? *You* get to have a pet but not me?" he said, mirroring Baltsaros's earlier thoughts. The astonishing outburst revealed the outrage that Jon had been suppressing thus far. Obviously, Jon had overheard the captain and his first mate earlier that afternoon and was not happy about it.

And why should he be?

The captain looked flatly at Jon, concerned by his vitriol but not wanting to appear touched by it. Baltsaros licked his bottom lip, choosing his words carefully.

"Tom is none of your concern," he said slowly. "Please do not mistake my interest in you for permission to openly criticize me."

Jon's dark brows came down over his eyes, and he placed his hands on the table, pushing himself up out of his chair. As he leaned forward over the table, Jon stared hard at Baltsaros.

"Do you want me to lick your boots, Baltsaros? Cower every time you raise your hand? Is that what you want from me?" he asked, his voice quiet and angry.

Tilting his head slightly, Baltsaros scrutinized the fierce young man. There was definitely steel buried in Jon, steel and darkness enough to compete with the same inside Baltsaros. He sighed softly and motioned to the chair behind Jon.

"Sit," he said grimly.

Jon waited a moment before resuming his place at the table, all the while looking distrustfully at the captain.

"It *is* my ship, Jon. I am the captain. My word is the only law here," he said.

Anger flashed quickly again in Jon's blue eyes.

"If your word is law, then why not just *order* me to get down on my knees in front of you and... and..." he stammered, having come to the very edge of a thought that stymied the flow of his words.

Baltsaros stood and walked around the end of the table. Jon watched him with a touch of fear on his face; eyes widening, he turned in his chair to face the man as he approached. Baltsaros leaned against the edge of the table and crossed his arms over his chest.

"Are you quite done with your tantrum?" he asked.

Jon frowned at Baltsaros; the muscles worked in his jaw as his nostrils flared slightly. Jon nodded sharply once, his eyes sliding away from Baltsaros's face.

"Now, before your sudden descent into madness, I was trying to explain something to you," the captain said, his eyes tracing Jon's profile. The younger man wouldn't look at him... out of anger or embarrassment? "There are things you do not understand, Jon. Believe me when I say that I am a man unused to having his authority challenged; I simply will not let you come into my life to suddenly claim superior knowledge of how to run my crew or my personal affairs."

Jon shook his head and laughed harshly.

Baltsaros reached out with a hand and grabbed Jon's jaw, turning the other man's head towards him. Jon gasped at the sudden contact. Baltsaros smiled ruefully, dropping his hand.

"I do not want you to chastise me for things that you only have the faintest notion about. You're not stupid, Jon. Rash reactions like yours just now, based solely on emotion and assumptions, will get you killed in a world like mine," he said. "Like *ours*."

He looked down at the colourful arabesques in the rug below his booted feet. When he raised his eyes again, Jon was looking at him curiously, almost all resentment gone from his youthful face.

"I took care of Tom *like you requested*, didn't I? He shouldn't bother you again. I threatened him with something... well... something I shouldn't have." He waved at the air with one hand, pushing the thought away. "Tom has been my companion for nearly four years. He's an excellent first mate when you get past all of his audacious chaff... he keeps everyone in line and makes my job that much easier. I trust him—" Baltsaros raised a hand when Jon started shaking his head. "I do. I have to. After all, I spend a good portion of the night unconscious next to him," he said, chuckling.

Jon looked uncomfortable.

"I'm sorry. I know. It's probably difficult for you to understand. However... as inexperienced and as... conventional as you are, you have to realize that you're not a blushing maiden, and I'm not an evil pirate king here to sweep you off your feet and force you to resign your body to me." Baltsaros ran a hand through his hair, pushing the long strands away from his face. "So... do not criticize me. However, I will accept, and cherish, your *informed* opinions. You matter to me, Jon. But you'll have to get past this jejune notion of what that means," he said, his voice kind. "I don't want you to submit to me. Nor lick my boots," he said, grinning. "Unless that's something you like doing, of course." He shrugged and was pleased to see a bit of humour come back to Jon's face.

Jon shook his head, the smallest of smiles turning up the corners of his mouth. Baltsaros was suddenly breathless with the memory of those lips capturing his own. He reached forward and grabbed the front of Jon's shirt.

Jon was so startled that he didn't even try to fight as Baltsaros pulled him out of his chair. Still leaning against the table, the captain moved his feet to either side of Jon's as he drew the captivating young man against him. When Jon started to resist as his hips came into contact with Baltsaros's inner thighs, the captain let go of him, holding his hands up to either side in a gesture of surrender. Jon was so close that Baltsaros could easily see the rapid pulse in his slender neck; his eyes were so utterly conflicted that it made the captain's breath catch in his throat.

Don't hurt me, they said.

Baltsaros lowered his arms slowly; wrapping them around Jon, he was glad to see that he was not going to pull away. Instead, Jon moved into Baltsaros's embrace like a ship finding safe harbour after a long storm. The captain sighed and held tight to the slender body in his arms, Jon's face buried in the crook of his neck. So much pain. So much confusion. If Jon wasn't careful he would rattle himself to pieces.

Or would he?

Baltsaros leaned his cheek against the mess of brown curls.

"I'm a hypocrite, Jon," he murmured. "I ask you to accept my arrangements, yet I can't bear the thought of you in another's arms... I would kill them for touching you."

Jon let out a small groan, almost a whimper, and turned his head so his lips rested against the side of Baltsaros's neck. The captain felt his heart hammering fast against his ribs, a rapturous, warm surge rising up through him at Jon's tentative touch. Baltsaros bit the corner of his lip, and looked up at the ceiling, trying to find restraint inside of himself. He desired nothing more than to do what he just said he wouldn't: sweep Jon off his feet and take from him what he wasn't yet prepared to give.

Baltsaros shuddered slightly when Jon started to kiss his neck and was astonished when he felt his teeth graze him softly. Maybe the young man was more prepared than he thought. However, when he lowered his hands to grab Jon firmly by his backside to pull him tightly against him, the other froze.

Sensing that he was already pushing Jon's limits, Baltsaros sighed again and kissed the side of his head.

"You can have your dog," he said into Jon's hair and was charmed when he felt the younger man's lips curl into a smile against him. "But keep him out of the way. He's your responsibility."

Baltsaros smiled at the memory as he stood on the dock, arms crossed in front of him. That had been two days ago. It was maddening that he had yet to kiss Jon, never mind strip him bare and drive him mad with passion. Jon was proving to be a difficult code to crack. Baltsaros would be lying to himself if that didn't make him more enticing.

He lowered a hand to the front of his pants and adjusted himself; lately, his cock felt like it was constantly semi-hard. He was beginning to hurt.

"Where do ye want them?" asked Tom, rolling the barrel of fresh water up the dock to where the captain stood.

Baltsaros frowned and did a few calculations in his head.

"Put half in the storage behind the crew quarters and lash the rest up on deck like we did last year," he replied. "There should be enough room for the extra barrels."

"Aye, Da," said Tom, and grunted as he started pushing the barrel up the gangplank.

Baltsaros turned his head, watching the muscles of the first mate bulge with his efforts.

"Tom. You were gone quite a long time. Did you have any trouble?" he asked.

Tom frowned and shook his head as he heaved the barrel onto the deck and then stood panting, one tanned forearm coming up to dash the sweat out of his eyebrows.

"No trouble, Da. Just stopped for a pint is all," he said, not even having the decency to look guilty for having delayed his work in the name of a drink.

Baltsaros scowled at him and shook his head. Tom winked in return, leaning down against the barrel once more.

The captain saw that Jon, dressed in borrowed long-clothes that included a cloak with a hood, was coming down the deck towards the gangplank. Tom stopped rolling the barrel to watch the dark-haired man walk by; taking an exaggerated step back-wards out of Jon's path, he looked at the captain and smiled.

Tom and his games, Baltsaros thought. The young brute was incapable of taking anything seriously for very long.

Jon made his way down the planks and looked at Baltsaros. He seemed both excited and extremely nervous. The captain reached into his pocket and pulled out a small bag of silver.

"This will be enough to hire a horse. You should be able to make it to Portsmouth by sundown," he said, handing the money to Jon. "I know you said that your stepfather was glad to be rid of you, but I'd be cautious. He lost quite an asset in you."

Jon looked down at the leather purse in his hands, fingers pulling restlessly at the string that held it closed.

"Thank you," he said.

Baltsaros reached out to clasp the back of Jon's neck, drawing him against his shoulder.

"I wish you would take someone with you," the captain said quietly.

Jon shook his head and looked up into Baltsaros's eyes.

"It'll be fine. I'll be back before you have a chance to miss me," he said with a grin.

Baltsaros smiled grimly.

"Nevertheless..." he said. "Come back to me, Jon. That's all I ask."

Jon's face went serious, and he nodded. He leaned forward to press himself against the captain quickly before he spun on his heel, trotting down the wide dock towards the small fishing town where they were anchored.

Baltsaros watched him go with a faint worry tightening his chest. He turned his head to look at Tom, who had also stopped to watch Jon depart. When he saw the captain's eyes on him, Tom grinned and started to whistle a jaunty tune as he continued to roll the barrel down the deck.

12

THE BLACK BRIGAND

*My father is the jailhouse. My father is your
system... I am only what you made me. I am
only a reflection of you.*

— CHARLES MANSON

Jon squeezed his knees against the sides of the grey mare as
he looked down at the town of Portsmouth. It was nearly
dark, and some of the larger buildings, like the taverns and
whorehouses, had already lit their lanterns against the falling
dusk.

The horse *whuffed* softly beneath him, and Jon reached down
to pat her side as they came to a stop.

"I know, I know. I'm a terrible rider," he said, smiling ruefully.
The mare bobbed her head as if she understood, pawing impatiently at the ground with a hoof.

Jon wanted to wait until it was fully dark before making his
way through town and up the hill to the ancient, mouldy castle
where he hoped to find Brutus.

As restless as his steed, the young man fiddled with the hilt of the long knife at his hip, wishing suddenly that he had taken the captain's advice and brought someone along; at least then he'd have another person to talk to while waiting for the sun to sink down across the water.

He frowned, pulling out the captain's short double spyglass—something Baltsaros had called *binoculars*—to focus on the crumbling ruin that had been his home for so long. Part of him felt foolish for how incredibly furtive this all was; for all that he knew, Reginald thought Jon had simply run away and was glad for it.

"I suppose I *did* run away, though," he said, and the mare's ear flicked back to listen to him.

It had been nearly a month since that night in the brothel; even if Reginald *had* been looking for him, the old soldier must have presumed by now that Jon wasn't going to return. And, so what if Jon was spotted by Reginald? What's the worst that could happen? Reginald would ask him to stay? Though the captain voiced concern about Reginald's reaction to the loss of his charge, Jon couldn't believe for a moment that his stepfather could make him stay. There was nothing for him in Portsmouth; his future lay in much stranger places.

As if bored by his musings, the mare leaned her head down to nibble on some grass. Jon sighed and put the binoculars back in his bag, deciding he had waited long enough.

Now or never.

After pulling the hood of his cloak up, he clucked his tongue at the horse, coaxing her forward and down towards the softly glowing lights of the harbour town.

Baltsaros was sitting up behind the ship's wheel, drinking strong coffee and rum from a tin cup. The nights were starting to get cold, and he was anxious to get sailing across the wide ocean towards home.

Home.

He laughed. Strange to think that a place where he spent so little time could be considered "home." He took a sip of the warmly soothing black drink and narrowed his eyes at the activity below him.

From the sutler in town, they had purchased almost everything needed to make the long journey, and he expected the shipwright in the morning to replace the rotten boards that plagued the aging ship. Everything was coming together for the trip.

From where he was sitting, Baltsaros couldn't see Tom, but he could hear the first mate barking orders to the ship's hands somewhere below.

"—shake a leg, or so help me gods, ye'll kiss the gunner's daughter! Don't be daft... Here, who taught ye to tie a bloody rope? Fuckin' hell, love... This is more twisted than a demon's cock..." laughed the lusty, young mainlander.

Baltsaros chuckled to himself. The captain was starting to think that maybe he could find a balance between the two young men who fanned his desires so disparately.

After more cursing and shouting, Tom finally appeared at the foot of the stairs leading to the upper deck; heedless of the chill in the air, the first mate was shirtless as usual. Tom's skin shone slightly in the yellow light of the lantern, a thin sheen of sweat covering his muscled torso; lugging heavy supplies on board was backbreaking work, and the first mate never hesitated to help out with even the toughest of tasks.

Smiling up at the captain, the first mate pulled a dark cheroot from behind his ear and stuck it in the corner of his mouth. A match flared in his hand; in the brief light, the captain could see that Tom was covered in streaks of grime. As the smoke wafted out of his nostrils, Tom picked a bit of tobacco off his bottom lip and narrowed his eyes roguishly at Baltsaros.

"Permission to come up, Captain," he said, a cheeky grin dimpling his face.

Baltsaros laughed.

"Permission granted," he replied. He watched as the younger

man took the steps two at a time, coming up to sit next to him. As he leaned back against the wide seat, Tom looked up at the bright stars and breathed deeply, obviously glad for the moment of rest.

The captain plucked the burning cheroot from between the first mate's callused fingers and put it to his own lips. He inhaled and blew out a plume of smoke, watching it rise up into the night sky.

"If everythin' fits where it should, we'll be ready to leave by tomorrow evenin', Da," said Tom, reclaiming the slender cigar.

Baltsaros frowned. Never mind that weighing anchor at night was impractical; it was premature.

"We'll sail when all hands are back on deck, Tom," he said to the young man lounging catlike by his side and watched as his first mate sucked in another lungful of smoke. "That includes Jon."

When Jon saw the poster tacked to the high gates that stood at the edge of town, he knew something was wrong. Under the rough sketch of a gaunt man with black curls, read the words: *Wanted for murder most foule, Jon "The Black Brigand." Rewarde for capture.*

Jon nearly choked on the surprised laughter that burst out of him.

The Black Brigand?

He stared at the poster, not believing his eyes. After a moment, he frowned; the paper was not yet faded by the sun or rain, which meant it couldn't have been there for more than a day.

What the hells?

Though there was no doubt in his mind that it was meant to be a drawing of him, Jon squinted again at the picture, wondering whether anyone could possibly recognize him in it.

Nevertheless, he tugged on his hood to cast more shadow on his face and nudged his horse forward.

Murder? he thought anxiously; this did not bode well. All thoughts of a relatively peaceful encounter with Reginald, should the two cross paths, were now dashed. The faster he was able to leave, the better.

Thankfully, the route through the small harbour town was not long. Jon spotted a few more of the posters up on storefronts, but the main thoroughfare was mostly empty; the few who walked down the packed-dirt road did not even look in his direction.

When Jon reached the far side of town, he had the mare climb as high as the First Wall. He looped the horse's reins around an old metal support that probably used to hold up the gates, back before they were taken away... or stolen to melt down. Jon would go the rest of the way up on foot, better able to hide in the shadows on the barren hillside alone than atop a horse.

He began picking his way over the rocks and mounds along the roadside, trying not to stumble or twist an ankle in the dark. While he had taken this path many times, he couldn't remember ever having done it on a night so black.

After a while, Jon heard a bark of laughter up ahead and stopped in his tracks, listening. He heard the soft rattle of chain mail and the creak of leather as someone further up the path moved about.

"—you're not fucking serious," said a deep male voice, chuckling quietly. There was the sound of metal on metal and another tinkle of chain mail.

A reedy voice replied.

"I swear it! She stood right there next to him while he was at the bank teller. Said she needed to feel the money in her hand before she'd fuck—*Who goes there?*"

Jon had accidentally kicked a small stone while trying to circumvent the two men; it rolled down the steep slope, clattering against the rocks that dotted the hillside.

Before Jon could react, one of the men pulled open a covered lantern and shone it down the path. Jon lifted a hand against the sudden, blinding brightness. Utterly exposed, he stammered.

"I'm no one. I just got lost. Please, I'll be on my way," he said, taking a step backwards; there were spots in his vision as he stumbled over the uneven terrain. In dismay, Jon heard a shout from one of the men and then grunted as his arm was nearly wrenched from its socket.

As he struggled against the large man, Jon tried desperately to remember his fighting lessons with Calum. He kicked a leg forward into the other man's knee and used the soldier's own body weight to pull him down over his shoulder. When he successfully executed the simple manoeuvre, and his attacker landed with a thump, Jon thought he might actually have a chance to escape. However, he was almost immediately surrounded by more soldiers as they came running at the shouted alarm.

Jon held his arms out to either side, ready to try fighting his way out of the ambush, knowing full well that it was incredibly foolish; there was little hope that he would emerge from this a free man. The worst part, thought Jon, was that he *knew* these men; he had grown up with them. There was no way they would mistake him for anyone else.

As if reading his thoughts, a tall, hawk-faced man wearing an iron helmet (*Christopher? Christian? What was the man's name...*) peered at him, holding a lantern aloft in his lobstered mitt. The man smiled.

"Hello, Jon," he said, his voice oddly deep for a man so gaunt.

He nodded to someone over Jon's shoulder, and the younger man felt cold metal clamped around his wrist.

Baltsaros turned the page of the book resting against his bare stomach and put his arm back behind his head. He was reading a first-hand account of the early history of the large landmass to the far south. Though fascinating, the vocabulary was so archaic that Baltsaros was starting to lose the thread of the narrative.

Suddenly detecting the scent of sandalwood soap and a hint of tobacco smoke, he looked up and saw that Tom was leaning in the doorway to the stateroom, watching him with arms folded across his wide chest.

The captain frowned.

"What is it, Tom?" he asked.

The first mate smiled and pulled himself away from the door-jamb, walking on silent feet across the thick rugs towards him.

Baltsaros shut his book and sat up. He watched the first mate walk towards him with the grace of a panther. It was immediately obvious that Tom had taken a bath; though that in itself wasn't unusual, the fact that his first mate had actually put on a shirt for once was odd.

"What do you want, Tom?" asked Baltsaros, curiosity wiping away any irritation at being disturbed.

Tom just smiled and kneeled down on the edge of the bed. Slowly leaning forward, he lowered his head and softly kissed the instep of the captain's bare foot.

Baltsaros almost gasped at the astonishingly intimate touch. He shook his head as the first mate's hands slid up the leg of his pants, kneading the captain's calf muscle as he pressed his lips to Baltsaros's naked ankle.

"Tom, what in the world has gotten into you?" Baltsaros asked, slightly breathless and charmed by Tom's strangely tender advance. He watched as Tom crawled up towards him, pushing the captain's legs apart and bending his head down to Baltsaros's bare stomach.

Groaning as Tom's warm mouth slid wetly against his skin, Baltsaros pressed his head back on the pillow. Tom's hands came up to stroke the captain's chest as he kissed along his ribs, his tongue leaving wet trails on Baltsaros' skin.

As the staggering passion rose up in hot, pulsing waves in Baltsaros, so did too a tiny thorn of suspicion.

He opened his eyes, chest heaving as he watched Tom seduce him softly and with more care than Baltsaros had ever seen from the rough youth. Tom's lips closed over one of the captain's nipples, and he flicked it gently with his tongue.

Shifting his hips at the growing discomfort in the front of his pants, Baltsaros sighed, a slight frown on his face.

Something felt incredibly wrong.

With more than a little regret he finally pushed Tom up and away with a large, sun-darkened hand against his shoulder.

"Tom, I asked you a question," he said, trying to control his breathing and ignoring the fact that one of Tom's hands was stroking the inside of his thigh through the black leather of his pants.

The first mate smiled softly at him and shrugged.

"Nothin', Da. Just thought ye might want some company now that Jon is gone. I thought ye might like it if I was like this," he said and went to lean back in to resume his caresses.

Baltsaros's sense of wrongness intensified. While Tom was incredibly thorough when it came to his physical relationship with the captain, it had always been pure, glorious, brutal *fucking*. Not this... lovemaking.

With a tight grip on Tom's shoulder, Baltsaros continued to hold him back. He saw anger flash quickly in Tom's blue-green eyes.

"What, Da?" he asked, the corners of his mouth turning down as he clenched his jaw.

"You speak as if Jon is gone for good," Baltsaros said softly, watching Tom carefully; and, there it was: a sliver of guilt in the first mate's eyes.

"Well, what if he doesn't come back?" asked Tom, shrugging again. "He might not, ye know. Maybe he's run off... found himself missin' his old man. Maybe he fell off his horse and broke his neck."

The captain felt a pang of alarm; this was more than wishful thinking on Tom's part.

"Tom, what did you do?" he asked slowly, digging his fingers into his first mate's broad shoulder. The momentary look of uncertainty on Tom's face was replaced with defiance; smart enough to know that he was caught, Tom shoved Baltsaros's hand away and sat up.

"I had to, Da. He was makin' ye strange! Ye don't see it, but I do —" He choked when the captain's hard fist slammed into his throat.

Tom fell backwards off the bed and landed hard on the floor, writhing and fighting for breath. His tearing eyes went wide when Baltsaros planted a foot on his chest, standing above him with his teeth bared in an expression of savage fury.

"Tell me," said the captain, his voice deadly calm. "Tell me all of it."

13

HOMECOMING

Jon rubbed at his wrists. The iron shackles that bound him were cold and thick, leaching the heat from his blood without ever growing warm themselves. They'd taken his cloak and his boots and left him to shiver alone in the dark cell; Jon sat hunched on a dirty pile of hay, avoiding the damp walls of the dungeon.

Home, sweet home.

The rotten-meat odour of old blood and the acrid scent of heated metal sat thick under the trapped-human smells of piss, shit, and vomit. Even having worked for so long in the castle's dungeon, the odiferous cocktail of misery and pain that bombarded his senses was making Jon feel ill. He had no idea how long he'd been there; it felt like hours, but for all he knew it had been less than one.

Where is Reginald? he thought.

Someone had to come by sooner or later and let him talk to his stepfather. As he shuddered and pulled his knees up, Jon's brain ran wild. Why was he wanted for murder?

Jon stood on the shore of a black sea with water so calm it looked like glass. The rocks beneath his bare feet hurt him, but he couldn't move. He stood rooted there, watching as the ship sailed away from him. The wake it left behind was churning up the water blood-red. Looking down when he felt a sickening tug, Jon realized in horror that there was a dripping, tendon-like rope coming out of his chest. He could feel himself unravelling from the inside, the rope pulling out everything he was, bit by bit, in a long, swaying line across the water. The other end of the strand was tangled in the claws of a giant black lion that stood on the quarterdeck, watching him with sombre eyes.

J on startled awake at the loud bang on the metal bars. For a half second he forgot where he was; memories of a different cage flooded his mind until he realized he was cold and damp, something he had never been in Baltsaros's care. He lifted his head and peered blearily through the thick bars of his cell at the dark, stony face of the captain of the guards.

"Hi, Reginald," he said quietly.

His stepfather's brow was low over eyes narrow with suspicion.

"Jon," Reginald said.

It wasn't much of a greeting. Jon had the uncomfortable feeling that his stepfather was livid. He got slowly and painfully to his feet, the cold having cramped up his muscles during the long wait. It was well after midnight; he had already heard the changing of the guards some time earlier. Holding onto the iron bars, he looked out at the man who had raised him on a diet of duty and disappointment.

"Reginald, I didn't kill anyone. I don't know what's going on," Jon said. "You've got to believe me."

Reginald pressed his lips together a moment before answering.

"Where the hell have you been for the last month?" he asked, his voice harsh.

Jon frowned. He had been kidnapped and then recruited by pirates; no matter how he worded it, the answer would guarantee him a spot in a gibbet, feeding the crows with his flesh. Pirates were a scourge, according to Reginald, and deserved no better. Jon knew the captain of the guards wouldn't make an exception for him, regardless of their relationship.

Reginald slowly crossed his arms across his barrel chest while Jon tried to put together a plausible story in his head.

"I just… took up work on a fishing boat. I'm sorry but it was very… sudden," he said, wincing inwardly at how ridiculous he sounded.

The old soldier's eyebrows lifted, and he nodded slightly.

"After you spent all that silver, I take it?" asked Reginald.

Jon blinked.

"What silver?" he asked, confused.

His stepfather tapped a finger to the side of his wide, grizzled jaw.

"The silver you stole from the *Rose Garden*," replied Reginald drily.

"What? I have no idea what you're talking about." Jon backed away from the bars, feeling a little lightheaded.

Reginald stood glowering at him for a moment.

"I suppose you're going to tell me that you didn't kill those girls either?" he asked, his head tilting slightly.

"Reginald, for fuck's sake, tell me what the hell is going on?" said Jon, a note of panic creeping into his voice. "What girls? What silver?"

His stepfather took a deep breath, scrutinizing Jon.

"The day you disappeared from the brothel, a large quantity of silver disappeared along with you. I really couldn't believe you would have done something so incredibly stupid." Reginald paused, his dark-brown eyes locked on his stepson's face. "We searched for you, but you had disappeared without a trace. Do you have any idea how it feels to be the head of the city guards and have everyone think your son is a petty thief?" He paused, scowling at Jon. "Not good at all."

Jon kept shaking his head slowly at Reginald's words. One of his crewmates had to have stolen from the brothel that night; it was the only explanation.

Reginald leaned forward and wrapped his hands around the bars.

"I really thought you'd run off for good or gotten yourself killed. Then, this morning, two women were found down by the pier, their throats cut. I had to send a few men down to the inn to keep the peace. Someone had whipped the crowd there into a frenzy with stories of this 'Black Brigand' who was going from town to town, raping and killing women over the last month. One sailor swore up and down that he had seen the murderer with his own eyes and that he matched your description perfectly. He also said that this killer's real name was 'Jon' and that he was the son of a lawman. Keller at the print house made up those posters with your face on it. You can imagine what kind of mayhem that caused. Jon, I nearly had a riot on my hands," said the gruff, old soldier, his face grim. "Everyone thinks you're the murderer."

Reginald let go of the bars and began to pace back and forth in front of Jon's cell.

"You've always been a strange one... I've always thought there was something wrong with you. And then the headaches started, the confusion... your constant refusal to do your job. Was it all just a sham?" He stopped and glared hard at the man in the cage again. "Now you're standing there telling me you just, what, decided to change jobs and didn't bother to *tell anyone?* I... don't think so."

Jon's eyes had narrowed at the mention of the sailor.

"Reginald, was this sailor from the mainlands? Built like an ox?" asked Jon and then pointed to his face. "Scar through his right eyebrow?"

Tom...

"I am asking the questions!" yelled Reginald through the bars, his spittle spraying the man in the cage. "Jon, tell me where the fuck you've been and why I shouldn't have one of your old colleagues work you over for a while?"

Jon closed his eyes and swallowed hard. He had to get out. He had to get word to Baltsaros. Jon felt helpless. He opened his eyes and stared hard at the man on the other side of the bars.

"Reginald, I'm innocent. I told you, I was working on a boat. Maybe I didn't say anything because I thought you didn't give a damn whether I was alive or dead unless I was doing your job for you. I didn't steal any silver, and I sure as hells didn't kill any girls."

Reginald frowned but nodded slowly after a while.

"I'd like to believe you, Jon, but you're not giving me much to go on. The husbands of those two women are calling for you to be hanged. Tomorrow. Be glad my men caught you before someone else did." Reginald looked suddenly a little sad and looked away for a moment. "If Eleana was alive to see you behind bars…"

The corners of Jon's mouth turned down; he felt a little pain in his chest at the mention of his mother.

Reginald sighed and turned back to Jon.

"All right. Give me the name of this boat, and I'll see if I can get someone to corroborate your story."

Jon felt his heart sink to his stomach.

"It… It doesn't have a name," he said quietly.

"What do you mean it doesn't have a name?" asked Jon, sitting across the table from Baltsaros for the morning meal. "What kind of pirate ship doesn't have a name?"

The handsome older man took a bite of bread and lifted one shoulder up in an easy shrug.

"My ship, I suppose," he said and smiled, his gracefully curved lips stretching wide in amusement.

Jon frowned and shook his head.

"I thought it was illegal to go into port without a name. Or a flag… which you don't fly either," he said, remembering the first time he had seen the small, sleek warship in the harbour.

Baltsaros nodded.

"No flag, no name: no docking. But silver and gold buy many privileges," he replied. When he saw that Jon was dissatisfied with his answer, he laughed. "She's a ship… just a tool, Jon. Would you name your hammer? Your eating knife?" he asked, his eyes merry.

Jon shook his head.

"But I also don't call my knife *she* either," he replied.

While Baltsaros's smile didn't leave his face, his eyes went strangely flat for the span of a heartbeat.

"The ship used to have a name. Now it doesn't," he said simply and took a sip of coffee.

Jon nodded and looked back down at his food, feeling uncomfortable. Though he wanted to ask more, he felt his questions were touching the edge of a strange pain inside the captain; it was obvious that he didn't want to talk about it further.

L ater, Jon asked Katherine about the ship's lack of name. They had been practicing with wooden swords, and the lithe woman was slightly breathless when she answered.

"Did you ask the captain?" she asked, wiping the sweat from her neck with a handkerchief.

Jon grimaced slightly. He sat down on a crate and rubbed at the red marks that Katherine's stick had left all over his arm. She was fast and vicious with her attacks; even though he had the longer reach she somehow managed to disarm him over and over again.

"I tried that. He wasn't very forthcoming," he admitted.

Katherine sat down on the gunwale and looked hard at Jon. After a moment, she spoke in a low voice.

"Well, it's a sort of mystery. The captain's never really given anyone a straight answer." She laughed suddenly. "You're going to come to the realization very quickly that he's rather... unconventional. But he makes us rich, so we don't ask too many questions." She pulled off the leather thong tying her braid and raked her fingers through her raven-black hair. "I'll tell you the only thing I know for sure. Baltsaros is the second captain to hold this ship. The one before was his uncle and... There was a mutiny led by Baltsaros. It was successful, obviously," she said.

Jon frowned.

"What happened to his uncle?" he asked.

Katherine shrugged offhandedly.

"Captain Baltsaros killed him."

J on had given up trying to force the pin out of his shackle by tapping it against the wall when the guard, a man he didn't know, came and threw water over him at the sound of metal against stone. Shivering so hard his teeth were chattering, the soaking wet young man was still trying to come up with a credible story. However, the look Reginald had given him when he had said the ship had no name was enough for him to believe his efforts were in vain. Reginald was caving to public pressure; Jon would most likely be hanged the next day.

He laughed to himself, a small, sad sound echoing in the darkness. He'd only just started to really feel alive. As he turned over on his side, awkwardly trying to wrap his arms around himself despite the short-chained manacles, Jon felt tears threatening to fall. Tom had to be responsible.

Fucking Tom. If Jon got out of this alive, he would kill Tom.

But... Maybe they'd already left without him.

Closing his eyes tight, Jon took a deep breath and finally let himself think about the captain. When he grit his teeth against the hopelessness that washed over him, Jon realized that touching his feelings for Baltsaros was like tearing open a wound.

Why am I so foolish? he thought.

The sanctuary that lay in the captain's arms was intoxicating. His dreams were constantly filled with what *could* happen... Yet when given the chance, Jon had instead gone on a mission to save a dog.

As he sat shuddering in the cold darkness, Jon knew he was a coward. The desires that Baltsaros brought out in him were intimidating; he felt completely stripped of armour in the captain's presence, and it scared him just how much *he liked it*. A soft sigh escaped from his throat as he remembered how gently the captain had held him in his strong arms. Baltsaros had lowered some of his walls, and in return, Jon had run away. There was no denying that the intriguing man left Jon breathless and aching, staring miserably at the stained mattress above his head in the crew quarters as he imagined the captain and his first mate falling into each other's arms, night after night.

Tears ran down over the bridge of Jon's nose and down his cheek onto the matted straw beneath him. Why couldn't he just... give in?

It was too late now.

J on was muttering softly to himself hours later in the gloom of early morning when he heard quiet footfalls approaching. Startled, he looked up as a dark figure crept towards the bars. There was a gasp.

"Oh, my god. Jon, you're alive!" said a familiar voice.

He lurched quickly to his feet and pressed himself to the bars. The relief that flooded through him made Jon feel wildly giddy, his heart careening in his chest.

"Kat! You have to get me out of here!" he said quickly, his voice hoarse. Jon could see her eyes darting all over his face as if in shock to see him.

"What's wrong?" he asked.

She just shook her head and squeezed his cold fingers through the bars.

"Later," she whispered. "I have to find the keys."

Jon nodded and pointed up the dark hallway.

"The guards play cards and drink down that way. It's the only place in this hell that isn't damp and cold. There will be at least two," he said hurriedly. He heard the rasp of metal as she pulled her short sword from her belt, a dangerous glint in her brown eyes. "Be careful, Kat," he said, but she had already turned and was running fleet-footed down the dark passageway.

Soon Jon heard a muffled yell but no shouts of alarm. It seemed like only minutes before Katherine was back at the front of his cage, her face creased in a wide smile.

She quickly undid the lock and opened the door, pulling him into a tight embrace. Jon, his hands still shackled together in front of him, could only lean his head down onto her shoulder in return. Katherine pulled away and frowned into his face.

"I don't have time to get these off of you," she said, one hand on the manacle on his wrist. "Are you all right? Can you run?"

Jon nodded, and they made their way swiftly down the dungeon hallway to the winding stone stairs. With Katherine's hand on his elbow, they ran up the staircase and emerged into the courtyard in little time. The sky had only just lost the deep black of night; Jon could easily see the silhouette of the mouldering castle when he looked up.

Katherine tugged at him to move faster, and Jon gasped in pain as a sharp rock cut into the bottom of his foot. Thoughts of the dream came back to him as he lurched forward, crossing the rocky ground to the stables; they hadn't left him after all.

When Jon saw where they were going, he pulled back on Katherine's arm.

"There aren't any horses!" he whispered but was amazed when

he heard a snort and whickering sounds from the other side of the slatted wall.

"Well, there are now. Quick!" said Katherine, and yanked open the door.

When he frowned into the dark space, Jon could see that almost every stall was full.

What is going on? he thought as he stepped gingerly over the uneven ground.

The wind was knocked out of him an instant later when he landed on his back on the stable floor. At the sound of Katherine's sword leaving its scabbard again, he struggled in panic against the weight of the dog on his chest, trying to get his breath back. Finally, he sucked in a shuddering lungful.

"Stop! Stop!" he said hoarsely. "Katherine, no, it's ok... Stop! Aaagh, Brutus! Down boy. Get off of me." He strained against the mastiff's huge neck as the dog drooled into his face.

Eventually, Brutus rolled off Jon and sat, wiggling like a puppy, tongue licking his lips and whimpering as he waited for his long-lost master to reach out to him.

Jon saw that the massive dog was dirty, and his fur was matted. As he stroked a hand slowly down Brutus's shivering sides he felt the dog's ribs sticking up through his thin skin.

"Oh, I'm so sorry, buddy. I'm so sorry I left you." His chest felt tight as he crooned softly at the huge dog that leaned into his touch. Jon felt tears come to his eyes.

"Jon, we really have to go. Now. Someone will notice soon that the castle is short a few guards at the gate. Get up! Now!" The slim woman hauled Jon to his feet and pushed him towards the large tan destrier in the stall ahead.

He watched as she swiftly saddled the horse, her motions practiced and sure. Getting him up on the huge horse with his hands still bound proved to be awkward, but soon they were on their way.

Jon bounced uncomfortably behind Kat, his arms looped around her to keep him steady. He saw with dismay that the sun was nearly up; if they didn't hurry, the morning guards would discover them.

At that moment he noticed the pennants flying above the walls; Lord Barton was in the castle.

"Kat…" he said. "I think we're stealing the lord's horse."

The pirate turned her head to the side to look at him. She had a wide grin on her face.

"Good!" she said, laughing.

However, a loud horn blast from above split the air, and Jon heard Katherine curse. They were spotted.

"Hyaaahh!" yelled Katherine, and the destrier leapt forward, almost knocking Jon loose.

As he clutched the narrow waist of the woman in front of him, Jon fought for balance as the giant horse raced out of the courtyard towards the castle gates.

"Hyaah!"

With the woman's cries, the horse went even faster, careening down the steep hill. Right before Jon closed his eyes in terror at their breakneck speed, he saw the bodies of the guards at the gate, their blood pooling in the thick mud.

It was a crazy ride, every moment feeling like he was going to slip off the horse and drag Katherine down with him. Jon's breath lurched in his chest each time the horse's hooves struck the ground, and he was rigid with panic.

Soon, however, the destrier began to slow as they left the town of Portsmouth behind. Finally, they went down to an easy trot when they reached the crossing of the highroads. Even though the horse was carrying two, it seemed they had been swift enough to leave their pursuers behind.

When he saw that Brutus was keeping up with them, Jon smiled; he could breathe again. After a moment, Katherine's words in the dungeon came back to him.

"Why did you seem so surprised to see me if you were coming to rescue me?" he asked her.

She shook her head.

Jon wished he could see her face.

"It wasn't a rescue attempt," she replied over her shoulder. "It was a fool's errand, really."

Jon frowned.

"What do you mean?" he asked, confused.

"Tom told the captain you were dead," she said, her tone grim.

"He's dead. He's fuckin' gone. Ye can forget about him, Da," said Tom through swollen lips.

Tom's words had opened a great, yawning pit inside of Baltsaros. With his jaw clenched tight, he smashed his fist into his first mate's face again.

"How?" he asked, his voice a deadly calm. Jon couldn't be gone. Not yet. Not this way. When his first mate didn't reply right away, he grabbed the younger man around the throat and dashed his head hard against the floor.

"I… I paid a man," sputtered Tom, his left eye almost swollen shut. "I paid him to kill that little shit the second he got to town. And he did it! He killed—uhff!" His head rocked back against the hard wood planks as Baltsaros's fist connected again with his jaw. Tom moaned, but a slow grin soon spread his split lips.

The captain growled. Wrestling for self-control, he slowly stood up, backing away before he could end Tom's life.

"Yer cabin boy's feedin' the fish, Da. He's fuckin' dead!" yelled Tom from the floor. The first mate started to laugh but ended up choking as he coughed up blood. After he wiped his mouth, Tom finally closed his eyes and lay there breathing heavily; tears ran freely down his cheeks.

Baltsaros stared down at his first mate a moment longer before walking to the door. He looked out and saw Katherine nearby.

"Katherine, could you please bring two strong men to my quarters?" he asked in a low voice when she came towards him.

The tall woman nodded, her eyes widening almost imperceptibly at the blood on the captain's shirt.

Baltsaros turned back to the room and stepped over the man on the floor, sitting down in one of the dark wooden chairs.

Jon. Dead.

The words echoed in his head, devoid of sense. It was a... shame. He swallowed hard. When the woman returned with two deckhands, Baltsaros pointed to Tom.

"Take that to the brig," he said and watched as they lifted the unresisting Tom off the floor. He held up a hand as Katherine turned to go. "A minute, please?" he asked.

"Aye, Captain," she replied, crossing the room to stand in front of Baltsaros.

"Tom had Jon killed," he said quietly. He felt so strange.

Katherine's hand came up to her mouth.

"What? How?" she asked in shock.

Baltsaros looked down at the swollen knuckles of his right hand.

"He says he paid someone. I wish I didn't believe him," he replied, shaking his head.

Dead.

Baltsaros realized that he was sitting in the chair that Jon normally took, and he pressed his lips together hard. Why should he care? He felt a light touch on his arm and glanced back up at Katherine. She was looking at him with sadness in her eyes. No... It was more than that... There was sympathy there too.

"I'm sorry, Captain," she said softly.

Baltsaros frowned. Sorry for what? He felt pain in his hand, and strangely, in his chest.

"Tom's a pathological liar," she said. "Do you really have any proof that Jon's actually dead?"

Baltsaros shook his head.

"When have you known Tom to lie about killing someone?" he asked softly.

J on breathed quickly in astonishment as he listened to Katherine recount what had happened.

"You've certainly made an impression on the captain," said the woman in front of him. "He's not the kind of man to waste resources on a gamble."

Closing his eyes, he leaned his forehead on the leather of Katherine's vest. He heard her chuckle softly.

"And... I know he's made quite an impression on you," she added.

Jon felt like telling her to make the horse go faster. He needed to see Baltsaros. To... thank him. His heart lurched in his chest.

"Jon, just be careful, ok?" Katherine said after a few minutes.

He lifted his head and frowned.

"You've said that before. Why? What's wrong with the captain?" he asked.

"He's not like other men," she said after a long pause. "I've never met anyone who was so completely untouched by the violence they did. Hells, even Tom gets drunk after killing someone. But not the captain. He just goes on."

"I know he's dangerous," replied Jon.

"Yes, he is. But that's not quite what I mean. He's just... completely indifferent to people. They interest him like bugs interest little boys. Do you understand what I mean?" she asked.

Jon chewed on the inside of his lip. He had seen the strange flatness in Baltsaros's eyes many times; occasionally Jon felt as if the captain were a large, curious predator just sizing him up for a meal.

"Yeah. I think I do. But, I've seen something else in him," he said, remembering the emotion in Baltsaros's words.

Come back to me, Jon.

"Just be careful, ok? I've sort of grown fond of you, you know," she said and squeezed his arm.

Jon was about to reply when he saw that they had reached the port town where the ship was docked for supplies and repairs; when he saw the familiar shape of it out in the small harbour, Jon felt slightly breathless.

Baltsaros grunted as he pulled the new rope through the pulley, lifting the heavy sailcloth. The sun was warm on his bare back, and the physical work made him feel good. After yanking down hard one more time, he finally tied the hemp rope in a looping knot around the metal cleat.

The shipwright had found less damage than Baltsaros had thought he would, and with the captain pitching in with the labour, the crew had been able to finish up the preparations early; at this pace they would be ready to sail well before the sun set. He straightened and wiped a hand across his eyes, looking towards the road into town for what felt like the hundredth time. He had told Katherine to search along the road for signs that Jon was simply late, to only as far as Portsmouth before turning back.

If Tom was telling the truth, Jon would have died in town. If he wasn't, and Jon had stayed of his own volition, Baltsaros didn't care to hear of it.

She should have been back by now.

As he forced his eyes away, he stooped to pick up the rest of the rope that was tied in a wide bundle and heave it up onto his shoulder. He crossed the deck and dropped his load on the extra supplies that would be stored below deck.

Stretching his shoulders, Baltsaros smiled wryly to himself; he was going to be sore tomorrow. He had been spending far too much time in sedentary pursuits since Tom had taken over as first mate. However, that time was now over. He could no longer trust the spiteful creature locked in the brig; but, as much as he wanted to kill him, Baltsaros couldn't.

The captain realized that his gaze had turned again to the road, and he saw that there were figures on the pier now, coming towards the ship. When Baltsaros picked out the huge dog with them, his heart thumped hard once in his chest; he shaded his eyes and watched as Katherine and Jon approached.

Jon...

The captain stepped up onto the gunwale to quickly get by the milling sailors and ran a few steps along the edge to jump down onto the wide gangplank. He walked down onto the pier and stood there, eyes glued on the dark-haired young man.

Jon was in manacles.

All the fury and fear that Baltsaros had locked away seared through him then; it was as if he were a howl of rage trapped in human form.

However, when he saw the raw emotion in Jon's wide blue eyes, staring desperately into his own, dizzying relief suddenly extinguished all of Baltsaros's burning anger, leaving him strangely weak. He staggered slightly, taking a step forward.

Jon was not dead.

Jon had come back to him.

Baltsaros closed the distance with only a few long strides; but, when he was near enough to reach out and touch Jon, he faltered. It was daunting to make that final move across the small space; it was stepping into the unknown.

Jon stole the breath from Baltsaros when he suddenly bridged the gap and captured the captain's mouth with his own. Baltsaros gasped into the kiss and bent his head to it, his hands on Jon's face, in his hair, down his back, grasping at him tightly to pull him closer still.

Mouth open to Baltsaros, Jon took him in; when their tongues moved together they were lost souls found once more.

There was nothing else but Jon, this broken puppy, this

dangerous wolf pup, in his arms. Baltsaros wanted to devour him with his kiss and protect him forever.

This was the very heart of madness.

Baltsaros gladly let himself be pulled down into it, unexpectedly made whole with this homecoming, this birth of something previously untasted. Baltsaros groaned and bit softly at Jon's lips; the younger man whimpered, pressing himself hard into the captain's fierce embrace.

When he finally broke the kiss, Baltsaros looked down at the boy in his arms. Jon's eyes were filled with new awareness, pupils wide with desire. After a moment, his chest tight with strange emotion, Baltsaros rested his bruised lips against Jon's forehead and whispered into his skin.

"Never leave my side again."

14

NO QUARTER GIVEN

J on winced as Beard tried to use the mallet to remove the metal spikes from his manacles. The skin around his wrists was sensitive from being rubbed for hours, and though the big man was trying to be gentle, it was still somewhat painful. Chewing on the strange bread that Beard had given him, meat and cheese baked directly into it, Jon turned his head towards the quarterdeck to watch Katherine and the captain discussing ship matters.

Baltsaros.

Jon blushed slightly, thinking about all the eyes that had been on them kissing out in the open; he still couldn't believe his own recklessness or the captain's reaction.

Smiling, he turned his head back to the giant working to free him. Jon was filthy, starving, and in pain, yet filled with a steady pulse of giddying emotion; it was hard to do anything but grin like an idiot.

T he first few minutes on board had been a whirlwind. After making sure that Jon was in no immediate danger of collapse, Baltsaros had ushered him up the gangplank, a strong arm around his waist. Completely dispelling any fear that Jon had overstepped his bounds by kissing him, the captain had embraced him again briefly in full sight of the crew. Sitting Jon down on a crate, Baltsaros had murmured a quick apology before running off and yelling to the deckhands to weigh anchor.

There had been an incredible flurry of activity as all hands on deck had worked to get the ship away from the dock and out to sea. In amazement he had watched as the captain himself helped hoist the lines to square the sail for their departure, muscles bulging and straining in Baltsaros's arms and broad back as he bent himself to the lowly shiphand's task.

M etal clanged down to the wooden planks, Jon's wrists finally free. He gasped in relief and rubbed at the redness around one arm, smiling at Beard.

"Thank you," Jon said.

The giant man sat there looking at him appraisingly for a moment; Jon was almost startled when the craggy face finally split wide in a smile of large, yellowed teeth.

"Welcome," came the rumbled reply. The giant then stood up and clapped Jon on the shoulder, causing the younger man to cough in surprise, before taking off at a lumbering run down the deck.

Brutus, fast asleep in the sun, was curled up like a giant cat on the deck; he would be ravenous when he recovered from their arduous flight.

Jon looked up and saw that Katherine was now behind the wheel. Earlier, with zero ceremony, the captain had promoted her to first mate, and the astonishment was still plain on her face. Jon pressed his lips together. His mind kept leading him back to Tom, but he was not ready to think about the treachery just yet.

Soon they were underway, leaving behind the piled rocks of

the harbour and cruising through open water. However, Jon saw that instead of sailing away from the island, they were tacking to circumnavigate it.

He frowned, finding it curious, but was startled out of his thoughts at a light touch on his shoulder. Looking up, Jon was rendered breathless by the man standing above him.

Baltsaros's hair was windblown; dark-blond wisps of it had escaped the leather tie at his nape and were whipped up by the strong sea wind. Indoors, the captain's eyes had always seemed a deep brown, nearly black, but in the bright afternoon sun, Jon could see that there was more amber in them than he had thought. The corners of Baltsaros's eyes were crinkled as he stared down at Jon, a wide smile on his bowed lips.

"Come with me," he said simply, helping Jon to his feet.

The change of lighting between the deck and the captain's quarters was jarring; Jon felt blind for a few moments and stumbled against one of the chairs in the middle of the room.

Baltsaros's arms came up quickly around him.

It was a visceral shock, this sudden, warm, bronze skin enveloping him so protectively. Jon's heart crashed against his ribs. Now that his hands were free, they came up and grasped the older man around his smooth, muscled waist. He suddenly felt shy as his vision focused and saw that Baltsaros was looking into his eyes with unmistakable desire.

Slowly, as if afraid he would pull away, the captain brought his mouth down to Jon's in a soft, open-mouthed kiss, Baltsaros's tongue questing out to touch the tip of his in a way that was so tender it made him shiver. Baltsaros pulled away.

"Are you all right?" he asked, his eyes darting over Jon's face in worry.

Jon felt a tightness in his chest.

"Yes… I am. I am now. Your touch just makes me…" He swallowed. "Makes me *want*." He felt his words were awkward, but he was amazed when the captain's eyes went dark with emotion, and the man bent again to his lips.

This kiss was fuelled by frantic passion.

Baltsaros twined his fingers in the dark curls at the base of Jon's neck as he savaged his lips.

Jon groaned into the kiss, all his uncertainty being devoured by the fire that burned inside him at the captain's rougher handling. Jon felt crazy with desire, fingers digging into Baltsaros's skin as if he could press himself further into the other man's flesh. In a frenzy to feel Baltsaros's skin against his, Jon began pulling the soiled linen shirt out of the waist of his trousers.

The captain broke the kiss and took a step back to watch Jon strip his torso bare. There was the barest flash of anger in Baltsaros's face when he saw the mottled bruising that covered Jon's gracefully muscled chest; the castle guards had not been kind to him. After taking the shirt from Jon and tossing it aside, Baltsaros bent low and started kissing the dark marks on his skin, his tongue licking at the bruises as if to wash them away with his spit.

The sound that came out of Jon's mouth at the exquisite, unfamiliar sensation was part whimper, part sigh.

Suddenly, it was all too much for him; he felt himself start to shake, and in dismay Jon realized hot tears were slowly running down his cheeks. He quickly pushed Baltsaros's head away from his chest, his fingers snagging awkwardly in the captain's hair and sending the leather tie to the floor.

Baltsaros's eyes widened when he saw the distress that his touch had caused in Jon, and he straightened, his long, dark-blond hair hanging loose around his angular face. Frowning thoughtfully, he drew Jon against his chest to cradle his head in the crook of his neck, hands stroking slowly but firmly down his back.

Jon felt utterly foolish and lightheaded, and there was a deep ache in the pit of his chest; he felt that he was letting the captain down by acting so ridiculous. Jon was so naïve to think that he could just be that brazen and confident...

A shuddering sob erupted out of him, and then he couldn't stop. Jon cried hard against the shoulder of the man who had torn him from his home, who had forced freedom on him when he was too scared to take it himself.

All the while Baltsaros held him tight, his hands caressing Jon's shaking body. The man was silent; Jon was so caught up in his own misery that he couldn't tell what the captain was thinking, and that piled more pressure on his already overloaded emotions.

In alarm, Jon realized that Baltsaros was pulling him back towards the bed; he panicked, fighting weakly against the powerfully built captain.

"Stop it, Jon. Hush. You're having an anxiety attack. Come... I won't hurt you," said the captain, holding firm onto the struggling young man.

Jon felt Baltsaros's calm voice slide like a wedge into the tightening confines of his fear. Slowly, Jon let himself be led to the bed. The sheer terror he felt must have been clear on his face when Baltsaros bade him to lie down; the captain's own had gone serious in concern.

Jon closed his eyes and lay back on the soft bed, his heart beating high and fast in his chest; it was as if the air in the room was too thin to breathe.

When Baltsaros crawled up next to him, Jon took another shuddering breath and held it. Baltsaros stroked a hand slowly across Jon's body as he moved closer still, pulling the unresisting young man onto his side until Jon's cheek rested against his chest. Jon could hear the rumble of Baltsaros's voice and the slow, regular thud of his heart right against his ear.

"Jon... Just breathe. There is nothing I want from you that I cannot wait for. You are safe here. My dear boy, you've been through a terrible ordeal, and you haven't slept in over a day. Everything will be all right. Just breathe. Listen to my voice..."

Between the captain's low voice and the soothing sounds of his calm heartbeat, Jon began to feel himself relax. Baltsaros was right. He had been beaten, thrown in jail, accused of murder, and had faced the looming possibility of his death by hanging... all on little sleep and absolutely no food or water. However, he felt it didn't excuse how he was acting.

Jon opened his eyes and moved his head away from Baltsaros, looking up into the man's enigmatic face.

"I'm sorry," he said softly.

Baltsaros frowned at the boy in his bed and shook his head.
"You haven't done anything wrong, Jon," he said.

After a moment, when he felt that Jon was calmer, Baltsaros placed his open hand on his flat stomach and stroked the skin there with his thumb. Jon's breath hissed out between clenched teeth, and the captain felt the muscles tense under his palm.

"This. This is what I do not understand," Baltsaros said softly, curiosity colouring his words. "Has *no one* ever touched you?"

Jon pressed his lips together, and he shook his head.

Baltsaros propped himself up on one elbow to better look at Jon's face.

"I don't just mean sexually. I mean... at all? Has no one touched you in friendship? In compassion?" he asked, fearing he knew the answer. Still, he was dismayed when Jon closed his eyes and shook his head again.

From lips thin with grief, Jon whispered the truth.

"Not since my mother..." he said. There was deep shame in his voice.

Baltsaros felt a terrible anger well up inside him for this beautiful, broken creature that lay against him, shivering at his touch. Jon had told him that his mother had died when he was a small thing, a boy of four. Baltsaros would see Reginald pay for this. Even he, cruel life that he'd had under his uncle's care, had known warmth among the crew.

"But, what about everyone else in the castle?" he asked, his eyes watching the crease between Jon's brows deepen.

Jon shrugged slightly and opened his eyes. The captain was amazed at the depth of pain that lay trapped inside his gaze. Had no one loved this boy?

"Some of it is Reginald's fault. Some of it is my fault," said Jon, shaking his head again. "It really doesn't matter."

Baltsaros laughed harshly, and Jon frowned up at him. The grieving boy with no one to turn to had grown into a man with incredible empathy and no ability to control his own emotions; someone who craved being touched like a man craved water in the desert without even recognizing it. Jon was so drawn in on himself that it was a wonder he had made it as far as he had in this life. Baltsaros licked his bottom lip, thinking.

There is that steel within him.

Jon watched Baltsaros with wide grey-blue eyes.

"I think it matters," the captain said quietly. "And, I think you matter very much to me."

When he saw that tears threatened to spill again from the boy's stormy eyes, he pushed away the fury that was burning inside him and leaned down to touch his lips softly to Jon's.

The young man eagerly lifted his head to the kiss, tensing only slightly when Baltsaros resumed stroking the skin of Jon's stomach. Soon the kiss deepened, and the passion of earlier was slowly reignited.

Jon started moaning softly as Baltsaros's skilled fingers became bolder in their caresses, and the captain felt himself stir as the boy beneath him gasped in pleasure when his nipples were pinched gently, and then harder.

Baltsaros moved his mouth down to Jon's throat and bit down softly there, curious to see what his reaction would be; he was charmed when he felt Jon shudder and dig his fingers into his lower back. He had been surprised on that drunken night to realize that Jon was a virgin, but hadn't truly grasped how deep the boy's lack of experience went. There was a thrill running through him as he realized he would be the one to initiate Jon to these new sensations, this dizzying world of pleasure.

With Jon groaning and straining up against Baltsaros's body, the captain decided to go further. The captain slid his hand softly down Jon's smooth chest as he pulled his head back, resting up on his elbow again to watch Jon's face as he surrendered to Baltsaros's touch.

The captain's hand slowly made its way down past Jon's navel to the lines where his pelvis dipped alluringly beneath the grey trousers. As he slid a finger under the waistband of Jon's pants, Baltsaros leaned down once more and shared the young man's breath for a moment until Jon's body relaxed anew. More fingers slid under the coarse material at Jon's waist.

The dark-haired youth had his eyes shut tight and his lips slightly open; Baltsaros could see his tongue moving against his teeth in time to the older man's motions.

Finally, the tips of Baltsaros's fingers made contact with the smooth, rounded head of Jon's erect cock. He had expected him to shrink at his touch but was amazed when Jon moved his hips up, pressing firmly into the contact.

Jon's teeth were worrying at his bottom lip softly, and Baltsaros brought his face down so he could bite at the corner of his mouth.

Groaning, Jon opened to Baltsaros and kissed him deeply. However, when the captain's fingers slid further down Jon's shaft, the dark-haired youth hissed a sharp breath and stopped Baltsaros with his hand.

Baltsaros pulled his head back and frowned. Jon was almost panting, his face and neck flushed with desire, but still he held onto Baltsaros's wrist. *Please,* said his storm-grey eyes.

"Do you want me to stop?" Baltsaros asked quietly.

"Yes. No. I don't know," said Jon honestly. More colour mounted in his cheeks. "I don't know how to be," he confessed.

Baltsaros nearly laughed, but he knew it would be misunderstood by the vulnerable youth. Instead, he shook his head.

"Just *be,* Jon," he said.

After a moment and with obvious hesitation, Jon's hand came

up to brush the long lock of the captain's hair back over his shoulder; he pulled Baltsaros back down to his mouth. Their tongues moved together, and Jon's stubble scratched at Baltsaros's lips.

Jon suddenly turned his head slightly.

"I... won't last long," he whispered hoarsely.

Baltsaros could almost feel the young man's embarrassment in his hot skin, but it was permission. He buried his face in Jon's neck, almost dizzy with his own desire. However, this was for Jon. There would be time later for other things... Right now he needed to concentrate on the shuddering body against his.

He slowly withdrew his fingers and proceeded to unbutton the waist of Jon's pants; pulling back the flaps, he pushed down on the linen garment underneath.

Jon let out a small whimper and wrapped his arm around Baltsaros. Sighing softly at the nakedness under his palm, Baltsaros slowly curled his hand around the hardened length that had come free from the confines of Jon's clothing. Jon's erection was slimmer than his own but of a similar length, and he groaned surprisingly loudly as Baltsaros began to run his hand along its length. With Jon's rapid pulse against his lips, he quickly stroked the young man's cock.

"That's it," he whispered against the skin of Jon's neck when he began thrusting his hips in time to Baltsaros's moving hand. "That's a good boy."

Jon's breath was hoarse and loud in the darkened room; his sigh turned into a sob at Baltsaros's words. In next to no time, he felt Jon's body strain hard, falling out of rhythm suddenly as his hands grasped desperately at Baltsaros's shoulders, nails scratching at the captain's skin. There was a surging in the hard shaft that Baltsaros held, and he felt Jon's seed spill over hot and slick onto his fist, sliding in wetly between his hand and Jon's twitching cock.

Jon moaned loud, a completely uninhibited sound that lasted on and on as he continued to thrust into Baltsaros's hand, his body rocking in time to inner pulses as he came hard against his captain's body.

Baltsaros kissed Jon softly and deeply until he started to relax and his breathing slowed. When he raised his head to look at Jon, he saw that there was a sheen of sweat that covered the young man's smooth skin and made dark curls stick to his forehead.

Jon opened his eyes, his pupils large as he looked at the captain. A slight frown furrowed his brow as he licked his lips.

"Do you want me to…" he asked, sounding uncertain and once again shy.

Baltsaros felt a pulse in the half-hard mound in the front of own his pants but shook his head and laughed.

"No, no. You are completely exhausted. You'll sleep now. I have things to do above deck," he said smiling.

Jon's face was soft with drowsiness as he watched the captain get up and cross the room. He gasped slightly when Baltsaros returned with a wet cloth and wiped Jon's chest and stomach, being gentle over his spent cock. Jon's soft fingers, not yet rough with hard labour, grasped gratefully at the captain's hand.

With half-lidded eyes, Jon looked into Baltsaros's and smiled sheepishly. Swallowing hard, Baltsaros was confounded by the fierce devotion he felt towards this dark-haired creature of sadness and want. Never before had he felt this need to… cherish.

Smiling, he squeezed Jon's hand, and the young man let go, closing his eyes. Baltsaros pulled the quilt on top of Jon and, without a thought, kissed him lightly before turning to go.

J on, wake up. I have something to show you.

Jon's eyes fluttered open. It was dark in the room, a single candle burning in the middle of the mahogany table. He was brought back to the first night he had spent in these quarters; squinting, he could just see the cage across the room. There was a noise to his right, and he smiled, remembering. Jon reached out his hand and rested it on Brutus's big blocky head.

"Hey, boy," he said softly. The dog snuffled at his hand.

Frowning, he wondered whether he had dreamt the captain's voice. He sat up slowly and saw that the door to the stateroom was open. After swinging his feet over the edge, he stood somewhat shakily, using the dog as leverage. When he realized his pants were still unfastened, Jon felt the strangest combination of emotions: embarrassment, elation, confusion, and something that brought a swiftness to his heart that he couldn't put a name to.

He chuckled and rubbed a hand over his hair.

"Brutus, what have I got myself into?" he asked, and scratched the dog's soft ears.

Fastening his pants, he saw the captain's long black coat was draped over the edge of the table, obviously meant for him. Jon put it on. It was slightly too big, the captain being broader and taller than he was, and smelled like the commanding man who wore it: sun, salt, and something spiced and exotic.

He pulled the coat around him tight and went out into the night.

"Jon, come up," called Baltsaros.

Jon lifted his head and saw that the captain was up on the quarterdeck. He walked to the stairs and climbed up, his bare feet cold on the wooden stairs. Baltsaros met him at the top and embraced him tightly. The autumn air was brisk up on the high deck, and Jon was glad for the coat. He saw that the captain wore a long-sleeved, red leather doublet over a black open-necked shirt.

"Come see," said Baltsaros, a strange urgency in his voice. He pointed to lights off the starboard.

Jon frowned.

"What is it?" he asked, confused.

The captain laughed.

"I suppose you've never seen it from this angle," he said. He passed Jon the telescope he held in one hand, and Jon felt a momentary pang of guilt for the captain's lost binoculars.

He lifted the eyepiece and saw that he was looking at a small harbour town beneath a high hill. At first he didn't understand, but when he saw the barely visible silhouette of the castle up above the town, he realized he was looking at Portsmouth. Jon's mouth went dry.

"What are we doing here?" he asked in dismay, a half-dozen strange scenarios coming to mind at once. Was the captain handing him back to his stepfather? He looked at Baltsaros. Was this all some kind of cruel joke?

When the captain saw the utter confusion in Jon's eyes, he laughed abruptly, shaking his head, taking him into his arms again.

"So quick to mistrust, Jon?" Baltsaros asked softly, pressing his lips against the young man's temple. "Just watch…"

Jon kept his eyes on the town, seeing nothing but darkness and twinkling lights. He frowned. What was he supposed to see?

Then the night exploded.

Eye-wateringly bright streaks split the castle walls; balls of fire, like giant orange blossoms, erupted from the burning ruins. Jon could see the giant clouds of black smoke, blotting out the skies, the sounds of the explosions reaching his ears a second after they happened. He blinked, and there were bright spots behind his eyelids.

The castle is on fire.

He looked away, back to the captain's face. The older man was staring at the conflagration with a grim look on his face, the flames reflected in his dark eyes. Jon turned again to the burning castle in awe. It was beyond comprehension.

"Did you do this?" he asked in a hushed voice.

Without looking at Jon, Baltsaros nodded. A moment later he tore his gaze away from the fires across the water; his eyes were narrow in amusement.

"Well, not me personally. You have Billy and Jim to thank for the show," he said smiling, his teeth white against his dark face. The twin brothers worked the 32-pounder carronades at the front of the ship, and it seemed that they also knew something about explosives.

"Baltsaros," said Jon quietly. "There were women and children in the castle too."

The captain shrugged.

"My men made sure that there were no innocents within," he said and looked back to the burning ruins.

He is lying.

That, or he didn't believe any of them to be innocent. It was as clear as day to Jon: the captain had just murdered a castle full of people and didn't care in the least.

Jon turned and watched the flames lick the sky. Baltsaros had done this out of revenge. Searching inside himself for the horror and sadness that should have been there, Jon was astounded to find nothing.

The captain had done this *for him.*

And it felt glorious.

15

ROPE'S END

Destruction, hence, like creation, is one of Nature's mandates.

— MARQUIS DE SADE

Jon woke up from dreams of Reginald burning.

He sat up slowly and rubbed his face. The self-assurance that he had gone to sleep with the night before had become slightly smudged with trepidation.

A dangerous man indeed.

However, looking over at the captain lying next to him, Jon had to smile.

After the fire had started to burn low, the two of them had nearly tumbled down the stairs in their haste to get to the privacy of the stateroom. There, Baltsaros had once again coaxed Jon's desire to the very edge; however, this time he had delayed Jon's final plunge by releasing him and instead, kissing him roughly on his mouth, chest, and neck until the keen edge of pleasure's knife was dulled. Then he would start up again, hand stroking Jon's cock skilfully, building up his ecstasy until he reached the very cusp only to stop once more.

Jon had been frantic with need, his lips whispering *please* over and over against Baltsaros's neck, each breath a sob. Finally, when it felt like he could take no more, the captain had pushed him down flat and moved down his body to close his mouth over the end of Jon's cock, sliding his lips over the sensitive head and down his hard shaft. Jon's hands had taken on a life of their own as he pressed the captain's head down against him, fingers snarled in the man's long hair. It had been a mind-shattering release when Jon had cum hard into Baltsaros's mouth, each thrust a rough-edged, liquid pulse of pleasure.

Afterwards, he had lain there breathless, watching Baltsaros as he sat back on his heels between Jon's legs. Being with Baltsaros was like dying and being reborn; there was no other way he could describe it.

When he saw that the captain's eyes were darkly shadowed, and his face was taut with blatant hunger, it occurred to him then that Baltsaros was stronger than he was; he could take whatever he wanted from the younger man. At the shocking thought, Jon had felt a finger of fear touch him, and... It had excited him. However, the captain just smiled down at Jon before crawling up next to him and pulling the covers over the two of them. Sleep had found both men quickly.

J on stood quietly, not wanting to rouse the captain. After only a slight hesitation, and with a small smile, he pulled the captain's black shirt over his head and tucked it into his own grey trousers. On quiet feet, Jon left the captain's quarters, Brutus at his side, and headed below deck.

. . .

With a plate of food in one hand, Jon stood in front of the metal cage deep in the belly of the ship. The man in the back of it was crouched with knees to chin. When Jon stepped closer, a pair of fierce green-blue eyes looked him up and down.

"Have ye come to kill me, little man?" asked Tom, his voice hoarse from disuse. Jon walked right up to the front of the cage and placed the plate on the floor, sliding it through the opening at the base of the bars.

"No. Just to bring you your breakfast." Jon took a step back and sat down cross-legged on the floor. "And to get some answers."

Tom laughed harshly.

"Ye can keep yer fuckin' breakfast, love. I ain't hungry."

However, the way Tom's eyes had followed the food belied his words.

"Don't be a martyr, Tom. It's unattractive," said Jon, glibly.

The beaten pirate raised his head and grinned.

Jon gasped at the extent of the burly young man's injuries. Half of Tom's face was a mess of dark bruising, his left eye had a burst of dark red in it, and his lips had a deep split on one side. Jon could see that what he had assumed was grime was actually flaking dried blood that covered Tom from his matted dirty-blond hair to where his torso disappeared behind his bent knees.

When Tom finally uncurled and reached forward for the plate of breakfast, he did it with a grunt of pain; it wasn't only Tom's face that had taken a beating. Taking some egg up with his fingers, Tom began wolfing down the food.

Jon sat quietly just watching Tom eat.

The muscular young man's ocean eyes kept flicking back up to Jon's face in curiosity as he devoured his breakfast quickly. He was soon done and slid the metal plate back across the floor where it clanged against the bars. Tom sat back, his elbows resting on his knees as he looked at Jon. The ex–first mate burped and then smiled.

"So what can I do for you, dear Jonny? Ye've come to gloat? Did ye poison my food?" he asked, finishing the piece of bread in his hand in one bite.

Jon pressed his lips together and frowned at Tom.

"I just want to know *why* you told the captain you had me killed. Why not just tell him the truth?" he asked.

Tom looked away. After a long pause, Jon saw the man's broad shoulder come up in a minute shrug.

"Tom, why not just kill me? From what I've heard, it's something you do well... Why the roundabout way of getting me captured? Why bother?" he asked; the question had burned in him from the moment that Katherine had told Jon of Tom's assassination claims.

Tom looked back to Jon and grinned.

"Aw, Jonny, so did ye wind up in the slammer?" he asked.

Jon leaned forward.

"I did. I would have also swung at the end of a rope if Katherine had not come to rescue me."

At this Tom's eyes went wide, his astonishment real.

"I thought yer da was the lawman?" he said slowly. "He'd a let ye hang?"

Jon nodded.

"The man's a coward. And he's not my father... He's only the man who married my mother."

Tom frowned and looked down at the floor.

"So he's a real cunt, aye?" he said after a long pause. He raised his eyes back to Jon's. "That's somethin' we have in common, isn't it? Our da's can't stand us." An odd look passed over Tom's face. "Listen, love. It wasn't my intention to have ye killed. Truly. I thought yer da would never believe ye killed those skirts. I figured ye'd wind up in a cage somewhere... just long enough to get ye out of my life." The words were spoken in complete truth.

Jon was about to respond when he heard boots behind him on

the stairs. He turned his head and saw that Baltsaros, his face completely expressionless, was standing at the door.

"Jon, come away from there," he said quietly.

Jon got to his feet, his brows drawn in confusion.

"That's it, dog. Obey yer master," laughed Tom from his cage.

Baltsaros narrowed his eyes at his former first mate.

"Take him out of there," he growled.

Two deckhands came forward, jostling Jon out of the way to open the cage. With some difficulty, they managed to pull the big man out.

Jon leaned against the wall, his eyes on Tom; he almost gasped when he saw an incredible change go through the muscular brute. Tom had gone rigid with fear, his breath sounding loud in the small space. Following Tom's line of sight, Jon was aghast to see a heavy leather whip looped in the captain's hand.

Dragging Tom behind them, the two deckhands pushed past Jon again and followed Baltsaros up the stairs to the upper deck. Jon went with them, swallowing hard.

Tom struggled frantically as they tied him to the mast, arms spread wide to either side. He kept up a steady repeating plea that made Jon ache with the sound of it:

"—please Da please don't I didn't touch him Da please please don't oh god Da please please I didn't touch him please..."

"Tom just said I'd been killed so you'd leave me behind! He didn't figure on Reginald wanting to hang me. Please... Don't do this, Baltsaros... He didn't touch me. He didn't think I'd be killed," Jon said, a hand on the captain's arm.

Baltsaros looked down at him, his eyes cold.

Jon tightened his grasp and tried to find the loving, tender man he had shared a bed with last night in the terrifyingly glacial creature that stood before him.

"The result would have been the same, Jon. He would have been responsible for your death," said the captain, pushing the younger man back a few paces. "Now get out of my way." Baltsaros nodded to Old Calum who came and began pulling Jon away from the captain.

"He's absolutely terrified," Jon said, his voice harsh, and it was true. Tom was trembling and pale as he stood waiting for the captain to mete out his punishment, still whimpering his pleas over and over.

Baltsaros shook Jon off and took a few steps towards the man at the mast.

Defeated, Jon yanked his arm out of Calum's hands and went to stand next to Katherine.

An imposing black-clad figure in the bright morning sun, Baltsaros stood a good five paces away from Tom. He dropped the looped length to the deck with a thud, holding the heavy handle of the whip in his gloved hand. His arm came around in a wide circle above his head, and then the whip cracked out, a red line appearing on Tom's broad back as if by magic. The scream that rent the air was born of pure terror and pain.

Jon felt the blood freeze in his veins.

Crack!

Crack!

Crack!

The whip kept coming, over and over again. Tom's back was a mess of dripping red lines as the captain skilfully changed his grip and approach not to have the braided leather come down in the same place twice. Tom's shrieks became cries and then groans as more lines appeared; Baltsaros began grunting with exertion as his arm came up for the next stroke and the next.

Jon looked around and saw that most of the audience had trickled away. Those who had stayed seemed glued to the spot by horrified fascination. Behind him, Jon heard Katherine let out a soft cry.

Tom had suddenly sagged in his restraints, and his body no longer twitched when the leather continued cutting into him. The captain's face had taken on a look of soft ecstasy as if he were caressing Tom instead of whipping him to death.

Jon felt ill. He took a few steps forward.

"That's enough, Captain," he said loudly. "Stop it." His voice seemed to break through to Baltsaros, and the man blinked and staggered slightly, dropping the whip to the deck in a seeming daze; he looked at Jon, eyes wild. Then, without a word, the captain walked past him and made his way slowly to his quarters, closing the door behind him. The crew stood in silence a moment longer, rife with uncertainty.

Katherine was the first to step forward when Jon's legs refused to move. She went up to Tom and felt at his neck for a pulse.

"He's alive," she said, looking up at Jon with brown eyes wide with horror. It seemed that her dislike for the cheerful brute did not extend to torture.

The breath that Jon had been holding whooshed out of his lungs and time resumed. Everyone scattered to their various jobs, two of the younger cabin boys already coming forward with bucket and brush to scrub away Tom's blood.

Gingerly, Jon tried to undo the knots holding the big man to the mast, but the weight of him had pulled everything taut. He pulled the knife out of his belt and sawed at one of the ropes, thankful to see that Katherine was working at the other. When they had Tom down on the deck, Jon looked around for someone to help. No one would meet his eyes. However, a large, friendly hand soon grasped his shoulder; Beard leaned down and picked up the insensate Tom in his arms like he was lifting a child, carrying him towards the stairs.

When Jon saw they were going back to the brig, he pulled on Beard's arm.

"No... somewhere soft," he said. Tom had paid his dues.

The huge man looked at him in confusion and shrugged, not understanding. Katherine said a few words in another language, and Beard shrugged again, shaking his head. His voice rumbled out a reply, and Jon saw Katherine press her lips into a hard line.

"He's right, Jon," said the woman. "Tom stays in the brig until the captain says he's free."

Baltsaros lay on his back on his soft bed, his eyes closed. First the loss of control at Jon's return... That he would kiss another man, with obvious passion, in front of the crew was out of character, but now this? He would have kept whipping Tom until the man died.

As he took a deep breath, he tried to clear his mind. His feelings for Jon were beginning to take a toll on him, his composure full of cracks and his self-control... He grimaced and pressed the heels of his hands against his eyelids. Baltsaros needed to sort out the mess his mind was becoming. A balance would have to be found, but giving up what he had found with Jon was not an option.

Baltsaros heard the door open, and he almost groaned out loud. Jon's soft footfalls came up to the side of the bed and stopped.

"You almost killed him," Jon said softly.

In another man it would have been an accusation, but Jon was just stating a fact. Baltsaros didn't say anything for a long time, hoping the young man would just go away. After an interminable silence, he finally moved his hands and turned his head. Jon stood next to the bed, a deep crease between his dark brows.

Baltsaros sighed.

"I know," he said. When Jon's face didn't change, he looked away. "Jon, because of his lie, *I thought you had died*. He had to be punished."

"Don't say that like you didn't have a choice," said Jon. "Sitting in the brig would have been enough. You must have known how the whip would affect Tom."

Baltsaros nodded.

"It's the only thing he's afraid of," he said softly. "I broke a promise today."

The word *promise* had never meant much, just a means of getting others to do things for him. The captain thought back to his uncle; the man had not left a single mark on Baltsaros's skin, but the terror had been the same. He sat up and reached out for Jon. The young man let himself be pulled into Baltsaros's arms. The captain had done damage today, both to Tom and to Jon, but he didn't think it was irreversible.

"Please, Jon," he said simply.

J on frowned at Baltsaros. The man was obviously in distress, but it stemmed from confusion rather than regret. With a deep breath, Jon lifted his hand and touched the side of Baltsaros's face. He saw no remorse, no guilt in his captain's brown eyes; yet, there lay a deep tide of emotion in them. A complicated man. Part monster, part gentleman.

When Baltsaros's hand started sliding up Jon's back, he closed his eyes, giving in to the caress.

His lover.

"Fix this," Jon said, opening his eyes. He tangled his fingers in Baltsaros's hair and stared hard at him. "If you can find it in your-self to forgive Tom, it would be a great gift to me."

Baltsaros frowned.

"Tom can't be trusted," he said.

Jon smiled at the irony.

"Well, neither can you," he said. Jon watched Baltsaros take in his words with a look of consternation.

After a moment, the captain nodded. The troubled look had left his face. He then spoke quietly.

"Do you trust me, Jon?" he asked.

The younger man ran a hand through his dark curls, thinking. Did he trust Baltsaros? The man lied. He killed people. All while wearing a mask of affable charm. No... He didn't trust Baltsaros, but it didn't change how he felt.

"Yes," said Jon, lying; he realized that, strangely, his answer mattered to Baltsaros. The captain's face softened, and he pulled

Jon down to his mouth. Jon kissed Baltsaros hard, bending the older man's head back. He felt the captain's surprise at his rough handling and smiled against Baltsaros's lips. Jon was changing. But, for the better? He did not know.

Tom.

Jon pulled away from Baltsaros.

"I'm going to go see if Tom is conscious," he said, not waiting for the captain's permission.

Baltsaros stood.

"Hold a moment. I'll give you something for his back," he said, walking to the cabinet. The captain handed him a bundle of dried leaves with the instruction to get a container and hot water from Cook. Jon was to wash the wounds, apply a thick salve, and then plaster over the area with the rehydrated leaves.

"Why don't you come with me?" Jon asked.

Baltsaros frowned.

"No, Jon. I'm still… angry."

J on stepped down the stairs, carefully carrying the metal container with the leaves in it. He set it down next to the cage and unlocked the door with the key Baltsaros had given him. Picking the container back up, he walked to where Tom was lying on his stomach on the hard cot with his head towards the wall and knelt down. With a cautious hand, he reached out to touch the prone man's shoulder.

"Tom?" he asked in a whisper.

"Go away, love. Just… Go the fuck away," said Tom.

Jon realized that Tom was crying, and he felt something in his heart twist at the bigger man's pain. After putting down the bucket of warm water and the container with the leaves, Jon pulled the small pot of salve out of the pouch at his waist. Without another word, he began to softly clean the torn skin of Tom's back.

16

UNCHARTED TERRITORY

T hings quickly fell into routine for Jon. He would wake up, sore from work on the ship and somewhat tender from Baltsaros's caresses, and make his way to the galley. After grabbing breakfast for Tom and himself, he would head down to the brig and eat, cross-legged on the floor of the cage.

Tom wouldn't touch his food while Jon was there; in fact the man on the cot hadn't turned his head to look at Jon the entire time he had been taking care of him. However, when Jon returned in the evening with another meal, the morning plate was always empty. After Jon had eaten, he would open the pot of salve and gingerly apply more on the prone man's wounds.

The muscular young man was healing quickly; Tom was a hale and hearty brute... at least in body. How Tom's mind fared was what worried Jon the most; apart from telling him to go away that first day, Tom hadn't spoken a word to him, or to anyone else.

Afterwards, Jon would get to work. Sometimes it was in the kitchen with Cook, but most of the time it was above deck for general upkeep. Once that was done there would be target or sword practice with Katherine, and later, hand-to-hand fighting lessons with Old Calum. Then it was a quick trip to the galley to pick up Tom's supper and back to the brig to drop it off, checking on the state of the silent man's wounds again while he was there.

However, his nights belonged entirely to Baltsaros.

Jon would clean up and meet the captain in his quarters for the shared evening meal. There they would talk at length over supper, Baltsaros obviously pleased with Jon's healthy appetite and quick mind. The topics varied: ship matters, geography, politics, history, literature... But eventually, the conversation would inevitably wind down as a different kind of hunger grew in the two men.

J on looked down into his glass of wine and frowned. The captain and he were discussing the history of the midland isles where Jon grew up, something that usually fascinated him. However, the way that Baltsaros kept looking at his lips when he talked was distracting him; he couldn't stop thinking about what Baltsaros would do if he suddenly leaned across the table to kiss him.

Jon nodded, not actually hearing the captain's last words, and suddenly realized that the other man had stopped speaking. Jon glanced up.

"Am I boring you, Jon?" asked Baltsaros. Though the captain's face was serious, his eyes were lively with amusement.

Jon shook his head, smiling.

"You could never bore me," he said.

The man stood slowly and held out his hand to Jon.

"Come to me," he said softly.

No matter that Jon had shared Baltsaros's bed for over a week now, the man's sheer confidence and graceful masculinity still made him strangely shy. Heart hammering in his chest and limbs awkward, Jon got up and walked self-consciously towards the man who had captured him, body and soul.

When Baltsaros's strong arms came around him, however, Jon's shyness dissipated like fog in the bright morning sun; he reached up and cupped the older man's face in his hands, bringing his mouth close to Baltsaros's and teasing it with light brushes of his lips. Jon loved the way the corners of Baltsaros's jaw fit in the palms of his hands, his thumbs against those sharp cheekbones as he nudged the captain's mouth open. Baltsaros closed his eyes and sighed into the kiss, his fingers quickly pulling up the bottom of Jon's shirt to run possessive hands over his soft skin.

Any time they were together during the day, no matter how brief, the captain peppered him with small touches: a hand on his shoulder, a light tap of his fingers on Jon's tanned forearm, his hip pausing briefly against Jon's in the course of their shared labour.

You are mine, said these touches. *You are mine, and no one else's.*

In the sombre light of the captain's quarters, those words repeated themselves loud and clear in the way Baltsaros gently withdrew from Jon's grasp and slowly undressed him with deft fingers until he stood naked. The first time Baltsaros had done this, Jon had felt he would die from embarrassment; he was a skinny, pale thing compared to the captain. However, reluctantly raising his eyes to Baltsaros's when he was asked to, Jon had been astounded by what he saw there: *Baltsaros found him beautiful.*

The rush of emotion that had coursed through Jon with that realization had brought hot tears to his eyes. Baltsaros had quickly stepped forward and kissed him hard, taking his breath and tears away.

As then, the roughness of the captain's leather pants and stiff brocade vest against Jon's skin made him acutely aware of his nakedness, and this vulnerability excited him. Jon shivered as the captain's warm hands slid down his back to his buttocks, pressing him firmly against the black leather and the prominent hardness beneath. It was intensely erotic, and it brought out a shameless-ness in Jon.

He pushed himself into Baltsaros, his own stiffening length rubbing against the unyielding folds of the captain's pants. Taking one of Baltsaros's hands, Jon slid it between their bodies and pressed the captain's palm hard against his erection, biting softly at those curved lips that constantly drove him to distraction.

Baltsaros began stroking him slowly, his own excitement obvious in the pulse that hammered against Jon's tongue as he ran his open mouth down the side of the captain's neck. When Baltsaros's hand became slippery with the pearls of desire beading at the tip of Jon's cock, he growled low in his throat and started working his own fastenings loose with the other hand.

However, Jon pulled out of Baltsaros's grasp and dropped to his knees on the colourful rug, quickly unlacing the captain with nimble fingers. Looking up into Baltsaros's face, Jon was bolstered by the surprise he saw there and smiled.

Eyes dark, Baltsaros unbuttoned his vest, pulling it and his shirt over his head as Jon began kissing his exposed skin. The curly patch of hair that covered the captain's chest and stomach was surprisingly soft, and Jon ran his hands over it, feeling the hard muscles underneath Baltsaros's skin. The captain's hand came down to cup the back of his head as Jon's mouth moved lower down, his lips and tongue against the curved lines of Baltsaros's groin.

Jon started to falter, but Baltsaros's fingers pushed at him gently; before he could lose his nerve, Jon started tugging down the leather at Baltsaros's hips, finally freeing the captain's cock. It bobbed out at him, hard and thick with a wide head. Jon's hands had been on it many times, stroking it until the captain gasped and moaned in his grasp, but never his mouth. This was uncharted territory.

Hesitantly, Jon leaned forward and kissed the root of it, licking softly at its underside as he lifted it up with a hand. Above him, Jon heard the captain sigh as his fingers began running through his dark curls. Jon slid his tongue along its length and pressed his lips against the ridge where the bottom of its swollen head met hard shaft; after lapping at it gently, Jon finally opened his mouth and slid his lips over the head of Baltsaros's cock, sucking it down.

Jon looked up and felt a surge of desire when he saw the

captain's flushed face and half-lidded eyes. Baltsaros's tongue licked at his bottom lip, teeth grazing the soft skin there as he watched Jon take in more of his cock. Shuddering, the captain threw his head back with a hard gasp as the young man swallowed the hard length down, only to pull back and tease at Baltsaros's cockhead with tongue and gentle teeth.

As he held the root of Baltsaros's shaft in one hand, Jon began sliding his grasp along it tightly in time to his mouth's movements, building up a steady rhythm. He used his tongue to add pressure and friction to the head of it on every pass, and Baltsaros moaned softly, broken words coming from him between hard breaths.

"Jon... Gods, where did you... oh, like that... that... yes..." Baltsaros's hand began pushing insistently at Jon's head, snagging in his hair, as his hips rocked with every deepening plunge of his cock down the other man's throat.

Jon gagged at the onslaught, pulling his mouth away more than once, only to return and try to force the captain's cock further.

Baltsaros's other hand came around to clasp Jon's head, and he finally lost control over the situation as the captain's lust made him rough.

Suddenly Jon couldn't breathe, and tears came to his eyes. He began to panic...

I'm going to suffocate... I can't do this...

But then something happened: Jon decided to let go and surrender himself completely.

Throat wide open to Baltsaros's cock, Jon again felt vulnerable... *Baltsaros was fucking his mouth.* Jon shuddered and moaned; incredibly, an overwhelming desire surged through him as his fist closed over his own hard cock bobbing between his thighs. Stroking quickly in time to Baltsaros's thrusts, Jon found himself soon nearing the edge. He lifted his eyes to the man abusing his throat and felt the balance tip within as he saw the bestial look on Baltsaros's face.

Jon came *hard*.

The exquisite pulsing pressure mounting in his groin spread like a crackling fire through him as the first thick spurts of cum pumped out of his cock. Not able to cry out or suck in a deep breath as the pleasure coursed through him in hot waves, he felt giddy and crazed as he stroked himself quickly, not even caring that the captain's thrusts were hard and the hold on his head painful.

All at once, Baltsaros was cumming too. With a deep grunt, the captain abruptly slowed his motions, matching the pulses from his jerking cock as he spilled his seed into Jon's throat. The thick, yolky bitterness filled the younger man's mouth, and he almost gagged again, but instead swallowed the cum down, once… twice.

Finally, the captain sagged back against the edge of the table, his hands going soft in Jon's hair as he panted, eyes closed.

Jon let Baltsaros's spent cock slide out of his mouth, moving to lean his head against the captain's twitching thigh for a moment. Jon was breathless and filled with a warm ecstasy that buzzed slowly through his limbs. When his heart had begun to slow, he sat back on his heels and looked slowly up at Baltsaros in a daze.

The older man was smiling down at him.

"You made a mess on my rug it seems," he said.

Jon looked down with alarm, but the captain just laughed.

"It's all right," said Baltsaros, reaching down to pull Jon to his feet. With the captain leaning on the table, they were the same height. Baltsaros's hand came up, and he ran his thumb along the edge of Jon's tender lower lip.

Jon stared wide-eyed into Baltsaros's brown eyes, and he brought his hands up to the man's waist, feeling the cooling wetness of the captain's soft cock against his.

Baltsaros leaned forward and kissed Jon gently.

"Did I hurt you?" he asked.

Jon shook his head; he felt strange and wanted to tell Baltsaros, but didn't know how to express it. It was like he felt… *free…* But that made no sense to him.

The captain frowned slightly.

"Why are you looking at me this way?" he asked slowly, his accent making the words hiss softly.

Jon shook his head again. There was peace inside him. He lifted his hand to Baltsaros's face and touched the captain's lips with his fingers before bringing his own lips against them once more. Baltsaros held him tight, his open mouth warm against Jon's as their tongues slid against each other. Jon felt like crying or laughing; he couldn't tell which.

Baltsaros grinned and pulled back.

"You're shaking, and your pulse is erratic... Are you quite sure you're all right?" he asked.

Jon had to smile. He shrugged. This time the captain laughed out loud.

"You look drunk," he said and pushed away from the table. After taking the disoriented man by the arm, Baltsaros steered him towards the bed where they ended up sprawled on the soft coverlet with Jon's head against the captain's chest.

Finally his mind was starting to feel more normal as he lay there, Baltsaros's fingers idly stroking his shoulder and back.

"You are definitely something," said the captain, his voice rumbling against Jon's ear. "That was... exceedingly pleasant."

Jon pulled at Baltsaros's chest hair and smiled.

"Yes," he said.

Baltsaros looked over at Jon sleeping next to him in the wide bed and frowned. What was it about the slender, dark-haired, young man that *pulled* at him so? Part of it had to be that Jon could be a wide-eyed innocent one moment, and the very next, a wanton, naked sylph with the skills of a consummate lover.

For a strange moment earlier, when his cock was being so expertly handled, the captain had been sure that looking down, he would see Tom's sea-green eyes staring back at him instead of Jon's.

It was utterly fascinating; Jon spent so much time trying to "read" people and situations that he began to mimic his subjects. Baltsaros was convinced that Jon wasn't even aware of it.

Baltsaros slid off the bed and padded to the door to open it. The moon was a bright sliver in the night sky, but he couldn't see many stars. Cold air blew against his bare skin, and he breathed deep.

Was that it? Was he so deeply enchanted by the serious young man simply because Jon, unlike others, could actually *see* him? And could, perhaps, become more like Baltsaros?

The idea had merit.

It would be interesting to see what happened as time went on, and Baltsaros wondered if there was anything he could do to increase the effect.

When he glanced over his shoulder at the slumbering boy in his bed, Baltsaros's face softened. No, there was more to it. At the very least, the captain felt extremely protective of this fascinating creature in his bed. Something about Jon made the captain ache... And as painful as it was, Baltsaros craved it night and day.

Baltsaros smiled to himself; the way Jon had stared at him afterwards, like he had been nearly driven mad with passion, made the captain eager to have the young man on his knees again soon.

Keeping the door open a crack to air out the stuffy room, Baltsaros then made his way back to bed, pausing only to pinch the flame from the candle between thumb and forefinger. He crawled up beside Jon and curled himself against his side, pulling the coverlet up to shield them from the cool night air.

J on, balancing two plates and a mug of beer while he descended the dark stairs the next morning, was astounded to see Tom watching him from where he sat on the cot.

The muscular pirate stood and approached the bars, reaching out to hold the plates while Jon forced the iron key into the stiff lock.

Jon smiled, and Tom raised an eyebrow at him, shaking his head, but a small grin curved to one side of his mouth. Jon sat on the floor and Tom sat on the cot, both men immediately digging into the food on the metal plates. Not knowing how to break the silence, Jon just chewed his bread and took a swig of beer before passing the metal mug to Tom.

The big man took a long pull, swishing the beer in his mouth before swallowing it down. As he leaned forward with a large, scarred hand on his knee, Tom looked at Jon appraisingly.

"The least ye could fuckin' do, lovey, is not come in here reekin' like ye've been fuckin' all night long. It's enough to put a man off his feed," he said.

Jon felt the heat in his cheeks; but, before he could stammer a response, Tom just slapped his leg and started laughing, his blue-green eyes twinkling in merriment.

17

STAUNCHING THE WOUND

*"Love is, after all, a selfish thing; and it throws a
black shadow on anything between which and
the light it stands."*

— BRAM STOKER, THE JEWEL OF SEVEN
STARS

It was obvious, at least to Jon's eyes, that all was not right
with Tom. On his release from the brig the previous day,
Tom had been full of his usual bluff good humour, but Jon
immediately saw it for what it was: an act.

Sitting atop a stack of crates as he fixed some netting, Jon
frowned to himself. He could see the muscular young man from
his perch—now just a regular deckhand—laughing with someone
near the front of the ship. It looked strangely off to Jon, even from
this distance. Getting close to Tom since he'd been freed was difficult, as the man seemed to be giving both him and the captain a
wide berth; however, he had seen enough in the last day to know
that though the burly man still swaggered and joked, his blue-
green eyes had gone dull, and his shoulders tensed at even the

smallest sound. Just yesterday, when a board fell over with a loud crack, Jon had seen Tom freeze in his tracks, hands going to white-knuckled fists at his sides. It was as if the lusty fire that had burned bright in Tom had been extinguished.

Jon's eyes kept being drawn to Tom as he worked.

Out of worry or out of sheer curiosity? he wondered idly.

Suddenly the knife Jon was using to cut into a tangle slipped and sliced through the meat of his palm; dropping the net and knife to the ground, he sucked on the bleeding cut and winced. To be fair, not everything was right with him either if the dream from this morning was any indication.

The castle was burning. Jon coughed into the crook of his arm as he tried to see through the thick smoke. He could hear screaming, but he couldn't tell where it was coming from. Walking forward he was almost hit by a burning ceiling beam. He had to find Reginald. More screaming. There was a whoosh, and the old, threadbare tapestries turned into sheets of flame. Maybe Reginald was in the tower. Jon made his way to the stairs leading up and was dismayed to see that there were piles of charred bones in the way. Picking his way over them, he saw the skull of a child. Many children. All the bones were small and fragile, crumbling to black dust as he walked over them in his bare feet. Strangely, though the bones were still smouldering, they didn't hurt him. He climbed up and up, much higher than he thought the tower went. There was a low sound, like the beating of a giant heart coming from the other side of the large wooden door.

"Reginald?" he called. "Reginald, are you there?"

He thought he could hear his stepfather's voice. He put his shoulder to the door and pushed against it hard. Slowly the door opened, but it was as if he were pushing at something through treacle. Finally, it gave way, and Jon stumbled forward. He saw that he was in an unfamiliar, bare room... not the one he had been expecting. The captain of the guards stood in the corner, facing the wall.

"Reginald?" he called loudly. "Is that you?"

His stepfather didn't move. Something behind Jon nudged him, and he realized the great black lion had followed him here. He took a step forward.

"Yes, yes, just this last one and then we can go, right?" he asked.

The nose of the giant lion nuzzled the back of his neck softly as Jon struck the match in his hand, throwing it at the man standing in the corner. As if Reginald were made of dry straw, the older man burst into bright flames.

J on woke up, choking and drenched in sweat, the phantom smell of burning flesh still thick in his nose. Breathing hard, he clawed at the blankets and sat up, Baltsaros's arms coming around him quickly in the dark; as always he was grateful for the man's instantly calming presence. The dream, incredibly vivid just a moment ago, had already started to fade as he took a shuddering breath, shaking his head to try to clear it. Jon hadn't seen Reginald's face.

Was he the burning man?

He brought a hand up to clasp Baltsaros's strong forearm and leaned back, the captain a solid comfort behind him. When Baltsaros brought his lips to the side of Jon's neck, something nagged at him for a second, but then it was gone. All that was left was the uneasy sense that he should feel *something* about Reginald's death, and of those that perished with him in the fire; however, Baltsaros's warm breath against his skin gave him shivers, distracting him from his dark thoughts.

"It was only a dream, Jon," said the captain's enchanting voice in his ear. "Come, lie down… You're safe here with me."

Jon let himself be pulled back down into the soft mattress, Baltsaros's hard body against him. Questing out with a hand, he felt for the other man's face and ran his fingers along his stubbled jaw before shifting forward to bring his mouth into contact with

Baltsaros's. It was hours yet until morning, and Jon wanted nothing more than to forget the dream completely.

J on stared in dismay at the cut on his hand. It wouldn't stop bleeding. After climbing down off his perch, Jon went in search of something to staunch it. Perhaps Baltsaros had something in that cabinet of his.

However, on entering the captain's quarters, Jon was suddenly uneasy; even though he was essentially sharing the room with Baltsaros, Jon still felt very much a visitor here.

Squaring his shoulders as he took a few steps forward, he tried to push away the feeling that he was trespassing. As usual, the large room was sombrely lit and Jon, eyes sliding over the curved walls of the captain's quarters, thought again about how peculiar that was.

By his reckoning, the room had to be about twenty feet at its widest and at least eighteen feet deep, and the whole was poorly lit by two small portholes to either side; even the room where the gunpowder was stored had better lighting than the captain's room.

He frowned. Jon walked slowly around the table and stared at the top of the far wall. Standing on his toes, Jon narrowed his eyes; he had noticed before that there was a decorative cornice above the map and the crest, but from this close, it could almost pass for a window ledge.

With his undamaged hand, Jon dragged one of the heavy chairs over and stepped up onto the wine-coloured cushion. When he peered at the space above the cornice, he saw immediately that the wood was of a different type than the walls. Recalling that ships like this often had a row of windows at the back of the forecastle, Jon lifted a hand up and touched the wood paneling above the ledge. He pushed and it gave a little. It wouldn't take much to pull the thin sheet of wood away.

I wonder why it's cov—

"Jon, what are you doing?" came the captain's voice from behind him.

Jon started; he'd been so focused on what he was doing that he hadn't heard Baltsaros's boots at the door. Jon felt the heat mount in his cheeks, his heart beating a little faster. When he turned to look at the captain, he felt both embarrassed and a little fearful.

Baltsaros's face was grim, and the lines at the sides of his mouth deepened as the muscles moved in his jaw. His eyes, usually warm when he looked at Jon, were flinty and suspicious.

Jon shook his head.

"I'm sorry. I just... It's so dark in here all the time. I wanted to see why..." he said, his voice sounding a little high in his ears as he scrambled down off the chair. In dismay he saw he had left a dusty footprint right in the middle of the velvet cushion.

Baltsaros's eyes travelled over the dirty cushion, up over the soiled knees of his grey pants, past the grime and blood on his linen shirt, and stopped at Jon's face, his brown eyes narrow.

Jon swallowed. One didn't need to be particularly empathic to see that the captain was not pleased with him.

"I'm sorry," he said quietly and dropped his eyes to the floor, not sure what else to say. He heard Baltsaros sigh and was gratified when the man's hand came up after a moment to cup Jon's chin, lifting his face back up to meet his eyes.

"You're a mess," The captain said simply.

Jon felt like a small, dirty child, and the thought rankled him.

"You don't need to climb all over my furniture like a monkey. Why not just ask me why I've covered the window?" asked Baltsaros, the grip on Jon's face tightening slightly.

After swatting the captain's hand away, Jon's brows came down dark over his eyes.

"Because asking you questions is a study in frustration," he said. "Besides, I'm here nearly as much as you are. I figured I have some right to climb on the furniture if I have a reason to."

Baltsaros stared at him for a moment and abruptly started laughing, his eyes warm once more as he clasped Jon's shoulder.

"Yes. Yes, I suppose you do. I've invited you to climb into my bed... Why not on the chairs too?" he said, smiling.

Jon shook his head in disbelief.

Cold and hot.

Though he tried, he could never quite predict the captain's reactions. Then, Jon saw the captain frown and followed his gaze down, grimacing when he saw what Baltsaros was looking at.

"My dear boy, you do have a penchant for getting bodily fluids on the rugs," he said, his brow furrowed but his tone light. "Why in gods' names are you bleeding?"

Jon, having gone red from the memory of being on his knees in front of the captain that first time, laughed awkwardly and held up his palm. The cut was deep and still dripped blood slowly.

"I cut myself," he said lamely.

Baltsaros nodded.

"I can see that. Sit down, I'll need to put a few stitches in or else it won't close properly," he said, pushing Jon towards the chair he had dirtied.

He blanched at the captain's words.

"Stitches? Is that really necessary?" Jon asked, staring down at his wound.

Baltsaros laughed as he rummaged through a drawer in the teak cabinet. After pulling out a little box with brass trimmings, the captain dragged a chair close to Jon. He placed the box on the table and opened it; inside were a variety of metal instruments, bits of fabric, and what looked like thread.

Jon watched as Baltsaros walked away to pour out a healthy amount of dark rum into an earthenware mug from the bottle atop the cabinet before coming back to sit down.

The captain held out the mug.

"Drink," he said.

Jon's stomach fluttered uneasily at the smell rising up from the dark liquid; since that drunken night with Tom, Jon hadn't been able to drink rum without feeling ill. He took the tiniest sip and shivered, but Baltsaros reached a hand out and pushed the mug back up to Jon's lips.

"Drink it all, you foolish thing. This is going to hurt," said the captain.

With his eyes closed, Jon drank the rest of the burning liquid down in a gulp, his insides roiling in response. Soon, however, a warm, syrupy feeling began to spread out from his chest. What had Tom called him? A lightweight? Jon opened his eyes; he already felt flushed.

Baltsaros was watching him with a curious expression on his face, and his brown eyes held a small note of desire in them. Baltsaros reached for the cup and stood to refill it, bringing the bottle to the table on his return. However, before passing it back to Jon, he wrapped his large hand around the younger man's wrist, quickly tilting the mug over the wound and splashing some of the liquid directly into the cut.

"Ahhhh! Fucking hell!" yelled Jon, jerking in his chair; the wound in his hand was on fire. "Oh gods, that hurts! You could have warned me, you sadist."

Baltsaros grinned and let out a short chuckle. The older man then leaned down, and Jon watched wide-eyed as the captain's tongue slid warmly over his fingers, tasting the runoff of rum and blood that dripped from them. It felt both bizarre and strangely arousing knowing the captain was tasting his blood, and Jon closed his eyes at the sudden hard pulse of lust in his groin. It amazed him that Baltsaros could effortlessly make such a thing so erotic.

"Is that better?" asked the captain, his voice amused.

Jon opened his eyes and quickly nodded his head, feeling a little dizzy from the rum and Baltsaros's soft, mobile tongue.

The captain sat up, a distracted smile on his face as he started rummaging in the small box. The young man watched him, a little breathless but no longer scared. Baltsaros's stark brow furrowed as he seemed to vacillate between two different hooked needles, both appearing alarmingly thick to Jon.

Nervous, he drank deeply from the mug, enjoying the warm glow of courage that the rum brought with it.

The captain's gracefully bowed lips, the top one jutting out a little further than the bottom, curled slightly when he noticed how intently Jon was watching him. Clasping Jon's arm softly, he smiled, showing his sharp teeth.

"Don't worry. It'll be over quickly," he said, pulling a thread, presumably catgut, through the small hole in the needle. "Now ask me."

Jon frowned.

"Ask you what?" he replied, confused.

Baltsaros laughed.

"Anything you'd like. I didn't realize that I was such a frustrating person to question," he said.

Jon's breath hissed between his teeth as the needle hooked through the skin of his palm. He had to look away.

"All right... Why is the window covered up?" Jon asked, his voice unsteady as Baltsaros pulled the needle through the other side of the cut.

The captain laughed.

"The short answer is that there *is* no window. Hasn't been for a long time," he answered, knotting the thread and cutting it with small scissors.

Jon turned back to look at the captain and frowned.

"What do you mean? What happened to it?" he asked.

"Ah. Well, that is the long answer," said Baltsaros, a small, somewhat sombre smile on his enigmatic face. "I broke it. Well, *them,* rather. Originally, there were five panels of stained glass depicting scenes from an old religious text." He leaned forward and poked Jon again with the needle.

The young man was so intrigued that the pain seemed dulled.

Or maybe it's the rum?

He frowned. But what would make Baltsaros break windows? It seemed like a childish thing.

Baltsaros nodded.

"Strange for me to break windows? That's what you are thinking, is it not?" The captain chuckled again. "Jon, there's no bizarre mystery. Simply put, once the ship became mine, I intended to destroy it... out of revenge. You might say that I decided to start with things that reminded me of the man who held the ship before me—"

"Your uncle?" interjected Jon.

Baltsaros pressed his lips together and nodded, glancing up at Jon with dark eyes before returning to his work.

"I see that little birds have been filling your ears... Yes, my uncle. The man was loathsome. Religious. Fanatical. Twisted and depraved. Filthy. I could go on..." Baltsaros shook his head. "My parents died when I was a boy of seven. I lived in an orphanage until the age of nine. I found solace in helping the nurses with the sick and had lofty aspirations of becoming a doctor. Then, this man appeared at the orphanage gates one day: my uncle. Were it not for the fact that he was the very image of my departed father, I would not have believed him to be family, so different was his disposition. He took me away from the simple life that I was living and brought me here."

Finished with his stitches, Baltsaros sat back in his chair and gestured to the walls around him.

"Thus began my life at sea. I was... exceedingly angry, and for a very long time. My uncle tried to find ways of terrorizing me into complete obedience but consistently failed. I had no respect for the man; his crew was slovenly and the ship was disorderly. Calum could tell you of that time... He was there. Finally, I took the ship from him on my sixteenth birthday." Baltsaros's gaze shifted to the boarded up windows. "It was fully my intention to burn the ship or take her apart board by board... But then time passed. I found myself thinking of ways to improve the way the ship was run. I... removed the crew that I deemed disloyal or problematic..."

Jon swallowed at the word *removed*, knowing full well that their bones probably rested at the bottom of the sea as a result of Baltsaros's culling.

"And went to work cleaning her up. I thought that once I had a good crew and a well-maintained ship I could sell her off and return home to pursue my earlier dreams of becoming a doctor." Baltsaros pursed his lips, eyes focused on nothing for a moment. He then reached out to close the small wooden box of surgical tools and stood, holding it in his hands. "But here I am still," he said quietly.

"You're a better doctor than the one we had back home," Jon said.

A man now dead, he remembered.

Baltsaros started to laugh and went to put away his instruments.

"That is most definitely not a compliment, Jon. The man probably still used dung and rusted knives..." he said. Baltsaros took the mug from Jon's outstretched hand and poured some more rum into it, taking a deep swallow himself before returning it to his dark-haired patient. "Everything I know, I taught myself through books and experience," said the captain. "But I could have been more. Instead, I've been holding onto my role as captain, year after year, getting older and more mired as time goes by." A few seconds passed in silence.

"It's because you enjoy it. Immensely. I see it all the time. You're good at it, and it suits you perfectly," Jon said softly, his words made plain by the rum in his blood. "I think it's past time that you fixed the windows and gave this ship a name. Cut your ties with its history."

He watched as Baltsaros's eyes went flat for a moment, his features smooth. Jon shook his head, understanding the crux of the problem.

"You're not trapped, Baltsaros. This is not your prison... This is your home."

Baltsaros looked at Jon appraisingly.

His home.

The boy was right. This old ship was much more of a home to him than where they were sailing to; and, it had been so for almost three decades. Baltsaros could leave at any time... But he *chose* not to.

He sighed and reached forward to take Jon into his arms, a comforting gesture for both of them. He rested his lips against Jon's high forehead and frowned.

"You're completely right," he said softly. The anger that he had kept stoked for the man who had mistreated him so long ago wasn't even real anymore, just old habit. At this point, the ship had been his for far longer than his uncle had held it.

Baltsaros smiled and ran his hands down Jon's back, fingers bumping over his ribs.

"Your home too. I haven't been fair to you, have I? My quarters are yours... if you're to be my consort," he said.

Jon pulled away and looked at Baltsaros, dark brows low over his blue eyes.

"*Consort?* Is that what you call it?" he said. "Is that what Tom was to you?" Baltsaros saw the anger and the outrage that Jon kept tamped down and hidden suddenly rise closer to the surface.

"Don't, Jon," he said, lifting his hands to Jon's shoulders.

The younger man struggled out of his grasp, stumbling awkwardly against the chair and slamming the wrong hand down on the table to steady himself. Jon let out a cry and cradled his arm to his chest, furious eyes staring at Baltsaros as though he were the source of his pain.

Irritated at Jon's mercurial nature, the captain clenched his jaw and swallowed down the urge to dash his head against the table.

He saw Jon's eyes go round suddenly, wide with disbelief. He realized in amazement that the young man had caught the barest glimpse of his thought.

"Why are you angry with *me*, Baltsaros? Don't I have the right to be fucking furious at *you*? You're the one who just neatly slid another peg into the hole left behind by Tom. You want me to play house with you? I had to watch you lose control and nearly kill Tom. He's... not well, Baltsaros. Neither are you. Gods... What the fuck am I doing here?" Jon's words were followed by a strangled moan, and he rubbed at his face.

Baltsaros felt a little offended.

Out of control?

True. However, Jon was the source of Baltsaros's lapses. He sighed inwardly.

"Jon, sit down. I think you've had a little too much rum," he said.

Jon stared at him, fury distorting his face.

"I'm not drunk," he growled, taking a step forward. When he swayed slightly, the anger in Jon's eyes faltered. "Ok. Maybe a little tipsy... But that doesn't change the fact that I'm not dealing well with your treatment of Tom. Tom, who I am not even *allowed* to talk about, correct?" Jon sat heavily in the chair, the passion behind his outbursts winding down as a sadness came over his features.

The captain knew well enough that whipping Tom had been excessive, but what was done was done. Earlier that day he had tried to have a few words with his former first mate, but the muscular youth shied and cringed away, sea-green eyes wide with fear and pain. Maybe Tom would come around, maybe not. Only time would tell. He hadn't figured on Jon becoming strangely attached to the dangerous ex-slave.

Baltsaros walked around Jon, coming up behind him to put his hands on his shoulders. Jon stiffened but didn't pull away.

"I feel strange. Like I'm losing myself, Baltsaros," said Jon quietly. "I'm all right as long as I don't think about anything too deeply. If I do, it's as if a giant hand is squeezing my heart. I'm overwhelmed... And all I see ahead is more tragedy. More death. One minute I... I can't think of anything but how you make me feel. Inside." The back of Jon's neck was flushed, and Baltsaros felt strangely touched by his words. "At that moment, everything is rosy... Life is wonderful, and my heart swells with happiness. But if I lift the edge of those feelings, there is nothing but a blackened, rotting sea underneath."

Jon's shoulders shuddered slightly under Baltsaros's palms, and the captain stroked the muscles under his thumbs, brow furrowed in concern.

"I'm afraid of being pulled down into it. Am I a fool?" asked Jon, almost to himself.

Baltsaros ran a hand up the side of the young man's neck, and Jon leaned the side of his face into it. There were no answers that Baltsaros could give him; he was glad that Jon couldn't see the confusion that the captain knew was plain on his face.

"I'm... sorry," Baltsaros said softly, the words as sincere as he could make them.

Jon shrugged and let out a shaky breath. After pulling Baltsaros's hand away from his face, he moved it to the open neck of his shirt and slid it between the material and his skin.

Curious, Baltsaros stroked the soft skin of Jon's chest, fingers closing over the puckered nipple as he felt the young man's heartbeat quicken under his palm.

Jon sighed softly and bent his head back, looking up at the man above him.

"Baltsaros, I'll be your consort. Really, whatever you want from me. Just... Help me forget these dark thoughts for now," he said.

Looking down at Jon's stormy-blue eyes that were filled with sadness and resolution, Baltsaros wished again that he could just pluck out the pain that plagued him.

As he leaned down to place a soft kiss on Jon's lips, Baltsaros thought of a perfect distraction, one where he would have the opportunity to expose the inexperienced young man to new pleasures. When he broke the kiss, the captain rounded the chair and got down on one knee in front of Jon.

Jon frowned at him, obviously suspicious of Baltsaros's sudden smile. The captain raised his wounded hand to his lips and pressed a kiss onto the cut gingerly. The younger man winced but didn't pull away.

"There is one place where I would like to take you, Jon. It won't make everything better, but I believe it could help," Baltsaros said, the change in course already being plotted in his head as he spoke.

"Where's that?" asked Jon, curiously.

"The whorehouse at the edge of the world," replied Baltsaros, his grin wide.

18

THE JEWEL

Jon pulled down on the sleeve of his dark-blue shirt and then ran a hand through his hair, shifting his weight in the new boots Baltsaros had given him.

"Jon, it's a whorehouse, not the cave of a fire-breathing dragon," said Katherine, laughing at his nervousness. "Just relax."

He looked up at her and frowned.

"Easy for you to say. I've never been to one," he replied, rubbing the skin of his freshly shaven jaw. *And I've never wanted to... especially now,* he added silently.

Katherine leaned a hip against the side of the cannon and crossed her arms over her chest.

"That's not entirely true, you know. Didn't we *find* your scrawny ass in a whorehouse?" she asked, a mocking smile on her lips.

Jon grinned despite how tense he felt. "Scrawny?" he asked, arching an eyebrow at the first mate. "I was working. Not... uh... being with a lady." He coloured slightly.

Katherine grinned wide.

"Ha! 'Being with a lady'? That's rich. And yeah... sure you were working... spreading those little cheeks of yours for cock and earning good coin, I hear?" she said, teasing Jon.

The blood was hot in his face, and he threw a mock punch at her arm. He hated the fact that no matter how long he stayed in the company of rough men (*and women,* he thought), he was still so easily made awkward by a crass remark; Katherine in particular loved that she could make him blush so effortlessly.

"What are *you* going to a whorehouse for, anyway?" he asked, eyeing her outfit.

Katherine was still wearing her tightly laced black pants but had put on a dark-green shirt with a drawstring neck and wide sleeves. Sliding alluringly off one shoulder, it showed off her smooth, tanned skin. It was her turn to raise an eyebrow at Jon.

"What do you mean?" she asked.

Jon blinked. Sticking his foot in his mouth was an oft-used talent of his.

"I, uh... didn't realize you... liked... uh..." he stammered.

Katherine's brows came down over her almond eyes.

"You didn't realize I liked *what* exactly?" she asked, her tone challenging.

Jon shook his head, confused.

"Wait... Are there boy whores?" he asked meekly.

"O' will ye stop teasin' the boy, missy," said Calum, his gapped smile bright against his dark skin, "or 'e's like to faint away dead o' shame."

The old man was dressed in a garish orange shirt and had shaved and oiled his head. Jon watched as Calum touched the money pouch at his belted waist with the tips of his fingers before turning to make another circuit of the boat; he wasn't the only one who was anxious about the visit to the whorehouse. However, the current that ran through the crew was excitement rather than the dread that Jon felt. He started when Katherine clasped the back of his neck, shaking him slightly.

Her eyes were narrow in merriment as she smiled somewhat crookedly at him.

"I'm sorry, Jon. I'd love to 'be with a lady' as you so charmingly put it, but my lady back home would have my hide. Lying is not one of my strong suits... And besides, I don't want to lie to her. I'm just going for drinks and a massage... And maybe a game of dice, if the mood strikes," she said, releasing him.

Jon furrowed his brow.

"I thought you said you were married to the owner of a tavern... ohhh..." he said. He squeezed his eyes shut when understanding dawned, and then looked at her with a flustered grin. "I'm sorry. I'm a backwards peasant. I assumed your... uh... wife was a man. Women just don't normally own anything but brothels where I come from," he finished lamely.

Katherine winked at him.

"And most are lucky to own even those, I take it? Ah... Thus is the plight of the lowly woman in most of the world, Jon," she replied.

"Lowly," repeated Jon, shaking his head. "I'd hate to see the state of the next man who calls you 'lowly'." He laughed.

A piercing whistle split the air, and Katherine turned her head aft, looking for the captain.

"I've got to go," she said. After spotting Baltsaros's tall, dark figure, she started walking with long strides towards the rear of the ship.

Tom was perched on the gunwale a few yards away, separate from the rest of the men, with one leg through the ratlines that stretched up to the yardarm. Because he was in direct line of sight, Jon had seen how the ex–first mate's head had snapped up at Baltsaros's whistled call. A little sadness had tugged at him when Tom had blinked his green-blue eyes and frowned before shaking his head to resume cleaning his nails with his long knife, shoulders bent.

Jon's lips were set in a hard line as he watched him; he was utterly confused when it came to Tom. While truly wanting to help him, Jon knew that the only way to do so would be to heal the rift between Tom and Baltsaros.

As he looked down, Jon frowned and picked at the scab on his healing, itchy palm. Even if he *could* somehow make things better between the two men, he wouldn't. It would mean having to share Baltsaros. Jon clenched his jaw, a raw feeling in the pit of his stomach. *Like he would have to share Baltsaros tonight.*

Miserable and tense, Jon watched as the tip of the peninsula came into view. Baltsaros had explained that the whorehouse wasn't literally at the edge of the world (because there wasn't one, according to the captain) but was simply at the most southerly point of the continent; it was the last stop before the wide expanse of deep ocean.

Jon shifted awkwardly again in his new boots; the *Jewel*, as the brothel was actually called, was a much fancier affair than the *Rose Garden*, and the crew was decked out in their finest clothing. Brutus nudged at his hand, and Jon scratched his ears distractedly.

"Poor Brutus. You get to miss out on all the *fun*," he said, his voice tight.

At a roar of laughter, Jon looked over his shoulder; someone had broken out the rum, and a few of his shipmates were miming what they hoped to accomplish that evening. Sighing, Jon turned back and clung onto the ropes, watching the twinkling lights over the still water as he stroked the dog's soft head.

The town was a large one, easily five times the size of Portsmouth; and, sitting right at the edge of the harbour was a large, well-lit building that was fashioned to look like an elegant castle with high towers and smooth stone walls. Hearing a quiet step behind him, Jon knew before the hand came to rest on his lower back that it was the captain.

"That's the *Jewel*. The harbour is too narrow and shallow for us to anchor there, so we'll be going out in the jolly boats. Try to look as though you're not being led to your doom, please," Baltsaros said, his accented voice near Jon's ear.

Shrugging, he fought the urge to lean into the captain; he didn't want to give Baltsaros any satisfaction. He was thoroughly unhappy that the decision had been made for him.

"**A** whorehouse?" asked Jon, his eyes wide. "You want to bring me to a *whorehouse?*"

Baltsaros leaned back at Jon's vehemence, his eyes going stony and dark, two chips of obsidian in his angular face.

"Yes. And it's not up for discussion," replied the captain.

Jon gaped.

"Wh-why? How is going to a brothel going to help anything? No, Baltsaros. It's out of the question," he said, incredulous.

The captain stood, and looked down at Jon. After a moment he reached out with a hand and stroked his cheek, his face still and serious.

Jon tensed slightly at the touch; however, the warmth had already returned to the captain's eyes.

"Jon, you just said you would give me anything I wanted. I want this," Baltsaros said, smiling softly. "Besides! It'll do the men some good!" he added and abruptly turned away from Jon before he could argue.

As he strode quickly out of the room, Baltsaros was already calling out the course change to Katherine, leaving Jon, pale and distraught, behind in his quarters.

Jon watched the ship recede in the distance, Brutus's shaggy head peering sadly over the top of the quarterdeck railing. At that moment Jon decided to come back in the next life as a dog, if he had any choice in the matter. Brutus might be sad to see his master go, but at least he didn't have to be subjected to the whims of a madman.

As if sensing his thoughts, Baltsaros's arm snaked around his waist, and he leaned in to start murmuring against Jon's neck. It was some odd bit of history about the town they were nearing, but he couldn't pay attention. Oscillating between hope and fear, Jon was driving himself to distraction.

Maybe we're here, as Katherine said, to game and drink? Maybe a massage? A massage is nothing to be afraid of. But what if Baltsaros meant we're going to... What if he wants me to... do something with a whore? What if I have to watch him? Watch him touching someone else...

Jon groaned out loud and lowered his face to his hands.

Baltsaros just chuckled and patted Jon on the back lightly, making him angrier by the fact that the captain seemed to be enjoying his distress.

Soon the boat bumped up against the floating wooden dock, and the men disembarked. Jon, the last to get off the boat, almost stumbled as he stared up at the building. From this close he could see that the entire castle was faced with an almost pearlescent, veined white stone, and that every window was glazed; it was absolutely beautiful.

Baltsaros took Jon's arm and steadied him, pulling him forward after the rest of the crew. As they approached the colossal wooden doors, men in costumes resembling elaborate guard uniforms bowed and pulled them open.

Jon knew his mouth was agape, but he couldn't help it; they had just walked into a scene out of a dream. The space was *huge*. Rising up on either side of the room were immense, curving staircases with crowds of people going up and down or simply standing there watching the action below. The rest of the open area was an eye-dazzling array of candlelit tables on tiered platforms with an immensely long bar in the back, the coloured bottles of liquor behind it somehow brightly backlit. Above it all hung the biggest chandelier that Jon had ever seen, with dozens upon dozens of candles in it.

Everything was reflected a hundredfold in the mirrors that were found everywhere the eye rested. And the women... There were so many! All of them were in elegant garb that somehow managed to be extremely revealing while only hinting at what was hidden underneath.

When he felt the captain's fingers tighten around his upper arm, Jon turned to him. He must have looked like a fool because the captain started laughing and shaking his head, leaning forward to press a kiss against Jon's temple.

A tall figure draped in layers of diaphanous fabric suddenly appeared before them, pale face covered up to the eyes. Jon couldn't tell if it was a man or a woman; the voice of the graceful figure was melodious and completely asexual. The captain nodded his head in response to words Jon couldn't understand, and then the figure glided away. He watched it go, trying to see curves beneath the flowing material but failing; it was disconcerting not to know what was beneath those robes.

Looking over at the men and women sitting at the tiered tables, Jon spotted Tom. The muscular young man was sitting alone, drinking. As he watched, Tom lifted his sea-green eyes to Jon over the edge of his cup, his eyebrows lifting slowly as he swallowed down his drink. Tom lowered the cup and tilted his head slightly at Jon, his eyes questioning.

Jon realized that he probably looked terrified. He furrowed his brow at the other man and hunched his shoulders; across the wide space, it felt like Tom had grasped his plight. The other man, a small smile curling only to one side of his mouth, shook his head and shrugged before looking back down at his cup. However, Jon could see that he was frowning, thinking about something.

When he raised his head again, Tom pointed to his eye and then to Jon.

I will watch out for you.

Jon felt a small pain in his chest, a twist of poignant emotion towards the other man at this simple gesture. He gave a tiny nod, swallowing hard. Baltsaros then tugged at his arm again; the draped figure had reappeared, and they were being led towards one of the colossal staircases.

Jon turned his head quickly back to Tom and locked eyes. The burly young man smirked, though his eyes were sad, and pushed his chin up with a callused finger before he patted at his broad chest, miming taking a deep breath.

Chin up and breathe, Jon.

Jon sucked in a lungful of air, and Tom was gone, blocked from view by the giant columns that flanked the wide stairs as they ascended.

Baltsaros and Jon were brought to a large room on the second floor. The walls were covered in dark, embossed paper, somewhere between black and purple. There were large windows along one wall, surrounded in wide, ornamental white frames. The carpeting, a dizzying pattern of vines, red on black and purple, was incredibly thick underfoot. To one side of the room, there was a strange, bench-like chair with no back, one side of it raised higher than the other, and it was to here that the two men were led.

Jon sat awkwardly in the middle of the plush red satin and clutched his hands between his knees. Baltsaros, however, reclined against the higher end of the chair, one leg bent off the side of it, knee resting against Jon's, with the other leg stretched out behind him.

After a moment, a door opened to one side of the room, and a beautiful, buxom woman approached them on mincing steps, her hair an extraordinary shade of red.

"Captain Baltsaros! It is always such an incredible pleasure to have you here with us! It has been far too long," she said in a lilting accent that Jon did not recognize. Jon smelled an intoxicating blend of spices and flowers as she leaned forward to clasp Baltsaros's outstretched hand with her long-nailed fingers. Her gaze flicked to Jon, momentarily confused, but she covered it with a gracious smile.

Where is Tom? asked her eyes.

"My name is Fresia," she said, lowering her eyelashes demurely.

Before Jon had a chance to stammer out an awkward reply, Baltsaros rescued him.

"This, my darling, is Jon. He will be joining me tonight," he said, his voice amused.

Jon swallowed and tried to bend his mouth into a smile that seemed sincere.

Fresia straightened and laughed throatily.

"A pretty thing you are, Jon. My girls will fight over you!" she said. She turned her head and motioned to a servant standing against the far wall. The tall, fair-skinned youth, wearing only a loincloth, came forward holding a silver platter in his hands.

"An appetizer, my dears? To whet your passions?" asked Fresia, her hand plucking the lid off a high ceramic jar. There were things that looked like Tom's black cheroots in it but narrower and papered in red.

"Of course," said Baltsaros, and he picked a few out of the jar.

Fresia smiled and bowed low, her cleavage shown to good advantage by the cut of her black dress.

"I will be back with the girls in a moment. Please, enjoy yourselves," she said and left the room in a swirl of perfume.

Jon, frowning at the strange cigars, watched as the captain slid two into the breast pocket of his black vest and put the third to his lips; the young servant came forward again quickly to put a flame to the end of it.

Baltsaros drew smoke into his lungs and closed his eyes, his hand waving the boy away. Nervously, Jon watched as Baltsaros took in another lungful of the smoke and blew out a plume; the smell of the burning herb was sweet and tangy at once and made Jon's nose itch. Curious, he watched a strange softness come over the captain's face.

What is this?

"Here, Jon," said Baltsaros, offering the red cheroot to him.

Jon shook his head, though he was intrigued by the change in the captain. It was as if all the tension had gone out of the older man's limbs, and he exuded a sense of deeply relaxed contentment.

"Please, Jon. Don't say no without trying it. At least once," said Baltsaros, sitting up slowly, a soft smile on his face.

Biting at the corner of his lip, Jon took the small burning thing between his fingers and looked at Baltsaros uncertainly. The captain, his eyes crinkling in good humour, watched as Jon put it to his lips and inhaled. Instantly, he was overcome with a coughing fit, tears springing to his eyes as his lungs burned. A glass was pressed into Jon's hand by the lithe servant boy, and he drank down the sweet juice within, Baltsaros's large hand stroking his back.

"I'm sorry," Jon said in embarrassment, his head spinning a little.

In response Baltsaros narrowed his eyes and leaned forward for a kiss.

Eyes darting to the servant, Jon tensed... and felt instantly foolish. Why would anyone care in this sort of establishment? When he opened his mouth to Baltsaros, he felt a strange tingling in the back of his mind and a soft heaviness in his limbs.

Baltsaros pulled away, his eyes lingering on Jon's mouth a long moment before he looked back up.

He was mesmerized by how big the captain's pupils were as he stared at him. Feeling odd but strangely good, Jon smiled at Baltsaros; maybe this would be ok after all.

After licking his lips, Baltsaros lifted the cheroot, inhaling deeply again; however, instead of blowing the smoke out into the air, he clasped the back of Jon's head and pulled him in for another kiss, exhaling slowly into his mouth.

Jon breathed in the smoke; this time it was less harsh, having been softened by Baltsaros's lungs. He tasted cinnamon, cloves, and something reminiscent of pine. Almost instantly, Jon's head began swimming, and he clutched at Baltsaros in a panic. He heard the captain laugh, and his strong hands pulled him close so that Jon was lying with his head on Baltsaros's chest.

Thu-thump, thu-thump, thu-thump.

He could hear the captain's heart beat loud in his ear, yet

somehow it was far away. He felt cold and then incredibly hot. Licking his lips, Jon started to get a little nauseous. The carpet was moving slowly in his vision, the red vines crawling across the floor. He shivered.

"Jon... don't fight it. Just breathe," came Baltsaros's voice from somewhere.

Breathe, said Tom.

Jon narrowed his eyes; there was a ringing in his ears and then a sickening feeling of falling. Jerking his limbs out to catch himself, Jon realized he hadn't moved. Then Baltsaros's hands were in his hair, down his back... pulling the blue shirt out of his pants and stroking his skin, pressing into the muscles that always seemed sore from ship work. He closed his eyes and realized that the falling feeling had settled into a gentle rocking sensation; he was light as a feather and felt great.

When he opened his eyes again, he pushed himself up and away from Baltsaros; he was startled to see a row of girls standing in front of them, all bare-breasted and absolutely beautiful.

When did that happen? he thought in wonder; he had only closed his eyes for a few seconds.

Baltsaros reached for Jon again and slowly lifted the shirt over his head as if he were a child.

Jon shuddered a little as the material left cool trails on his skin, the drug in his system amplifying all his sensations. Frowning slightly, he looked over at Baltsaros, but the man was eyeing the row of girls. Jon turned his gaze to them again. No two were alike, and he found himself wondering how many variations there were to beauty.

Gasping when Baltsaros's mouth touched the side of his neck, Jon felt the captain's tongue come out to taste his flesh, and he shivered again. A flash of disgust crossed the pale face of a blond-haired girl for a split second, and Jon reddened. However, she quickly hid her feelings and smiled coyly when she saw Jon's blue eyes on her.

Baltsaros nipped the skin of Jon's neck gently with his sharp teeth before murmuring softly to him.

"Which one would you like, my love?" asked Baltsaros.

My love.

Jon's heart sped up at the words. Though he knew that to the captain it was probably a meaningless affectation, it made Jon feel a little weak. His breath hitched in his chest as Baltsaros stroked his stomach, and pinched his nipples. Jon watched in amazement as the cheeks of a dusky-skinned beauty with dark-blue eyes became suffused with a pretty pink blush.

"The girl in blue," he said reverently. She found them alluring and wanted to see them kiss… and more. Were he and Baltsaros so enchanting in their caresses?

In wonder, Jon found that his cock had started to harden, and the outline of it was clearly visible through his pant leg. Baltsaros's fingers had discovered it and were stroking him slowly through the thin fabric. When he looked up, Jon saw they were alone with the girl, and she was smiling.

"Come, beautiful men. Come," she said, the motions of her hands fluid in the air, like birds.

Baltsaros untangled his limbs from Jon's and rose, pulling the young man to his feet. They followed the girl through a hidden door in the wall to a room with a large bed and plush armchairs. This room was papered and carpeted entirely in red, the furniture made of a pale wood and upholstered in pure white.

Upon reaching the centre of the room, the girl turned around and slowly unknotted the blue silk at her waist, letting the thin material slide down her tawny thighs.

Jon felt Baltsaros's hands come around him from behind; sliding down his ribs and meeting at his belt, the captain's quick fingers made short work of the knot, followed by the buttons of his pants. Shockingly, Jon was rendered naked in front of the girl and he gasped, his bare cock standing out stiffly from the dark thatch of hair between his thighs.

Baltsaros kissed down Jon's spine, making him step out of his pants and boots before coming back up and wrapping his large hand around Jon's shaft, stroking him. Jon could feel the captain's chest soft against his back and wondered suddenly when Baltsaros had taken off his shirt; time was passing in strange fits and starts.

Watching them with large eyes, the girl touched her tongue against her top lip as the captain ran his hand over Jon's length, his hard grip making the head of the younger man's cock swell. Jon shuddered as Baltsaros moved against him, the captain's mouth sucking and licking at the sensitive skin of Jon's neck; his senses felt completely bombarded.

He was almost panting with desire when the girl came forward to sink to her knees in front of him, her tongue coming out to lap at the head of his cock. Hand clutching the root of Jon's shaft, Baltsaros fed it into the girl's open mouth.

Jon whimpered and clutched both at the girl's head and Baltsaros's thigh, firm against the back of his own. This was so outrageous and delicious, Jon thought as he began to thrust himself wantonly into the girl's mouth, held there by Baltsaros's strong hand.

The build-up of pleasure went on and on, and Jon was moaning between loud huffs of breath, the sweat running down his skin.

"It's the drug, Jon," murmured Baltsaros, when he realized Jon was becoming frantic. "It sharpens the appetite but staves off climax so that pleasure can be drawn out."

Jon nodded but closed his eyes; he wasn't sure how much more he could stand.

As if sensing that Jon needed respite, Baltsaros pulled him away from the girl and led him to a big armchair next to the bed. After pushing Jon down into it and leaning down to kiss him, Baltsaros then turned towards the girl. His long fingers quickly undid the laces at his crotch as he walked, kicking off his boots and then the pants that had fallen from his hips.

The dark-skinned beauty, her lips red and wet from pleasuring

Jon, rose smoothly to her feet and submitted readily to Baltsaros's rough kisses.

Jon gasped, a strange mixture of desire and jealousy gripping at him as he watched Baltsaros thrust his tongue into the girl's open mouth; the captain's hands slid under her buttocks to lift her up against his pelvis where Jon could see Baltsaros's hard length slide against the skin of her belly. As one they collapsed on the bed and the older man groaned as he angled himself between the girl's legs and pushed his thick cock swiftly into her wetness.

Glued to his seat, Jon watched with wide eyes as the captain began fucking the girl with smooth, fluid motions of his hips. Jon breathed heavily, his hand on his cock; the agony in his chest was blossoming anew at the horror and beauty of it.

Baltsaros was powerful and graceful, his muscles moving rhythmically and sinuously under tanned skin slick with sweat. The girl began moaning, the sound completely sincere when the captain brought a hand forward to do something between her legs as he plunged his hard length into her.

Jon gritted his teeth and stood unsteadily, his cock throbbing in his grasp. He walked to the bed and slid a hand down Baltsaros's hot flank, lust sinking its teeth hard into Jon as he felt the captain move under his hand. Furious and ecstatic at once, Jon grabbed at Baltsaros's jaw and turned the man towards him, savagely capturing the captain's bowed lips in a frenzy.

The girl beneath Baltsaros let out a shuddering cry, and Jon felt her tense through the man's body.

This was insane. Baltsaros pulled away from Jon and stood, his stiff cock wet and shiny from fucking the girl. On her back atop the white duvet, the lovely whore lay panting and flushed.

Jon watched her for a moment and then clenched his jaw, knowing what Baltsaros wanted from him. He slid a hand under the girl's back as he climbed on top of her, Jon's hand guiding his cock into the wetness that Baltsaros had so recently plundered. Shuddering and gasping, Jon thrust himself into the girl hard, her smooth, wet insides squeezing at his cock as it moved within her.

But... this was wrong. It was the wrong body beneath him.

He turned his head and saw that Baltsaros was lying beside him on his stomach, his arms folded under his head as he watched Jon fuck the whore. The captain's eyes were dark, pupils huge... But his mouth was set in a hard line, and Jon understood that Baltsaros was no longer enjoying this. All Jon could see was confusion in the other man's face.

Immediately pulling away from the whore, Jon stood back, panting hard. Propping herself up on her elbows, the girl frowned at him as he caught his breath, worried that she had done something wrong. Quickly, Jon walked to the clothing discarded on the deep-pile carpet and fished around in the coin pouch that was tied to his belt. He came back to the girl and placed three large gold coins on her curved belly.

"Please. Leave us," he said quietly.

The whore's eyes went huge; it was an incredibly large sum, and she moved swiftly to obey though there was a touch of disappointment on her face as she left.

Jon turned to Baltsaros.

Watching him quietly from the bed, Baltsaros frowned but stayed where he was.

The drug was still coursing strong through Jon, and he wanted nothing more than to run his hands over the man's bronze skin to wipe away all traces of the girl's touch. He walked towards Baltsaros and slid a hand up his muscular calf, feeling the captain tense slightly under his palm; in dismay he realized that his fingers felt rough against Baltsaros's skin now that the sweat of his exertions was drying.

Frowning, Jon looked around, an idea taking shape in his head. When he spied a small, stoppered bottle of liquid on a dainty table next to the bed, he scooped it up in one hand and peered at it curiously. When Jon opened it and saw that it was filled with softly scented oil, he smiled. After climbing up onto the bed, he moved to straddle the captain.

"What are you doing, Jon?" asked Baltsaros, his voice sounding strangely unsure. However, the man didn't move as Jon settled himself down just behind Baltsaros's hips.

"I have no idea," said Jon, truthfully; he just wanted to feel the captain's strong body under his hands. Pouring a little of the oil into his palms, he rubbed them together to warm it before laying his hands flat against Baltsaros's broad back. Jon slid his hands up and over the hard muscles, marvelling at how smooth the captain's tanned skin was. He pushed his thumbs into Baltsaros's back, following the natural curves beneath his hands and was gratified when the captain let out a deep groan.

"Gods, Jon. That's lovely," said Baltsaros, closing his eyes and smiling.

Pleased with himself, Jon kneaded and pressed at the captain's muscles, eliciting moans of pleasure from the man beneath him. However, there was something dreadful gnawing at Jon, poisoning him and casting a shadow over his mind.

Baltsaros seemed to sense Jon's darkness and spoke softly.

"What is it?" he asked.

Jon started shaking his head but then stopped; he realized he was fed-up of being constantly kept off-balance. Breathing deep, he spoke in a quiet voice that belied the emotions that threatened to choke him.

"I don't know what you were trying to accomplish here, but I'm not your whore. I'm yours... but not like that." He pressed hard into Baltsaros's back with a knuckle at a pressure point Calum had shown him, and the man beneath him let out a grunt of pain. His own words, finally spoken aloud, fed into the anger he had been holding back. "I mean it, Baltsaros. I don't want to be with anyone but you. Don't you *ever* make me fuck someone else for your pleasure again. Never."

Baltsaros reached back with one hand and tried to free himself from the painful pressure Jon was exerting, but the young man grabbed his wrist and wrenched it up, his angle giving him the advantage over the other's superior strength.

"Also... I may be yours but understand here and now that *you are mine.* Learn to keep your cock in your fucking pants or *I will end this.*" Jon finished, his heart hammering in his chest.

A few seconds passed, sickeningly empty of Baltsaros's response, and Jon began to feel his courage crumble; he was completely devoted to the man but couldn't bear the thought of having to live through this perversion again...

Then, Baltsaros nodded.

It was such a simple thing, this up-and-down movement of the head, but it brought with it a relief so intense that it made Jon's eyes sting with tears. The older man was frowning, his eyes closed and his breathing strangely hoarse. Jon released Baltsaros's arm and resumed his caresses after a moment with a sureness to his hands that hadn't been there before.

Baltsaros's brow smoothed out and he sighed; eventually relaxing under the younger man's palms, he groaned softly at Jon's efforts.

As Jon slowed his movements, the massage became increasingly erotic. Pouring more oil onto the man's lower back and buttocks, Jon found himself becoming incredibly aroused by the fact that Baltsaros was pinned beneath him; in response to these thoughts, his cock stirred from the softness it had settled into. Jon watched as the blood surged into it, his cock sliding along the cleft of Baltsaros's buttocks and getting slippery with oil as it lengthened.

This honestly hadn't been his intention when he started to massage the older man, and Baltsaros tensed underneath him. However, he became almost dizzy with desire when he felt Baltsaros shift his hips ever so slightly so that Jon's cock rested unambiguously between the cheeks of his ass. With no small amount of trepidation, Jon experimentally pressed his shaft into the warm, oiled furrow and was rewarded with a tiny movement of the other man's hips; Jon gasped, and his cock twitched from the sensation. Kneading the flesh of Baltsaros's buttocks with fingers and palms, Jon began to thrust himself slowly against the man, his cock sliding easily over the oiled crevice.

It was divine... And Jon wanted more.

As if reading Jon's thoughts, Baltsaros began rocking his hips and moving himself against the young man with more vigour until finally raising himself high enough that Jon's cockhead began rubbing at his puckered opening.

Was this permission to... Jon couldn't finish the thought; it was too much. His mind took a tumble, and lust claimed him completely.

After raising himself up, Jon quickly parted Baltsaros's thighs with his knee and placed himself between the older man's legs. Jon felt a shiver go through the man beneath him as he caressed Baltsaros for a moment with a thumb slick with oil. Baltsaros lifted himself up on his knees in response, and Jon swallowed hard. With his cock in one hand, he pushed the swollen head of it hard against the rough mouth of Baltsaros's narrow passage and gasped as the exquisite tightness stretched open and engulfed him. He slid slowly inside Baltsaros's body as the other breathed unsteadily beneath him; feeling the hot, slick muscles envelop him completely, Jon groaned and began moving within.

Baltsaros shuddered as Jon's cock battered into him, thrusts coming harder as the younger man climbed the steep slope of his mounting pleasure. Jon's words and hands had opened up a raw weakness within him... And he clutched at it.

Baltsaros now belonged to this lithe, dark-haired creature that fucked him with an urgency and passion born of staggering emotion. He himself could never attain it... This depth of feeling that came so readily to Jon. However, he could hold onto this strange ache, this rift inside his deformed soul that belonged to Jon *and only to Jon.* And thus he thrust himself back against the assault. In attempting to possess Jon, he himself had become completely and totally ensnared.

He gasped when Jon suddenly pulled away. However, it was only to coax Baltsaros onto his back so that Jon could enter him anew while kissing him deep, tongue questing for the possibility of shared rapture.

When Jon reached between their bodies to grasp Baltsaros's cock, the captain felt a slow pulse of pleasure start to course through him. He was made aware of a sensitive point inside him as Jon's length continued to slide steadily over it while the younger man's strong hand stroked him to hardness. Soon Baltsaros was moaning into Jon's open mouth, pulling the breath from the other man's lungs as he shuddered with his own advancing climax.

Jon suddenly cried out, his body going rigid as his cock twitched deep inside Baltsaros. The thought of Jon spilling his seed within him sent Baltsaros careening over the edge of his own orgasm, his muscles tensing as the hot fluid gushed out of his cock in thick bursts, coating Jon's hand and his own chest as he cried out with the sweetly agonizing pulses of release.

Jon's breath sobbed out of his chest, and he soon collapsed on top of Baltsaros, spent and trembling.

Baltsaros felt a keen joy, an incredible lightness within him, and started chuckling as he ran his hands softly over Jon's slick back. The young man raised his head blearily and looked at Baltsaros with a curious lift of his dark brows. The captain clasped Jon's face with his palms and kissed him softly.

"See... didn't coming here help?" he said, teasingly. Jon tried to frown but instead just bit the captain's lip with a wry smile; a moment later he exhaled hard as his softening cock slipped wetly out of Baltsaros, and he shuddered, putting his head back down against the older man's neck.

For a long time, the two men just lay there entwined, bodies cooling as the sweat dried on their skin. Today had definitely not gone how Baltsaros planned. Sharing a woman with Tom had always been a lusty affair that returned them to a fixed point in their relationship, and Baltsaros had mistakenly thought that the same would happen with Jon. He had not been prepared for what had happened instead.

As he frowned up at the ceiling, Baltsaros realized that this somewhat botched attempt at reconciliation had in fact changed everything. Baltsaros smiled. Though the path leading to it had been unexpected, the end result had brought the two men closer together. It was intriguing.

After a while Baltsaros could tell that Jon was falling asleep by the slowness of his heart and a slight twitching of his limbs. In contrast, he felt completely electrified; Baltsaros slowly shifted Jon off of him and onto the soft bed.

"Jon..." he said softly, and the young man's eyes opened a crack.

"Mmhmm?" Jon replied.

"Did any of the girls seem put off by me touching you?" Baltsaros asked, curious.

Jon's face took on a sleepy frown as he thought.

"Mmm yeah. The busty blond. The one in uh... pink," he replied, his eyes closing again. There was a line between his brows, but Jon was so close to sleep that he didn't question Baltsaros.

The captain nodded and smiled, stroking Jon's hair away from his high forehead.

"I have to obtain something, but you can rest here for a while... Can you make your own way back to the boat?" he asked.

Jon nodded, his features relaxing into slumber.

After flicking the edge of the comforter over Jon, Baltsaros slid off the bed and went in search of his clothes.

It had been some time since Baltsaros had obtained a fresh heart, and the particular brand of excitement reserved for the hunt slowly began to build inside him.

19

BAAL'S HEART

It is not the strongest of the species that survives,
nor the most intelligent that survives. It is the
one that is the most adaptable to change.

— CHARLES DARWIN

Through the hazy veil of half-sleep, Jon heard the sound of someone clearing their throat and realized that he wasn't alone. He lifted his head and blinked sleepily as the memory of where he was coalesced in his mind. At another soft sound of movement, Jon looked towards the foot of the bed.

Lounging in one of the plush white armchairs, with a wry expression on his handsome face, was Tom. Jon sat up slowly and frowned, rubbing his eyes as he held the white duvet against his nakedness.

"What are you doing here?" he asked hoarsely.

Tom's eyebrows went up.

"I said I'd watch out for ye, didn't I?" answered the burly pirate, his smile crooked. "Was beginnin' to think ye'd sleep all night." He slapped his hands together and then made beckoning motions.

"C'mon, lovey. Let's getcha out of bed and back on the ol' tub before *he* thinks ye've run off, shall we?" Tom said with a feigned cheerfulness. He was pale with fatigue, and Jon sensed that Tom had spent the evening drinking alone, though he seemed far from drunk.

Jon felt a pang of shame wash over him and shook it off.

He coughed into his fist, realizing that the herb he'd smoked earlier had made his lungs rough, and he felt a little lightheaded. He watched curiously as Tom suddenly slid out of his chair, striding quickly across the thick carpet to a stand holding a crystal ewer.

After pouring some water into a glass, Tom returned to Jon with it, holding it out in one large, scarred hand.

"Here, pup… Ye'll feel a little bit poorly for a while. Smokin' *char* for the first time ain't all fun 'n games," said Tom with a sardonic grin.

Jon ducked his head in embarrassment and took the cup, drinking down the water gratefully; it was cool as it ran down his throat, and he felt immediately better for it.

"Thanks," he said quietly, deciding that he was glad for the bigger man's presence. "What time is it?" It felt like days had passed since he had crossed into this room with Baltsaros and the girl when it could only have been a few hours. He swallowed hard as sudden, vivid memories of Baltsaros gasping and moaning beneath him brought heat to his face. Jon clutched at the duvet; had he really…?

"It's late," said Tom, interrupting his thoughts. "Past the time ye should'a been back on board. Now up, young Jonny."

Jon nodded and tried to get off the bed while holding the heavy comforter around him.

"Where are my clothes?" he asked weakly, not seeing them on the floor. He stumbled forward, and the material jerked out of his hand, stripping him suddenly bare in front of Tom.

The ex–first mate let out a long, low whistle, and Jon blushed furiously.

"Here," said the other man.

When he glanced up, Jon saw that Tom had his clothes in one fist and was holding them out to him. Desperately trying to seem unconcerned by his nakedness, Jon took a step forward and pulled his clothing out of Tom's grasp.

"Yer lookin' good, lad," said Tom, his voice soft.

Jon turned to scowl at the bigger man as he was shoving a foot into his pant leg, but he saw nothing but frank admiration on Tom's rugged face. He looked down at himself.

It was true; the demanding physical labour required of him aboard the ship had packed hard muscle onto Jon's slight frame. His shoulders were wider than they once were, and his arms bulged with definition; though Jon would never be the power-house that Tom was, nor as broad and sculpted as the captain, he was a far cry from the pale, weak thing that had first joined the crew.

"Uh, thanks," he said self-consciously, though he realized he was sincerely pleased with the compliment. He tugged up his pants and buttoned them at his hips before pulling the shirt over his tanned chest.

Tom stood up and Jon, still fumbling to tie his belt, followed him through the hidden door.

As the two men made their way down the broad staircase, Jon saw that the first floor of the brothel was still busy even though dawn was reaching out to pull away the cover of night. Near the tall wooden doors, Jon caught a glimpse of the dark-haired girl that had knelt before him on the soft carpet.

Feeling strangely cocky, he winked at her and was rewarded with a shy smile. He turned his head and saw that Tom had stopped to watch him, a thoughtful look on his face.

The big man set his jaw and motioned to the exit with an impatient tilt of his head; Jon quickly left after him through the high doors and out onto the wide, cobbled street that led to the wharf.

"Ye've changed, Jon," said Tom gruffly, looking askance at him as he caught up.

Jon glanced at Tom in surprise, but the muscular deckhand continued down to the floating dock where the ship's small rowboat was waiting for them. Jon climbed in and sat on the wooden bench, a small smile on his face; the last time he'd been in this boat with Tom, he'd been terrified with a bag over his head.

After pushing them away from the dock, Tom settled down between the oars. His countenance was serious as he took them up in his hands, his large shoulders bulging with the strain as he began pulling the oars through the dark water.

"You've changed too," said Jon softly after a while. "I don't think you've ever called me just 'Jon' before."

Tom frowned and nodded, not meeting Jon's eye. Apart from grunting occasionally with the effort of rowing, Tom was mute.

Jon sat watching him, a troubled look on his face.

"Tom, are you all right?" asked Jon after a few minutes.

Tom's sea-green eyes flicked up to Jon's face, and he was astounded by the hurt he saw there.

"I'm fine, love. I'm fine," said Tom, his words a blatant lie. "And, if ye don't fuckin' mind, yer the last fuckin' person I want to discuss my bloody problems with."

His words were an admonishment, and Jon clenched his jaw, conceding with a tight nod of his head. The rest of the short trip back to the ship passed in complete silence.

Baltsaros felt Jon wake when he slid his arm around his warm body in the dusky light of early morning, his own skin slightly cool from being outdoors.

"Mmmm," Jon sighed and pushed back against him, lithe and soft skinned. "Where were you?" he asked sleepily.

Baltsaros pressed his lips against Jon's shoulder.

"It's a surprise," said the captain, smiling as he traced his fingers along the other's side.

Jon laughed softly.

"Oh good. It better be something nice," he mumbled.

Baltsaros expected Jon to fall back asleep but was surprised when he slid his fingers around Baltsaros's hand instead, pulling it down his stomach to where his cock was slowly beginning to unfold itself.

"I was wondering if I could be excused from duty today, Captain," Jon said with a jesting coyness that Baltsaros had never heard from him before. The young man pressed the captain's hand hard against the stiffness in his groin. "I think I'm coming down with some sort of illness." Jon continued with exaggerated worry in his voice. "Feel this... Does this feel healthy to you? Am I dying?"

Baltsaros laughed out loud at the silliness. His fingers encircled Jon's cock, and he stroked down against the hardening flesh, eliciting a pleased groan from the younger man. As he kissed Jon's neck, he touched the tip of his tongue against his warm skin. Jon had never been playful before—eager, yes, but not with this mischievous forwardness. Baltsaros was intrigued. After sitting up and rolling Jon over onto his back, the captain frowned down at him.

"I'm not sure," he said, playing along with Jon. "Does this hurt?" He stroked Jon's gracefully curved cock a few times and then stopped to run his thumb back and forth over the head of it softly when a wetness beaded at the tip; Jon shuddered and let out what was nearly a yelp.

Baltsaros grinned and licked his thumb. He pulled the rest of the coverlet away from Jon's naked body. Gone was the shyness that had plagued the serious young man before; a lusty confidence was in its place as he lay there, unashamed beneath Baltsaros's appreciative gaze.

Jon reached out with impatient hands for Baltsaros and pulled the man on top of him, his legs trapping the captain against his body, his cock hard against his stomach.

"I suppose we can stay in bed a while," Baltsaros said against the underside of Jon's jaw. The young man laughed throatily in response as he clutched at Baltsaros's hips, moving slowly beneath him.

J on glanced over at Baltsaros, sprawled out on his stomach on the wide bed. Grinning, he rubbed at the bite mark on his shoulder and shook his head. Baltsaros was always enthusiastic in his lovemaking, but this time he had left Jon feeling exceptionally loose limbed, albeit a touch sore in a few places; Jon's instigation had certainly brought something out in the captain.

He was still astounded by his own behaviour; Jon couldn't remember a time in his life when he'd been so bold. His growing confidence was making him increasingly aware of a strength of character that years of isolation had hidden from sight... as well as a deep appreciation for the more carnal aspects of life.

Staring down at the gorgeous naked man that he had claimed as his own, Jon debated climbing back into bed to wake him for another round, but the grumbling in his stomach was getting ridiculous. Besides, the captain was exhausted and probably appreciated the chance to sleep; the man had been out all night.

Doing what?

Jon pushed the nagging thought aside and groped around on the floor for his discarded pants, pulling them on quickly once he found them. When he spotted a black shirt of Baltsaros's that he coveted, Jon pulled it from the back of the chair where it was hanging.

Frowning, he was dismayed to find it stiff with something. When he rubbed at the hardened patches, Jon's fingers came away peppered with tiny brown flakes; there was a shiny quality to them that he instantly recognized and, lifting the shirt to his nose, he smelled a meaty, coppery tang mixed with the captain's scent.

Jon turned to look at Baltsaros again; the man had no injuries, where had all this blood come from? Slightly discomfited, Jon draped the shirt back over the chair. He would ask the captain later; surely there was a logical answer.

Shaking his head, Jon dismissed the worry that threatened his good mood. When he found his own grey shirt crumpled on the floor, he pulled it over his head and went in search of something to eat in the galley, thoughts of whorehouses and murders scratching faintly at the back of his mind.

T om was once again avoiding him.

Jon sat in the shade, pressing down with the handle of his knife on the caulked rope between the wooden boards, mending the deck's weatherproofing as he watched Tom.

The muscular deckhand, a heavy roll of sailcloth on his wide shoulder, climbed nimbly up the ratlines to the leeward spar to replace the upper topsail. It was really a two-person job, but Tom was somehow able to manage it on his own.

Baltsaros was right: Tom was an incredible asset to the ship. He was strong and agile, and, having spent the bulk of his adolescence as a slave in the mines, not afraid of hard work. The mostly friendly, competitive nature of the crew often saw others trying to match Tom's herculean efforts, something that greatly benefited the ship as more work got done as a result.

Jon flipped the knife in his fingers a few times and sat back, staring up at Tom high above. He watched as the other man skilfully attached the sailcloth to the buntlines while standing balanced in the foot loops. It was a dangerous job, yet Tom did it fearlessly. Jon smiled and shook his head; his own worth on the ship would never extend to something so perilous.

Jon laughed when he heard the clatter of nails on wood and watched as Brutus raced down the deck towards Beard. Having found some old saddlebags on board, the huge man had somehow shortened them to fit the mastiff. Jon looked on as Beard pulled two metal flasks from the dog's saddlebags and gave him a piece of dried fish in return. Brutus sat on his haunches and chewed the salty treat happily. The intelligent dog had quickly learned to deliver messages and items from one side of the ship to the other, and his courier service had proven to be an amusing diversion for the crew. Jon smiled and watched the dog turn and make the return trip before bending himself to his task once more.

About an hour later, while putting more caulk between the boards, Jon noticed Baltsaros at his usual spot at the rear of the ship. For a moment he thought about joining him up on the quarterdeck; however, unless work took him there, Jon had no business being in a place reserved for higher-ranking crew. That he was Baltsaros's lover—his *consort*—didn't change anything. It was bad enough that his shipmates alternated between plying him with small gifts to win favour and teasing him about being Baltsaros's cabin boy; Jon didn't want to call more attention to himself by going where he didn't belong.

He stood and dusted off his pants. The captain's room, on the other hand, was fair game since Jon had moved all of his belongings there. As he walked aft towards their shared quarters, Jon spotted a small boat approaching from town and assumed some shipmates had paid another visit to the brothel while they were still in the vicinity.

He stepped over Old Ben, who was sleeping against a rigging chest, and made his way to the rounded door between the staircases going up to the raised quarterdeck. It was dark inside the large room as usual, and Jon was glad for it; though nights were getting increasingly cold as winter approached, days still tended towards high heat around this time.

When his eyes adjusted, he saw that the captain's quarters were as fastidiously tidy as usual; there was no sign of the bloodied shirt. Jon crossed the room to the ice chest, craving some of the cold, fresh water Baltsaros stored there; his lungs still felt a tad raw.

When he pulled the pitcher out, he saw a lumpy package of something wrapped in paper on the lower shelf. Jon smiled. Perhaps this was the surprise? Baltsaros certainly lived up to his promise of feeding Jon every exotic thing he could come up with.

After replacing the water, he closed the door and walked to the bed, drinking down his mug of water. His head still felt fuzzy from lack of sleep; surely he could lie down for just a few minutes…

A loud crash woke Jon.

He gasped and sat up, looking around in alarm. There was a banging and another crash from above. He glanced up and saw that the room was strangely bright, the boards having been pulled away from the broken windows. Two strange men stood on wooden cases, hammers in hand.

Crash.

Another piece of wood went flying, and Jon slid off the bed, taking a few steps back.

What in gods?

He heard a laugh from behind him, and turned, startled to see the captain standing there with a smug smile on his angular face.

"Serves you right, sleeping on the job," said the captain dryly.

Jon was mortified, wondering how long he had been out. Tom hadn't exaggerated when he said that the aftereffects of the drug were long lasting; he could have slept all afternoon and only woken at morning. He ran his fingers through his curls, though his hair had gotten long enough that it no longer stood up at all angles from the habit.

"Sorry," Jon said quietly.

Baltsaros frowned and shook his head.

"I should put you over my knee for such laziness," he said softly, his eyes glinting with mischief.

Jon swallowed hard, his blue eyes wide. The thought of Baltsaros punishing him, especially in a way so intimate, had instantly elevated his heart rate. He almost groaned out loud; it was all Jon could do not to reach for the captain right there and pull his body against him. Lust was like a constant burning ember waiting only for the tiniest breath to fan it into flame; Jon had a hard time remembering what it was like before he was a slave to this perpetual, demanding hunger.

Baltsaros narrowed his eyes at Jon, sharp teeth visible in his wide smile.

"I see," he said simply, obviously gratified by Jon's breathless reaction.

Jon had to look away before he made things worse.

"What's going on?" he said in an unsteady voice, gesturing towards the men.

Looking pleased with himself, Baltsaros turned his eyes towards the workers.

"This is the surprise... I took your advice. These clear panes are only a temporary measure," he said as he watched one of the men hold up a greenish pane of thick glass to the empty window frame. "When we arrive in Madierus I will have some new stained-glass windows made up by the men who crafted the ones for my home there, but in the meantime I thought you'd be pleased with the change nonetheless," Baltsaros continued and lifted a hand to grasp the back of Jon's neck, his thumb lightly stroking the soft skin behind his ear.

Jon shivered slightly with the touch, his skin breaking out in gooseflesh.

"That's not all, however. Come and see the rest," said Baltsaros, smiling.

As he stared at the captain, Jon felt like he was seeing glimpses of a younger man through Baltsaros's uncharacteristic excitement; it was like a heaviness that Jon hadn't even realized was there had been lifted from the man.

Baltsaros led Jon out of the room and up the stairs to the very back of the ship. Below them, hanging on the wooden bench the men used for painting the sides of the ship, was another worker that Jon did not recognize. The man was painting words in red on the black of the ship's hull, and Jon could see that it would read *Baal's Heart* once the letters had been completely filled in.

He frowned in confusion and looked up into Baltsaros's clear brown eyes.

"What does it mean?" he asked.

The older man's tanned face creased in amusement.

"It is the root of my name, Jon. It means 'lord' or 'god' in an ancient language. And, as you pointed out, this is my home and thus my heart. I thought it was fitting, don't you?" Baltsaros said, looking up.

Jon followed his gaze and was amazed to see a flag flying from the post above them. On it was the same black silhouette of a roaring lion on a red field found on the crest within the captain's quarters, but here it was superimposed on a compass rose. Jon grinned wide.

"Lord, indeed," he said, raising his eyebrows. He laughed. "Yes... yes, definitely. I think it's fitting," he agreed. "It's a noble name and completely worthy of this ship."

This time he didn't hold back, forcefully drawing the captain in for a passionate kiss.

20

BLOW THE MAN DOWN

Baltsaros pulled away after only a moment, strangely tense. As he held Jon away from him distractedly, the captain studied the horizon with a furrowed brow.

Jon frowned and looked out at the clear water, not seeing anything amiss. Then he noticed that Tom was standing on the gunwale below them, his body also straight and tense as he stared in the same direction as Baltsaros.

"What's wrong?" asked Jon, worried.

The captain licked his lips and glanced down at Tom. The two men shared a look and Baltsaros nodded.

"What is it?" repeated Jon, the fact that captain and his ex–first mate were suddenly acknowledging each other's presence striking a nervous chord in him.

The captain looked at him, but it was a half second before his eyes focused on Jon's face.

"It might be nothing. It might be a storm," he said.

Jon tried to shrug nonchalantly.

"We've been through storms before…" he said but stopped at the concern on Baltsaros's face.

"Not a storm like this, Jon," replied the captain, his fingers digging into Jon's bicep. "Go below. Make the rounds and see that everything is secured. I don't want loose crates and barrels on deck if this is what I think it is."

Jon tried not to be hurt at being dismissed so hastily but moved to obey the captain's orders. Tom met him at the foot of the stairs and pointed to starboard.

"Tie anythin' that rolls or slides, lovey. We're in for one hell of a wild ride if the wind doesn't shift," he said, his brow creased over his ocean eyes.

Fear was beginning to take hold of Jon; what kind of storm could rattle the two stalwart men like this? He nodded and watched as Tom took off at a sprint in search of Katherine. When he squinted his eyes at the line where sea met sky, he still couldn't see any indication of a storm. However, he had to trust the pirates' instincts. They knew the sea, after all. He jogged along the side of the boat, pausing to secure loose lines and to tie down crates.

Jon was soon satisfied that at least one side of the ship was tidy and secure. Turning aft, he saw the workmen leaving in the small boat he had seen earlier. At the bow, deckhands were already turning the capstan to weigh anchor. Were they going to try to outrun the storm?

Katherine stood close by, hands on her hips as she frowned at the horizon.

"I don't see it," Jon said, walking up to her.

She turned her head and smiled.

"Neither do I, to be honest, but I've learned that if both Tom and the captain say there's a storm coming, you can bet your soul that there will be a storm," she said, her face serious. "I want you out of the way when this thing hits, Jon. The last thing I want anyone to worry about is you getting washed overboard." She reached out and grabbed his shoulder. "I know I normally tell you not to look so afraid, but this might be bad. Just heed me, ok? Keep to your quarters."

"Why are we lifting anchor? Isn't it safer here?" he asked, confused.

Katherine shook her head slowly.

"It would be safer if we could actually get into the harbour, but we're too big for that. If we stay here, all that will happen is the chain will snap or get pulled through the hull of the ship as we get buffeted around like a leaf in a windstorm. And then we'll get dashed against those rocks. No—it's better to face a hurricane on the open sea. For now, can you head to the galley while things are still calm? Help Cook secure things down there. The last time we got hit badly we ate shitty rations for a week because no one had time to lock everything up tight," Katherine said, smiling though Jon could see how worried she was.

"Yes, sir!" he said and squeezed the hand on his shoulder before leaving her to continue her watch on the horizon.

J on was rolling the last barrel into the big locker beneath the kitchen when the room got ominously dark. The portholes, showing blue skies only a moment ago, were now a deep grey, almost black.

Cook shoved him aside and quickly jammed the door closed, passing a loop of rope through the handle a few times before tying it tight. When he turned to look back at Jon, his eyes were wide.

"Go, Jon. Find somewhere to hole up and pray," he said, pushing him towards the door.

Jon's heart beat hard in his chest as he ran out of the dark room.

W hen the first gale hit the ship, Jon was struck with the gut-wrenching terror of being at sea during a storm. There was a high wailing noise that shrieked through the corridor as he frantically climbed the stairs to the upper deck; the ship was shuddering and swaying, making it hard to keep to his feet. Panting with the exertion, Jon just couldn't believe how sudden it all was.

When he reached up and pushed at the door, Jon was certain that someone or something was on it; however, after yelling with no response, Jon realized it was just the force of the wind holding it closed. When he finally got it open, he was instantly soaked as a blast of rain smacked hard into him, thrown by the furious winds. Jon coughed and wiped the stinging water from his eyes, terrified and unsure of which direction he was facing. He struggled onto the wooden planks and then stumbled as the ship pitched hard to starboard.

On his knees in the pouring rain, he gaped at the scene in front of him.

It was dark. Not night dark, but a howling, living darkness made up of swirling rains and black shapes.

There was a bright flash of lightning, and Jon made out the colossal wave just before it hit the ship. Frigid salt water crashed down on top of him, and he struggled to find something to hold. His hands closed on nothing and he panicked, his mouth full of water as he choked and groped around him.

The water receded, and they tilted precariously back, riding another huge wave high into the air. The ship creaked and groaned, shimmying slightly before she dropped suddenly out of the air, smacking down hard onto the water beneath. The wind was knocked out of Jon, and he writhed on the wet deck, trying to take in a breath. Finally his lungs expanded, and he drew in a shuddering breath.

Why in gods did I leave the galley? he thought in horror.

When the next lightning bolt flashed, he realized he was facing aft. He heard someone yelling behind him, and a loud crash. The ship rode up yet another wave, and Jon braced himself, ready for the next impact. There was a high squeal of something sliding against metal, and the ship yawed suddenly backwards.

Jon was utterly petrified, but he knew that he had to make his way to the captain's quarters; the door to belowdecks was lost somewhere behind him. On hands and knees, he crawled across the slippery wood. Where was Baltsaros in all this? Surely the captain knew what he was doing, having been through this before, but Jon was scared nonetheless.

The ship shivered under his palms, and Jon realized they had gone sideways again as yet another wave crashed down over the ship. Jon cried out as he was swept backwards, and for one sickening moment, he was free falling before he hit the deck.

Jon knew he was turned around, but with no lightning and most of the lanterns knocked out by saltwater, he had no way of figuring out which way to crawl. Thankfully, his hand made contact with something a moment later, and he breathed a sigh of relief. However, his reprieve was cut short when he realized that he was against the side of the ship and that there was nothing between him and the raging sea except for the low gunwale. He felt around for rope or a hand-hold but again found nothing. Sobbing in desperation, Jon tried to cling to the slick wood.

Up went the ship, and down again with a hard impact. Jarred momentarily from his spot, Jon slid against the deck. Raising his head, he thought he could see the outline of the quarterdeck right in front of him and decided to make a run for it. He lurched to his feet and took a few steps forward before he realized that the ship was tilting to starboard again. The wave crashed down hard, and Jon felt himself being lifted up into the air with the force of it. He windmilled his arms, trying to find something to hold onto, but it was too late; Jon was dashed against the side of the ship and swept upwards. All he could see below him was the churning, frothing maw of a sea gone mad. Feeling himself slide over the edge with nothing to hold onto, Jon realized he was going to die. He hung, terrified, on the edge of the yawning blackness for a half second before he began to fall...

...only to be pulled backwards by something hard around his waist. He choked and clung to the arm that was holding him as he was dragged across the deck. A few times he and his rescuer were blown down to the planks, but Jon was picked up, over and over again until they reached a sheltered corner.

When he wiped the water out of his eyes, Jon realized that the man holding onto him, one strong arm looped around his waist while the other held onto the stair railings of the quarterdeck, was Tom.

The ship creaked and groaned again, but this time when she landed, Tom was supporting him.

"It's goin' to be ok, mate!" shouted Tom over the wind. "She's already startin' to lose steam."

By "she" Jon assumed that Tom meant the storm. Jon felt limp against Tom, his heart careening wildly in his chest. If Tom had not reached out when he did, Jon would have been sucked down into the cold, black depths, surely to drown in the indifferent embrace of a mindless sea.

The ship went up and down, side to side. Sometimes Jon wondered how she hadn't capsized yet. Through it all was Tom, a wide hand on Jon's lower back as he held them steady in the small shelter of the staircase.

Strangely, the ship's wild movements seemed to take on a regularity, and Jon started to climb out of his terror. The lantern that hung swinging from the wall above hadn't yet been doused by water, and Jon could see Tom's face in the meagre, swaying light. The big man's eyes were narrowed against the water that dripped from his hair as he stared off to the side, watching the patterns of wind and rain with a keenness born of experience; the muscles worked in his broad jaw, and Jon saw that his lips were pressed in a tight line.

When Jon shivered hard he suddenly noticed that Tom, bare chested as usual, was still radiating warmth even though completely soaked with cold seawater. Tom was the very essence of summer at sea, with his blue-green eyes, and the sun's heat coming off his bronzed skin. Just like the sea, he was callous and dangerous... yet...

Shivering slightly, Jon lifted a hand and placed it flat against the bigger man's chest.

Tom's eyes swung to Jon's, wide with surprise.

Jon couldn't tell if it was the storm making him crazy or if he was just reacting to being saved, but he didn't care. Tom's skin was so warm under his palm, the hard muscles moving under his touch as the broad-chested man shifted his stance. Tom was just staring down at him with a frown, his eyes searching Jon's with distrust and confusion. The storm receded in the distance as he felt his heart ache at the look on Tom's face. Jon lifted his other hand to place it against Tom's stubbled cheek and felt him recoil.

Frowning, Jon tried again, reaching this time for the back of Tom's head, his fingers sliding through the short, wet hair at his nape. He watched as Tom blinked at him, his heart beating hard against Jon's palm.

Tom wrenched his head out of Jon's grasp and yelled something, but it was swallowed by the wind.

Jon shook his head, not understanding.

Tom stared hard at him, his forehead creased in seeming helplessness. When he finally leaned forward to Jon's ear, Tom looked as if he was stepping into the path of a loaded gun.

"Are ye *tryin'* to get me killed, love?" he shouted at Jon.

He caught the slight catch in Tom's voice and realized in astonishment that the powerful young man holding him was afraid. However, despite his words and fear, Jon felt Tom slide his thumb slowly against his lower back as he pulled back to look at him.

Jon's world imploded.

Tom was the last man on earth that he should be touching, yet Jon's desire became a living thing; pierced through with a dreadful emotion, it was shoving him headlong to where promises were broken and trust thrown away. He shivered as he stared into Tom's gaze, captivated by ocean-coloured eyes that were utterly heartbreaking. The man was almost terrified, but as he leaned into Jon's touch, Jon knew that Tom was caught up in the same fever that gripped him.

It was utter madness.

Wanting to laugh and cry at the same time, Jon knew he was at the very epicentre of a storm that was stronger than himself; there was something in this that was so agonizingly important that he was completely powerless to stop himself. Jon felt like weeping as he reached up and pulled Tom's mouth to his own.

Tom went rigid for a moment, and Jon felt his shock. However, Tom's fingers began clawing at Jon as he pulled him closer, leaning hard into the kiss.

Jon was breathless as Tom savaged his mouth, his kisses rougher and more frenzied than Baltsaros's. Jon's hands slid around the man's broad back, and he held on as Tom fed all the hurt and misery of his heart into the passion of his embrace. Tom's mouth tasted of anise and saltwater; his rough stubble burned Jon's lips, but he didn't care.

Tom released his hold on the stairs and wrapped Jon in arms that felt like steel, pushing him hard against the wall and tonguing deep into his mouth. This was sin and redemption at once. There was a savagery to Tom that Jon suddenly understood; he'd dismissed Tom as being an unfeeling brute when in fact it was nearly the opposite.

Jon thought his heart would shatter as he felt the layers of Tom's pain come away, wishing this kiss could heal the deep wounds that were nearly crippling the big man. Still Tom came at him hard, the heat of his body melting into Jon's cold skin, driving the passion of their kiss into a dizzying pinnacle of want and desperation.

With an audible groan, Tom pushed Jon away slightly, his chest heaving. The handsome brute shook his head, his eyes dark with desire and a hint of his old waggish smile on his lips. He cupped Jon's face with surprising gentleness in his big, callused hands and brought his mouth again to Jon's ear.

"Bloody hell, Jon," he said, his voice husky and deep. "He'll strip the skin from my bones, ye daft thing."

Jon shuddered; Tom's breath was warm against his neck. He turned his head and placed his lips next Tom's ear.

"I'm sorry, Tom. Oh gods, I am so sorry... for everything," he said and pressed his mouth against the skin of Tom's neck. Jon felt the bigger man's groan against his lips as Tom's strong arms tightened around him again, pressing their bodies together in their small sanctuary away from the storm.

Tom's voice was once more in Jon's ear, rough with emotion.

"Yer a bloody fool, love. It's not yer fault that the man has no heart. I just wish—"

There was a shout and a crash.

Tom's head swung away, and Jon felt the man's body tense.

Jon thought he could hear someone screaming. Tom looked back at Jon, his eyes wide with concern. He noticed then that the rigging chest, and the crates that were normally stacked next to it, had slid across the deck and were leaning against the door to the captain's quarters; there was no way he could get to safety.

Tom's hands tightened around Jon's hips, and the first mate's brow creased as he thought hard for a moment. Quickly, Tom reached for his own belt, untying it and passing it behind Jon.

Jon held onto Tom's shoulders as he felt the man's fingers slide one end of the belt through his own. Tom pushed him back and did something with the ends of the leather before stepping back, a wide grin on his face.

Jon frowned and looked behind him; Tom had secured him to the railing so that he wouldn't be swept away. He laughed, turning his eyes back to Tom.

The burly deckhand's handsome face went serious once more, and he leaned forward to press his lips to Jon's for an instant before jogging away to investigate the yelling. Tom turned after a few steps and pointed to Jon, grinning impishly. He mouthed one word: "Stay!" and winked, taking off towards the stern as the storm's winds lashed against him.

Jon caught movement out of the corner of his eye and saw the silhouette of someone turning away above him on the quarter-deck; however, his thoughts were instantly swept up by the storm as another huge wave crashed over the side of the ship, Jon struggling to keep to his feet as water swirled around him.

The night was long and terrifying. Again and again Jon heard shouts in the distance, and once he was sure that the ship would rattle herself to pieces, so loud was the creaking and popping sounds coming from the deck. However, he stayed well secured in his place, thanks to Tom's belt through the railing behind him.

Finally, the wind seemed to lose interest in the ship, and the waves became gentle. The sky was lightening, and Jon realized that the clouds were fading away, leaving twinkling stars behind. The storm was over.

Jon was shaky and his ears were ringing in the comparative silence that descended over the ship. Jon fumbled behind him and worked loose the knot in Tom's leather belt. It came away, and Jon saw that Tom's long knife was still within its sheath.

He was suddenly filled with a mixture of excitement and dread when he thought of the stolen moment beneath the stairs. However, now was not the time to worry about it; Jon saw in dismay that the deck was a mess of broken crates and scattered detritus. From the looks of it, some rigging had fallen from the foremast and one of the carronades had burst loose from its moorings before rolling down the deck. It was against the base of the mainmast and, in mounting horror, Jon realized that the pile of cloth that was crushed between the heavy cast-iron and wood was actually a body.

He quickly ran forward to see if the man was still alive.

When it finally came up over the battered *Baal's Heart*, the sun shone down on a sadly diminished crew. Three men were dead from injuries sustained aboard, and another five were missing.

Tom was numbered among those presumed swept overboard by the fury of the storm.

21

BREATHE

Jon paced back and forth across the colourful rugs, his hands holding his head as if it were about to fly apart. With his mind reeling and his heart full of jagged cuts, Jon let out a low, frustrated growl between clenched teeth. He stopped and turned to the man sitting at the table; Baltsaros was watching him, eyes untouched by emotion and arms crossed over his chest. There was nothing human in that face. Jon felt tears dampen the neck of his shirt.

"Don't you fucking feel *anything*, Baltsaros?" he asked harshly, his voice breaking on the captain's name. He laboured against the sharp pain in his chest, a burning tightness that threatened to break into hard sobs. Tom's last words kept playing in his mind:

The man has no heart.

Those words had never been so true as they were in that moment when Jon stared at the glacial creature watching his torture with an air of staid curiosity. Jon shuddered and resumed his pacing, overwhelmed with fury and anguish.

"Jon. I don't understand why you're acting this way," said the captain quietly. "Tom wanted you out of his way and would have done everything in his power to achieve that... eventually. He would not be carrying on about your loss were your positions reversed."

He swallowed hard, remembering the way Tom had held him so tight and the slight tremor in those massive arms when Jon had groaned into his open mouth... The way they had clutched at each other in the swaying light of the lantern; days later, Jon could still feel the heat of Tom beneath his skin. He closed his eyes, and the floor beneath him rocked, not from the ocean's swell, but from the deep exhaustion and hunger that hounded him.

Lightheaded, Jon quickly opened his eyes only to see the floor rushing towards him. Before he hit the carpet, Baltsaros's arms came up around him, catching him, and Jon leaned his face against the soft, dark material of the captain's shirt, gritting his teeth. He was burning with an inner turmoil that threatened to choke him.

Jon hadn't slept in two days, not really... not since the storm.

When it had become clear that Tom was amongst the missing, Jon had fought against it at first, denying the truth; it was more than he could bear. He had then spent hours with his eyes sweeping back and forth, searching the choppy waters for any sign of the lost man. It was only after jerking awake on the wooden planks of the deck earlier that day, after exhaustion momentarily claimed him, that Jon had remembered something that froze him to the very marrow of his bones.

He'd just had a fleeting dream of a giant lion looming over him, its shadow spreading like oil across the deck; he recalled then that someone had been standing above as Tom and he clutched at each other in the shelter of the staircase.

Had Baltsaros seen them?

A fist of ice had opened up inside Jon at the thought, its fingers sharp and long. Had strong, surefooted Tom, a seasoned sailor, simply fallen into the water?

J on swallowed against the bitter bile that rose up in him at the horrifying alternative that was churning in his mind... that Tom had been pushed. As he shuddered, Jon clutched at the strong arms of the man holding him gently.

Did Baltsaros know?

Jon already knew what the captain was capable of.

Don't think.

When Baltsaros's hand touched his head, brushing his hair back softly, Jon wanted to scream. Lying in Baltsaros's arms, all Jon could think about was Tom...

The man already tried to kill Tom once.

...lying in a murderer's arms...

Don't think.

He couldn't confront Baltsaros without revealing his trespasses; Jon's lungs were on fire.

Breathe, said Tom.

Jon opened his eyes wide, new bricks sliding into the walls around his soul, and looked up into Baltsaros's face. The captain was gazing down at him with concern as he ran his fingers through Jon's rough brown curls.

"It is a terrible thing when the sea claims someone," said Baltsaros quietly.

He could tell that the man was trying to understand the source of the anguish that threatened to drown Jon; he looked desperately for any sign that Baltsaros was hiding a terrible deed.

Would I know if he was? thought Jon miserably. He let himself be pulled to his feet and felt as Baltsaros began tugging his shirt out of his pants, the captain's warm hands stroking up his sides as the material was lifted up. Obligingly, Jon raised his arms, and Baltsaros pulled the shirt completely off.

Wordlessly, Baltsaros unbuttoned Jon's pants and undressed him, frowning at the young man's complete lack of reaction. The captain pushed Jon towards the bed, and he lay down on the sheets, his eyes staring at nothing. Quickly ridding himself of his own clothing, Baltsaros climbed up onto the bed and pulled Jon against him.

Jon closed his eyes and breathed deep. The captain's body was strong and warm around him; the thatch of soft hair on Baltsaros's chest felt nice against his torso, and the captain smelled alluringly of wind, musk, and sandalwood.

Baltsaros's fingers stroked Jon from thigh to shoulder and along his arm with gentle touches that were feather soft.

Breathe in, breathe out.

Jon felt like he was breathing for the drowned Tom, lost somewhere beneath the ocean's waves just as a new flame had started burning within him.

Baltsaros's mouth was hot against Jon's neck as he slid his tongue softly up to trace the lines of his jaw.

He frowned; sex was the captain's solution to everything.

Breathe in, breathe out.

Tom's hands on his face.

Baltsaros's hands on his skin.

Jon felt himself drifting on the sensation of Baltsaros's hands ghosted by Tom's as he counted his breaths. When the captain pushed Jon onto his back and began kissing down his chest, he felt the slow burn of desire begin to warm his loins. He didn't want it.

Tom and his tragic blue-green eyes at the bottom of a blue-green ocean.

Jon gasped and was brought back to the present when Baltsaros's wet tongue slipped between his legs; lapping upwards, the captain licked the wrinkled skin of Jon's sensitive sack, tongue broad and firm as his mouth manipulated the round forms within.

Measured breaths became quickly forgotten as Jon shamefully surrendered, tangling his fingers in Baltsaros's hair and arching his back off the bed as he pushed the older man's head firmly against him.

Tom began slipping beneath the waves and out of his grasp as Jon sighed the captain's name.

"Oh gods, Baltsaros... more... please..." he said in a whimper.

Baltsaros continued to lick slowly, his tongue leaving wet trails on the insides of Jon's thighs, along the lines of his pelvis, teasing so close to his cock and returning to tongue his scrotum; gently nudging Jon's legs further apart, he then pulled his mouth away from the younger man to wet his finger with spit.

Jon raised his head and frowned, his chest heaving. When he guessed Baltsaros's intention, Jon felt a pang of fear-laced excitement. With his eyes locked on Baltsaros's, Jon pressed his lips together and nodded; Baltsaros smiled as he slid the finger inside him, and Jon breathed a long moan, trying not to tense.

Slightly shaky from the foreign sensation, Jon watched as Baltsaros trailed his tongue along the bottom of his cock to the underside of its head, the long finger stroking gently around a tingling, pulsing point of pleasure deep within.

"Fuck... oh gods," Jon gasped, his chest heaving. This was ecstasy bordering on agony. The finger inside him, slowly starting to move directly over this unfamiliar sensitive centre, added a keen-edged intensity to what Baltsaros was doing with his tongue. He panted and pushed back hard on the captain.

"St-stop. It's too much," Jon groaned.

Baltsaros lifted his head, his dark eyes curious. Heedless of Jon's words, he pressed a second finger to his puckered entrance, stretching him open further. Jon gasped and dug his fingers into the sheets beneath him, a shudder running through his body as his head fell back on the bed; his hips moved automatically with the slow motion of the captain's long digits probing inside him.

Jon gritted his teeth. His cock was rock hard and throbbed in a way that was almost painful, a long string of clear fluid stretching out between its tip and the base of his stomach as the shaft bobbed up in response to Baltsaros's inner caress. He squeezed his eyes shut, a low groan rasping out of his chest with every long stroke of Baltsaros's fingers.

He suddenly realized just how heavily Baltsaros was breathing and raised his head, looking helplessly at him. The captain was flushed, his pupils huge with desire; he gazed wonderingly at Jon.

"I could make you peak just like this, couldn't I?" Baltsaros said, sounding amazed.

Jon swallowed reflexively, words failing him as the pleasure mounted and spread, only to fold back on itself and surge forward again. He licked his lips and gasped again as another rush of pleasure sluiced through him; he reared back on the pillow and groaned loud.

"You're unusually receptive," said the captain, a note of surprise in his low voice.

Jon shuddered when he felt Baltsaros lean forward again to touch his warm tongue to his stretched opening, sliding softly beside and between the two fingers moving languidly inside him, slickening them anew with spit. Jon's breath sobbed out of him, and he reached for his cock, frantically wanting release; however, Baltsaros's hand stopped him.

"No. I want to see how far I can take you," said the captain softly. Jon moaned in desperation, but his breath caught in his throat as a third finger started to pierce him. Jon whimpered and clutched hard at the hand Baltsaros had placed on his chest to hold him down. This hurt... He felt like crying out as the tightness strained over Baltsaros's knuckles... And then it didn't, his passion taking over, loosening his muscles.

As Baltsaros fucked him smoothly with his fingers, Jon felt the pressure mount in his testicles, each little slap of his cock against his taut stomach a little explosion of sensation. Jon felt himself open up; flush with lust and ripe with desire, he held his breath a moment and clutched at Baltsaros.

"Baltsaros, I can't anymore... please... I-I want you inside me," Jon said, his words made plain by the hunger that tormented him;

the idea had been building in his head since that night in the brothel.

Jon heard Baltsaros exhale hard before pulling away. He opened his eyes and lifted his head in dismay, wondering why he'd been abandoned and saw that Baltsaros had just retreated as far as the cabinet to fetch something; the captain was back on the bed in a moment.

The older man poured out a small amount of oil into his hand and smoothed it over the head of the thick cock jutting out stiff and veiny from the curled hair between his legs. His other hand stroked Jon's thigh and glided up his leg to grasp his hip, his thumb rubbing against the skin there in a distracted way as he passed his hand over his own length. When Baltsaros's shaft was shiny with oil, he thumbed some into the crevice of Jon's ass, pressing him open to smooth some within.

Jon whimpered and obligingly lifted his knees up, grasping the backs of his thighs. He was terrified of the prospect of Baltsaros's wide cock inside him, yet there was nothing in the world he wanted more.

Tom...

Jon gritted his teeth and growled out a hard breath, wanting to drown the emotions that kept seeping through the walls he had erected.

After shoving one arm under his waist, Baltsaros grunted as he lifted Jon's hips up and pulled a pillow beneath his buttocks, raising him up and opening him further by pressing back on his thighs.

Jon closed his eyes, his heart thudding hard against his ribs, as he waited for the final assault.

Baltsaros's fingers were on him again, pushing into him, spreading the oil, readying him. When the head of Baltsaros's thick cock finally touched him and started to force his way into Jon's body, he cried out softly.

However, while there was pain, it was quickly overshadowed by the pleasure of feeling full of Baltsaros's hard length. The captain pushed his greased cock to the very hilt into Jon's body and groaned.

With hungry hands, Jon pulled Baltsaros down onto his chest to feel the man's weight above him as the cock inside him started gliding back only to slowly stretch him wide again.

With his own oversensitive length trapped between their bodies, rubbing and sliding through the slick trail it left on their skin, Jon was soon crying out, a single, open-voweled syllable repeating over and over out of his raw throat as he quickly came hard; he spilled over onto his stomach with hot pulses as his passion hit a frantic peak, dissolving him with a searing, shattering explosion of sensation and release.

Baltsaros gasped in response, thrusting himself hard, his brows furrowed and his mouth open as his cock was enveloped and milked by the tight throbbing of Jon's orgasm. Baltsaros grunted like a beast, his pounding gone wild as he came deep inside Jon.

J on pressed his mouth against Baltsaros's neck and tasted sweat on his lips. He was almost uncomfortably sore and incredibly tired, but his mind wouldn't stop its relentless churning. Caught directly between his feelings about the loss of Tom and the suspicion that Baltsaros had played a part in it was this profound emotion he felt towards the man at his side.

Baltsaros sighed happily and ran his fingers down Jon's back, scratching gently at his skin.

"Jon, do you realize how very unique you are?" the captain murmured sleepily.

Despite how perturbed he felt, Jon had to smile; this was the way he liked Baltsaros the best: sated and gentled... It made him seem more human.

After a long pause, Baltsaros spoke again.

"I'm sorry that Tom's death causes you so much pain, Jon.

And... I'm sorry that saving you is a debt I can never repay to him," he said, his voice soft.

Jon closed his eyes and pressed his forehead against the side of Baltsaros's stubbled jaw, feeling torn and weary. Jon knew the captain didn't understand, and that the words *I'm sorry* meant next to nothing. However, that Baltsaros was even volunteering them was enough for Jon to clutch to.

He stroked his hand over Baltsaros's broad chest and nodded, his lips pressed together and his brow furrowed. Tom was gone; he had to think more rationally...

Maybe it's for the best.

Instantly Jon felt sick to his stomach with the thought, but it was true.

Baltsaros woke when his outstretched arm failed to make contact with another warm body. He opened his eyes and lifted his head. When he saw that the room was empty and the door closed, he frowned. Brutus was also not at his place on the folded blanket next to the bed.

He sat up and stretched his back, spine popping with his movements. Baltsaros then dragged one of the blankets over his wide shoulders as he stood. Reaching down to touch himself, he smiled; his cock had a delicious soreness to it. Jon had definitely surprised him tonight.

After padding across the floor in his bare feet, Baltsaros opened the door to his quarters and looked out. He knew it was too early to feel the difference, but it already seemed that the night air was getting warmer as they headed south.

Curious, he climbed the stairs to the quarterdeck above and saw that Jon was asleep, huddled on the floor fully clothed next to his oversized dog.

Brutus raised his head slowly and looked at the captain sedately with eyes that reflected the light of the moon.

Baltsaros rubbed his jaw and stared at Jon for a moment. Now that Tom was gone, maybe Jon would stop worrying about the former first mate. As he shook his head slightly, he walked forward and pulled the blanket off his shoulders, leaning over to place it over the curled body of his young lover.

When Baltsaros turned and looked at the seemingly endless stretch of water behind them, he found that his own mind had turned to Tom.

22

FIRE IN THE BLOOD

The captain pulled the lumpy package out of the icebox and placed it on the table, laying it on the thick wooden slab he used to protect the table's surface.

Jon, stinking of rum and tobacco, watched him bleary-eyed from the bed.

Three days had passed since the storm, and Jon was still in the throes of his mysterious bereavement. This morning Baltsaros had found him slumped over some crates after a long night of gambling and drinking. It was completely out of character for him, and it baffled Baltsaros; Jon seemed bent on mimicking the man he was mourning.

Baltsaros eyed the pale, sickly looking Jon and wondered if he should make up a tonic for his hangover or just let him suffer.

"What's that?" asked Jon.

Baltsaros looked back down at the package and began pulling apart the twine that held it together.

It's almost a waste, he thought. After pushing open the paper, he held up the contents of the package to Jon.

"It's a heart," he said.

Baltsaros turned it over once in his hands, remembering how

warm it had been when he plucked it from his quarry's chest. It was so cold now, and it was too late to eat it raw; the storm had ruined that opportunity.

Jon sat up slowly, his mouth drawn down in a grimace.

"Why do you have a heart in your ice chest?" he asked, his voice hoarse. "What kind of heart is it?"

"Deer," lied Baltsaros smoothly, smiling at Jon.

Jon slid off the bed, his bare feet silent on the thick rug as he came to Baltsaros's side. The odour of liquor was a miasma around him, and he smelled of sour sweat.

"Where did you get it?" Jon asked. The young man was looking down at the heart curiously.

Baltsaros had a sudden vision of Jon covered in heart's blood, and it brought with it a little pang of desire. He ran his hand up Jon's side, smiling when he saw the goosebumps his touch caused.

"I went hunting the other night," said Baltsaros.

The blond woman's legs flashed white as she ran away from him, stumbling over branches and slipping on leaves. The blood pounded hot inside his chest.

Jon leaned into Baltsaros, and the captain could feel little tremors going through his body.

"Oh, I wondered where all that blood on your shirt came from," replied Jon. "But... Where's the rest of the deer?"

Baltsaros chuckled. The body would have been disposed of as per the arrangement with Fresia; the management at the Jewel catered to almost every proclivity of their vast and varied clientele.

"I only needed the heart. It is a custom among my people to eat fresh heart raw at the beginning of a long journey. It brings good luck," said Baltsaros. "But this one isn't fresh anymore. I suppose I could make sausage with it."

Jon looked at him askance.

"I didn't take you for the superstitious type," he said, his dark brows high.

Baltsaros reached up and touched the tips of his fingers to Jon's stubbled cheek.

"Call it… tradition, then," he said softly.

Jon's eyes were bright blue in his pale face this morning. Baltsaros was glad once again that he had convinced him to repair the windows in his quarters; the added light was a welcome change.

Charmed by Jon's unselfconscious nakedness and the way he licked his lips when Baltsaros touched him, the captain felt lust sink her claws into him. He pushed the heart and cutting board aside and pulled Jon around so that he was against the table, facing him.

Jon frowned, and Baltsaros felt a touch irritated; the same look of suspicion had crossed his face often over the last few days, and it was beginning to wear on the captain.

He grazed his fingers over the solid muscles of Jon's chest and down his hard abs, stopping to tug softly at the line of dark hair that led to the thatch around the younger man's cock. Baltsaros was pleased to see that Jon was starting to harden at his touch.

When he looked back up, he saw that Jon's suspicion had been replaced by half-lidded desire. Gently pushing his legs apart with his knee, Baltsaros stepped closer and leaned into him, kissing his neck and grinding his pelvis hard into Jon's stiffening cock. Jon groaned softly, his hands clutching Baltsaros's buttocks to pull him in harder.

Obviously, whatever was bothering Jon wasn't enough to make him refuse the captain's advances.

Baltsaros ran his hand up Jon's back and tangled his fingers in the brown curls that now fell to his shoulders. He pulled a handful of it into his fist and tugged hard.

"Ow… You're hurting me," Jon said, wincing.

Tom would have never complained at such treatment unless the captain wanted him to. Frowning, Baltsaros pushed away the thought and looked piercingly at the young man.

"Jon, I want you to stop your nonsense. You have not slept in my bed in three nights. Whatever it is that is going on in that pretty head of yours, put it to rest. Now," he said, his voice intentionally harsh.

Jon closed his eyes, a deep line forming between his brows.

"If you fall apart every time we lose a man, you will be less than useless to me," Baltsaros continued. He slid the thumb of his free hand along the line of Jon's jaw, down to his throat and felt him swallow twice. "And... I do not like to share you with ghosts," he said.

Jon's eyes opened, and he looked startled.

Guilt?

Baltsaros could smell desperation on Jon's skin and a little fear.

"Put away your demons, my love. They serve you badly."

Jon stared at him, an inner struggle trapped in his wide eyes. Then Baltsaros watched a shift take place. It was as if Jon had come to some decision; the lines in his face smoothed out, and his whole countenance changed like a man putting on a different mask. Baltsaros wondered idly what it cost Jon to bury his emotions every time he surrendered to his captain's wishes.

"As you wish," Jon said softly.

Baltsaros smiled and leaned in to kiss Jon. After a heartbeat's hesitation, Jon kissed him back, his tongue questing into Baltsaros's open mouth. The captain released his hold on Jon's hair and savaged him with the heat of his mounting passion, eliciting groans of pleasure as he pressed himself hard against his lover's body. His constant desire for Jon was like fire in his blood.

There was a loud knock at the door.

Baltsaros pulled away from Jon with a groan.

"Come in!" he yelled.

Jon's eyes were wide, his body having gone rigid against Baltsaros.

"Wait... I'm..." he started.

The captain chuckled.

"Katherine has seen her share of naked men, Jon," Baltsaros said as he watched his first mate open the door and step inside.

The lithe woman took in the scene with raised eyebrows, eyes pausing for a brief second on the heart, but made no comment. Tom would have said something completely inappropriate. He also would not have knocked before entering.

Baltsaros frowned to himself. Why was he thinking of Tom again?

"Yes, my dear?" he asked.

Katherine's face was solemn.

"Jim's hanged himself," she said simply.

Baltsaros nodded. He had been expecting something like it; the young gunner had lost his brother Billy in the storm, and the twins had been close.

"Thank you. Can you take care of it? I'm sure you can think of a few things to say to the men," he said, dismissing her.

She frowned and nodded before leaving the room.

When he looked back at Jon, the young man was staring at him, expressionless.

If you fall apart every time we lose a man, you will be less than useless to me.

"I guess that's just one less mouth to feed," said this new version of Jon as he reached for Baltsaros to pull him back into a fierce kiss.

J on cried out as Baltsaros bit him hard on the shoulder. He was trapped under the bigger man, his arms pinned beneath his chest as Baltsaros rubbed his thick cock along the furrow of Jon's ass.

It was maddening.

He thrust his hips up and back against the captain's hard length and whimpered.

"Please," he begged. "Just fuck me already." His cock ached to be touched, but he couldn't move his hands, and Baltsaros would only tease his ass slowly. Jon shivered and groaned, getting what little stimulation he could from the bed beneath him.

Again Baltsaros bit down on his flesh, his sharp teeth closing on the back of his neck. Jon yelped and shuddered.

"Please," he repeated. He had seen male cats bite females on the back of the neck as they mated, and the thought aroused him even more. Baltsaros's cock slipped past his sensitive, puckered opening again, and Jon gritted his teeth.

Baltsaros had been keeping at him steadily, pushing him close to orgasm only to back away, for what had to be over an hour; Jon was starting to lose his mind.

"Please, Baltsaros. Please. I can't," he panted into the coverlet.

Baltsaros remained silent and slowly tongued the spot he had bitten, continuing to slide his cock in the greased cleft of Jon's ass.

"Please fuck me," Jon whimpered again. He clenched his eyes shut, the word *please* starting to flow like a mantra out of a throat dry from panting.

Chuckling softly above him, Baltsaros shifted his hips slightly and moved his hand away from Jon's shoulder. The coolness that came from the sudden loss of contact there made Jon aware that both he and the captain were covered in a sheen of sweat. When Baltsaros shuddered slightly, it dawned on Jon that he had been teasing himself just as mercilessly.

After working his hand beneath Jon's stomach and down to where his erection pressed hard into the bed, Baltsaros took him in hand. Jon moaned at the contact and continued his plea. Another shift of Baltsaros's hips brought the wide head of his cock into contact with Jon's asshole, and Jon gasped, his begging coming to a strangled end.

When Baltsaros started to push into him, widening his narrow passage, Jon almost cried out in relief.

Thank the gods, no more teasing.

He clenched his jaw against the pain; Baltsaros was so big. However, as before, when the head of Baltsaros's cock rubbed against the hard, sensitive spot within him, a keen pleasure started to radiate out of his loins like warm molasses. With Baltsaros's hand firmly around Jon's cock, he let his body go limp as the hard length of the captain's shaft opened him up; but, once his cock was buried deep inside Jon, Baltsaros stopped moving.

Jon groaned.

"Please, no. Baltsaros," he gasped in dismay, "Please, please, no more. Gods, no more..."

"Hush," said the captain, his voice low.

Jon tried to shift his hips to force movement within him, but the man held him still. Jon thought he would start to cry.

Thus began another extended stretch of teasing, the pleasure mounting and receding agonizingly slow as Baltsaros moved his hips in tiny, staggered motions, his cock gliding minutely inside of Jon.

It was a long time before Jon was finally allowed to cum.

When he did, his whole body shook with the force of it as he sobbed loud, the ecstasy crashing through him hot and sweet. His cock throbbed and pulsed, again and again, sending thick gouts of cum onto the bed beneath him, Baltsaros's hand stroking and squeezing with the same rhythms of his orgasm.

The relief was so intense that Jon felt like he ceased to exist for a moment; his awareness shrunk down to a knife's edge, becoming the cock that twitched and jumped in Baltsaros's grasp.

The captain had gone rigid, his groan of pleasure long and low, as he spilled his seed into the younger man. Face pressed hard into the crook of Jon's neck, Baltsaros urgently moved his hips as he rode the tide of his own orgasm, and Jon could feel the man's heart hammer against his back. Finally, the only movement was the heaving of their chests, and only the sound of breathing broke the stillness in the air.

Jon felt almost delirious, and he ached to clutch Baltsaros to him. As if hearing Jon's thoughts, Baltsaros slowly pulled out and lay down next to him with a sigh, his arms reaching out. Jon turned on his side and curled against the broad chest, his forehead resting against the base of Baltsaros's neck.

"Thank you," Jon said quietly.

There were tears in his eyes and they soaked into the sheet beneath him. Baltsaros's hands stroked his back, and he felt the man nod.

"That was gorgeous," said Baltsaros, sounding somewhat dazed. A floodgate of raw emotions opened inside Jon, and he shivered and wept against the captain. He had been conquered and then set free. The word love was right at his lips.

"Jon... Don't cry," Baltsaros said softly, his fingers stroking the back of Jon's neck. "Why are you crying?" The captain seemed suddenly younger to Jon somehow, a note of awe in his voice.

"Because... I need you," whispered Jon after a moment. "I needed this. I needed you. You came for me. You claimed me. No one has ever made me feel these... things you make me feel. I don't ever want it to stop." As he spoke, Jon realized that no matter what Baltsaros did, he would stay by his side; though he would lose his soul, piece by piece, by the things he would be forced to endure, this is where he belonged.

When Baltsaros next broke the silence, Jon felt his heart skip a beat.

"Jon, I would walk through fire just to hear you speak my name," murmured Baltsaros. "And although I don't understand it, I would be a lesser man without you here with me."

23

DEAD IN THE WATER

*Absence diminishes mediocre passions and
increases great ones, as the wind extinguishes
candles and fans fires.*

— FRANÇOIS DE LA ROCHEFOUCAULD

Jon frowned and looked down at the potato he was peeling.
He and Calum were on kitchen duty for the day, and they
were going through what seemed like the very bottom of
the barrel. The potato in his hand was slightly soft, and it had
black spots on its wrinkled skin. They had been sailing southwest
for nearly a month, and their provisions were running danger-
ously low.

Though the storm had robbed them of supplies, they hadn't
restocked before leaving for Madierus. Baltsaros had done the
calculations and had pointed out coldly that the missing or dead
men could not eat; what food and water they had once the storm
cleared was ample for the reduced crew.

The captain had not counted on the long weeks with no wind.

Grimacing, Jon cut another rotten piece out of the potato, flicking away in disgust the little white worm he had uncovered.

Calum laughed, and Jon looked up.

"What?" he asked.

The old man shook his head and pointed to the wriggling thing on the floor with the end of his knife.

"Soon ye won't be throwin' away good meat like that, son," joked Calum, chuckling to himself.

Jon's stomach roiled at the thought.

From what he could tell, they were still a few weeks out from the island of Madierus. However, every time he pressed the captain for exactly how far they were, Baltsaros's eyes flashed to anger, and he went stonily silent.

Jon knew that the captain would be sitting up on the quarter-deck right now, just staring out at the still water, his face drawn and eyes hooded.

When he looked over at Calum, who was cutting up the rest of the carrots, he remembered that the old pirate had been on this ship longer than Baltsaros had.

"Has this happened before?" he asked, curious.

Calum sucked at his bottom lip a moment and then nodded.

"Aye. A few times. The worst was when yun' Baltsaros had just come aboard," he said. "We was sailin' to the north and got caught in open water, nary a breeze for the cloth. Dark times."

Jon's hands slowly continued their work as he listened to Calum's story.

Many years before, when Calum was in the prime of his life and newly widowed, he had joined the crew of the *God's Hammer*—as it had been known in those days—to escape prosecution.

Before becoming a pirate, Calum had been part of the standing army for the mainland kingdom. His job had been to train new recruits in different hand-to-hand fighting techniques, something he had learned from his father, a man of dubious employment.

Calum's wife, on her way to visit a sick friend one evening with fresh-made bread and soup, fell prey to a man who mistook her for a prostitute. The man, a well-known aggressor of women, simply slammed her head against the wall when she refused his advances, and the woman died shortly after from her injuries. It was not hard for Calum to track down the murderer, a small lord, and beat him to death with his bare hands.

On the run and with a warrant on his head, there were few choices to him that appealed as much as becoming a pirate.

Calum had been on board working as a simple deckhand for a little over two years when Captain Romas went to retrieve his brother's orphaned boy. It was that summer, a few months after the nine-year-old Baltsaros first came aboard, that Romas had decided in a moment of fanaticism to sail from the midland isles to the lowest tip of the northern continent.

The last-minute course change was fuelled by a rumour that barbarian tribes were threatening villages along the coast and converting them to heathen ways. Romas, being a man who considered himself on God's *one true path*, was incensed by the rumours. He put both his ship and crew in the path of pure folly by sailing them north through a barren sea with few provisions during a time of year that was known for fickle winds.

Calum had watched in dismay as the sails held less and less wind in them every day until they finally went flat and listless. Soon the crew began running out of provisions, and things became strained on the ship.

Since Baltsaros's arrival, Calum had been watching the frail, fine-boned boy with the dark eyes and high cheekbones; Captain Romas, though couching his adoption of Baltsaros as familial duty, seemed hell-bent on breaking him. Romas was under the impression that the boy was somehow tainted and in need of saving, a theme that the religious man was obsessed with.

Night and day, young Baltsaros was set to backbreaking

labour; the tasks were often extremely taxing on the boy's health, and he would be frequently found pale and listless at the end of his shifts. However, the captain would shove him awake with a boot only a few hours later and set him on some new, more onerous task. Hard work, said the captain, would save the boy from the devils within.

Baltsaros always bent his head to his work without complaint; the only sign of outrage towards his treatment was a dark fire that burned in his eyes. When Baltsaros wasn't working or sleeping, he was found on his knees in the small chapel; more than once Calum had seen the boy kneeling through the open door as his uncle exited, his hands re-buttoning the front of his pants.

Calum felt pity for the boy and wanted to help, so he waited until the next time the captain went ashore to approach Baltsaros. His offer of fighting lessons had been met with a long, hard stare, one that was strangely calculating for one so young. In the end, Baltsaros had nodded his head curtly and extended his hand to the older man.

Thus began their longstanding alliance.

At first Calum worried that the lessons, in addition to Baltsaros's duties and the meagre sleep he was afforded, would begin to take their toll on the fragile-seeming lad. However, the graceful young boy took to the lessons like a fish to water, and they seemed to give him energy rather than sap it; a new fire burned within Baltsaros.

It was during this windless drifting in the barren northern sea that Baltsaros first used his new skills against the captain.

A fight had broken out between the men in the lower deck, a squabble about the size or quality of rations, and the galley was trashed as a result.

Captain Romas put the three men responsible into the brig; he then dragged young Baltsaros by his neck to the galley and shoved him down to the floor, wanting him to clean up the mess.

At least that's what the captain had intended.

Instead, as Romas went to fling the boy down, he was flipped over into the air, landing hard on his back in the mess. Calum had been there to see the older man staring up in shock at the boy who stood above, a fierce grin on his elfin face.

That afternoon, Baltsaros was sealed in one of the big rain barrels with a few cannonballs and thrown overboard. The barrel was dragged slowly behind the ship by a rope tied around it for nearly two hours. When it was finally hoisted back on board, Baltsaros was unconscious and lifelessly cold from the frigid northern waters.

Calum had been surprised that the boy had recovered. This was to be only the first of many, many times that Baltsaros was lowered into the cold water over the course of Romas's captainship.

As the horror faded from Baltsaros's eyes that first time, Calum noticed something new about him; where Baltsaros had been sober and quiet before, he was now curious and driven. The secret lessons between Calum and the fine-boned lad also took on a different aspect; while Baltsaros worked to hone his physical skills, he asked countless questions of the older man about the ship, the captain, the crew, and the world in general.

He became a more charming version of himself with the other men, winning small friendships onboard. Calum asked Baltsaros what had changed, but the boy wouldn't say.

A week after the incident, the captain dragged the three men from the brig and set them kneeling, side by side, on the deck in front of the crew. There was no longer enough food to feed all of them, and, in a misplaced attempt to further terrorize Baltsaros, Captain Romas was making the young boy choose which sailor was to walk the plank.

Calum had stood quietly in the back of the crowd, watching Baltsaros's face grow cold as he stared into his uncle's eyes. Without a word, the boy pulled the knife from his belt and quickly slashed the throats of all three men before Captain Romas had a chance to stop him. The instant the last body fell limp to the wooden planks, a great gust of wind was felt. It soon filled the sails, and the ship was quickly on its way again; a great cheer had gone up among the crew despite the ruthless killing of the men.

That was the last time Captain Romas publicly tormented the boy.

Baltsaros's workload increased ever more, and his punishments became more frequent, but the first nail in Captain Romas's coffin had been forged that day. The wind, while coincidental, had elevated the boy in the superstitious minds of the crew; their growing admiration and loyalty for Baltsaros was what had made the mutiny possible seven years later.

J on licked his lips and swallowed.

"So Baltsaros was not always this... ruthless? You think his uncle pushed him to it?" he asked Calum when the story was done.

The old man frowned at Jon.

"I wouldn'a say that, lad. The cap'n... 'E's always been different. I think whatever 'e seen in the deeps just freed what 'e already was. Though I known 'im for near thirty years, I wouldn'a call 'im a friend, see?" The dark-skinned man peered thoughtfully at Jon a moment. "But... I never seen 'im treat a man the way 'e treats ye, Jon. It's none of me business what ye two get up to behind closed doors but outside of 'em... Well, I'd call what ye have friendship."

Jon grimaced. The relationship between him and the captain had become strained as the long weeks passed. Baltsaros had started acting strange; he did nothing but drink and stare out at the water all day long. Aching with worry, Jon desperately wanted to break through the captain's isolation.

"Calum. I... uh... do you..." he started, unsure about how to word the question that still haunted him.

The old man just looked back down at the carrot he was peeling and waited patiently for Jon to form his question.

"Do you think the captain could have killed Tom if he saw him doing something he was forbidden to do?" he asked quietly.

Calum's eyes flicked up to Jon's face with interest. However, the old man was canny, and Jon saw that he wouldn't be pressed for more information. After chewing his lip for a moment, Calum spoke.

"The cap'n wouldn'a kill the boy, no. There's reasons, but it ain't my place to say," he said, his rough voice equally low.

"He would have killed him that day with the whip," Jon pointed out.

The old pirate shook his head right away.

"Aye, perhaps; ye did stop 'im, but I'm likin' to think he'd a stopped hisself. That boy Tom was angrier than a bag full o' cats when 'e come aboard, and it was the cap'n who gentled 'im. No, lad. The cap'n wouldn'a kill Tom," he repeated firmly, looking back down at his hands.

Jon knew that the old man believed his words.

The younger man flipped the potato back in the bin, and Calum glanced back up quizzically as Jon stood.

"I... need to... I'll be back," he said quickly. He strode through the big doors to the galley and rinsed his knife in the basin of standing water that Cook kept there for that reason. He held the long blade flat in his hands and looked down at it.

Tom's knife.

He ran his fingers down the bone hilt, over the markings there, wondering as always what they meant. With his eyes closed, Jon pictured the big brute in his head, the impish grin and the rough hands that had held his face so gently. Jon would never be able to ask him. For all he knew, the big man was rolling in his watery grave knowing that Jon had claimed the knife as his own. Jon smiled sadly at the thought but put his feelings for the dead man away for later.

He needed to see the captain.

B altsaros frowned at the cloudless blue sky and took another sip of the rum and cold coffee from the cup he held in one hand. The wind had to blow soon... But did it even matter now? The sun beat down hard on the captain; he had changed from his customary leather pants to the black linen ones he favoured when sailing to the summer lands, but he was still hot. His torso was bare and his chest hair was dark with sweat. He ground his teeth in frustration.

Why is there no wind?

He turned his head when he heard the soft steps approaching. Jon padded up the stairs and came to stand in front of Baltsaros.

"What do you want, Jon?" he asked, his voice weary and annoyed.

"Come. The ocean can wait," Jon said.

The captain's stark brow raised slowly. He drank down the rest of the liquid in the cup and stared at Jon.

"Not now," he said and turned back to the water and the lack of wind. When Jon's hand curled around his bicep, he wasn't prepared for the anger that crashed through him. He flung his arm out to push the other away... but found himself suddenly flat on his back on the wooden boards.

Jon stood above him, a frown on his face.

"I said come," he repeated.

Baltsaros bared his teeth and sat up.

What is this?

In amazement, he watched Jon simply turn his back and walk down the stairs. Despite the outrage he felt, the captain decided to follow.

When Baltsaros entered his quarters, Jon was standing in the middle of the room, his arms crossed over his chest. He'd taken to wearing a sun-bleached pair of green pants that were cut off just below the knee and, like most of the crew, went shirtless in the tropical heat.

Baltsaros noticed for the first time that Jon was now wearing his hair tied back in a short tail, the dark-brown curls falling softly down the back of his neck.

"Do you know how frustrating you are?" Jon asked when Baltsaros stopped, his face unreadable.

Baltsaros frowned; he didn't have the patience for Jon's ridiculous complaints. The gracefully muscled young man just continued to stare hard at Baltsaros and, after a long minute, the captain's eyes widened.

"You want me to admit that I'm frustrating?" he asked, confused.

He watched the muscles move in Jon's jaw and realized that the man was furious. Baltsaros reached up and rubbed the shoulder that had hit the deck when he'd been unexpectedly thrown down by Jon.

"Jon, I don't have time for this," Baltsaros said and turned to go.

"The wind won't start to blow just by you staring at it. You have plenty of time," said Jon, his voice low and angry.

Baltsaros turned back to the young man in astonishment.

"You think we're going to die, don't you?" Jon asked.

They stood a long time, staring at each other in the sun-dappled room. Finally, Baltsaros clenched his jaw and nodded. It felt strangely good to be admitting it.

"Why?" asked Jon, taking a step forward.

"Even if the wind were to start blowing right now, we would not have enough food or water to last us until we reached Madierus. There is still a great, empty expanse of ocean between us and the island," Baltsaros said softly.

What had made the island so appealing was also its downfall. It was hard to get to because of the paucity of surrounding islands; getting to the small tropical island was no easy task, even for the most seasoned sailor. That it was just a tiny green dot in a wide sea of blue, so very easy to miss, was something that Baltsaros counted on when it came to his enemies; *Baal's Heart* had unfortunately fallen prey to the same dangerous isolation.

"Was that so hard?" Jon's blue-grey eyes searched his face.

"I don't understand," Baltsaros replied slowly. What was Jon trying to accomplish?

"You tell me *nothing*. Do you realize that? Almost everything I know about you comes from talking to other people. I know how you like to have your cock sucked," Jon's face coloured slightly. "But I know next to nothing about what goes on in your head. I've been asking you for days whether we were close to our destination—a place I know nothing about, I might add—and you wouldn't say. Am I not worth answering? Am I not asking the right questions? *What's wrong with you?*" asked Jon angrily.

Baltsaros felt the heaviness in his chest press at him.

"There is nothing wrong with me," he replied curtly.

"That is utter bullshit. For one thing, you haven't come near me in over a week. That in *itself* is cause to worry... And I *am* worried," said Jon, re-crossing his arms.

Baltsaros opened his mouth to refute the claim but realized that it was true; apart from sharing a bed for sleep, the men had not spent any time together. With his lips pressed together Baltsaros scowled at Jon.

"I've been preoccupied with the fact that we will never reach Madierus. The death of an entire crew is not something to be taken lightly," he said, speaking slowly to stress his irritation.

"And yet you could," said Jon, pointing at him. "Do you want to make me believe that you would actually care if everyone died around you, including me?"

At this Baltsaros started shaking his head; Jon spoke the truth but for one thing.

"I would care very much if you died, Jon," he said softly, but Jon narrowed his eyes at the captain.

"I wonder if you would," Jon said, his voice flat with restrained emotion.

Baltsaros pressed his lips together and sighed softly.

"That's not what I care about at the moment," Jon continued. "You're angry. I can feel it. I can see it. You're *furious*. And do you know why? *Because you're not in control.* There is nothing you can do to make this ship move any faster."

Again, it was the truth. Baltsaros felt his jaw tighten.

"I'm not an idiot," said Jon. "You brought me on board to use my powers of observation… And this is me observing a captain that is so caught up in a battle against nature and his own past that he's driven himself half-mad. Do you know that you've called me Tom three times in the past few days?" Baltsaros frowned. "You've barely eaten, you haven't bathed, and you've been treating me like I'm just a bedwarmer. This is not your uncle's ship; this is not the northern sea. There are plenty of fish in the water… We'll make do. We're not going to starve to death."

Baltsaros shook his head.

"We don't have enough fresh water… It's impossible."

Is it?

"Then why not kill off some of the crew?" asked Jon, his eyes suddenly shrewd. "That would save some water."

Baltsaros's eyes went wide. Was Jon serious?

"You know why you won't? *You're not your uncle.* You haven't failed anyone. You may not actually care about anyone on board, but you'll do your best to keep them alive, won't you? Because that's what you do." The young man fell silent again.

Baltsaros's head was starting to hurt, and he looked down. What did Jon know? The frustration and anger of the past few days felt like they were bleaching Baltsaros's bones; he wanted to kill something.

"Baltsaros… Why did I have to learn from Calum that you were horrifically abused? Why not just tell me these things?" Jon's voice had softened when he spoke up again.

The heavy, burning sensation in Baltsaros's chest rose to his throat, the blood singing in his ears.

"The man is dead. What does it matter?" he growled.

"It matters because you've spent your entire adult life trying to prove to yourself that you're not your uncle," Jon retorted. "And that you don't need anyone but yourself."

Baltsaros lifted his head and stared at Jon. When had he ever needed anyone else?

You need Jon.

The boy was the source of his weakness.

Is he?

Baltsaros felt strangely dizzy.

"It occurred to me for the first time today that you might not actually know when you're suffering. You're so fucking damaged that you can't even tell when you're acting strange. Calum said something earlier that I found interesting. He thinks you've always been this self-possessed, unfeeling creature, but that you saw something in the cold depths that brought out a new strength in you. Is he right? What did you see, Baltsaros?"

Baltsaros was back in the barrel again, staring wide-eyed into the solid blackness that surrounded him and shaking so hard that his teeth felt like they would break against each other. Blinking hard to clear the vision, Baltsaros walked unsteadily to the bed and sat down on the edge.

"I saw myself," Baltsaros said quietly. "And it scared me."

Jon took a step towards Baltsaros, and the older man held up a hand.

"Don't," he said. "I'm not well. You're absolutely right."

As he shook his head and frowned, Jon continued to approach.

"I'm not afraid of you," he said.

Baltsaros grimaced.

"You should be. I'm not a good man," he muttered. "I might hurt you. The urge exists within me." However, he leaned his head gratefully against Jon's smooth side when the younger man reached him.

"Listen to me, Baltsaros. You once told me that you would cherish my informed opinions. Well, this is an informed opinion: you have made the best out of what you were granted at birth. I know it's proof that there's something deeply fucked up about me, but I wouldn't have you any other way. Fate has thrown us together for some reason... Now can we please proceed to the stage in this partnership where you start actually sharing with me?" Jon's fingers rubbed the base of the captain's skull, exactly where the tension was the worst.

Baltsaros closed his eyes. *Partnership.* It meant an equality between two individuals.

"I... will try," he said slowly, testing out the idea. He heard Jon exhale hard.

"Good," Jon said.

Baltsaros turned his head so that his cheek rested against the taut muscles of Jon's midriff. The idea that he could need someone was still very foreign to him, but Jon's words rang with truth, and he felt it in the pit of his stomach. They stayed this way for a long time, Baltsaros leaning against Jon's side while the other stroked his hair. Though he still felt on edge, Jon's presence was soothing. The boy was right.

"Did you kill Tom?" asked Jon suddenly.

Startled, Baltsaros's eyes opened, and his brow furrowed. He pulled his head away from Jon and stared up at him in confusion.

"Why would I kill Tom?" he asked, bewildered.

Jon fiddled with the leather thong in Baltsaros's hair, his storm-grey eyes troubled.

"We embraced," he said, his voice barely above a whisper.

Baltsaros felt a sharp pang of something in his chest but shoved it away.

"And you think I killed Tom because I knew about it? *This* is what's been bothering you?" Baltsaros asked, astounded. He sighed when Jon nodded and pulled his hands out of his hair, opening them up against his lips to kiss his palms.

"No. I did not kill Tom. Nor would I kill him now, were he alive at this confession," he said quietly. With a feeling like he was venturing out into strange waters, he offered up something else.

Why not?

"I... miss Tom," Baltsaros said.

It was true. Since Tom's death, his mind kept turning over and over again to his former first mate, no matter how he tried to still

279

his thoughts. It was honestly no surprise to him that he had called Jon by the other man's name. He missed the easy connection he had with Tom, the way that they were almost constantly in sync, working together like two pieces of the same machine aboard the ship.

He missed Tom's rough hands, his unquenchable desire, his love of pain. His feelings for the muscular youth did not run nearly as deep or even in the same direction as they did with Jon, but they were there.

When he looked up, Baltsaros saw that Jon's eyes had gone glassy with tears; he stood and wrapped his arms around the young man. Strangely, the captain felt like he had just sacrificed a small part of himself with that concession. The thought shook him.

Jon suddenly tensed, and Baltsaros pulled away, eyes darting over the young man's face with worry. Had he said too much? Was Jon about to launch into another angry tirade against him?

"What is it?" he asked. Baltsaros watched in amazement as Jon's face split into a wide grin.

"Can't you feel it?" he asked, his voice high with excitement.

Baltsaros started to shake his head but stopped.

From the open door came a strong, cool gust. The wind had started to blow.

24

LANDWARD HO!

J on pulled himself out of Baltsaros's arms and ran out the door, feeling ridiculously excited. When he got amidship, Jon was amused to see that the rest of the crew had stopped what they were doing and were standing quietly on deck, just feeling the breeze.

The ship was moving again.

Seemingly at once, everyone started jostling against each other, running to stations that had long been unmanned because of the lack of wind. Then all heads turned to the quarterdeck, and they waited in a hush.

Baltsaros stood a long time holding his sextant, facing the sun hanging above the horizon. When he pulled it away from his eye, the captain's smile was wide.

"All right boys, helm's a-lee! We need to tack some to the south. But… We are on our way home!" yelled Baltsaros, laughing.

Katherine grinned and then turned to the crew.

"You heard him, you lazy curs! Let's get this tub turned due south. Square the sails! Bring a spring on her cable!" she shouted.

Jon ran to the gunwale and started to climb the shrouds. Turning his head as he ascended, he caught the captain's eye. Jon could tell that the man was still worried about supplies running out before they made land, but at least he was smiling, something that he hadn't seen in what felt like a long time.

Baltsaros winked at Jon, his face creased in a sharp-toothed grin. For the first time in weeks, Jon didn't feel anxious or lost; instead, he was filled with hope.

"And… hells… Splice the mainbrace! I think we all deserve it!" yelled the captain, calling for rum to be distributed to the sailors. A great cheer went up through the crew, Jon hollering with them.

On the captain's bench, up on the quarterdeck, Jon lay with his head in Baltsaros's lap. He gazed up at the stars and was, as always, filled with wonder at their astonishing number. He knew there were no more stars above the ocean than there had been above his small harbour town, but something about them seemed more awe-inspiring from the deck of a beautiful ship.

A moving ship.

He turned his head and saw that Baltsaros was watching him, his dark eyes catching the light of the hanging lanterns. The captain seemed quietly amused.

Jon smiled.

"What?" he asked.

The corners of Baltsaros's eyes crinkled with his sudden grin.

"I'm happy," said the captain, a tiny shrug lifting his shoulder.

Jon nodded.

"Good. More rum please," he said.

Baltsaros chuckled and tilted the flask carefully, pouring a trickle of the dark amber liquid into Jon's mouth.

After swallowing it down, Jon turned to look at the stars again; he was feeling similarly loose limbed and happy, a state enhanced by the spiced rum they were sharing.

"The wind is strong. At this rate, we may make it home before we have to eat Brutus." said Baltsaros.

Jon looked to the captain and gasped in mock horror.

"Don't even joke about that, you savage," he said. Jon knew there was a good chance that they would be miserable and hungry for the last few days of the trip; however, that was later. Tonight, everything was perfect.

"Tell me about Madierus," Jon asked.

Baltsaros lifted his head and looked at the stars. His long, light-brown hair hung loose over his shoulders, and his relief at their progress had stripped years off his sharp features.

"It's a beautiful little emerald of an island," the captain said softly, his accent exotic like the land he described. "The harbour is actually a naturally deep lagoon. When the ship is anchored there, no one can see her from the waters beyond; it's a perfect hiding place for us. The water is so blue and so warm that it will literally make your heart ache with its perfection and the sand so white that you will think you have gone blind to colour. The island itself is an old, dead volcano; it's incredibly lush, lots of coconut and palm trees. We planned the town further back from the harbour and built it up to mimic organic shapes so that the buildings don't take away from the natural splendour. It's really quite something. Everyone has their own gardens, but there is a plethora of fruit everywhere growing wild. The figs are especially good."

Jon smiled, his eyes closed trying to picture this paradise; it was strange to think that he hadn't known what a fig was half a year ago.

"Where do you live?" he asked. "Though I suppose I should be asking where do *we* live since I'm to join you in this fantasy. Describe it."

When Baltsaros didn't respond, Jon opened his eyes. There were deep lines in the captain's forehead as his eyes searched the dark waters; he seemed to be struggling with the answer.

After a long minute, Jon slowly sat up and looked at the captain, a feeling of dread coming over him.

"What are you not telling me?" he asked.

Baltsaros's mouth twitched, and he rubbed his hand over the

short stubble of his chin. When he looked over at Jon, his eyes held a desire for forgiveness in them.

Jon's heart sank. His entire relationship with Baltsaros seemed doomed to be one long strand of misunderstandings, lies, and personal struggles linked together by small jewel-like moments of clarity. Was it ever going to get easier to love the unpredictable captain?

Love? asked Tom's voice in his head. *That's unwise, ducky.*

Jon frowned at the phantom in his mind; perhaps he'd had too much rum already.

"Baltsaros? What is it?" he asked, disturbed by the man's apprehension.

"It's going to sound far worse than it is, Jon. Believe me when I say this," Baltsaros said and took a long pull from the flask he held, the chased silver flashing with reflected light.

Jon waited silently, his hands curled into fists in his lap.

"There's a beautiful castle built into the mountainside. It has high stained-glass windows and graceful arches covered in colourful mosaics; the inner courtyard is one of the most breathtaking things you will ever see, with its reflecting pools, fountains, and orange trees. The smell alone..." He stopped, a small smile on his face. "That's where I live. Where *we* shall live."

Jon frowned and shook his head.

"So you're really an evil pirate king after all?" he asked, his tone artificially light. He didn't understand why Baltsaros was treating this information with such trepidation; Jon had grown up in a castle, albeit an old decrepit one. Being a king or a lord was a good thing, no?

As he laughed a little harshly, Baltsaros nodded his head.

"Yes, I am indeed king. Of a very, very small kingdom. It's a ridiculous affectation... and not one that I would have chosen myself. I like to think of the island as being the same as my ship... all men and women equal..."

"Baltsaros," Jon whispered. What was the man working up to?

"I never desired to be king..." Baltsaros said finally, looking desperately into Jon's eyes. "...but my wife desired to be queen."

Up on his feet before he realized it, Jon stared down hard at Baltsaros.

Told you so, said Tom, chuckling.

"Wife? When the hell were you going to tell me you were married?" he choked out.

Baltsaros's hands were up in supplication. Jon could see he was saying something, but he was so caught up in the shock of the confession that he couldn't understand the man. It had never crossed his mind that the captain might have a wife.

Baltsaros rose and grabbed at Jon to pull him into his embrace. Jon struggled against him, the other man's more powerful arms trapping him tight.

"Please, Jon. Listen to me. This changes *nothing.* You must understand me," said Baltsaros, his mouth right near Jon's ear.

Jon brought up his knee hard in the captain's groin and gasped in relief as the man released him. He reeled back against the railing, his eyes wide.

Baltsaros groaned; he was bent over and clutching his pearls in his hand. Breathing hard, the captain croaked out a few words.

"That was uncalled for," Baltsaros said, his voice hoarse. When he glanced up at Jon, his face was drawn with pain. "I should have you keelhauled," he joked weakly.

Jon shook his head, the immediate shock of the news beginning to recede.

"When were you planning on telling me?" he asked, furious.

After a moment, the captain scooped up the fallen flask and sat back heavily on the bench, rubbing at his crotch.

"Honestly? If I could have gone our entire lives without ever telling you, I would have. However, I was planning on simply introducing her to you when we arrived," he said, wincing as he shifted slightly on the hard bench. After taking a sip of rum, he held the flask out to Jon.

He just stared at the captain's hand for a moment and then

sighed, crossing the planks back towards Baltsaros. Pulling the rum from the older man's grasp, he drained the rest of it in one long gulp. The spicy liquid burned his throat going down, and Jon welcomed the feeling.

"Why would you do that to me?" he asked, his voice harsh.

Baltsaros's eyes went flat for an instant; his habit of dropping all expression when he was attempting to speak plainly was one that Jon had begun to recognize. From his experience it either meant the captain had something worse to say or that he wanted to make sure that Jon understood him fully.

Thankfully, in this case it was the latter.

"You will see when you meet her. It's a marriage of convenience. A political and financial partnership... nothing more. There was no point in telling you ahead of time. I wanted you to see with your own eyes that she holds me in contempt," said Baltsaros quietly. "Especially with your gift, it should be obvious that there is no love lost between us. And, as I said, it changes nothing between you and me."

Jon eyed him a moment; it was about as genuine as Baltsaros got. He turned around and sat back down on the bench, resting his elbows on his knees as he leaned forward, trying to absorb the information.

"Still. Baltsaros... You should have said something. Sometimes I think you have only the vaguest notion of what it means to be honest. Are there no words for honesty or truth in your language?" he said. He heard Baltsaros sigh before the man's warm hand touched his back.

"I'm sorry," said the captain.

No, he's not, said Tom.

Hush. Go away, Jon thought hard at the ghost in his head. He could have sworn that he heard Tom's laughter faintly in the night air. Definitely too much rum.

Baltsaros was looking at him curiously, and Jon just shook his head.

"I'm going to bed," he said. "I'm tired, and I'm trying not to be angry at you." Jon lurched to his feet and took a few steps towards the stairs. He stopped with his hand on the railing.

"Are you coming? I demand restitution for the wrongs you have committed against me," Jon said solemnly.

He was gratified when, a moment later, Baltsaros's quiet steps followed him down.

K atherine cracked the wooden sword hard against Jon's ribs, and he yelped, falling over.

"Gods, woman! You don't have to be so damn rough with me," he said, rubbing the welt on his skin that he knew would soon be a bruise.

Katherine swung the practice sword a few times at him, barely missing his head.

"You think that's rough, young man? Can you picture the mess that a real sword would make of you? Get your guard up. Jon, seriously... You're sloppy," she said, her expression one of amusement.

Jon groaned and pressed his fists against the boards before getting his feet under him. Before she had a chance to react, he sprang forward from his crouch and had her pinned to the deck in an instant, her practice sword spiraling overboard to sink below the choppy green waters. He grinned down at her, but Jon was soon in great pain as she managed to snap her wrist free and jab her stiff fingers at his throat.

He coughed and writhed on the deck as she laughed.

"What? You don't think I learned under Calum as well? I know your tricks, pup. The next time you try to pin me like that, you'll be following that wooden sword overboard," she said, pushing at him with a long-toed bare foot playfully.

When Jon managed to suck enough air into his lungs he started to laugh.

"I hate you," he said, smiling. "You're a terrible excuse for a woman."

Katherine kicked him hard in the side and then sat down on an empty crate, wiping the sweat from her face.

Jon joined her after a moment, thankfully accepting the small bladder of water that she offered. There was not much fresh water left on the ship; every drop counted, and hoarding was met with stiff punishment. Jon looked up to where the captain was watching them with obvious amusement and scowled.

Baltsaros smiled and looked away.

Chuckling softly, Katherine shook her head.

"Goddess, you two are pathetic," she said, smiling.

Jon felt his face get hot. He sat awkwardly for a few moments, frowning down at his hands.

"He told me about his wife," he said and lifted his eyes to watch her face.

Katherine's eyebrows shot up, and she pursed her lips.

"He did? Well, scupper that," the woman said, her gaze flicking up to Baltsaros for a second before her dark-brown eyes settled back on Jon.

He felt himself tense.

"You knew? Gods, of course you knew... Why the hell didn't you tell me? You all know, don't you? Have you all just been laughing at the poor naïve boy this whole time?" he asked, his tone peevish.

Katherine reached over and squeezed his arm.

"Nah... I wasn't laughing. I'm actually surprised he told you already," she said.

"You are?" Jon replied. "Isn't it the kind of thing that you should mention when you're... uh... fucking someone?" he said, feeling uncomfortably crass.

Katherine laughed and leaned her shoulder against his, a friendly touch.

"You are doing way more than just fucking, my dear," she said, her grin sly. "But yes... I would have waited until you met the ice queen herself before telling you I was hitched to a cunt colder than the northern sea. Seeing in person how much they loathe each other would have dulled the shock of the news somewhat, I think. Now you just get to dwell and go all miserable, creating scenarios in your head."

Jon huffed out a short, bitter laugh; the image of Baltsaros and his wife in the marriage bed had already started plaguing his dreams. However, with Katherine backing up what the captain had already claimed, Jon felt slightly better. Maybe Baltsaros was right. Maybe it didn't change anything.

He sighed.

They would be there in a fortnight if the wind and weather held, though the fresh water would only last another week at best. Jon shoved the thought from his mind and stood, flexing his shoulders.

"Find me another sword, woman." he said and ducked when the lithe woman levelled a punch at his head.

J on was taking a caulk on deck when he heard the first shout. Opening his eyes blearily, Jon looked around, wondering what it was that had awoken him. When he heard nothing further, Jon crossed his arms more firmly over his chest, nudging his head back against the gunnysacks that he had piled in the shade of the sails. No sooner had Jon closed his eyes than he heard another shout. It sounded like one of the cabin boys was yelling.

Jon sat up, blinking sleepily. There it was again; this time Jon heard the words clear as day:

"Ship! Ship off starboard! Sail ho! Sail ho!"

Jon rose to his feet and padded towards the side of the ship to squint at the horizon. True enough, there was a dark smudge in the distance.

A small thrill of excitement shivered through him as it always did when they approached another ship. The crew was down to the barest of rations; the "us or them" mentality that came with attacking other ships would be magnified due to their current vulnerability. There was a good chance that the other ship would be in the same dire straits; perhaps their supplies would be just as low.

Jon glanced up at the captain. Baltsaros stood with the spyglass to his eye, assessing the other ship. After a moment he lowered it, his face serious as he rubbed his jaw in thought. With their reduced crew, dead front gunners, and out-of-commission front starboard carronade, the captain was being cautious.

However, after a moment Jon saw Baltsaros nod at Katherine. The captain's eyes then swept the deck, settling on Jon. With a beckoning hand, Baltsaros called him up to talk over plans.

B altsaros stared hard at his men. After a long silence, he spoke, his voice ringing out over the assembled crowd.

"We are down to the last of our rations," he said, his dark eyes running over the crew. "This means we go hungry very soon, and we still have over a week to go before we make land. However, there is a ship, a large galleon, just at the horizon. Catching up to her will cost us time... And she may actually have nothing to offer us. Could be that she's in worse shape than we are. So... I leave it to you. What say you, men? Do we take the chance and try our luck with plunder, or do we sail home and tighten our belts?"

Though the captain was unquestionably in charge, it always astonished Jon when he asked his crew to pick their fate. This was the closest thing to equality that Jon had ever seen, and it amazed him that it happened at the behest of a man devoid of a natural moral compass, who only pretended to have an interest in the lives of his men.

After some muttering and nodding, the crowd settled down. Beard was the first to raise his hand. In the tense silence, they all heard the giant speak one word in his booming voice:

"Attack!"

. . .

Getting to the other ship actually proved to be somewhat difficult. They lost nearly a day tacking back and forth against the strong headwind. Jon spent the time reviewing again and again the role he would play in the initial attack. Since their numbers were so low, they would all have to play multiple parts. Jon, his worth deemed unusually high by the biased captain, would hang back as the crew boarded the ship; he was to man the two remaining carronades along the starboard side.

Powder, pound, ball, light, and duck were the instructions given to him by his fellow gunners. He felt a little ill.

Finally, the other ship was close enough to hail. She was a huge, multi-tiered thing, four masts and an aft castle that towered high above the quarterdeck on their own ship. The ship was heavy in the water and unwieldy; it boasted of a cargo hull full of something.

"Ahoy!" yelled Katherine when the two ships were close enough. There were no men on deck, and the ship was strangely quiet. Katherine waited a moment before repeating her cry. The second time brought about some movement in the stern of the ship, and they spotted a man scurrying for cover behind barrels.

"Go away!" was the shouted reply.

Jon frowned. Something felt off. Katherine was facing the captain, discussing the use of grappling hooks, when Jon spotted someone else on board the heavy ship. The figure ducked back belowdecks but not before Jon had seen the bright red, weeping rash on the man's cheeks. He swallowed hard, his heart sinking.

"Captain," he said loudly.

Baltsaros turned to look at him, his stark brows high.

"We have to get away from that ship," continued Jon nervously.

Frowning, the captain closed the gap between them, coming to stand next to Jon.

"What do you see, Jon?" he asked, looking out at the galleon.

"I think the men on board are infected," he replied. "It looks like the weeping plague."

Baltsaros closed his eyes, the disappointment plain on his face. It was all for naught; they would only bring death to the *Baal's Heart* if they boarded the other ship.

He was startled a moment later when Baltsaros's eyes snapped open, his hands coming down on Jon's shoulders.

"Your mother died of the weeping plague, didn't she?" he asked Jon, his fingers digging into the younger man.

Jon nodded.

"Did you contract it?" Baltsaros asked, staring at him intently.

Jon frowned.

"Yes. But a mild form. Why?" he replied.

With a laugh, Baltsaros dragged him forward and kissed his forehead.

"You're immune," he said happily.

J on tied the rowboat to the end of the rope ladder and heaved the heavy bag over his shoulder. He made his way carefully up the side of the hull and dropped down over the high gunwale.

A few feet away were the two men they had been communicating with. Covered in horrible, weeping sores and obviously skeptical about Jon's immunity to the disease, they kept their distance. The younger of the two, a swarthy man with dark curling hair and a deep frown on his high brow spoke first.

"I'm Malik," he said hoarsely, his thin lips blistered from the disease. He pointed to his companion, a middle-aged man with ashen hair and a slightly amused look on his face, one brow raised in curiosity. "This is Nathaniel."

The older man sketched a quick bow.

"Welcome aboard the *Maiden's Bounty*," said Nathaniel, a touch sardonically. "We would have rolled out the red carpet for you, but, as you can see, we're feeling rather poorly at the moment."

The man had friendly hazel eyes and a slight gap between his front teeth. Jon found himself smiling back; the man was immediately likeable. With a grunt, Jon dumped the burlap sack down on the boards.

"Well, I'll have you mended in no time," he said. The sack was full of ointments and tinned poultices that the captain had made up. Jon hoped it was enough. "In return for some supplies," he added.

Malik crossed his arms.

"You can have anything you want. We won't need it soon enough," he said, fatalistically.

Jon frowned and looked around.

"Where is the rest of the crew?" he asked. A vessel of this size would have a crew upwards of two hundred men.

Nathaniel laughed harshly.

"You're looking at it," he said.

Jon's eyebrows shot up, and his heart thudded hard in his chest. All of a sudden Baltsaros's insistence that he was immune to the horrible plague was a slim comfort. What if the captain was wrong? As he attempted to still his fear, Jon looked from one man to the other.

"All right. Let's see what you got."

A few hours later, Jon yanked off his gloves and waved to Beard across the water. The huge man started pulling the rope that was tied to the stern of the small rowboat, now piled high with supplies enough to last the crew for the rest of the journey home.

When he turned back to the two men, Jon was dismayed to see that Malik was slumped against the mast, obviously suffering greatly. Baltsaros had explained that the disease was transmitted by tiny, invisible creatures in the fluid that oozed out of the red sores. Once a person was infected, the disease progressed rapidly, normally killing within five days though often sooner.

Malik and Nathaniel had been sick for four days so far; Jon hoped it was not too late to save them. The fact that they were still alive seemed to point to the men being resistant to the disease; perhaps they were part of the small percentage, like Jon, that wouldn't be carried off by the plague.

N early a week passed. Thankfully, the captain had been right about Jon's immunity because he didn't fall ill himself as he nursed the two men back to health. Malik, being sicker, had a close brush with death, but he soon recovered.

When Jon ushered them aboard the *Baal's Heart*, he wasn't prepared for the thunderous cheering and applause that met him as he stepped up and over the side of the ship.

As Katherine explained with a dimpled smile, not only had he saved the lives of Baltsaros's men, he had made two valuable additions: Nathaniel was an experienced cartographer, and Malik had just finished his apprenticeship as shipwright.

Blushing, Jon accepted the tankard of dark beer and grinned sheepishly. When he looked up he saw Baltsaros atop a large crate, his arms crossed over his chest and a proud smile on his face. The captain nodded.

Good job.

Jon felt warm all over, and he blinked hard a few times to dry the tears that had sprung up in his eyes at the unexpected and hearty welcome. As he held his cup aloft, Jon looked over the crowd and smiled wide.

"May the wind fill our sails, and the calm waters spur us on quickly!" he yelled. "Landward ho!" He drank down a great gulp of beer, some of it running down his chest. The voices of all the men rose up as one.

"Landward ho!"

25

THE TIES THAT BIND

*The main difference between a cat and a lie is that
a cat only has nine lives.*

— MARK TWAIN

J on looked down at himself and sighed.

"Is this really necessary?" he asked. "I feel ridiculous." He lifted up the corner of the sleeveless blue tunic, its long hem decorated with strange abstract black and gold shapes.

Baltsaros frowned at him and straightened the collar over the loose, gathered white shirt underneath.

"Yes," he said simply and began to tie a silken black sash around the younger man's waist.

Jon obligingly moved his arms out of the way and watched the captain's face as he dressed him in the strange outfit. Ever since the island of Madierus had come into view the previous evening, Baltsaros had been acting preoccupied. While everyone else aboard seemed to be in a near-frenzy of excitement, the captain just seemed weary and distracted.

Jon chewed the inside of his lip.

"I never thought I would say this... But I'd rather be naked," he said, smiling.

While it was said in an attempt to lighten the captain's mood, it was largely true. After so much time spent wearing nothing but a pair of thin trousers, Jon felt hot and uncomfortable in so many layers. However, he was pleased that his jest made Baltsaros look up and grin, an easy humour glinting in his dark-brown eyes.

Jon loved the captain's face. One minute, it was a stark, almost cruel landscape; the next, it was creased into a charmingly guile-less smile. The corners of Baltsaros's eyes crinkled attractively when he was amused, the lines accentuated by a long life of squinting against the bright sun while at sea. Jon could see that Baltsaros had shaved close; the skin of his chin would be soft if Jon were to reach out and touch it now. Jon knew that later today it would be rough like sandpaper and leave red marks on his neck when Baltsaros kissed him there, and he *would* kiss him. The captain had reiterated this morning that nothing would change between them, that their relationship was sacrosanct as far as he was concerned. Jon held on to that promise like a man with a purpose; he would be damned if he would stand for anything else.

"I doubt very much that you would like to appear in the nude in front of my court. Are you so proud of the stripes you have earned?" Baltsaros said, roughly grabbing Jon's backside with a large hand and squeezing.

With a gasp, Jon leaned into Baltsaros to try to escape the pain; it had been two days since his "punishment", and he was still incredibly tender. Jon felt a shudder of desire go through him with the sensation, and he heard the captain laugh softly against him. Eyes closed, Jon replayed in his mind the lesson he had learned.

J on frowned.

"You don't think you deserve to be punished for dropping one of my books overboard?" asked Baltsaros, his teeth sharp and eyes dark. "That one in particular will be especially hard to replace."

Jon was confused because his senses were telling him that the captain was exaggerating the book's worth in an attempt to justify punishing him. Baltsaros's face was angry, but there was the barest hint of humour in his hooded glare.

Nervous, Jon licked his lips and shook his head.

What are you up to?

"I already said I was sorry. It was an accident," he said calmly.

While the captain had playfully penalised him in the past for what he had deemed were minor infractions, the punishments meted out were always in the form of long drawn-out sessions of almost torturous sex where Jon was held on the brink of orgasm, leaving him a shuddering, sobbing wreck in the aftermath.

This was different.

Baltsaros had something else in mind, and it both terrified and excited Jon. He was willing to submit to Baltsaros but only within reason. The problem was that he and the captain had different ideas of what was considered reasonable.

"I disagree, my love," said Baltsaros. Jon immediately felt a little helpless. *My love.* The words always took away part of his resolve, though meaningless they were; the captain knew this and took full advantage of it. "You disobeyed me in that you brought the book outside to begin with. I told you that the pages were fragile."

Jon shook his head.

"How am I supposed to keep track of all your ridiculous rules?" he asked, his dark brows high.

Immediately he regretted using those words. Baltsaros's face took on the cast of real anger for a split second. Knowing how talented he was at digging his own grave, Jon pressed his lips together and waited silently. Though the mischievous glint returned to Baltsaros's eyes a heartbeat later, Jon grew incredibly wary of what the unpredictable man had in mind.

After taking a step back, Baltsaros crossed his arms.

"Strip," the captain said, his voice quietly authoritative.

With his head tilted slightly at Baltsaros, Jon fumbled at his belt; starting to feel some anticipation break through his reservations, he stepped out of his pants and started to approach the captain. However, Baltsaros held up a hand and stopped him.

"*Kneel.*" It was a hissed order. The captain's face was set in dangerous lines.

Jon's breath hitched in his throat, and he dropped immediately to his knees on the soft rug. A little relieved when the captain smiled, Jon was confused when he didn't come any closer.

Instead, Baltsaros walked to the chest at the foot of the bed and opened it up, looking for something; Jon watched him curiously, heart beating swiftly in his chest. Finally, Baltsaros straightened and came towards Jon with something in his hands. It looked like the captain was holding a few bundles of something red and a piece of dark material.

Though he began to turn around in place on his knees as Baltsaros stepped behind him, Jon stopped when the captain made a sharp, discouraging sound.

What is this? thought Jon, excitement and trepidation making his pulse race further.

He shivered slightly when he felt Baltsaros's hand on his shoulder and was surprised when he heard the other man sink to his knees behind him.

"It's time for a lesson in obedience," purred the captain in Jon's ear.

His throat went dry, and he felt his body react as strongly to the words as if Baltsaros's hands were on his cock instead of just painting shapes with his fingertips on Jon's back. Surprised at his own breathless desire, he nodded quickly.

"Good boy," said Baltsaros and kissed Jon lightly on the side of his neck, right where his pulse was jumping under his skin.

The captain slowly stroked his hands down Jon's arms, and then forcibly bent them behind his back. Jon's first instinct was to struggle, but he quashed it, curious to see what Baltsaros intended.

Good boy.

The words had caused a warm sensation in his loins, and he realized that yes, he wanted to be a good boy. The thought was strangely thrilling.

Behind Jon's back, Baltsaros positioned his arms and hands so that his forearms were parallel to each other, his fingers clasped around his elbows. Jon then felt Baltsaros move one hand away to start looping something around his left wrist.

Jon gasped; the captain was tying him up. A bit of panic was added to the symphony of emotions playing inside him, and Jon cleared his throat.

"W-what are you doing?" he asked timidly. Baltsaros didn't answer but passed the rope around again. Jon felt the bundle of it brush against his back softly, and he shivered again. Baltsaros slid the rope up over his shoulder, the length tickling him gently; it was a sharp contrast to how it bound his arms tightly, biting into his skin.

Working in silence, the captain brought the rope up over his other shoulder, beside his neck, and back down again. Slowly twisting and knotting as he went, Baltsaros's strong hands stroked Jon's skin each time before he slid the rope into place.

Jon found himself holding his breath and releasing it in time to Baltsaros's short caresses. The red hempen rope became a knotted net that covered him from shoulder to hip, binding him tight. The panic he had felt earlier started to diminish as Baltsaros's hands lulled him with their steady, rhythmic movements. However, when Baltsaros paused to tie the soft, dark strip of material over Jon's eyes, fear robbed him of breath for a moment.

"Baltsaros, no! This isn't ok. I'm not ok with this. Untie me. I can't breathe. Please!" he panted, a kind of hysteria gripping him as he started to struggle.

Baltsaros's hands came around him quickly, holding him still. Jon could feel the captain's broad chest against his back and his warm breath on his neck. Robbed of his sight, he had an increased awareness of Baltsaros's hands on his skin; in the warm, dark silence, Jon trembled as the tension slowly leached out of his body, held there by the man who knew exactly how to defeat him with pleasure.

When Jon felt calmer, the captain gently released him, returning to the patterns of rope he was creating. No longer fighting his bonds, Jon felt a curious peace settle over him; Baltsaros was showing him yet another way to surrender.

With his head bowed, Jon breathed a shuddering breath; the experience was pushing his emotions to the surface. He felt vulnerable, subjugated—completely under the control of a powerful man for a single purpose: Jon knew he existed in this moment only to please Baltsaros. He was at the mercy of the captain's whims... And it was intensely arousing.

Jon moaned softly when Baltsaros's hands began passing between his legs, pushing them further apart to wrap his thighs in lengths of rope. Aching for the captain's touch, Jon trembled when Baltsaros finally reached around him to softly stroke the stiffening cock hanging between his legs.

The captain soon had him coaxed to full hardness, and Jon began to thrust his hips, pushing himself with eagerness through Baltsaros's fingers. However, Jon whimpered when the captain stopped his efforts short.

"Baltsaros..." he started but then tensed as he felt a length of rope being passed behind his testicles and around the base of his cock. He held his breath as Baltsaros pulled it tight and looped it around once more, tying it off.

With a gasp at the sensation, Jon felt his cock, held ramrod stiff by the rope constricting the blood flow, begin to throb in time to his heartbeat. When a long time seemed to go by with no further contact from Baltsaros, Jon began to worry anew. The only thing he could hear of the other man was his slow, measured breathing. What was he doing?

Jon panted hard and leaned forward, frustrated. Was Baltsaros just staring at Jon? The ropes binding Jon were unyielding and the silence echoed on. Was this the punishment? When he rocked back on his hips, his bonds tightened around his thighs and chest and he gritted his teeth.

Baltsaros's hand was suddenly on him, pushing him forward.

Losing his balance, Jon landed on his chest and cheek with a grunt. He raised his hips slightly to adjust his cock beneath him, and the carpet scratched at the engorged head, causing him to groan from the sensation.

"Please, Baltsaros," he said softly. He heard the captain chuckle quietly.

Baltsaros spread Jon's legs wide on the carpet, and he held his breath in tense anticipation; but, when something cold and hard touched his skin, sliding up the back of his thigh and tapping his left buttock gently, Jon's eyes flew open in shock behind the blindfold.

"Please, *my lord*," said the captain, correcting him quietly, a natural edge of command in his voice.

"You want me to call you lord?" asked Jon quickly, confused. It seemed a ridiculous request, but whatever it was that Baltsaros held in his hand struck his skin a second later; the pain was intense, and the bound man cried out in surprise and fear. He coughed and panted hard, squirming on the carpeted floor.

"Well?" asked Baltsaros.

Jon swallowed and stammered.

"Is that it? You're my lord? Please, I don't underst—" His words were cut off when the cold thing cracked hard against the sensitive back of his thigh. Jon yelled loud; the place where he was hit was a thin line of agony, like he had been cut with a knife. It dawned on him suddenly what he was supposed to say.

Aye, that's it. Don't think, lovey. Just obey, came the voice of the phantom in Jon's head.

He pressed his lips together to hold back the sob that threatened to spill from his throat. Jon shook off the pain and whispered hoarsely:

"Please... my lord."

In response, Baltsaros laughed and stroked the switch down the curve of Jon's spine giving him a moment's respite, and tapped again at the meat of his backside, as if testing the target for resilience.

Jon whimpered.

"You were disobedient," said Baltsaros. "You were disrespectful of my belongings."

CRACK! CRACK!

Jon choked on his scream, pressing his face hard into the carpet. His skin was on fire. The captain hit him again hard on the buttocks and the backs of his thighs, and Jon felt frantic from the pain.

"Please, my lord!" he yelled. "Please!" What else could he say?

The switch slid into the cleft of Jon's ass, gliding coldly against his perineum before tracing the bottom edge of his buttock. The flesh there felt inflamed.

"Please, my lord," he said softly, panting. The weapon left his skin and he groaned in relief.

The heat from his welts and the adrenaline pumping through him were stimulating him in a strange way. He had feared the initial pain when the switch came down, but when it faded, Jon began to anticipate the next strike. He found himself wondering how much he could take and whether Baltsaros would test his limits. Jon felt a thrill go through him at the thought. He swallowed hard a moment later when he heard the captain drop back down to his knees.

"Please, my lord," he repeated, his voice weak.

His ankle was grasped hard in a big hand, and Baltsaros bent it back to secure it to the bindings around Jon's thigh, doing the same with Jon's right leg. Jon shifted on the rug; he was almost completely immobilized, legs splayed open on the floor.

He tensed, waiting for the captain to do something, anything to him... But nothing happened. Grinding his teeth in frustration, Jon turned his head, questing blindly behind him. All he could hear at first was that Baltsaros's breathing had gotten heavier. When a moment later he realized that he could now detect the shushing noise of skin passing over skin, Jon's eyebrows rose, and his heart skipped over itself in his chest.

Baltsaros was pleasuring himself.

The realization was both shocking and intoxicating, and Jon's cock surged harder in reaction. With his legs spread wide, he was perfectly exposed. The captain would be looking down at him, at the opening between his legs and at the markings that would be livid against the pale skin of his thighs and buttocks.

Jon closed his eyes and tilted his hips back a tiny bit, imagining Baltsaros's dark eyes focused on him. Not knowing whether Baltsaros was going to fuck him was driving Jon crazy. All pain was forgotten. He pictured the captain's thick cock and the man's hand sliding over it. The head would be purplish and stretched full, shiny with the pearls of fluid that would be beading at the tip.

Jon groaned and shuddered. The sound of Baltsaros stroking his cock got louder and faster, and Jon could feel the presence of the man near his skin. When he shifted his hips up again, presenting himself to the captain, Jon licked his lips and waited.

Baltsaros let out a low growl, and Jon felt something hot hit his skin and run down the cleft of his buttocks, getting cooler as it dripped onto his testicles. Jon gasped when he realized what was happening. Another spurt of hot fluid landed on his flesh. Then another.

Baltsaros was breathing fast and hard as he spilled his seed onto Jon's spread ass.

Jon moaned; it was incredible that something that should have been a degrading act was instantly and agonizingly erotic to him. With a deep grunt, Baltsaros shot a last jet of cum directly against Jon's puckered opening and collapsed forward, his chest landing on the younger man's bound ankles.

Jon panted against the pain of Baltsaros's weight on his stretched limbs, but the delicious contact of the captain's cock on him was keenly pleasurable as the man stroked the head of it through the cooling mess between his legs for a moment, spreading it over his skin.

Too soon, Baltsaros pushed away though not to leave Jon cold on the floor. Instead, the captain's hands swiftly began unravelling the pattern of knots, and Jon gasped as his twisted limbs were quickly released. He felt shaky and confused, aroused yet distraught. The blindfold was pulled away from his eyes, and he looked in despair at Baltsaros.

The man's face was slightly flushed as he pulled Jon back up to his knees to undo the ropes binding his chest and finally his arms. Jon felt like a rag doll, limbs tingling and weak.

Baltsaros's dark eyes met his, and Jon felt a little breathless at the emotion that flitted there: a deeply possessive adoration.

Jon's heart ached.

"You enjoyed punishing me?" he asked quietly, reaching out to touch the captain's cheek.

Baltsaros leaned into his hand, smiling.

"Oh Jon, very much so. You were exquisite," he said, his voice affectionate. Baltsaros slid his fingers over the dented, red markings on Jon's chest, left behind by the tight bindings. "You were perfect," he said, his voice soft.

Jon felt curiously proud.

When Baltsaros's hand finally closed over Jon's hypersensitive cock, still bound tight with rope, he hissed between his teeth at the contact. Arching his back, Jon gratefully submitted to Baltsaros's ministrations. The captain curled around behind him and pulled Jon back against his chest, stroking him swiftly and firmly.

"You're a good boy," Baltsaros murmured into Jon's ear, and he was swept up into the waves of his own shattering pleasure.

After a quick kiss and a promise to look for each other in the coming days, Jon parted company with Katherine and ran after Baltsaros once they had made it to shore. The heels of his boots sounded loud on the smooth boards of the pier rising above the beach, and Jon longed to remove his uncomfortable footwear to feel the white sand between his toes.

The island was every bit as beautiful as Baltsaros had described, and Jon was already in love.

However, there was no time to explore. Baltsaros's wife, having been notified of their arrival, had sent a carriage to retrieve them, and it stood waiting in the shade of two giant fan palms. The carriage had already been loaded up with the chest containing their belongings, and the white horses nickered softly to each other as Jon approached.

The captain, with an air of strained civility, held the door open for Jon and then followed in after him. The inside of the carriage was stuffy and smelled of wood that had been left out in the damp too long. Jon raised his eyebrows at Baltsaros, but the older man just squinted out the window.

"Welcome to my city, Jon," he said softly.

Jon followed his gaze and gasped in amazement as they passed under a tunnel of greenery, emerging into a scene from a fairy tale.

It didn't resemble any city he had ever seen. The houses and shops were set far back from the wide, cobbled street, some almost invisible beneath the foliage. What he *could* see made his eyes widen; the low buildings had smoothly curved wooden walls, not unlike the hulls of boats. Windows were round, and the doors were painted in the same colours as the flowers that seemed to burst out from every corner.

"That is the *Grog Blossom* tavern," said Baltsaros, pointing a long finger at a squat, wide building with a flower mosaic around the entrance. "You'll find Katherine there if you ever need her. Her wife serves a wonderfully brewed white beer of her own design. I hope that she has some yet." Baltsaros smiled.

Jon could see through the tavern windows that it was a large, airy space; the entire back of the building seemed to be an open, covered patio, strung with what looked like colourful lanterns.

Baltsaros kept pointing out shops and houses, once even opening the door to lean out and shout a greeting to someone. When the captain sat back down, he was smiling wide; some of the tension that had been weighing him down seemed to have melted away as he was reunited with the beautiful island. However, as they approached the graceful castle at the foot of the volcano, Baltsaros's eyes once more turned cold.

Jon was filled with dread and not knowing what to expect had him feeling on edge.

The carriage stopped at a beautiful arched portico, and Baltsaros looked at Jon thoughtfully. The captain opened his mouth to say something but decided otherwise and instead just cupped the back of Jon's head, pulling him in for a soft kiss. When he broke away, Baltsaros stared hard into Jon's eyes, his gaze flicking back and forth as if testing his resolve.

"Jon. Don't worry. Please. This is my home, and I want it to be yours too," he said gently, his fingers squeezing Jon's neck warmly.

Unfortunately, Baltsaros's words just compounded Jon's fear. He had the sinking feeling that his relationship with the captain would be tested shortly. Wanting to appear confident, Jon nodded quickly and took a deep breath.

A moment later, they were standing in the middle of a beautiful courtyard.

Baltsaros had not been exaggerating; it was a small paradise in itself with its perfumed orange trees and bubbling fountains. The columns surrounding it were so high and light with their peaked arches that they seemed terribly fragile, like lace. Small circular patterns like the one on the coverlet in their quarters aboard *Baal's Heart* were picked out in blue and gold mosaics everywhere.

Jon was enthralled when he saw the big gold and red fish swimming under flat green leaves in a star-shaped shallow pool in the middle of the courtyard. He stopped to watch them a moment; however, with a hand on Jon's arm, Baltsaros tugged him forward as he took in the breathtaking sights.

Jon couldn't understand why anyone would ever want to leave this place.

They crossed the courtyard and came to a long, wide flight of white marble steps and entered the castle through high, narrow peaked doors with stained-glass starbursts in yellows and blues high above their heads.

"The woman does have taste," said Baltsaros, looking at Jon's round eyes with a wry grin. "I will allow her that much."

As he turned his head every which way, Jon somehow managed in his distraction to miss the fact that they were walking towards a dais at the far end of the great hall. When he felt Baltsaros shake him slightly, Jon faced forward and gasped at the sight before him.

Atop the low platform, flanked by sculptures of curved dolphins, was a woman and a young girl standing in front of two elaborate thrones.

The woman was beautiful.

Though obviously older than Baltsaros, her lovely, pale skin retained the smoothness of youth. Softly waved blond hair fell below her shoulders and framed a heart-shaped face; her full lips, the colour of raspberries, were turned up in a serene smile. Standing with a graceful elegance, hands clasped in front of her, she silently watched the two men approach and stop at the foot of the stairs.

Jon turned his gaze to the girl standing next to her. She was the prettiest child Jon had ever seen, a petite, shy-looking creature of five or six with long dark hair and huge blue eyes. Her expression was timid as she stared back at Jon, her small white teeth biting softly at her pouting bottom lip.

Can ye see? asked Tom.

Jon frowned. His eyes slid back to the woman.

"Hello, husband," she said, her blue-green eyes cold as she looked down at the captain.

"Hello, wife," replied Baltsaros, his voice expressionless.

Jon felt a little strange suddenly, like a cold wind was blowing against his neck, raising goosebumps on his arms.

What do ye see? repeated the ghost in his head.

Jon stared at the woman. She was looking over their shoulders, searching for something.

For someone.

"Where is he?" the woman asked, her nostrils flaring slightly with what Jon read as trepidation. There was something about the curve of her jaw and the height of her brow that reminded him of something.

"Abetha, Eloise... I'm terribly sorry," said Baltsaros softly. "Tom was lost at sea."

Jon's vision began to swim. He watched as Abetha put a graceful hand to her mouth, her blue-green eyes wide and startled. Her eyes. Eyes that Jon had looked into a thousand times, eyes that had often winked and narrowed in amusement at him. Eyes that had looked deep into Jon's with an emotion that tore him apart. Tom's eyes.

See?

Jon slowly turned his head to the captain, his mouth dry; his mind was staggering over itself in a hurry to make sense of it. Baltsaros was watching him, his face devoid of expression.

As he blinked back furious tears, Jon stared back at the man for a moment longer before turning on his heel and walking quickly out of the castle.

Baltsaros watched Jon's departure and turned back to his wife.

She stared at him with narrowed eyes.

"You were to keep him safe," she said, her voice strangely calm despite the fury in her eyes.

Baltsaros frowned and dismissed her by going down on one knee and opening his arms, his gaze fond as he looked at Eloise. The girl smiled and ran down the stairs, her little shoes clattering on the stairs. She threw herself into Baltsaros's arms and hugged him tight. He knew that the news of her brother's death wouldn't greatly affect her; Tom had been a near stranger to her, a brother in concept only.

"How's my little wildflower?" he asked; though his affection for the girl was real enough, he found it useful that Eloise's love for him rankled Abetha. It was such a petty thing but important if he wished to turn the girl against her mother in the future.

"You've gotten so tall!" he exclaimed, hugging her back.

She giggled against him, this exciting and charming father figure she only saw for three months out of the year.

He looked up into Abetha's angry eyes and patted Eloise's back softly.

"Why don't you go on and play in the nursery, my darling. We shall see each other at supper, yes?" he said in a cheerful voice.

The little girl pulled away and looked at him lovingly with her big blue eyes before obediently running off.

Baltsaros stood, dusting off the knee of his soft black pants.

"He was a grown man, Abetha," he said as he watched the woman he called his wife sit down on her gaudy throne.

She frowned at him.

"How do I know you're not lying, Baltsaros?" She asked, "We both know how fond you are of bending the truth. Tell me, did he truly die at sea, or did he perish at your hands?" She turned her head to the left and gestured to the servant standing there. A moment later, another servant quickly stepped into the throne room with two goblets on a tray.

Baltsaros accepted his with a nod and slowly ascended the stairs.

"I promised you that no harm would come to him. That is my

only failure: making a promise I couldn't possibly keep. Tom fell overboard during a storm. That is all," he said. Baltsaros took a sip of the rich red wine in his cup and stared down at Abetha.

She looked piercingly at him, turning her own cup in her hands before drinking some down. She then turned her head towards the great doors.

"I take it that this boy you brought into my home is a replacement for my son?" she asked, her quiet voice contrasting with the bitterness of her words. "He didn't know Tom was your stepson, did he? How thoughtful of you to present the information to him thusly. Tell me, Baltsaros... Does your young lover know you are a monster?"

Baltsaros frowned as he looked towards the doors.

"Yes, wife," he said. "He does."

26

IN ALL HONESTY

*"Of course I'll hurt you. Of course you'll hurt me.
Of course we will hurt each other. But this is
the very condition of existence. To become
spring, means accepting the risk of winter. To
become presence, means accepting the risk of
absence."*

— ANTOINE DE SAINT-EXUPÉRY, THE
LITTLE PRINCE

Baltsaros walked slowly down the steps and crossed the paving stones to the pond in the middle of the sunny courtyard. He eyed the boots discarded on the ground before sitting down on the wide stone ledge surrounding the water.

Baltsaros reached his hand out and placed it on the side of Jon's head, stroking the soft brown curls. Jon was lying prone on the edge of the raised pond, his blue eyes tracking the motion of the koi swimming under the lily pads. At Baltsaros's touch, he closed his eyes, and a furrow appeared between his brows.

With a sigh Baltsaros felt something he rarely encountered: shame. How could he explain to Jon that he had kept up the lie because he, unaccountably, had found himself unable to speak of Tom? That he had left it this long only because he knew that he would be *forced* to reveal the truth? Initially the lie had simply been used to keep the sheltered young man from bolting... But he had kept it up. Why? Had he not wanted Jon to think less of him?

He frowned and bowed his head. Baltsaros felt off-balance. Jon's words came back to him:

You might not actually know when you're suffering. You're so fucking damaged...

His hand was trembling slightly. He closed his eyes and breathed deep, reaching for that calm place that was always within reach and found that it was smaller and further away than it had ever been. When he opened his eyes again, he saw that Jon was watching him.

"Do you want to see our room?" asked Baltsaros quietly after a moment. Baltsaros saw that there was recrimination in Jon's eyes as he stared at the captain, but it was eclipsed by a profound weariness.

Finally looking away, Jon pushed himself up off the ledge, stooping to retrieve his boots before motioning to Baltsaros to lead the way.

Baltsaros stood and walked swiftly to the groin-vaulted, covered walkway on the left of the main entrance. Not wishing to subject Jon to Abetha's venom, he took a different route that circumvented the throne room, leading him to what he considered his wing of the castle.

With the silent Jon padding along behind him, Baltsaros made his way to the spiral staircase and climbed two floors. When they reached the landing, Baltsaros pulled open the heavy red door and saw with a frown that his wife had not wasted any resources airing or sweeping the long hallway. He guessed that his chambers had not even been readied for his arrival.

Petty witch, he thought.

Jon followed him down the hallway to the big doors on the right. After opening them, he saw that his suspicions were confirmed. The sitting room that fronted his bedchambers was stale and dusty. The only saving grace was that everything was covered in white sheets.

Jon passed him and looked around curiously, dropping his boots to the ground.

Baltsaros reached for the bell-pull to summon a servant and then walked to the large windows, yanking back the thick red velvet curtain. Sunlight streamed into the room, bringing the air alive with floating dust motes.

Raising his eyebrows at Baltsaros, Jon finally spoke.

"That woman really despises you," he said.

Nodding, Baltsaros crossed the room and threw open the doors to his bedchamber. He opened the curtains and started pulling the white dustsheets off the huge four-poster feather bed. Hearing Jon enter the room, Baltsaros turned to watch his reaction.

His eyes wide, Jon walked towards the bed. He reached out and touched the carvings on the tall posts. There were hundreds of fanciful and grotesque figures carved into the hardwood: mermaids, centaurs, giants, skeletons, and other fanciful creatures, all rendered in exquisite detail. Jon looked back at Baltsaros.

"This is... amazing. Who carved it?" he asked in awe.

"I did," said Baltsaros. "I started it the year I claimed this island as my own."

Jon frowned and turned away, stroking his finger down the flank of a tree nymph. After a moment, he spoke softly.

"You said he had no mother," he said, dropping his hand. His accusation was coloured by melancholy. The captain could hear the meaning underneath: *why do you enjoy lying to me?*

Baltsaros wanted to pull Jon into his embrace, to kill the pain with his kisses, but he knew if he tried he would be rebuffed. He looked towards the door when he heard footsteps and excused himself.

After telling the maids to take care of airing and cleaning the sitting room, he walked back to the bedroom and shut the doors behind him. Jon was at the window, gazing down at the gardens below.

"When I said that the devil pushed him out, it was... an exaggeration of what I consider the truth. Abetha has never been a mother to those children, Jon; and, she barely knew Tom. It wasn't a complete lie," he said, hoping his answer would mollify the younger man.

Jon turned to look at Baltsaros, his face twisted in scorn.

"Not a complete lie?" he said, taking a step towards Baltsaros. "Not a *complete* lie? What part of 'don't fucking lie to me' do you *not understand?*" The last words were a strangled shout.

Jon's hands were at the black sash around his waist, untying it as he took another step towards the older man.

Baltsaros tilted his head and frowned. Suddenly Jon came at him, his leg sweeping Baltsaros's feet from under him before he had a chance to step back. When he landed hard on the floor on his back, Baltsaros grunted and then coughed out his breath as Jon fell on top of him.

The two men struggled against each other, but Jon somehow had the advantage; Calum had taught the boy well. Baltsaros soon found himself lying on the handwoven rug on his stomach, his hands tied tightly behind him with the silk sash.

In all honesty, he hadn't fought very hard.

Jon yanked off one of the captain's boots and then the other, and Baltsaros gasped when what felt like Jon's knife slid coldly against his ankle.

Tom's knife.

He lifted his head and tried to see behind him. In dismay he realized that Jon was cutting through his pant leg. It was completely outrageous, and in just a few minutes, Jon had cut most of Baltsaros's clothing off, slicing the captain's skin a few times in the process.

Baltsaros closed his eyes and waited for what he knew would follow.

However, when he heard the bed creak, he frowned. He lifted his head, turning to face it, and saw that Jon was lying on his side watching Baltsaros over the edge of the mattress as he tapped the side of the blade against his cheek.

The young man's eyes were steely grey as he glared down at Baltsaros.

"Jon?" asked Baltsaros, confused. He'd expected Jon to take his anger out on his body, a mock rape to pay the captain back for his lies.

"So you really were fucking your son," Jon said simply.

Baltsaros groaned and closed his eyes, pressing his forehead down on the rug.

"Stepson, Jon. Not of my loins," he replied. "He was as much my son as Reginald was your father." When he looked up again at Jon, he was nodding thoughtfully.

"Why?" he asked, his tone challenging.

"Why what, Jon? Why was I fucking Tom?" he asked, starting to feel annoyed. He hated saying that name now; it brought with it the thrum of a surprising hurt found deep within him, one that brought up questions he didn't wish to think of. "It's… complicated. What was initially an attempt by Tom to wound his mother turned into something else entirely," he finally replied.

Something good.

Jon laughed.

"You want me to believe that Tom seduced *you?*" he asked, incredulous.

Baltsaros shrugged as well as he could.

Jon narrowed his eyes.

"Can you please untie me? I feel foolish speaking to you from the floor," asked Baltsaros, flexing his arms to test the silk binding his hands.

Jon shook his head.

"I like you right where you are," he replied, dancing the blade's tip over the side of the wooden box holding the thick mattress. "Why should I believe *anything* you say?" he asked, but Baltsaros could see that Jon's anger was starting to peter out.

"You shouldn't," replied Baltsaros truthfully. "I've given you no cause to trust me."

Jon laughed again, an ugly little sound.

"But... This is the last of the lies," Baltsaros added quietly.

Jon pushed himself up and sat with his legs crossed, looking down at Baltsaros with a thoughtful expression.

"Tell me, my love... Am I lying? What are your canny senses telling you?" asked Baltsaros. He put his head back down on the scratchy rug, his neck sore from looking up at Jon on the bed.

"Absolutely nothing," said Jon, candidly. "Baltsaros, was Tom even a slave?" he asked after a moment.

"Yes. Now untie me. Please," said Baltsaros and waited silently. He heard a sigh and was gratified when Jon climbed down off the bed. With a quick slice of the knife, Baltsaros was free. He sat up and rubbed his wrists. "Thank you," he said, and Jon nodded.

The captain stood, pulling the remains of his clothing off. As he looked down sadly at the shredded material, he shook his head.

"I really wish you hadn't felt the destruction of my clothes necessary," he said with a sigh and turned to Jon.

The young man had returned to his place on the bed, and after a moment Baltsaros climbed onto the mattress to join him. He was astounded when Jon laid his head against his shoulder. He drew his arm around him, and a warm feeling spread through Baltsaros's chest.

As if sensing the captain's relief, Jon shook his head.

"I haven't forgiven you," he muttered.

Baltsaros smiled. He ran his fingers over Jon's arm, tracing the shape of his muscles through the thin cotton of the white shirt.

"Yes," Baltsaros continued, wishing to dispel his misgivings. "Tom was most definitely a slave. An unknown party kidnapped him when he was seven years old and held him for ransom, but unfortunately, there was no money to free him. Tom's father was a lord, but only in title; the money had long been spent. The kidnappers, disappointed with the failure of their plans, then sold Tom in the slave markets; no one knew what happened to the young boy afterwards. Tom's father took to drinking, eventually hanging himself after a number of years," said Baltsaros, his voice grim. He stroked Jon's side slowly and continued.

"The rest of Tom's history with me you basically know, and it is the truth. He was seventeen when I found him, and it took almost half a year for him to tell me of his parentage. He believed his parents had abandoned the search for him... And in truth, they had. However, I decided to find them for myself. I have to admit that the reasons were selfish; I'd hoped that in the years that had passed, their finances would have improved. They had not, and the reunion with his mother was not a happy one... Ten years of being a slave had changed Tom. She was thoroughly horrified to see what he had become, and Tom felt it keenly. He was no longer a pampered little lordling; he was a man with the rough appetites and experiences of one much older." Baltsaros let out a low chuckle.

"In the end, he chose to stay on with me as a deckhand. We already had a certain rapport, though nothing yet had taken place between Tom and me that first year. But... I continued to visit his mother. She had a title, and I had money. It made sense at the time to ask her hand in marriage. Truthfully, I thought that it would go better than it did. Abetha is extremely intelligent and, as you saw, very beautiful. We have many things in common... But she very quickly turned against me. Taking on her son as a lover was the final nail in that coffin." Baltsaros closed his eyes and leaned his head back on the headboard.

"As intelligent as I think I am, I've made more bad decisions than I'd like to admit. I don't regret Tom, but I do his mother. This winter will be our five-year wedding anniversary. A complete farce." During Baltsaros's monologue, Jon's hand had crept up to the older man's stomach, and he played with the coarse, slightly greying hair there.

"Why not just leave her?" asked Jon.

Baltsaros sighed and pinched the bridge of his nose.

"Abetha has managed to make some powerful allies. Leaving her would be, ah… *unwise*," he replied. "I can't just kill her either; though, gods, would I enjoy that." Jon's hand stopped moving but resumed after a second. "She has 'contingency' plans, as she likes to put it," explained Baltsaros.

"I don't understand why she would want to stay married to you if she despises you so," Jon said.

Baltsaros shrugged.

"Money? Status? She covets my island? I honestly have no answer for you there."

"Eloise… she yours?" asked Jon after a moment.

Baltsaros shook his head.

"No." He felt Jon nod against his shoulder.

"And that's it?" asked the younger man.

Baltsaros squeezed Jon's shoulder.

"That's it," he replied. *For now.*

Jon pulled away suddenly and sat up; Baltsaros thought for a moment that the other had somehow heard him.

However, Jon just looked at him, his grey-blue eyes calm.

"You know, I wasn't going to fuck you just now," he said casually, and started flipping the knife in his hand the same way that Baltsaros had seen Tom do a thousand times.

The captain raised his eyebrows, surprised.

"No?" he asked.

"No. I was going to slit your lying throat," replied Jon softly, his face serene. Baltsaros's heart hammered a double beat that quickened his pulse. His mind started walking a thin line between alarm and desire.

"What made you change your mind?" asked Baltsaros, his voice barely a whisper.

Dangerous wolf pup.

Jon brought up a shoulder in a slow shrug.

"I remembered who I was. Maybe next time… I won't."

When he saw that Baltsaros believed his lie, Jon felt some of his confidence return.

A lie? asked Tom. *Are ye sure about that, love?*

Jon saw again the sharp blade in his hand as he knelt over the prone captain. One deep cut to Baltsaros's neck would be enough. No more waiting for the next twisted falsehood to reveal itself. It would be so easy... But the truth was that he would just as soon cut his own throat.

What is it like to be dead? he asked Tom, but the ghost was silent for once.

Jon blinked, clearing the visions away, and saw that Baltsaros was looking at him with desire plain in his face. Jon shook his head and had to smile; it was just like the captain to take a death threat as an invitation to fuck.

Baltsaros lay in a daze on his stomach on the bed.

Jon had forced him onto his hands and knees and taken him roughly from behind, sparing the captain no quarter as he pounded into him. In the end Jon had pulled out and ejaculated onto Baltsaros's back with a panting moan, the cum mingling with the blood from the myriad nicks inflicted on him as his clothing had been cut off.

Now lying flat, Baltsaros could see the stains on the white sheets and feel Jon's seed pooling in the crook of his back and running down his side.

As soon as his breathing slowed, Jon hopped off the bed and buttoned up his trousers, leaving Baltsaros to watch him exit the room without a backwards glance.

He lifted his head when he heard Jon address the startled maids.

"Once you've finished in here, please change the bed linens and air out the king's bedchamber. Also, I would like someone to run His Majesty a bath immediately," said the young man, his tone comfortably commanding.

Grinning, Baltsaros put his head back down on the bed.

Jon would forgive him again.

27

MADIERUS

Love is composed of a single soul inhabiting two bodies.

— ARISTOTLE

Jon picked at his food, his appetite gone; the interminable silence of the meal was making him ill. He glanced up and saw that Abetha was staring at him with a small, polite curve to her lips; Jon smiled weakly at her.

He looked over at Baltsaros, but the man was just staring into his wine cup, the lines of his face hard. The captain looked older, tired.

He turned his eyes to Eloise and winked at the wan child. She blinked her huge, blue eyes at him and smiled shyly back.

"Eat your food, Eloise," said Abetha suddenly.

The child started as if poked from behind and quickly lifted a forkful of the roast duck to her mouth.

Jon sighed and went back to scowling down into his own plate of food. He couldn't understand the woman's insistence that he join them for the shared evening meal. More so, he didn't know why Baltsaros hadn't let him refuse; though, if all mealtimes were so bleak and oppressive, Jon could see why the captain would want an ally present.

He took a sip of the wine, barely tasting it, and looked again at the queen.

She had narrowed her eyes and was watching him over the rim of her cup. Smiling serenely as she put it down, Abetha finally addressed Jon.

"So, Jonathan is it? You've been here a week now... Tell me, how do you like our little island, Jonathan?" she asked.

Jon took a bite of bread, made bland by his nerves, and shook his head.

"It's just Jon, please, Your Majesty," he said tensely. "I think Madierus is very beautiful, Your Majesty."

Eyebrows raised, Abetha looked over at her husband.

"He's a polite little thing, isn't he?" she said, her voice low and smooth as silk.

Baltsaros raised his head slowly and looked at her in confusion; his mind was obviously elsewhere.

Abetha's expression was haughty when she turned her green-blue eyes back to Jon, and he suddenly saw again the resemblance to Tom; he felt like he was being stared down by a giant, malevolent cat.

"Are you enjoying your stay here?" she purred at him.

Eyes flicking quickly to Baltsaros and seeing that he was watching his wife with no emotion on his angular face, Jon nodded slowly. She continued to ask him questions about his upbringing, his education, his taste in books and music. Jon answered all of her queries as straightforwardly as he could. Slowly becoming more at ease, Jon was completely unprepared for the question that followed.

"And... How are you enjoying my husband's cock? You know he used to fuck my son with it, don't you? Do you find it to your liking?" she said, her voice conversational. However, her eyes were now glinting with malice.

Jon gaped and pushed his chair back, scrambling to his feet. He looked helplessly at Baltsaros, his face hot with embarrassment and outrage.

"I... can't do this," he said, his voice choked. Jon took a step backwards and then turned to run; he had to get away from the pure animosity radiating from the queen. As he ran down the hallway he heard Baltsaros raise his voice in anger behind him.

"Abetha!"

W inded from the run and soaked from the summer downpour, Jon pulled the tavern door open. The place was half-full, most of the patrons sitting in the covered patio at the back taking advantage of the cooler wind that the rain had brought; the lanterns swayed in the welcome breeze, making the light dance to the rhythm of the raindrops.

Jon climbed into his usual high stool, putting his forehead down on the glossy wood of the bar. A soft hand ruffled his hair.

"Tough night, Jon?" asked Maya, her voice kind. Jon closed his eyes and nodded without lifting his head. "Beer or whiskey?"

The *Grog Blossom* was an interesting establishment that boasted quite a number of exotic choices; however, the beautiful proprietress had been quick to realize that Jon was a man of simple tastes.

"Both," he muttered, almost to himself. He heard Maya laugh a little sadly and pull her hand away to get him his drinks. Jon lifted his head when she placed a mug of her good brown beer and a tumbler of golden whiskey in front of him, and he sighed.

"Thanks," he said, grateful. He lifted the beer and took a sip, smiling at Maya.

She stood in front of him, wiping out a small bowl that he knew she would fill shortly with the little crunchy, salted dried fish that he'd grown fond of. Maya had her long brown hair in the messy knot at the back of her head that she wore when tending bar; her big blue eyes were friendly, and she smiled softly at him.

Jon smiled back; he had taken to her the moment they'd been introduced.

"Where's Katherine tonight?" he asked, looking around for the first mate.

Maya shrugged.

"Out with the boys," she said, referring to Malik and Nathaniel. "Though she should be back any time now."

The captain had the first mate working with Malik on modifications to the ship, and Nathaniel often just tagged along for company; Jon had a feeling that the two men still felt a little out of place among the tight-knit crew and their families on Madierus.

"So what did the witch do tonight?" asked Maya, putting her elbows on the bar as she leaned towards Jon.

Jon felt himself relax a little; where Katherine was high-spirited and had a dry humour, her wife was gentle, inquisitive, and very sweet. Jon found that they made an interesting couple; he couldn't imagine them arguing half as much as he and Baltsaros did.

"Aren't you afraid of what she might do if she hears you calling her a witch?" asked Jon, licking the foam off his upper lip.

Maya laughed and shrugged, her blue eyes mischievous.

"She's not well-liked, Jon. She might have a few staunch supporters, but the people are loyal to the captain," she said, taking a sip of her own beer. "You can't let her get to you. She's a harpy in a cage of her own devising."

Jon nodded. He still found it strange that no one outside the castle referred to Baltsaros as king, only captain. After knocking back his whiskey, Jon held out the glass for more.

At this Maya frowned slightly but turned to grab the brown bottle, pouring another few fingers into his glass.

"I was 'invited' to sup with her and her *husband* tonight. It didn't go well... And her *husband* did nothing about it," he said, bitterly. It irked him that Baltsaros seemed so dismissive of her rancour towards Jon. The captain kept telling him to just ignore the woman. In fact, that was the advice he had been given by everyone so far.

However, what people didn't grasp was the fact that the whole situation was hurting Jon. Regardless that Baltsaros was not sharing his wife's bed, he was still married to her, and it rankled Jon. He was being forced to endure the spite of a woman who absolutely hated him... merely to keep up appearances.

Even though almost everyone on the island knew and accepted the truth.

Jaw clenched, Jon blinked hard a few times, trying to dry his eyes before the shameful tears fell. Maya, ever observant, quickly reached out a hand and squeezed his arm.

He quickly told Maya what had happened over supper.

"You really love him, don't you?" she said quietly.

Jon felt his insides twist.

"Is it love? I don't know," he said truthfully. "Sometimes I think I'm just addicted to him. Or that he's cast some kind of horrible curse on me where I'm to follow him for the rest of my life, doomed to fall for his lies over and over again." He laughed sourly and drank his whiskey, exhaling hard as the liquid burned like fire down his throat.

This time Maya refilled his glass before he had a chance to ask for more. With a sad look, she tilted her head.

"His lies... Were they about really terrible things?" she asked.

Jon opened his mouth but nothing came out.

"I mean, I'm not condoning his lying, but... It seems to me that he lied to keep you from leaving him, correct?" Maya asked, her blue eyes guileless.

Jon closed his mouth and frowned.

"Didn't you lie to him about Tom? Aren't you *still* keeping from him the full truth of what happened?" she asked gently, her thumb stroking the skin of his forearm.

Her touch and the mention of his infidelity with Tom made

him suddenly very uncomfortable. He pulled his arm away and wiped his damp palm on the knee of his trousers.

"Don't make me regret telling you about that," he said defensively. "Aren't you supposed to be trying to make me feel better not worse?"

On his second day on the island, when Katherine had first introduced Jon to her beautiful and incredibly savvy wife, the trio had gotten very, very drunk on Maya's newest brew.

Over the course of the evening, the truth about Jon's indiscretion with Tom had come out. As it turned out, during the storm, the person above them on the quarterdeck had been Katherine. However, she only saw Tom walking away and hadn't thought anything of it. When Jon finally admitted that they had kissed and that it had brought with it a breathless, frantic emotion, Katherine had looked at him like he was crazy.

It was Maya who had stroked his hair that night as he lay with his head on his arms in the dark of the patio, weeping over Tom's death and asking over and over whether it was possible to love two people at once.

The memory still made him blush furiously.

Maya bit the corner of her lip, her dark lashes coming down over her big eyes. She looked away.

"I'm sorry, Jon. I am just laying out the facts," she said, walking to the side of the bar so she could lift the panel to get out.

Jon watched her come towards him, and he swallowed; he found himself unable to move as she put her arms around him in a hug. Maya smelled of spring flowers, and she was all curves and softness. He leaned his forehead against her shoulder and tried to keep his composure.

"I'm sorry things are so complicated for you, Jon. I wish I could do something to help," she murmured.

"Unhand my woman, boy," came Katherine's voice from behind him, and Jon started.

He pulled himself away, feeling strangely guilty. When he turned, Jon saw that the tall woman was grinning at him, her eyes narrow in merriment.

She walked forward and punched him hard on the arm before wrapping herself around Maya, dipping her low for an affectionate kiss. When Katherine released her, Maya laughed and swatted her wife with the back of her hand.

With the realization that all the tension had suddenly vanished from the room, Jon felt could breathe easy again. He glanced over his shoulder and saw that Malik and Nathaniel had accompanied Katherine back to the tavern and were arguing about something. Maya needed Katherine to help her with a barrel in the back, so Jon grabbed his beer and walked a little unsteadily to the table where the two men were arguing.

"I'm telling you. It can be done," Nathaniel was saying, pointing to a scrap of paper with a few notes and lines scribbled on it.

"Not sure it can, my friend. There would be an awful lot of pressure put on the hull by the ice. It might crack up before you got to the other side... And then what do you get? Stranded in an ice field—Oh hi, Jon. Care to join us?" asked Malik, kicking a chair back from the table.

Jon sank down into the seat gratefully and took a long pull from his mug.

"What are you guys arguing about? What ice field?" he asked, looking curiously at the paper in front of Nathaniel.

The older man, his hazel eyes narrow, pointed a finger to a series of small, joined circles arranged in a curve to one side of the writing.

"I think, if a ship was well stocked and modified to withstand continuous, small impacts on her hull, it could make its way through the passage in the Devil's Isles," he said, sliding his finger to the bottom of the drawing where there was a bigger gap between the circles.

Jon shook his head.

"I don't understand. What are the Devil's Isles?" he asked, confused.

Malik grinned and drank from his mug, sitting comfortably back in his chair.

"They're not really islands... more like a mountain range. They're spires that rise up high in the sky like the teeth of a giant sea creature," said Malik, gesturing up with his hands and twisting his face into a grimace.

Nathaniel laughed.

Jon could tell that there was probably more drinking than work done on *Baal's Heart* earlier this evening.

"So... No one has ever been past them. Or at least no one who has come back to tell of it," said Nathaniel, jumping back into the story. "However, there is a gap here that can accommodate a large vessel. The only problem is that the water that far south is completely frozen for most of the year."

Malik nodded. "A narrow gap of time for a narrow gap of water," he said, grinning at his own words.

Jon frowned at the drawing, scratching at the stubble on his cheek.

"Why not put a layer of beaten metal on the front of the ship?" he asked, looking up at the shipwright. "Where I'm from, it gets cold enough to freeze the water outside the harbour. We have ships called icebreakers that go around and crack up the ice, pushing it away to let boats in. They all have this... sharply bent layer of metal on the front," Jon said, putting the tips of his fingers together but holding his palms apart. "Like armour for the ship."

Nathaniel's head swivelled to Malik, his eyebrows high. However, Malik was shaking his head.

"I already thought of that. What do you take me for? It just can't be done! Not on the *Heart*. It will unbalance her way too much. Besides… Where would we get that much steel here?" he said.

Jon shrugged and then frowned.

"Wait… The captain is thinking of taking us there?" he asked, surprised. Baltsaros had made no mention of the trip.

Malik and Nathaniel shook their heads in unison.

"Are they going on about the Devil's Isles modifications again?" asked Katherine, walking up to them. She turned a chair backwards and straddled it, folding her arms along the top.

"Nathaniel, your crazy idea is a death wish. Seriously. Just drop it will you?" said the first mate, turning to Jon. "Don't listen to them… And don't mention it to the captain."

Jon furrowed his brow.

"Why?" he asked, curious. Katherine grabbed Jon's mug out of his hand and downed the rest in one swallow.

"It's just the kind of outrageous thing that the captain would want to try, given enough encouragement. And… I don't know about you, but I kinda like being warm and alive, no?" she said and grinned before calling to Maya for another round.

Baltsaros opened his eyes when he heard Jon's step outside the door. He had been lounging in the big comfortable chair in his sitting room reading a book of newly translated poetry while he waited for Jon to come home. At some point he had obviously drifted off and, as Jon opened the door, Baltsaros wondered how late it really was.

The captain cleared his throat to alert Jon of his presence and watched as the young man swayed into the room. He was noticeably drunk.

"Hi," said his wayward lover as he leaned into the door to close it. "I'm uh… Sorry it's so late. You waited up?"

Baltsaros watched him stumble slightly over the edge of the rug as he came towards the captain. He was surprised when Jon came to straddle him in the wide wingback chair and plant a sloppy kiss on his lips.

Baltsaros moved the book from his lap and fumbled to place it on the dainty side table before wrapping his arms around Jon's waist, pulling him closer. Jon tasted of beer and whiskey as Baltsaros nudged open his mouth, breathing in his warm breath. Pulling away from Jon after a few long minutes, he looked fondly at the inebriated boy in his lap.

"I'm the one who's sorry, Jon," he said, running his hand up the front of the young man's shirt to place it against Jon's heart; it beat quick and strong under his palm. "I dragged you into this. I should be doing more to protect you from her." He laughed a little contritely. "You'd think after all this time I would have learned to be more suspicious of her nature."

Earlier that day, when Abetha had asked him to invite Jon to the evening meal, he had thought nothing of it. Granted, he had been distracted; they were nearly three weeks late getting to the island, and he still hadn't finished working through the expense books. The pile of correspondence alone was daunting.

Jon's brows came down, a line forming between them as he looked at Baltsaros.

"She's very angry with you," said Jon, his face soft with drink. "She used to love you."

Startled by Jon's words, Baltsaros looked at him curiously. Abetha had loved him? To Baltsaros it had always been an arrangement that suited the both of them; that Abetha had felt something more had never crossed his mind... She was such a reserved woman.

"Why do you say that?" he asked.

Jon leaned forward and rested himself against Baltsaros, his cheek against the captain's shoulder.

"Mmm... the way she looks at you. Like she lost something. I guess she realized too late that you're incapable of love. Hmmm... misplaced punishment for her mistake. Something..."

Baltsaros felt Jon's body twitch slightly, and he realized that the young man was falling asleep.

"You think I'm incapable of love?" Baltsaros asked softly. When Jon didn't respond, the captain nudged him gently.

Jon sighed and nuzzled against Baltsaros's neck.

"I love you too," he said drowsily.

Baltsaros sat in the chair and watched the candle burn down as he held Jon against him. There was a tenderness inside him, one that could contain tears and laughter at the same time. It was lovely but also painful, the way that a limb waking up from lack of blood flow prickled and stung; Baltsaros cherished the feeling. As he stroked Jon's hair as he slept, Baltsaros thought of love and fate, the future and the past.

T he morning sun found the two men entwined on the great bed where Baltsaros had carried Jon when the candle finally died; the captain's arm held the younger man against him tight, both protective and possessive, as if afraid of ever letting him go.

28

A REVELATION

J on stood at the window watching Eloise and Brutus play a
game of chase. The giant mastiff leapt and trotted around
the little girl, and Eloise's spindly legs pumped quickly as
she ran and skipped down the garden path.

Though the panes of glass were thick, Jon could swear he
could hear her excited peals of laughter; he had a feeling that
Eloise did not laugh very often. Grinning wide, Jon watched as
Brutus let himself be caught, throwing himself almost dramati-
cally to the ground so that Eloise could crawl over his side: the
conquering hero slayed the evil beast.

Baltsaros's hand gripped his shoulder in passing as he walked
heavily to the big wooden desk across the room. At the sound of
an exasperated sigh, he turned to look at Baltsaros and saw that
the captain stood with his back to Jon as he leaned hard on his
knuckles over the pile of papers and letters that littered the desk.

"Why don't you have someone to do that for you?" Jon asked, approaching Baltsaros from behind. He put his arms around the other man's chest, resting the side of his head down on the captain's broad back. One of Baltsaros's hands came up to clasp his, and Jon heard the low groan of frustration directly against his ear.

"I don't know. I should. It will be at least the end of the week before I get through this. The worst are Abetha's records; the woman is so vague that every page I read requires an audience with Her Highness just to understand what I'm dealing with," said Baltsaros. "I need a break."

He straightened suddenly and pulled out of Jon's arms, turning around to look fondly at him, his brown eyes warm.

"How would you like to come for a hike with me? There is something I would love to show you," Baltsaros asked with a smile.

Jon had planned on asking Katherine if she needed help clearing more land at the back of her property. Turning farmer on her return home, the first mate now wanted to plant the seeds Jon had found in the cargo hold of the *Maiden's Bounty*; however, a hike with Baltsaros sounded leagues more enjoyable.

J on's arm was weary from swinging the blade over and over again to clear the path. It would soon be Baltsaros's turn to break through the foliage, and he was thankful for it. He hadn't realized that a hike would mean hot, tiring work as they struggled through what felt like virgin jungle.

Jon paused and lifted the waterskin hanging from his side, pulling the cork and taking a long swallow of the tepid water. With a glance behind him, he saw that the captain was looking curiously at a flat green leaf in his hands, turning it over and rubbing it with the back of his nail. Baltsaros was sweaty and bare chested like Jon but, unlike the younger man, seemed perfectly happy to hack and slash his way through the dense wilds of

Madierus. Jon watched as Baltsaros folded the leaf to put it in the bag at his hip, a new "specimen."

When he realized he was being watched, Baltsaros looked up and smiled, the corners of his eyes crinkling.

"Tired?" he asked Jon cheerfully. "I can take over now if you'd like. We're almost there."

The captain had yet to tell him where "there" was, preferring to keep it a secret. Jon hoped it wasn't just an interesting rock formation or a rare medicinal plant. He flipped the long, flat blade in his hand and passed it to Baltsaros handle-first in response.

Jon stepped out of the way to let the captain pass him and took another mouthful of water, following the older man through the narrow swath he cut out of the jungle.

Before too much longer, Jon thought he could detect a thinning of the foliage. The sun started peeking out between the green leaves, and soon Jon could see blue skies. Panting from the long climb, Jon frowned; he could hear something like a rumbling roar coming from ahead.

"What's that?" he yelled at Baltsaros. The tireless man had outpaced Jon by a good distance; at Jon's shout he stopped and wiped his forehead, putting his hands on his hips as he waited for Jon to catch up. Despite his weariness, Baltsaros's sharp-toothed grin was infectious, and he found himself smiling back.

"It's just up over this ridge," said the captain, his eyes bright with excitement. As soon as Jon was close, Baltsaros turned and resumed slashing at the vines though now it was barely necessary.

The rumble grew louder until finally the source of it came into view through the tall, skinny trees ahead.

As he stepped past the grinning captain, Jon's eyes went wide. He pushed through the last of the greenery and stepped out into a breathtaking scene.

In front of them was a waterfall, something Jon had only read about in books. It fell from a gap in the high lip of the volcanic crater above into a wide pool of water surrounded by smooth, sunken boulders and flowering plants; a pair of colourful birds flew by overhead, calling to each other as they eyed the intruders. Mouth agape, Jon stared up at the falling water. He realized that they had come around the west side of the volcano, climbing its slope as they went along.

"Where is the water coming from?" he asked, enthralled. The waterfall made a mist in the air around its base, and Jon could see pieces of a rainbow shimmering there.

Baltsaros wrapped his arms around Jon and sighed happily, looking up.

"I'm not exactly sure. There is a big freshwater lake in the crater, but it cannot possibly be replenished solely by rain. My theory is that there is an underground river that flows beneath the island and is somehow being forced up through the old lava tubes. Perhaps this is why the volcano stopped erupting many, many years ago? It is beautiful, is it not?" Baltsaros said, sliding his hands down Jon's torso. The captain's nimble fingers began tugging at the buttoned fly of Jon's trousers, and he gasped at the sudden contact when Baltsaros slipped his hand between material and skin to cup him firmly. Soon the captain had Jon stripped down to his bare skin, pulling his own boots and pants off in a hurry.

Having expected more in the way of caresses, Jon squawked in surprise when Baltsaros just shoved him hard. He flung out his arms but lost his balance, falling into the surprisingly deep and cold water of the pond. Coughing and spluttering as he reached the surface, he quickly ducked out of the way when he saw Baltsaros take a flying leap towards him.

The man resurfaced, his face creased in a wide, delighted smile.

Jon treaded water and grinned, bringing up his hand suddenly to splash the captain who, in turn, roared in mock fury.

It quickly escalated, the men cavorting and splashing in the pool, laughing and trying to drown each other in its chilly depths. There was no age difference between them, no dead lover, no bitter queen, no stack of responsibilities... No, they were just two boys playing in the warm summer sun of their own tropical paradise.

Jon, in trying to flee from Baltsaros, swam around to the side of the waterfall and found that there was an underwater ledge where he could stand. Panting from exertion, Jon grinned when Baltsaros suddenly popped out of the water beside him; the captain seemed part fish, able to swim for long distances underwater without breathing.

Laughing, Jon pulled the older man towards him and, buoyed by the water, he wrapped his legs around the captain's hips. Instantly their play took on the sharpened edge of lust. Jon looked searchingly into Baltsaros's dark-brown eyes, clasping the back of the man's neck.

The captain's face had gone serious, his mouth slightly open as he looked at Jon. There was suddenly a tiny comma, as if from pain, etched between Baltsaros's brows as he licked his lips.

Despite the loud splashing of the waterfall, Jon thought he could hear Baltsaros breathing.

Large hands coming up to hold his waist, Baltsaros leaned forward and brought his mouth to Jon's, hesitating for an instant before making contact. Though Baltsaros's lips were cold from the water, his tongue was warm as it touched Jon's; the contrast was intoxicating, and Jon moaned softly as he kissed Baltsaros.

There was a subtle difference in this embrace, a new poignancy that had not been there before, and Jon wondered what had changed. Clinging to the captain's body, Jon felt almost frantic with desire, and he shuddered when Baltsaros moved his hand to his cock, squeezing the hardening shaft.

However, despite the fervour of their embrace, Jon realized he was getting cold. He pulled away from Baltsaros and, with a backwards glance, swam to the sun-heated rocks on the far side.

Baltsaros followed him and climbed up to lie next to Jon on the warm boulders. The abrupt change in location had brought with it a slowing of their passion, and Baltsaros started just running his fingers slowly up and down Jon's body as the sun dried their skin.

The line appeared between the captain's stark brows again, and Jon frowned.

"What's wrong?" he asked. "You look like something's bothering you." Jon hoped desperately that it wasn't yet another lie to sour the relationship with.

Baltsaros shook his head.

"There's nothing wrong, Jon. You just..." He trailed off and closed his mouth, his lips pressing together hard for a second before he continued. "The other night when you came back from the tavern... You said you loved me," Baltsaros finished in a strange voice.

Jon brought himself up on his elbows and grimaced.

"Oh gods... I did?" he asked, aghast, and Baltsaros's eyes quickly slid away from Jon's face at his words.

When the captain looked back at him, his expression was distant.

Jon grasped the misunderstanding right away and sat up. He reached for Baltsaros and cupped his lover's head between his hands, fingers tangled in the captain's wet hair.

"No! It's not that! Baltsaros, *yes*. Yes, I meant it! Of course I meant it... I just hate that it had to come out when I was three sheets to the wind. I... love you. I do. Oh gods, how I love you," he said fervently, his heart in his throat as he spoke the foreign words.

The coldness in Baltsaros's eyes had melted away at his confession, and slowly he nodded, letting out a long exhale.

The captain suddenly leaned in to kiss him, pushing Jon back onto the smooth rock.

Jon gasped at the urgency that spurred Baltsaros's desire; the man reached up and slid a hand around Jon's jaw, leaning into his kiss as he pressed himself hard against his body. Baltsaros was demanding and rough, and Jon gave himself up completely to the captain.

When Baltsaros's hand worked its way between their bodies to clasp their cocks together and stroke them as one, Jon felt dizzy with desire. His breath panted out of his lungs and into Baltsaros's as the kiss went on and on, a confirmation of Jon's words.

When Baltsaros finally released him, it was to push apart Jon's legs and kneel between them. Baltsaros leaned forward and reached over Jon's head; when he sat back down on his heels, in his hand was the broken off end of a thick plant-stem that ended in a point.

After a momentary panic, Jon was relieved when Baltsaros just pressed his thumbs into the plant, splitting the skin and scooping a clear gel into his palm. Jon was confused. Was it a drug? His question was answered almost immediately.

"I need you. Now," said the captain hoarsely, eyes wide and desperate with his naked lust.

Jon nodded quickly and raised his knees, watching breathlessly as Baltsaros smeared the plant's juice over his thick cock. Without another word, the captain grasped Jon's hips and rapidly slid his lubricated cock in the furrow of the young man's ass a few times before angling himself with a hurried hand for the final plunge.

Jon yelled loud and arched his back in shock as the captain's cock drove hard into him; however, he swiftly started succumbing to Baltsaros's long strokes and groaned in response.

Jon's cock bobbed up from his stomach and he breathed hard. He grunted at the force with which Baltsaros ploughed into him and realized that his pleasure was climbing swiftly in reaction to the furious pace of the captain's fucking. He could already feel the pressure mounting for the final release in his testicles, and he started to moan and pant with Baltsaros's thrusts. He realized he was going to cum even though his cock was untouched, and he whimpered, pushing himself up on his heels to match Baltsaros's movements.

Fingers scrabbling at the smooth rock to either side of him, Jon felt the captain's thick length carry him over the edge of his climax, sending shocks through him as he cried out again and again.

"Oh gods, Jon," moaned Baltsaros, watching the younger man's cock gush out strings of pearly cum over his own taut stomach. Baltsaros's head snapped back, and he dug his fingers hard into Jon's hips as he was toppled by his own orgasm, the cries of his pleasure loud and unbridled in the green summer air of the jungle oasis.

T he sun was setting when the two men finally came within sight of the small village, and the lights twinkling from the buildings reminded Jon of the fireflies he used to watch as a boy. His hand was curled around Baltsaros's forearm as the captain led him out of the jungle.

Something had happened today that had made a mark on him, and he wouldn't soon forget this excursion. When Baltsaros looked back at him, Jon felt gratified and comforted by his warm smile. Now that his declaration of love was out in the open, Jon was both more confident and hopeful of the coming times. Though the captain hadn't responded in kind, the way he had reacted to Jon's words made him feel weak inside. Jon was filled with a joy that lightened his heart.

He and Baltsaros quickly ran through the castle gardens and, stopping to catch their breaths, they kissed and stifled their laughter when they saw the queen walk by, hiding from the woman they both wanted to avoid.

Suddenly the sky opened up with a heavy, tropical rain, and the men, now boys again, raced each other to the end of the covered walkway, pushing each other out of the way to gain access to the castle. Jon beat Baltsaros to the top of the stairs and wouldn't grant the captain entry to his rooms unless he pledged his undying loyalty to him.

Breathless and silly, the two men finally embraced in the sitting room when a draw had been called, the room lit only by the full moon shining in through the tall windows.

Baltsaros was the first to pull away, decrying the insistence of his bladder.

When the captain had gone, Jon walked to the bell-pull and yanked on it once; the captain's liquor cabinet was bare, and they were in need of some lighting. Before Baltsaros had returned, a spare boy of indeterminate age had already put a flame to the candles in Baltsaros's quarters, excusing himself to fetch a bottle of wine from the cellar.

When the captain walked into the room, he groaned.

"Why, Jon? Now I can see the infernal pile of rubbish that mocks me with its urgency," said Baltsaros, crossing to his desk. "It's bad enough that I get the correspondence for half of my crew; the fact that I get complete gibberish is just taxing."

The captain lifted up an envelope and held it near the flame of the wax candle burning on his desk.

"Take this one for instance... Its label reads 'The Black Brigand.' What does that even mean?" The captain scowled down at the letter and shook his head.

Jon's blood froze in his veins. He swallowed hard and took a step towards Baltsaros.

"Can I... Baltsaros, please can I see that?" he said, his voice unsteady.

The Black Brigand.

He couldn't remember if he had told Baltsaros what Tom had called him in the lies the jealous first mate had spread in Portsmouth. Katherine knew but... Jon broke the seal at the back and pulled out the single, folded sheet. The message was written in a blockish, unadorned hand:

Dear Jonny,

I thought you might like to know that a navy fleet passed this way. The man leading them was a dark-skinned fella with burn scars on his face and hands... I think you might know who that is? Turns out that killing a small lord in the shit-soaked, ass-end of a kingdom is enough to grant you a visit from the navy? Who knew? Bad news though, love: they know exactly where you are. Tortured it right out of Fresia, the fuckers. I'd get everyone ready for a small war, if you know what I mean.

    Regards,

—T.

J on's heart beat fast as he looked up into Baltsaros's eyes. "Tom's alive," he said quietly.

29

ENEMIES AND ALLIES

Baltsaros read the words again and frowned.

Gods be damned, Tom! he thought angrily.

A fleet? What did Tom mean by a fleet? Three ships? Five? The letter wasn't even dated; how in the blasted hells was he to know what to expect and when? The mail came but once a month from the nearest island, and there was no way a reply would reach Tom in time. Baltsaros assumed the "this way" in Tom's letter referred to the *Jewel*, given his mention of Fresia.

He rubbed his thumb over the initial at the bottom, picturing in his mind the way Tom's tongue poked from the corner of his mouth when performing the rare act of putting pen to paper.

Why address it only to Jon?

Baltsaros frowned and took another swallow of wine, looking over at the naked young man curled in slumber next to him. Baltsaros hadn't liked the way that Jon's blue eyes lit up at Tom's miraculous resurrection.

He scanned the message in his hand again. Why did he feel so... vexed by Tom's refusal to acknowledge him in his missive? After drinking down more wine, Baltsaros leaned his head back on the pillow and stared up at the colourful silks draped above his head. He had felt a keen, almost painful relief when Jon spoke his hushed words: *Tom's alive.* Jaw clenched, Baltsaros passed a hand over his tired eyes. Why had it turned so quickly to anger?

Unable or unwilling to go to sleep, Baltsaros slipped off the high bed and went to stand at the window; looking out at the pinkening sky, the captain attempted to turn his mind from thoughts of a hunt to soothe his rage to preparations for the possible battle to come.

J on drank down the beer in his mug and grinned eagerly.

With her lips slightly pursed, Maya frowned at him, her blue eyes softly reproving. She shook her head.

"I'm glad the man isn't dead, Jon… but aren't you being a little ah… openly optimistic about Tom?" she asked. "I'm really not seeing a reunion in your future, given what I know of your relationship with the captain. Please tell me you aren't seriously thinking of suggesting that you go find him." She wiped down the bar with her rag and watched sympathetically as his expression teetered on the edge of disappointment.

"Yes, Maya. I am. If Baltsaros sees Tom… maybe…" he said, his conviction faltering. If Baltsaros sees Tom… what? They all live happily ever after? He swallowed and looked down into his empty mug, blinking hard.

"Jon," said the soft-spoken woman, leaning across the bar to pat his hand. "I know you think you saw something in Tom; maybe it was real… Maybe it was just a fleeting thing. I only knew him briefly, but I honestly don't see anything good coming of wanting him back in your life. While I'll admit that he was handsome in a roguish sort of way, he was a known troublemaker with violent tendencies. Why not just be glad that he sent us warning when he did and let the rest go? You just said you had a good thing with the captain, why stir up old wounds?"

Somewhat chastened, Jon frowned and nodded.

Maya pulled the mug out of Jon's grasp and turned to fill it anew. When she slid it back in front of him, her eyes were narrowed with worry.

"Now… Tell me again the part about the navy," she said, sitting down.

That evening Jon found Baltsaros high up in one of the towers. The captain was at the window with his arms crossed, staring out over the water. At the sound of Jon's footfalls, he turned.

"Oh hello, Jon. You got my note," said Baltsaros, looking pleased to see him.

Jon crossed the room, gazing around him. The walls were covered in maps of all kinds. Some seemed to be reproductions or earlier versions of the one aboard *Baal's Heart*; others were details of the midland isles or the coastline of the northern continent. Jon assumed that many of them had been drawn by the captain himself though he spotted a few that were yellowed with obvious great age, the landmasses on them unrecognizable.

Jon stepped up to the heavy oval table in the middle of the room and saw that its surface was covered in sheets of paper with half-finished drawings of buildings and figures. Curious, Jon began to flip through them and was startled to come upon a sketch of his likeness. It was an image of him looking off to one side, his brows low over his eyes, his lips slightly parted as if deep in thought. Jon felt suddenly shy; the drawing was beautifully rendered.

When he lifted his eyes, he saw that Baltsaros was watching him curiously. He felt almost breathless with the sudden tightness in his chest; it always amazed him how his love for the captain came in bursts of blinding intensity that caught Jon unawares. He looked away quickly and cleared his throat, trying to ignore the lump that had formed there.

"So this is what you do when I wake up in the middle of the

night and you're nowhere to be found?" he asked, trying to make his voice light. With a glance back up at Baltsaros, he saw the older man nod.

The captain crossed to the table and gazed down at his drawings.

"I've been at sea for so long that I have problems sleeping when I'm ashore. It's too quiet, too still," explained Baltsaros with a small smile.

Jon tapped the drawing of him with his fingertips.

"Do I always look so grave?" he asked, curious.

Baltsaros's eyes narrowed appraisingly at him, and he shook his head.

"Not as often as you used to, no. However, while I dearly cherish your smile… It's the sober, pensive Jon that sticks in my mind when I have charcoal in my hand," Baltsaros replied quietly. "Perhaps it's just the medium that lends itself to solemnness."

Sighing, the captain looked again at the open window after a moment, his mind obviously occupied.

"I wish I knew how much time we had before Reginald arrives, if he comes at all," he muttered distractedly, walking back towards his post. The high vantage point meant the captain could see ships approaching long before they arrived, but the lack of time frame made for a frustrating wait.

The toe of Jon's boot brushed against something; looking down, he frowned at what he saw.

"Come with me; I would like to pick your brain about your stepfather, but I desperately require some sustenance. Shall we see what I can make for us in the kitchen?" said Baltsaros from behind him.

Jon looked up quickly and nodded. As he followed the captain out of the room, he threw another backwards glance at the paper in the shadows under the heavy table, Tom's smiling eyes peeking up at him from its crumpled surface.

Baltsaros leaned over the table in the great hall and pointed to the map.

"There are some old cannons that we can place up high... here in the rock face," he said, circling with a finger a spot slightly east from the castle. "I assume that the fleet will be approaching us from the north; however, if they decide to come around and land on the south side of the island, dragging those cannons up to the ridge will have been for naught."

Katherine folded her arms and frowned down at the map.

"You think they could come from the south?" she asked.

"The element of surprise. The man in charge was a soldier for a long time and a gifted tactician. I wouldn't put it past him to try to catch us off guard. They might also split the fleet and try for both. It will be hard to defend on all fronts if that's the case. While the letter we received did not outline the navy's intention, the fact that they tortured someone for the location of Madierus suggests that they are coming here with destruction and violence in mind. It could be that they are solely looking for me... But the man leading the fleet would see every pirate and their kin hanged. There are a lot of lives to protect," replied the captain, straightening. "They would have been here by now if the letter was written shortly after the storm, which isn't the case. However, it couldn't have been that much later, given that the letter arrived here with the last ship."

He sighed and pinched the bridge of his nose. He was feeling uncomfortably tense. Jon was completely right about his control issues; he had zero patience for unknown variables, and there were too many on his mind, his actions to blame for all of them. Not for the first time, he thought about how blowing up the castle at Portsmouth had been a terribly rash decision on his part.

To be fair though, how could he have known that killing such a small-town nobleman would spur an attack backed by the crown? Baltsaros had a feeling that Reginald's obstinacy was part of it. From what Jon had told him, the man had a streak of vengeance in him that rivalled Baltsaros's.

And then there was Tom.

Two men he thought dead suddenly resurrected in one fell swoop.

Quickly pushing away a sudden, sharp image of Tom from his mind, he clenched his jaw and swallowed as he lifted his gaze to Jon; he saw that the younger man was looking at him from across the table with sympathy in his grey-blue eyes. Baltsaros watched as Jon's face went pensive for a moment.

"How many people are on the island?" Jon asked, looking around.

"About two hundred and thirty at the moment, why?" Baltsaros asked.

Jon looked down, nodding thoughtfully. When he raised his head, Baltsaros could see that he had an idea.

"What if we sent everyone who is unable to fight onto *Baal's Heart* and out of the way? That way we can concentrate on the attack rather than worrying about kin," suggested Jon. "We'll have plenty of notice of the navy's arrival if someone keeps constant watch from on high, right? Enough time to load everyone onto the ship and take her out of harm's way?"

Baltsaros nodded.

"Yes, Jon. However, we need those guns. The ship is our biggest line of defence," he replied.

Jon pointed to the mouth of the harbour on the map.

"Let's say it's a fleet of four or five ships maximum, right? Probably being frigates or sloops, they'll be bigger and almost definitely outgun *Baal's Heart.* So why fight them on the water when they have the advantage? How many of them will be able to fit into the harbour? Two? At most? The rest will be out of range. What can they do then? Let's make them bring the fight to us," he said, smiling.

Baltsaros tilted his head slightly at Jon; the idea of removing the vulnerable from the equation certainly had merit. Seeing that the rest of the assembled group were all looking at him waiting for his response, Baltsaros nodded slowly.

The bulk of the population of Madierus was made up of the crew's family; of those, a good third were capable fighters. With the weak, young, and infirm out of the way and safe aboard the ship, the rest of them could certainly hold their own on the island. At the very least it meant that his men's loyalties wouldn't be divided.

"They'll still have two ships within firing range in our own harbour," Baltsaros pointed out.

Jon shrugged.

"I don't think there's any avoiding that. There will be damage, yes, but I think it's worth it in terms of lives saved," he said.

And that is what is important, said Jon's solemn grey-blue eyes.

Baltsaros smiled softly at his younger lover. Yes, that was indeed important. Jon was right that though Baltsaros largely felt indifferent to his crew, he had made a pledge dedicating himself to their well-being.

Baltsaros was not his uncle.

"What if we made it so that there were *no* ships able to enter the harbour," said a voice from the back.

Baltsaros frowned and shifted to see who was speaking. Nathaniel stepped through the gap that formed in the crowd, and Baltsaros looked at the cartographer with interest.

"How so?" asked the captain.

Nathaniel stood next to Jon and turned the map slightly, frowning down at it.

"At the narrow point here," he said, gesturing to the mouth of the harbour as had Jon. "Why don't we drop big rocks or boulders overboard at intervals with long ropes attached. Float some wood and plants at the ends of the tethers. See... We would make it look like there's a narrow land bridge closing off the lagoon—no way to enter. It'll only look real if the water is calm enough though," said Nathaniel, crossing his arms and furrowing his brow.

The captain grinned wide, picturing the result in his head. He clapped his hands once.

"Bravo! Good work. I think this could work. We'll keep *Baal's*

Heart outside the harbour while this happens. The jolly boats could load everyone on board and drop the last boulder when done. They will still come through in the end; all it will take is one boat trying to disembark on this 'land bridge' to see through the ruse, but I believe it will be enough to keep the ships out of the harbour," he said, pleased with the plan.

"If they choose to come from another direction, they'll have to come up on foot anyway. There's no way their guns could do any damage from the south or west. From the east, it wouldn't be much. But... Why not set up the old cannons on the beach instead of the rock face? It would be far easier, no? We could just hit them as they're coming at us?" said Katherine with a smile.

Jon's brows came down low over his eyes as he stood looking at the map.

"We still have to find a way to destroy the ships. Sink them. That way they won't return," he said, his voice thoughtful.

Malik, standing next to Jon, nodded and raked his hair back. He looked up at the captain, his dark brows high.

"I might be able to come up with something interesting if I can have a few men and the use of a small rowboat during the attack," said the shipwright. "I know more than a few ways to sink a ship... The trick is to get them to go down while on the run and not cluttering the harbour."

Baltsaros nodded and smiled. He was pleased.

"Good good. Katherine, can you please start organizing every-one? We will destroy these invaders!" he said loudly, and the crowd hooted and hollered. The captain slid his eyes fondly to Jon.

As the assembled group filed out of the room with purpose, Baltsaros leaned his hip on the table, watching Jon as he circled around to come stand in front of the captain.

"Do you think it will work?" Baltsaros asked.

Jon shrugged and reached for Baltsaros's waist, pulling himself flush against the captain.

"I'd say it's a fair bit of labour to prepare for something that might not even happen," Jon replied. "But yes, it's worth a shot."

Baltsaros closed his eyes as Jon placed his lips against his neck, warm tongue sliding up behind his earlobe.

"Yes; and, the idea of a land bridge is a good one. I think perhaps when this is over, we could look to making a permanent version... something with a false opening to let in the *Heart* but to dissuade others from trying," Baltsaros said and moved his hands down to grab Jon's buttocks, pressing himself against him. "We may start to get more unwanted visitors; there's no telling who else Reginald has told of our location."

At this Jon pulled his head back.

Baltsaros opened his eyes and saw that he was looking at him with narrowed storm-blue eyes.

"Why does Fresia know where Madierus is anyway?" asked Jon, confused.

Baltsaros shook his head at the young man's expression, grinning.

"We were an island full of men for a long time, and while that's fine for some," he said, pushing his pelvis playfully against Jon, "most were a touch lonely. Let's just say I imported some 'wives'."

His eyes went wide, and Baltsaros could tell Jon was running through the list of women he had met on the island.

"No," Baltsaros said laughing. "Ha! They weren't all whores, Jon—and they weren't all women! They came of their own free will; lots of the folks who immigrated were just tired of tyranny or repression. Now... Stop talking and go back to what you were doing just now."

J on felt a little rush of adrenaline as he swiftly unlaced Baltsaros's pants in the great hall. Despite the captain's assurance that the queen rarely ventured out of her rooms at this time, Jon still felt terribly exposed down on his knees on the hard marble floors.

Baltsaros's cock was a long outline under the tight black fabric, and Jon mouthed it, blowing his hot breath through the material. Baltsaros's hands were in his hair, pushing the back of Jon's head a little insistently as he was teased. He nudged at the flaps of material with his nose, pressing his mouth up at the soft mound between the man's legs.

Above him Baltsaros groaned quietly, spreading his legs a little further apart.

"Stop tormenting me, boy," said the captain, his voice rough with lust. Jon smiled and continued to kiss Baltsaros's cock through his pants; however, when the man shifted his hips, the unlaced flaps came apart, and Baltsaros's cock freed itself.

Baltsaros's fingers pulled hard suddenly in Jon's hair; he winced and looked up past the thick cock to the captain. Jon saw that, though Baltsaros was looking down, his eyes were distant, and his face was set in a fierce sneer.

Jon's heart quickened, and he slipped a hand down the front of his own trousers, aroused by the bestial look on Baltsaros's face. He placed his mouth under the purple head of the captain's stiff, naked cock and tongued the bottom ridge of it. The shaft bobbed up in response and Baltsaros let out a small, frustrated sigh.

"Open your mouth," said the captain, moving one of his hands to Jon's jaw. Baltsaros's thumb stroked the side of his neck. "Now."

Jon moved his hand over his own cock. Aroused by the captain's commanding tone, Jon kept teasing him with small licks and brushes of his lips over the sensitive head.

Finally, Baltsaros growled and curled his fingers around Jon's chin, forcing his mouth open.

Jon panted out an excited breath and tilted his head back, letting Baltsaros feed him his thick cock. As he shifted his knees on the hard floor, Jon struggled to grasp himself better in the tight confines of his pants. With Baltsaros thrusting himself into his mouth, Jon tugged at the front of his trousers, and a button went flying in his hurry to free his erection.

However, his desire became confused as Baltsaros began fucking Jon's throat with a punishing pace, moving to trap Jon's head between his large hands. With a firm grasp on Jon, Baltsaros grunted and slowed suddenly, forcing his length as far down as he could.

Jon gagged and tried to pull back, but Baltsaros held him in place, making him crane his neck further up. Unable to breathe, Jon grabbed Baltsaros's wrists, and there were tears in his eyes as he started to panic.

Baltsaros stared down at him, his face brutal and angry, and then started to thrust harder, bruising Jon's throat muscles as he gagged and fought desperately to free himself. There were spots in Jon's vision as he pleaded with his eyes at Baltsaros, his nails digging in and raking the skin of the captain's hands.

In response to the sudden pain, Baltsaros started as if coming out of a trance, releasing Jon and stepping back to stumble against the table.

Jon coughed and choked on his hands and knees, his head close to the floor; a string of saliva dropped from his lips to the marble tiles.

"What the fuck, Baltsaros?" Jon said hoarsely, when he had caught his breath. He looked up and saw that the captain was breathing hard, staring down at Jon with a confused expression.

Jon's throat burned and his jaw felt strained.

"What the hell was that?" Baltsaros liked being rough with Jon but never to a point so far past his limits.

Baltsaros's eyes went flat, and the muscles twitched under the skin of his stubbled jaw.

Jon wiped at his mouth with the back of his hand and pulled his pants back together, all desire flown with Baltsaros's excessive handling of him. He stood shakily and glared at the captain.

"What's *wrong* with you?" Jon said angrily, his voice rough.

"I... am sorry, Jon. I'm not sure what came over me," said Baltsaros, his accent slurring his words slightly in his daze.

Jon bit back another retort and took a deep breath. Something was seriously bothering the captain; there was a strange vagueness in his eyes that Jon had never seen before. At the memory of the crumpled drawing in the map room, Jon's face softened.

"It's Tom, isn't it?" he murmured, watching Baltsaros's expression closely.

The older man's brows came down as he tilted his head to the side like a large, bewildered creature, but Jon saw the minute crease appear and disappear almost instantly on Baltsaros's high brow.

That was it.

He dismissed the anger at his treatment, as well as the tiny pang of jealousy he felt at the former first mate's ability to affect Baltsaros from leagues away, and pressed on.

"Did you just... mistake me for Tom?" he asked, the idea coalescing in his head. "Baltsaros, I know Tom is alive, but—"

"Tom is alive?"

Jon blinked and swivelled his head in shock when he heard the voice come from across the room.

The queen, her eyes crackling with wildfire, stood haughtily in the open doorway.

Baltsaros snapped out of his stupor, pushing his cock back into his pants at the woman's startling presence.

"Abetha, what are you doing here?" the captain asked, his brow creased.

Jon blushed furiously realizing that the woman could have been here the whole time and he wouldn't have noticed.

"When were you planning on telling me?" she asked coldly, ignoring Baltsaros's question.

The captain grimaced and looked at Jon.

"Could you please excuse us?" he said, turning back to the queen.

Jon gritted his teeth at the summary dismissal.

"I'll be at the *Blossom*," he muttered, turning on his heel.

However, as Jon walked out of the room his mind was spinning. Baltsaros had once confessed that he simply missed Tom. Jon now realized that it was much more than that.

B altsaros frowned at the icy queen staring him down in the echoing great hall.

"I only just found out," he said, angrily.

"Baltsaros, don't you think the first person you should have told was his *mother*?" she asked, her voice low and measured as always.

Baltsaros looked down and started relacing his pants, his mind still on what had happened between him and Jon. For a moment… For a worryingly long moment, the boy kneeling at his feet had been Tom. He licked his lips, feeling off-balanced by the conflict of emotions that suddenly swelled up inside him. Then, just as quickly, they were gone again, leaving him barren and cold. All he wanted to be was alone with his thoughts.

"Don't pretend you are the least bit affected by Tom's life or death," Baltsaros said wearily, lifting his head. He saw that at his words, Abetha had raised her chin higher, a glimmer of wetness in her beautiful ocean-coloured eyes. Remembering Jon's assessment of the queen's feelings, Baltsaros realized in dismay that he may have indeed been wrong about the seemingly dispassionate woman.

"And what would a creature like you know of things like a mother's love," Abetha asked, her nostrils flaring slightly and her cheeks flushed.

"Or a wife's love?" Baltsaros asked quietly.

Abetha's brows came down quickly, and her lips thinned. As she turned to leave, Baltsaros called out as he walked towards her.

"Wait. Abetha," he said hurriedly. "Queen Bee."

She turned to him, a startled look on her face.

"You haven't called me that since those early days, Baltsaros," she said, her expression one of suspicion.

"Why didn't you tell me that this was more than an arrangement for you?" he asked, looking down at her.

She lifted a pale hand to her blond hair and brushed it aside, glancing away briefly with a deep line between her brows.

"Oh it wasn't, Baltsaros. I never intended it to be more. What kind of doting wife wants to pine for her husband for eight or nine months of the year?" she smiled, but it didn't reach her eyes.

Baltsaros frowned.

"Then why this animosity?" he asked. "Jon thinks you loved me." Abetha's eyes flicked away from his face, and he saw they were shimmering again with tears that would never fall.

She laughed softly.

"He's an observant one, isn't he?" Abetha said, her smile genuine when she looked back at Baltsaros. She sighed. "I will admit that I fell for your charms... And that I was imprudent with my thoughts of you during that first long absence. I don't know what I expected... But I certainly did not think that you would come here, to my home, to blatantly paw at my son before my very eyes."

Baltsaros thought of Tom, and he closed his eyes; the boy had stolen into his bed like a sylph and gifted him with pleasure in return for pain.

The great hall had gone suddenly airless.

"I did not 'paw' your son in front of you, Abetha," he said, his voice barely a whisper, trying to bring himself back to the present. "But my indiscretion was an unforgivable lack of respect. I do see that now... And it seems that I wounded you." Baltsaros opened his eyes and looked at his wife. "That you had an attachment to me beyond friendship never once entered into my mind."

At this, Abetha shook her head sadly.

"Baltsaros, we were never friends. Partners, yes. Friendly? Once, definitely. But never friends." She smiled again, and Baltsaros nodded, realizing the truth of it.

In light of this new knowledge, Baltsaros felt oddly driven to confide in the woman who had loathed him for so long; perhaps if her detachment could extend to his relationship with her son, she could help him to see...

To see what?

His expression was open and honest as he looked down at her.

"Tom is indeed alive. He sent a letter to Jon, and we found it only yesterday. Abetha, Tom and I had a falling out, and it was entirely due to my mishandling of my relationship with Jon. I was... excessive in my reaction towards Tom's misconduct," Baltsaros said hesitantly. "I am greatly relieved that he is alive," he continued, shaking his head. "But, I believe there is some troubling connection between Tom and Jon. And... I am having problems reconciling my... emotions." Baltsaros's voice sounded weak to his ears, and he felt strangely lightheaded as if he needed to sit down. Nonetheless, it was good to speak the words out loud.

Abetha's eyebrows had risen in astonishment during his confession. When he stopped speaking, she narrowed her eyes at her husband and looked searchingly into his face.

"How very uncharacteristic of you, Baltsaros. It seems that perhaps I misunderstood something about you as well," she said quietly. After a moment, Abetha tilted her head and appraised him thoughtfully. When she finally spoke, Baltsaros immediately noticed the change in the intelligent woman's tone.

"Would you care to join me in the gardens? I could have some of the white summerwine you love so much brought out. We should speak further. I think you and I need to start again if we're meant to be allies," she said, with a reserved smile on her full lips.

Allies? thought Baltsaros with surprise.

"That would be incredibly gracious of you, my dear," he said and with no small amount of relief, followed her out of the room.

THE BLOOD NEEDS

*Life is a battle between faith and reason in which
each feeds upon the other, drawing sustenance
from it and destroying it.*

— REINHOLD NIEBUHR

*The night was dark, the woods deep. At the edge of it, Jon stood watching
a big tawny cat prowl back and forth at the shore of a black sea, like it
was desperate to enter the water but afraid. Taking a step forward, Jon
realized that he was covered in blood and lifted his hands, trying to see if
the blood was his. He looked up and saw that Tom was there, an amused
look on his face.*

*"When I said he had no heart, I didn't mean for ye to give him yours,
lovey," said the big man.*

*Jon frowned and Tom pointed to his chest. Jon looked down and saw
that there was a huge hole cut out of his chest. Alarmed, he put his hand
over it, attempting to staunch the blood flow.*

*Tom laughed, shaking his head, and Jon saw that the young brute
had a matching hole. There was a flash of lightning, and the wind
started to blow.*

"Come!" yelled Jon.

Tom shook his head slowly and pointed to the edge of the water. In the tide were red objects, moving and flopping in the currents against the night beach. Jon saw that they were excised hearts and knew that his and Tom's had to be among them.

"No!" shouted Tom. "Ours are safe."

They were on the ship, and the giant black lion stood on the deck, eyeing them. From its bared fangs dripped blood, and Jon saw that the boat was littered with the dead. He turned away. Beyond the horizon rose the impossibly high, jagged teeth of a monster. From there came the sounds of a heartbeat, and Jon recognized it instantly as his.

The lion stood on the deck looking at him with fierce affection, claws dripping with blood.

Baltsaros stood on the deck looking at him with fierce affection, a bloodied knife in his hands.

"There," said Tom, pointing to the horizon. "There is where we must go."

J on groaned and pulled the covers over his head, but he could still hear Baltsaros arguing with Maya outside the door.

"He still doesn't want to see you, Baltsaros," said the proprietress of the tavern.

"I think we should leave that up to Jon, no?" asked the captain, his voice low and annoyed.

With a sigh, Jon sat up. He'd been hiding out in Maya and Katherine's spare room above the tavern for the last two days, avoiding Baltsaros. He still felt shaken and angry about the way that the captain had treated him. And the queen... Her eyes had been so violent.

Jon wasn't sure he could ever return to the castle.

He'd asked Maya to keep Baltsaros away so that he could sort out his thoughts; however, all he'd managed to do was work himself into a worse state thinking about Tom.

Tom and Baltsaros. Baltsaros and Tom.

He rubbed his eyes and stood up a bit unsteadily. The whiskey bottle that Maya had brought up for him was nearly empty on the chair next to the bed. He stumbled over his boot and pitched head first into the door, managing to catch himself at the last second before his face slammed into the wood. As he pressed his forehead against the jamb, Jon took a few deep breaths and unlocked the door, opening it a crack.

Maya held out a hand, her big blue eyes startled.

"It's ok, Jon. The captain was just leaving," she said. Her face was taut with anger as she glared at Baltsaros.

Jon shook his head tiredly.

"Let him in," he said softly. "It's fine. Really."

Baltsaros had turned to look at Jon through the opening, and he could see the effect his state had on the captain. Jon was shirtless, his hair tangled, his face probably pale and haggard. It had been a long two days, and he was certain he reeked of liquor and sweat.

The captain was staring at him with his stark brow raised, the surprise and worry looking out of place on the man's sharp-featured face.

Jon opened the door wide, nodding once to Maya to convey his gratitude before swinging it closed and bolting it shut again. He walked around Baltsaros, who stood like a statue in the middle of the room, and picked up the whiskey, collapsing onto the bed with it.

"Well?" Jon asked and took a swallow direct from the neck of the bottle.

Baltsaros looked down at his hands, a crease appearing between his brows. Taking a step forward, he went down on one knee in front of Jon, his head bowed.

"Jon, forgive me," said the captain, his voice quiet.

Jon goggled at Baltsaros for a moment before breaking into harsh laughter.

"For what? Being a sadistic prick?" he asked, shoving at Baltsaros's shoulder with a bare foot.

The older man fell to his rear on the wood floor but didn't look up.

Jon frowned and took another sip of whiskey before sitting up and setting the bottle down.

What the hell? he thought drunkenly as he stood.

"Forgive me," repeated Baltsaros. When the man raised his eyes to Jon's, he saw that they were wet.

Anger boiled up hot in Jon.

"No!" he said pointing at the captain. "Don't you *dare* do that!" Jon shouted and levelled an awkward kick at Baltsaros's side.

With a grunt from the impact of Jon's foot meeting his ribs, the man just frowned and held his ground.

"I need you," Baltsaros said simply.

Jon rubbed his jaw and circled around the man sitting on the floor. When Baltsaros made no other move to speak, Jon dropped onto the floor next to Baltsaros with a sigh and looked at him in exasperation.

"You're a fucking manipulative bastard. I don't believe those tears for a second," Jon said, shaking his head. He looked down and gritted his teeth, scratching at a dirty spot on his trousers with a fingernail. With a long sigh, he lifted his eyes back to the captain's. "Gods, don't you *ever* be that rough with me again. That was a really shitty thing to do. You're lucky I didn't bite you." He frowned at Baltsaros. "Is that how you treated Tom? No wonder he was afraid of you."

Baltsaros's expression went flat for a moment before he tilted his head quizzically.

"Afraid?" he asked, his voice confused. The captain's eyes went distant like he was remembering something. Incongruously, he chuckled suddenly.

Jon frowned.

"Can you believe that he used to beg me to use him that roughly?" murmured Baltsaros, his eyes refocusing on Jon's face. "He used to make me angry on purpose so that I would be violent with him. Jon, he loves to submit. I can hurt him and hurt him *and he takes it*... and loves every damn minute of it. No, Jon... Tom was only afraid of the whip. Not of me. Never of me."

Jon swallowed hard at the captain's words and thought back to the first time he heard Baltsaros and Tom from across the darkened room.

Baltsaros's eyes were warm and brown as he looked at Jon.

"Tom is beautiful and broken, Jon. He knows it and accepts it for what it is... And *there is nothing wrong with that*. Hells, he's better at coping than you or me," said Baltsaros, rubbing the spot where Jon had kicked him. "He soothed the beast inside me with his submission for so long that I didn't understand what was happening when he was gone."

As Jon listened, he shook his head; the night of the storm showed him a side of Tom that was rough-edged but desperate in its desire for love. Jon wasn't able to reconcile that with the picture that Baltsaros was painting of the muscular brute.

Jon's eyes went wide as he suddenly realized something through his haze: the captain was actually talking about Tom with what seemed like true affection.

"Baltsaros? What happened?" he said slowly, the whiskey in his blood making it hard to think straight. The captain's eyes were hooded and his face strangely bleak as he looked at Jon, and, for the first time, he felt honestly concerned for Baltsaros.

"I think I owe Tom an apology," said the captain quietly.

Jon frowned and stretched an arm out, grabbing the bottle to offer it to Baltsaros.

The captain accepted it with a laugh and drank down some of the amber liquid, grimacing.

"She could have at least given you something decent," Baltsaros said, smiling wryly.

Jon shrugged and ran his fingers through his dark hair, trying to untangle it while he thought. As he stared up at the rough-hewn undersides of the ceiling boards and beams, Jon tried to find the words that had eluded him for the past two days.

"Yes... You do need to apologize to Tom." He nodded. "Will we go find him?" he asked after a moment.

The captain licked his lips and took another swallow of whiskey.

"He may not accept my apology," said Baltsaros, looking sidelong at Jon.

Jon just lifted his shoulders.

"I think he will once he realizes you mean it," he responded. "And for once I really think you do." Jon took a deep breath and took the plunge, deciding to be painfully straightforward.

"I need Tom," he said.

Baltsaros closed his eyes.

I need Tom.

Three simple words, similar to the words he had spoken to Abetha in the gardens a few days prior: *I need Tom back.*

It had taken time for him to come around to that understanding. He had forgiven Tom a long time ago for the part he had played in Jon's arrest, but it was only sitting in the beautiful castle gardens, laying his words out to a newfound ally, that he had finally and truly understood:

Baltsaros was angry at *himself.* For his treatment of the sinfully gorgeous youth that had bent and finally broken at his hands. For the fact that he had dismissed Tom's affections so quickly. For the fact that he was utterly crippled when it came to understanding his own needs.

In the shade of the orange trees, Baltsaros had turned the idea around in his head and realized that he had truly wronged his former first mate. Abetha had looked sad when he had said as much. While speaking of her son in such a way had obviously made her uncomfortable, when the queen had seen how earnest he was, Abetha had sighed.

Then go to him, she had said.

Was it really that easy? Baltsaros put the empty bottle down. Jon made him crazy; this was something that he had come to accept. Baltsaros literally wanted to lock the young man in a cage sometimes, away from everyone else. It was an insane impulse and based on next to nothing, an urge that had stripped him of reason, time and time again.

He had *never* felt this way about Tom. In fact, one of his favourite things to do when in port was to throw women and men at Tom to see how well they could use the talented, submissive young man. It was all in good fun.

However, the fact that his former first mate was still alive had become something that was slowly burning him from the inside, rendering him nearly as crazy as Jon made him.

Tom was alive, yes. But was he well? Did he truly hate Baltsaros? It seemed that he would not be satisfied until he saw the young man with his own eyes. The realization that he needed Tom had been hard to swallow for Baltsaros; however, now that it was out in the open, he felt he could think straight again.

He frowned at the dark-haired youth who sagged against his side, made soft and vague by far too much whiskey.

Tom and Jon.

Once, he had hoped exactly for that. They were day and night, summer and winter; yet they weren't exactly opposites. Baltsaros frowned: could he accept that which he had forbidden? As he turned to look into Jon's half-lidded eyes, Baltsaros realized that he would have to try. Baltsaros hadn't enjoyed watching Jon fuck the prostitute like he thought he would; could he deal with watching Tom touch Jon? Watching Tom *fuck* Jon?

He was playing back that first drunken night with the two boys in his mind when he heard his young lover's voice break through his thoughts.

"Tom loves you," whispered Jon.

Baltsaros pressed his face against Jon's dirty, tangled hair. He nodded.

"Yes. I realize that now," he said softly. Such a blind spot for love. Did he love? Did he just obsess? What was this need that called to him? Blue-green eyes... storm-grey eyes. Bodies that moved beneath his hands, minds and hearts that somehow *meant* something to him. Baltsaros felt the impromptu urge to gift something to Jon.

"My marriage will be dissolved," he said. He felt Jon stiffen and watched him sit up sleepily.

Jon looked at him, confused.

"Won't she send more people after you?" he asked. Jon's eyes were large in his pale face, his skin slick from too much drink and not enough sleep. However, his seal-brown curls framed his face attractively and brushed the hollows of his collarbones in a charming way.

Smiling, the captain shook his head.

"No... Abetha and I have come to an understanding. One that should have come a lot sooner. She will stay on as queen. It is I who abdicates the crown," he said. "Abetha will continue to rule here... I honestly don't care. She's done it for the last five years during my absences and, as I have found out in the last day, does a rather spectacular job of it." He ran his hand up Jon's side, smiling. "I'll build us a hut on the beach for next year," Baltsaros said jokingly.

"But... her records?" asked Jon, pulling slightly out of the other man's grasp.

"Just a means of rankling me," replied the captain, grinning a little self-consciously. He reached out and placed his palm against Jon's cheek, his hand somewhat hesitant.

"We'll go find Tom when this is over. I promise you," he said.

Jon, brow knitted, looked at Baltsaros.

"Why?" he asked, his eyes hopeful.

"Because I need him too," he said and leaned in to kiss Jon's lips.

. . .

Baltsaros lifted his head off the pillow and frowned. Something had woken him up, but he couldn't hear anything. The bed was narrower and harder than he was used to, but the warm, sleeping body pressed tight against him made it more appealing than the softest feather bed.

Baltsaros smoothed Jon's stray hair out of his face, and he laid his head back down, curling protectively against the younger man. Baltsaros's arm ached slightly from the cut Jon had inflicted on him, and he smiled.

"It's a pact," said Jon, his eyes manic with the whiskey coursing through his veins. They were sitting on the floor in the dark, wrapped in the intense embrace of a hot, drunken night, the kind that fuelled desire and wrung promises from even the hardest of hearts.

Baltsaros frowned and looked down at the knife in Jon's hand; the young man was clutching his wrist with the other, intending on slicing through the flesh of his forearm.

"A pact?" asked Baltsaros, intrigued.

Jon nodded slowly.

"Yes… Soldiers would often do this back home to show their loyalty; it was a kind of pledge to always protect each other," he said with a rough emotion in his voice. "They would mingle their blood and be forever part of the other's life."

Baltsaros felt a strange sentiment rise up in him at Jon's words.

Forever is a long time.

He looked thoughtfully at Jon and then dipped his chin in permission.

The knife slid through the skin of his arm, a red, wet line that began weeping a moment after it appeared. The pain was nothing.

Baltsaros felt a strange excitement at sharing his blood with another man. When Jon quickly cut into his own arm, Baltsaros became keenly aroused. It was such an incredibly intimate gesture. Pressing his arm to Jon's, Baltsaros closed his eyes, imagining their blood mingling in each other's veins.

With a strangled moan, Baltsaros opened his eyes and crushed himself against Jon. Jon responded with equal passion, his mouth capturing the captain's in a savage kiss. They soon found themselves entwined on the bed, fumbling with buttons and laces, groping at sensitive skin, wet with spit and blood.

However, in the end their lovemaking was gentle and drawn out; curled into each other like spoons, Baltsaros had stroked Jon slowly to orgasm while buried deep within him from behind. Feeling soft and strangely fragile, Baltsaros's own climax had brought with it a resurgence of the tears that had glistened in his eyes earlier. He didn't understand but didn't question it, simply burying his face in the back of Jon's neck and breathing deep.

J on's eyes opened when he felt Baltsaros lift his head again.

"What is it?" he asked, his voice rough. The inside of his mouth was coated, and his head ached. Baltsaros raised himself up on an elbow behind him, his hand resting on Jon's side, thumb stroking the skin over his ribs. When he blinked his eyes shut again, Jon heard it this time, and his heart beat double.

It was the alarm bell.

Reginald was here.

31

DARKNESS FALLS

Baltsaros stood in the tower window squinting into the long telescope he had set up. There they were: three dots on the horizon.

Thank the gods it's not more, he thought grimly.

He swivelled the instrument to the mouth of the harbour where the last of the jolly boats was strewing long pieces of wood tied with vines and foliage among the anchored pieces of the false land bridge. Since they hadn't had time to complete the work, the captain hoped that the quickly cobbled-together solution would be enough to sustain the illusion. *Baal's Heart* would be leaving within the hour; Baltsaros was amazed and somewhat proud of the fact that everyone was so organized. Again he thanked whatever forces there were that they had found the letter when they did; the timing couldn't have been any closer.

Baltsaros smiled ruefully at his own inadequate preparations, having wasted the last two days on incredibly selfish pursuits.

Though, was that time really wasted? he wondered. He had successfully navigated the confused courses of his own mind to forge an alliance with a worthy collaborator.

After pulling his eye away from the sights below, Baltsaros

turned his head to the handsome, dark-haired young man who sat cross-legged on the floor next to him, trying to kill his hangover with strong, black coffee. Baltsaros had also managed to pull Jon closer to him with the promise of a sacrifice that excited him with curiosity. While he might not survive to see the fruits of what was sown these past few days, he was glad for what had happened.

Jon groaned and leaned his head back on the stone wall. When he turned back to the window, Baltsaros's grin faded, and he clenched his jaw. He felt no fear or worry for the coming battle, only a sense of deep outrage that a man such as Reginald could presume to trespass on Baltsaros's domain.

The captain would personally hasten the old man into the arms of death this time.

Jon swung the blade a few times, testing the heft of it in his hand. It was much better balanced than the practice swords that he and Katherine had spent months using aboard the ship, and he was pleased with how well it moved in his grasp.

Katherine, watching him with her arms crossed, nodded once.

"That'll have to do," she said.

Frowning, he made as if to poke her with the curved tip of the sword.

"Hey! I thought that was pretty damned good, considering whom I had as a teacher," he teased, trying to lighten her mood.

Katherine's lips were pressed together in a hard line, and there was a twitching tightness to her jaw that exposed her worry. She just frowned at him and nodded again distractedly.

"Yes, sure. Now go deliver the rest, Jon," she said and turned to give orders to the next man.

Jon, trying not to let the dread of the coming battle get to him, ran off with the armload of freshly sharpened swords. As he jogged down the wide, cobbled street that ran through the small village, Jon could see through the gaps in the foliage that the three ships were now visible to the naked eye.

The fleet, consisting of a galleon and two smaller frigates, were still a few hours away, but the sight of them made Jon's blood run cold. He could just imagine Reginald, fuelled by zealous revenge, standing high on the aft castle of the galleon staring at the small island through his spyglass.

Picking up the pace, he rounded the corner and descended the old coral-rock stairs that were a shortcut to the beach. As he ran down the uneven steps, he scared the small green lizards that were baking themselves in the hot noontime sun on the low wall. Jon breathed in deep the scent of pink frangipani flowers that bordered the narrow path down, wondering if he would live to smell them this night when they were at their most fragrant.

Caught up in his gloomy thoughts, Jon nearly stumbled when his foot sunk into the soft sand at the base of the stairs. As he looked around at the men working to position the six cannons, Jon spotted Calum.

The old man was sitting on a boulder, a dark hand the colour of walnut shading his eyes as he watched the coming fleet.

After dumping the swords beside Calum, Jon breathed heavily. He was still labouring under the effects of his overindulgence. Earlier, when Baltsaros had pressed him to sleep some more, Jon had been unable to relax enough to do so. Bent over with his hands on his knees, he looked over at Old Calum.

"Shouldn't you be aboard *Baal's Heart* with the rest of the old and infirm?" he asked jokingly. By attempting to make everyone else smile, Jon knew that he was just trying to make himself feel less afraid.

Calum cracked a wide smile, his missing tooth like a broken fencepost in the straight, white grin.

"Should'n'ye be there too, lad? Bein' a wee nipper like yerself... Yer bound ta get crushed underboot, nay?" laughed the old man.

Jon smiled and let himself fall backwards into the soft sand. If anyone could take a coming battle lightly, it was Old Calum. Jon lay looking up at the leaves of the coconut tree overhead and tried to clear his mind of worry.

Calum kicked his leg, and Jon lifted his head. The old man was holding a flask out to Jon, and he tried not to notice how Calum's hand shook; though it was from age and not from fear, it underscored the fact that they were facing an enemy with a scant, motley group of their own.

Jon took the flask from Calum, hoping it was anything but whiskey, and put it to his lips; he was thankful when the liquid that touched his tongue was sweet, spiced rum.

With *Baal's Heart* crammed to the gunwales and making the two-day journey to the next island over, Madierus's population now numbered one hundred and thirty-four men and women.

Jon was glad he had missed all the tearful goodbyes earlier; between the hangover and the fear, he would have been a wreck. It was better this way; he had managed to keep his head thus far.

One hundred thirty-four against how many? Four hundred? Five? he thought. It didn't seem fair that now that his life was filled with love and hope, it should be cut so short.

He took another mouthful of rum and passed the flask back to Calum. Jon laid his head back down in the sand and closed his eyes.

T t was almost dusk when the three ships loomed large just past the narrow mouth of the harbour. The captain stood on the roof of the *Grog Blossom* looking across the bay, his face stony and solemn.

The rest of the assembled group was quiet as they watched the three navy ships lower boat after boat over their sides, and Jon rubbed a hand over his face, the fear of the coming battle rearing its ugly head to bite hard at his guts.

Baltsaros, seeing the young man's terror, reached out and pulled Jon against him, a strong arm across his back. As he shuddered slightly in the captain's embrace, Jon tried to get ahold of himself. As always, Baltsaros's heart beat slow and strong in his chest; this time, however, it served only to highlight just how fast Jon's pulse was racing.

"Hush, my love," murmured Baltsaros, stroking Jon's dark curls against the back of his neck. "Don't be afraid."

Jon closed his eyes tight, wishing he had the captain's effortless confidence. They could hear the sound of horns in the distance, heralding the coming battle. Jon took a few deep breaths and leaned hard against Baltsaros.

The captain slid his hand down the younger man's back.

"If you assume that you will die today, you drag death to you as a cold, unforgiving stranger. Instead, embrace death like an old friend, for you will fight side by side with her; and, if death decides to choose you as her champion, you may yet live to fight, and love, another day," said the captain softly into Jon's ear.

After a few minutes, Jon slowly opened his eyes and realized he was calm. He lifted his head from the captain's shoulder and met Baltsaros's fierce gaze with his own. Jon felt ready, almost impatient, for the fight to start.

Baltsaros cupped the side of his face and ran his thumb over Jon's cheek before he leaned in to kiss him, maybe for the last time. The thought made Jon's heart pound harder, and he put all of his love into the kiss, without a care to those watching. Baltsaros's lips were insistent; the force of his ardour was an almost bruising embrace as he leaned in hard, breathing in Jon's breath as his own.

The false strip of land worked well to stall the coming boats; though the illusion was broken when the first boat to reach it tried to disembark onto it, two uniformed navy men sank immediately below the water. Only one man was pulled back into the safety of the boat, and the pirates amassed on the beach let out a roar. They had claimed their first casualty.

With the men on the boats trying to quickly untangle the floating mass of wood and vegetation to get past it, Baltsaros gave the order to start firing. The oldest of the cannons proved to be useless right away when her casing cracked, but the remaining five quickly started sending men to their watery deaths.

BOOM!

BOOM!

Jon thought he would go deaf from the noise, every volley a punch in the chest. After a few minutes, he was surprised when he could hear a strange whistling sound above the racket of the aged cannons and turned his head to Katherine to see if she could hear it too...

...only to see that her arm suddenly ended at the elbow as the small black ball bounced past them on the beach. Stunned into incomprehension by what he had witnessed, Jon watched the blood arc into the air as someone else was nearly cut in half.

Katherine fell to her knees, her face an almost comical mask of shock as she touched the bleeding end of her stump, and Jon looked on as she toppled over onto her side in the muddied red sands. He turned around and looked out over the water and saw a flash come from the side of the lead ship, then another.

The air was rent with screams, and Jon suddenly understood what was happening: they had underestimated the range of the galleon's guns.

"Get back! Get back!" roared Baltsaros from somewhere to his left. Shaken, Jon looked around and saw that the captain had picked up Katherine over his shoulder, motioning for him to follow. The air was filled with whistling as the small cannonballs bounced up the beach, throwing up sand and blood and wreaking destruction wherever they hit.

Jon snapped out of his daze and ran for the low wall; pulling himself up onto it, he reached down for the unconscious woman. Baltsaros handed Katherine up, and Jon hefted her onto his back as he struggled up the slope between the trees. The captain was beside him, lending a hand whenever Jon stumbled.

Soon they were at the tavern, but Baltsaros hastened them on. When they were far enough, the captain stopped him with a hand and helped lay Katherine down on the cobblestones.

From behind him, Jon heard Maya's strangled cry; he stood and turned to take her in his arms as she struggled against him. Stroking her hair, Jon watched as Baltsaros pulled his shirt over his head and cut into it with the short sword at his hip.

After tearing it into strips, Baltsaros twisted them together and passed the loop around the end of Katherine's bleeding stump. There was a pool of blood under her, and the woman was pale.

"A stick!" yelled the captain, and Jon let go of Maya, scooping up a thick twig from the side of the wide throughway. The captain pulled it from Jon's grasp with bloodied hands and passed it through the end of the loop, twisting it round and round to tighten the tourniquet around Katherine's arm, finally tying it in place when the blood had stopped flowing.

The woman's eyelids fluttered as Maya wept and stroked the side of her face.

Baltsaros lifted his eyes to Jon.

"Bring her to the castle. Abetha should have set up a space for the wounded by now. Maya... Maya—listen to me!" said Baltsaros loudly.

She turned to look at the captain, her eyes huge and scared.

"Maya, you have to get water into her when she wakes. She's lost a lot of blood. Nod if you understand me." Maya slowly nodded, and Baltsaros turned back to Jon.

The captain squeezed his arm and smiled tightly.

"Come find me after," said Baltsaros, his face set in hard lines.

Jon nodded and picked up the stricken woman again. As he made his way up to the castle with Maya, he heard the continued booming of the cannons on the beach; Jon sent a little prayer to the brave men and women who were manning them, out in the open and at the mercy of the naval guns.

. . .

The sounds of fighting reached his ears as he made his way through the dense foliage. The sun was starting to set, and the coming twilight would make it hard for them to see. To his left, Jon could hear what could only be a death rattle, and he hoped that it was coming from the throat of a navy man and not a friend's.

The big guns on both the galleon and on the beach had been silent for the last little while; there was nothing else to fire upon on the blood-strewn beach, and all the boats had made their way to land, disgorging men along the shore.

Jon, never a good swordsman and not much of a marksman, was put to work helping to haul the wounded to the castle. Every trip there and back was a harrowing experience for him; he hated leaving Baltsaros's side. It was as if keeping the captain within his sights would guarantee that the other man would live.

As he ducked beneath the long, spiny leaves of a huge aloe plant, Jon picked his way to where the captain was watching the fighting from a vantage point above the town square. Baltsaros was stripped to the waist, having sacrificed his shirt to Katherine's arm, and was covered in sweat and blood.

Jon could see that there was a long cut across the captain's chest, but it was only weeping blood slowly and didn't seem to be deep.

When Baltsaros spotted Jon, he jumped down from the low roof of the shed. The captain's eyes were wide and worried as he looked over Jon, and he felt both ashamed and touched that his well-being was the only thing that seemed to break Baltsaros's composure.

"Beard's dead," Jon said sadly when the captain reached him, and Baltsaros nodded. The giant man had taken a lead ball to the temple and somehow lived long enough to take down another three men before he had succumbed to his injuries.

While the odds were definitely in the navy's favour, the pirates of Madierus had managed to cut the invaders' numbers by over half. That still had them outnumbered at least two-to-one, but the battle wasn't over yet. Losing Beard was a terrible blow; however, the man had single-handedly killed a good thirty men on his own.

The great hall of the castle was filling up slowly with the wounded, and Abetha was running a tight ship with the attending servants. Almost all animosity between him and the intimidatingly self-possessed queen had gone away in light of the alliance forged between her and the captain, and the rest of it had dissipated over the course of the past few hours.

Jon saw how incredibly dedicated Abetha was to her subjects and how composed and undaunted she was by the horrors taking place. Jon had a feeling that the population's opinion of the queen would be changed greatly by her actions this day... if any of them survived.

"Abetha says that Katherine is trying to get back out to fight," said Jon, a grin on his face despite everything.

Baltsaros's face creased into a smile, and he laughed loud.

"She would," he said, shaking his head.

Just then the sounds of fighting got closer and Baltsaros's head turned, his eyes like chips of obsidian, flashing in the light of the setting sun.

B altsaros was torn between running into the fray and keeping back to protect Jon. This was the problem with attachments: they made you weak. Growling under his breath from frustration, he swung his head back to Jon and pointed up to the castle.

"I want you to remain with Abetha," he said, his words a command. Jon's face fell, and Baltsaros cursed under his breath. How to explain to him that to fight, Baltsaros needed to know that Jon was safe?

"Jon, please. Do as I say. Go to her. Protect her," he said, making his voice soft. Baltsaros didn't want to think about Jon being in trouble... Even now, an image of the young man pierced through by a sword was making his heart hammer fast in his chest.

Jon's mouth came down at the corners, and he shook his head.

"I won't leave you! I can fight!" he pleaded.

"For the love of the gods! Jon... Go. Obey me!" growled Baltsaros. "You'll be no good to me dead." When he just stood staring at Baltsaros, the captain lifted his sword and placed the point of it against Jon's right shoulder.

"So help me gods, I will cripple you myself to keep you safe." Baltsaros felt ill saying it, but it was true; he couldn't bear the thought of Jon dying. The sword trembled in his hand. "Please..." he said, his voice hoarse. He swallowed hard. "Please, I don't want to die knowing the pain of your death."

Tears coursed down Jon's face in reaction to the captain's words; he pushed the blade aside and stepped towards Baltsaros. However, he stopped when a group of navy men suddenly burst out from the alley beside the tavern, running towards them.

"Go!" shouted Baltsaros and was gratified when Jon finally spun on his heel to sprint up the road. A cold fury descended on Baltsaros as he watched his lover run before turning to meet his attackers' blades with his own, an ear-rending roar bursting from his throat as he submerged himself in the lust of battle.

J on stopped to watch a moment, his eyes stinging from tears and sweat.

Baltsaros let out a war cry and turned to the five men who had moved to surround him. The captain was a blur of motion as he hacked and parried with the long, straight sword he held in his right hand, while his left hand darted in like a snake to stab into his attackers with a short, pointed blade.

Jon cried out when he saw the captain take a cut to his thigh but forced himself to look away. He just couldn't watch his lover die.

He won't fall. He won't fall. He won't fall.

The words were a rapid-fire mantra coursing through Jon's head as he ran as fast as he could towards the castle, feeling like he was leaving his heart behind. He sobbed as he ran, the ache in his chest almost too much to bear.

However, when he reached the covered portico, Jon quickly ducked behind a column in alarm. Standing on the wide marble steps were two naval men holding long-guns.

How did they get through the line of defence? he wondered breathlessly.

At first Jon was rigid with panic, unable to move. However, when he heard Maya's scream, his body reacted by hurtling him through the courtyard like a madman, his blade swinging.

Through sheer blunder, Jon managed to knock one of the men backwards down the stairs while attempting to cleave into the second. His blade went wide, but the other man's gun went off as it landed on the marble, sending a lead ball straight up through the bottom of the standing man's jaw. Jon quickly spun around and slashed at the other man's throat, thankful when he saw that it was a killing blow.

After stumbling up the rest of the stairs, Jon ran through the entranceway and pressed himself against the wall next to the open door of a sitting room; he had heard Katherine's voice raised in anger and, a moment later, the low, growling tones of a man that Jon had hoped never to see again. There was the smack of flesh hitting flesh and another loud cry from Maya.

As he gritted his teeth, Jon tried to think of a plan. However, when his mind came up blank, he just took a deep breath and simply stepped over the threshold. Maya was on the ground, and Katherine was on her knees beside her, breathing heavily, a sword held up awkwardly in her remaining hand. She was glaring up at a man who had obviously struck Maya, but made no move to attack.

Jon guessed that the blood loss and the fact that the sword was held in her off-hand stayed her; the woman was probably expending all her reserves just holding the heavy blade aloft.

Abetha and her servants were nowhere to be seen.

With a shiver of revulsion Jon saw that standing in the middle of the room, with a mantle covering his head, was the man he had refused to call "father." He took another step forward.

At Jon's entrance, one of the navy men let out a sharp bark of surprise, and all heads turned to look at the intruder. Even from across the room, Jon could see that the entire left side of Reginald's face was a mass of burn scars, and the sight of it made him sick to his stomach; the old soldier resembled nothing so much as a melted candle.

"There you are, Jon," said Reginald pleasantly. "I'm glad you could join us!" The older man motioned for him to step forward.

Instantly, Jon was taken from behind by two of Reginald's men, his sword wrenched out of his hand. They pushed him further into the room, and Jon struggled in their grasp.

"I was just asking your collaborator here whether she knew of your whereabouts. She was unwilling to help at first so we decided to give her a little incentive," growled Reginald with a crooked smile.

Jon's eyes flicked to Maya's prone form and was glad to see that though the woman was unconscious, she seemed to be breathing easily. He moved his gaze to Katherine's face and saw that the wounded pirate was staring at him in anguish. Jon could see that she had broken out in a sweat; it wouldn't be long before she was too faint to hold herself upright.

"I take it by your lack of surprise that you were somehow alerted to our coming," Reginald said, shaking his head as he pulled at the edge of the hood he wore. "Now, I've been given to understand that you've taken up with the man who is wanted on a few dozen charges, not the least of which is the death of Lord Barton," said the old soldier-turned-privateer.

At this, Jon scowled. He cleared his throat and spoke up.

"I can't understand why the king would authorize such an incredibly stupid enterprise! Barton was a small lord. It seems completely blown out of proportion—"

Reginald suddenly lashed out and kicked a small table. It slid across the floor and crashed to its side, one of the delicate legs breaking off in the process.

"I'm sorry? Jon? What did you say?" asked Reginald, his scarred face bland as he tilted his head towards his stepson.

Jon blinked and frowned. Reginald's mind had obviously taken a beating along with his body.

"Let them go, Reginald. Just... Let them go. You want me... Don't hurt them," he said, lifting his hands.

Reginald's one eyebrow raised in his forehead.

"You?" the scarred man said, his face splitting into a grotesque grin. "No, Jon. I don't care about you. I'm looking for Captain Baltsaros. I'm to bring him back to the king for public execution. The rest of you... Well, I suppose we'll take care of you here once the prisoner is secured. Now," said Reginald, leaning into Jon's face. "Where is he?"

Jon recoiled from the madness trapped in Reginald's single, dark-brown eye and swallowed. Knifing through his fear was a brittle sadness that made his chest ache. He shook his head.

"He's dead," Jon said softly.

He must be. He willed himself not to break down.

"Your men attacked him in the town square."

He heard Katherine's sword clatter to the floor behind him, and Reginald bared his teeth at Jon.

"He can't be dead! I won't allow it!" the man shouted, his spittle hitting Jon in the face. "They're supposed to take him alive, dammit!" The barrel-chested man started walking back and forth in front of Jon.

The younger man heard the sound of another sword falling in the next room and frowned, but Reginald was too caught up in his fury to notice. As he allowed himself to feel a pulse of hope, Jon turned his head, straining to hear more.

The next few minutes were a confusing blur for Jon as he was suddenly dropped by the two navy men holding him, their hands quickly drawing their swords as they turned to face whatever it was that had startled them. Jon stumbled but did not fall, and he swivelled in time to see Calum and a few deckhands burst into the room.

Reginald stood as if frozen in stone for a moment, watching his men fight the pirates.

Jon fumbled at his belt; sliding Tom's long knife out of its sheath, he held it up to Reginald.

The older man turned, honest surprise on his burned face.

"Jon? What are you doing?" he said, putting his hands up.

Jon could see that the fingers of Reginald's left hand had fused into a shiny fist of scar tissue from the fire. "Oh, we weren't going to execute you! You're my son! Jon... Put the knife down." Reginald stopped mid-step when Jon's knuckles whitened on the bone hilt of the blade.

"Your son? Your witch hunt took the life of the only man who ever believed in me," he growled through his teeth. The sounds of fighting grew quiet around him as he stared down the old soldier.

Reginald's eye had gone wide at Jon's words.

"Believed in you? What was there to believe in? Just come home..." said Reginald and suddenly stepped forward, tackling Jon.

The two men struggled; Reginald had the advantage in size but, being crippled, wasn't quite able to grasp Jon to restrain him.

Gnashing his teeth, Jon let out a grunt and threw all of his weight against his stepfather; Reginald and Jon fell to the ground, grappling at each other. Jon's knife cut into Reginald again and again, but the man seemed immune to the pain.

Blood dripped down onto Jon's face when Reginald was finally able to pin him on his back. Jon bucked his hips but wasn't able to dislodge the heavy-set man who straddled him. After wresting his arm free from Reginald's good hand, he managed to push the man off his other arm to bring his knife up again.

Jon slashed at Reginald's neck, but the man grabbed his wrist, stopping it mid-arc. When Reginald squeezed, Jon felt small bones grind together, and he panted hard in pain and fear; he realized that the old soldier was far stronger than he was.

With an almost lazy movement of his hand, Reginald succeeded in turning the point of the blade towards the man beneath him and, without further struggle, buried it up to the hilt in Jon's chest.

Jon gasped and let out a soft moan.

Reginald glared down at him, breathing hard.

Jon thought it weird that he felt no pain, but the edges of his vision started to go a strange grey. Jon licked his lips and tasted blood, coughing weakly.

"No!" came a strangled cry from above.

Jon lifted his eyes, confused. It sounded like Baltsaros. If the priests were right, he would be seeing the captain again soon on the other side.

A moment later a hooked sword appeared to one side of Reginald's neck, and Jon watched in a haze as another blade passed cleanly through the stem of the ex-soldier's thick neck. Hot blood gushed over him like a red wave, and he turned his head away. Jon could only see a narrow tunnel when he opened his eyes again, and he imagined that he saw the face of Baltsaros above him, brown eyes wide with worry.

Jon smiled.

I'll see you soon, my love. His eyes slipped closed in the dark…

…and then Jon knew nothing else.

3 2

ENTR'ACTE

"Come!" yelled Tom. "Come back! You're out of the woods, love. Just sail to me..."

H is cheek was warm, and the light beyond his eyelids made the world bright red for a moment before he opened his eyes.

He looked up and blinked.

Above his head were the familiar sails of colourful silk draped over the high, carved posts of Baltsaros's bed. When he turned his head slowly, he saw that the curtain was pulled back from the open window, and the bright sun shone down on him; he could smell the orange trees and the sea air.

Shifting his shoulders slightly, he let out a groan; his chest was a tight, burning mass of pain. At the sound of his voice, he heard someone move beside him, and he turned his head the other way. Baltsaros was lying on his side, eyes closed in sleep.

Jon gasped and reached out a tentative hand, afraid to believe in what he saw. However, when the tips of his fingers made contact with the older man's brow, his heart leapt in his chest.

Baltsaros's eyes slowly opened, and Jon's vision swam with sudden tears.

Alive!

He watched Baltsaros's gracefully curved lips stretch into a relieved smile.

"Hello, my love," said the captain, his voice hushed.

Jon tried to move closer to Baltsaros, and he gasped again in pain.

Baltsaros quickly sat up and pressed down gently on Jon's shoulder.

"Don't move... You're badly hurt."

With a confused frown, Jon stared up at Baltsaros.

"Reginald?" he asked, startled by how hoarse he sounded. Images of the fight came flooding back to him. Hesitantly, he touched his chest, and his fingers encountered a thick bandage; he remembered how sickeningly easy the blade had slid into him.

"You're lucky to be alive," murmured Baltsaros, taking Jon's hand into his own and pressing his fingertips to his lips.

"How are *you* alive?" rasped Jon.

Baltsaros's brows came down in a startled frown.

"Me? Why wouldn't I be?" he asked, smiling.

Jon's eyes slid down Baltsaros's body, seeing for the first time all the bandages and bruises that covered the captain's tanned skin.

"I saw you get cut—" Jon started to cough, every spasm a fist of pain pummelling him hard.

Baltsaros quickly slid a hand beneath Jon's head and held a cup of water to his lips when the coughing subsided.

Jon drank the cool liquid down thankfully, washing away the slight taste of blood in his mouth.

Baltsaros lowered him back down on the pillow, and Jon realized he was famished. As if reacting to his thoughts, Jon's stomach growled loudly, and Baltsaros chuckled.

"Hungry?" he asked.

Jon nodded.

"I'm not surprised. We've been feeding you only broth while you were out. I think you might soon be ready for something a little more substantial," said Baltsaros, his face creased in a grin.

Jon closed his eyes and swallowed. He felt so groggy.

"How long was I sleeping?" he asked, looking up at the captain.

"Twelve long days," said Baltsaros, his eyes large and serious. "I thought I was going to lose you." Baltsaros's voice was rough with emotion as he looked down at Jon.

Twelve days? Jon felt himself tremble, and his breath hitched in his chest.

"Reginald managed to miss your heart and only just nicked your left lung. I had to keep you sedated so you wouldn't cough and open the bleeding wound in your lung further. Then a fever settled in on the fourth day, but amazingly you started recovering. There were a few times when I thought you were awake; however, you were ranting and raving about Tom, and hearts, and how we had to go to the Devil's Isles. You didn't even know I was holding you," said Baltsaros, his hand stroking Jon's hair softly back.

As he blinked sleepily, Jon turned his head and captured Baltsaros's hand, pressing it against his cheek.

"I love you," he said softly and promptly fell back to sleep.

Baltsaros watched Jon's eyes flutter closed and smiled. He felt more confident about the young man's recovery. Baltsaros decided then not to tell Jon exactly how close it had been.

When he placed his palm on Jon's forehead to check his temperature, Baltsaros was brought back to the first time he had touched the young man; it felt like a lifetime ago.

Jon frowned in his sleep and his mouth twitched.

Baltsaros pulled his hand back quickly; Jon was cool, and sleep was what he needed the most. He stretched out on his stomach beside Jon and laid his head down on his folded arms to keep vigil while the young man healed.

The sword sliced into his thigh, but Baltsaros knew instinctively that the cut was not deep. He simply spun in place, neatly shearing off the sailor's arm. It had been a long time since he had taken part in combat, and Baltsaros's muscles sang with pain and fatigue. However, he kept on, knowing that Jon would be safe in the castle as long as their line of defence held.

Grunting as he pulled the long blade out of one man's chest, he dipped low and slid his short sword through the back of another's ankle, crippling him. Baltsaros breathed heavily, the world narrowing down to the reach of his swords. Slash, duck, spin, stab; it was a graceful, deadly dance. Again a sword bit into him; this time it was his bicep. Shrugging off the pain, Baltsaros turned again.

Slash, duck, spin, stab.

More men came at him. Baltsaros fought for freedom, but it was more than that... He fought for friendship. He fought for love.

Jon...

The hilts of his swords became slippery and then sticky with the blood of his dance partners. As he turned and swept low with the long sword, Baltsaros pivoted on the ball of his foot, felling the men who came at him until finally... He stood alone.

Panting in the gloom of the open town square, Baltsaros wiped the sweat from his eyes; in a daze he stared at all the bodies around him. Blinking slowly, he raised his head and looked around, realizing there was a voice calling to him.

Jon?

However, the dark-haired man running towards him from the direction of the beach was Malik.

"Captain!" yelled the shipwright. "All three ships are being crippled as we speak, but someone spotted a boat docked far to the east. There's a path beaten through the brush... Nathaniel thinks there may be trouble at the castle—" Malik hadn't finished speaking before Baltsaros turned on his heel and ran full tilt up the cobbled road.

Jon.

On the way up to the castle, Baltsaros caught up to Calum leading a small group of ship hands in the same direction.

"Defences breached?" asked Baltsaros breathlessly as he slowed his pace.

"Aye, Cap'n. Queenie sent a runner down," said Calum, his voice low. The old man's left eye was swollen shut, and he walked with a slight limp, but he radiated a powerful ferocity. Beneath the lined skin and grey hair, Baltsaros saw once again the intense young man that had taken him under his wing on the *God's Hammer*.

The captain ground his teeth and nodded sharply, momentarily rendered speechless with worry.

Calum frowned and reached out to Baltsaros, his gnarled fingers digging into the captain's shoulder.

"Jon?" he asked, his face hard.

Baltsaros nodded again once.

"Well, Cap'n, let's go give 'em hell," growled Calum and took off again at a steady jog.

The captain pushed back on the fear tightening his chest and took off after the old man.

"The rest of it happened pretty quickly," said Baltsaros, watching Jon take another huge bite of the freshly baked bread. "Apart from the men in the room we found you in, there was a scattering of other sailors. However, Abetha, clever woman, had managed to poison over half of them by sending her servants to sprinkle dried moonberries in all the water jugs. Crude but effective. I have a feeling that Reginald's fleet may have been running out of fresh water by the time they reached us, given how quickly his sailors drank everything in sight," he said, chuckling.

"Calum and his men dispatched everyone quickly. I had no idea where you were; in our haste we passed right by the sitting room where Reginald was holding you. I backtracked when I heard Katherine's sword fall but was beset by a few of Reginald's men. I... thought the worst when I saw Reginald stab you. I was sure you were dead." Baltsaros rubbed his jaw, remembering for a moment the anguish that had coursed through him. "I cut off the head of that human wastrel, and... Then you moved."

Jon's fingers slid over Baltsaros's forearm, stroking the skin while he listened, as if unable to break contact even for a moment.

"The rest of the navy men?" Jon asked, chewing.

Baltsaros smiled.

"What rest? With their ships crippled and set ablaze, drifting out to sea... I don't think there are any more to speak of." The captain's face got serious. "We lost nearly a third of our number. The funerals are still going on. It's going to take a while to rebuild."

Jon nodded, his face sombre.

Katherine was recovering slowly, but it would be a long time before she would be able to fight again. Maya was fine, her broken nose mending nicely.

As a man who was not given to religious flights of fancy, Baltsaros was trying not to attribute their incredible victory to anything other than pure luck. However, he was having a hard time of it. He slid his arm under Jon's fingers to grasp his hand firmly. It truly felt like something had been looking down on them with favour.

Jon smiled softly and squeezed Baltsaros back. The younger man was pale and weak as he sat back against the pillows, devouring a meal of bread and thick soup, but he was gaining strength daily.

Feeling his heart swell in his chest, Baltsaros looked fiercely at Jon, and the dark-haired man frowned at him.

"What is it?" asked Jon, his voice alarmed.

Baltsaros licked his lips and swallowed.

"I'm just so very glad you're alive, Jon. So very glad," he said softly. "You are my everything."

J on walked slowly down the wide cobbled street. While his deep wound had healed well, he was taking his time as he was still prone to dizzy spells. Baltsaros assured him it was from having spent so much time in bed and not from anything permanent; Jon hoped the captain was right.

As he looked out at the harbour through the gaps in the tall palms by the side of the thoroughfare, Jon could make out the mizzenmast of the galleon sticking up from the water just past the mouth of the lagoon. While the frigates had burned a long time, drifting out into deeper waters, the bigger ship had succumbed quickly and went down within sight. Since it wasn't actually in the way, Baltsaros had decided to leave the mast where it was to serve as a warning to other ships that might come their way.

After all, Reginald had died without disclosing whether he had told anyone else of the island's existence or coordinates.

Jon pulled open the door of the *Grog Blossom* and winced as the motion stretched the scar tissue that graced his chest. Baltsaros had said that would pass too.

As he stepped into the large room, Jon smiled to see Baltsaros leaning over a large map, arguing good-naturedly with Nathaniel and Malik over the modifications that were taking place on the ship.

"It'll be harder to make her come about with all that extra width!" said the captain, lifting the mug of beer to his lips to take a deep swallow. "I like my ship sleek. You're making her into a fat sow!"

Malik laughed and shook his head.

"What? You prefer we get stuck in the ice? Your fat sow will be able to navigate the growlers and bergy bits!" he said, grinning at Baltsaros. "I'm sure of it." Malik spotted Jon approaching and smiled wide.

Baltsaros lifted his brow curiously at the shipwright and turned to look over his shoulder. The absolute pleasure that came over the captain's starkly defined face at seeing Jon made him feel weak. Quickly coming to Jon's side when Baltsaros saw him falter, the captain helped him down into a chair.

"Jon? Are you all right? What's the matter? You suddenly looked like you were going to fall," said Baltsaros, his eyes darting over Jon's face and chest.

Chuckling, Jon just wrapped his fingers around the back of Baltsaros's neck and pulled him close, capturing the captain's lips with his own.

"When you look at me like that..." he said softly after a moment, his blue eyes wide. "It feels like I'm home."

The captain's pupils dilated, and his eyes got dark with emotion.

Jon felt a pang of desire; the last month had brought a tenderness to their lovemaking that wasn't solely based on having to be careful of Jon's injuries. Jon craved Baltsaros's hands on his body day and night.

Baltsaros, sensing the shift in Jon's mood, opened his mouth over the younger man's again.

"Gods, you two are bound and determined to make me ill," drawled Katherine as she kicked Jon's chair in passing.

The captain frowned, lifting his head, and Jon had to laugh.

It was as if the battle had smoothed away all icy formalities between the crew and their captain. The mood was now, more often than not, warmly amicable, the men and women less afraid of lightly teasing the captain.

Jon smiled ruefully. Baltsaros seemed the better for it; it was nice to see him taken off the pedestal from time to time.

Katherine deposited one of the mugs in her hand on the table beside Jon before she sat down in another chair, crossing an ankle over her knee. She still held her amputated arm awkwardly against her chest as if afraid to bump it, but the coordination of her left hand had greatly improved.

"I can't believe you guys are actually going to go through with it. You're out of your heads... You all have a bloody death wish," she said, shaking her head. Katherine wouldn't be coming with them. Not only was her wound still on the mend, but Katherine had claimed that a quieter life helping to rebuild Madierus was more to her tastes.

However, Jon knew from Maya that the ex-pirate often woke up screaming in the middle of the night; the fight had been cut out of Katherine.

"Death wish! Please. We're only just going to attempt navigating through a narrow, dangerous pass in the Devil's Isles to reach goddess-knows-what on the other side!" said Nathaniel, smiling wide as his hazel eyes twinkled in merriment.

"If that's not a death wish, I don't know what is," replied Katherine, holding up her mug in salute.

Baltsaros had stood to turn back to the map and was flipping through the sheaf of papers that was stacked on it. The captain and Malik had collaborated to create detailed drawings of all the modifications that needed to take place for the dangerous journey.

"I'm still not convinced about this..." Baltsaros continued where the conversation had left off.

Katherine narrowed her eyes at Jon.

"What happens if Tom says no?" she asked quietly.

Jon took a swallow of beer before replying. Without Katherine as first mate, and the only other feasible candidates killed during the fighting, Baltsaros had astounded him by saying they would sail north to the *Jewel* to start their hunt for Tom as soon as Jon was able to travel. For such a dangerous voyage to the unknown, rationalized the captain, no one else would do.

Jon shrugged slightly, the motion causing him some pain.

"Tom won't say no," he said simply.

He can't, Jon wanted to say. *There is something incredibly important that isn't finished between us.*

However, he kept his words to himself. Katherine already thought him crazy for his affections towards the cheerful brute; he didn't want to make it worse by telling her that Tom was now calling to him nightly in his dreams. When he had confessed as much to Baltsaros, the man had just nodded, his expression guarded. It remained to be seen what would happen to their relationship when they found Tom.

Jon drained his beer and turned his thoughts away from his worries. Grinning, he held out his mug to Katherine.

"Barkeep, I believe I'll have another."

THREE-SIDED TAPESTRY

If you are not too long, I will wait here for you all my life.

— OSCAR WILDE

They left at the end of the month.

The hardest part for Jon was saying goodbye to Katherine and Maya; he would miss them terribly, and there was no way to know whether he would ever make it back to Madierus given the danger of the trip they were undertaking.

Katherine reiterated again and again that it was a fool's errand to attempt the journey past the Devil's Isles, but both Jon and Baltsaros were resolute.

The goodbyes were heartfelt and tearful; Jon wouldn't soon forget the friendships he had made.

In the end, he decided to leave Brutus behind with Eloise; the huge dog had become the lonely little girl's best friend, and Jon wouldn't think of separating them.

Abetha was gracious and reserved at their parting, but when the ship made its way out of the harbour, Jon looked back and saw that the queen was flying a banner of Baltsaros's modified family crest above the castle.

That first evening out, Cook made an astonishing discovery: in the big storage area below the galley were three huge casks of Maya's excellent wheat beer. While the crew drank and celebrated the start of the journey, Baltsaros kissed away Jon's tears before coaxing soft moans and sighs out of him in the dark of the quarterdeck above.

T he first stop on their long journey was to the neighbouring island to resupply and take on some new deckhands. They were short on so many posts, but there would be plenty of opportunity to learn duties and become a cohesive crew during the six-week-long trip to find Tom.

Baltsaros had sent word ahead so that little time would be wasted since they had such a narrow window of opportunity. If the weather held up, Baltsaros and Jon would have less than a week to search for Tom; any longer and they would miss their chance at making the crossing between the high spikes of the Devil's Isles while the water remained largely unfrozen.

If they were unable to locate the estranged mainlander, the crew would take a vote to see if they were willing to chance it without Tom's expertise or wait another season. After all, they might have found a worthy replacement among the new crew by that time, as unlikely as that was.

As if something wished to hasten their journey north, the wind blew steady and strong, and the trip was uneventful. Jon made some new friends aboard, but mainly kept to himself, the worry of finding Tom making him tense and quiet.

What if he was wrong?

. . .

J on stood up on the crates lashed to the mainmast, watching the peninsula come into sight nearly a week early. The sun was just over the yardarm, and the blue sky was dotted with clouds like fat, fluffy sheep. However, though it was warm, it lacked the open-mouth kiss of the southern islands' humidity.

His knuckles white as he held onto the rope above his head, Jon rubbed the healed scar on his chest and frowned. The letter that Tom wrote was months old now; there was no guarantee that the man was here.

But, where else could he be? Where else can we start? he thought.

This was a busy port town, making it unlikely that Tom was still here; he could have taken a ship to anywhere in the known world from this harbour. Tom was an expert sailor and power-fully built; finding employment aboard another vessel would be terribly easy for the burly, surefooted mainlander.

As he leaned against the mast, Jon tried not to let his thoughts spiral out of control again. The question that sat heavy in his heart had made his doubt an almost crippling thing:

Why hadn't Tom come to their aid?

Why had he simply warned them? There were so many reasons Jon could think of and most of them were negative. Every time he let his mind wander down that path, Jon found himself feeling raw and frantic by the end of the day; only Baltsaros's strong arms and mobile mouth were able to soothe the unease that trembled through him then.

Jon jumped down from the crate and ran to help turn the capstan so they could anchor outside of the harbour. The mood aboard *Baal's Heart* was one of nearly giddy excitement; while the goal of the trip north, before turning south again, was to find Tom, the captain had promised the crew a little fun.

However, since the sailors earned no wages, sharing equally in plunder instead, some of the newer ship hands were looking a little forlornly at the beautiful building at the edge of the harbour; *Baal's Heart* had yet to pillage another ship or take part in smuggling this season, so there was no plunder to be shared.

Jon grinned a little crookedly as he walked to his quarters, thinking about splitting up some of his own money to cover the cost of some drinks for them at the very least.

Jon opened the door to the stateroom and smiled at the sun streaming in from the stained-glass windows behind the captain. The five panels that showed the silhouette of a roaring lion in red standing above a mound of ivory skulls was somewhat morbid, but it was based on Jon's dreams, so he loved it. It made Jon feel like the ship contained a small part of his soul... like he truly belonged there.

Jon saw that Baltsaros had dressed in a dark-red shirt and his black leather pants. The older man stood straight, buttoning a charcoal grey vest over his shirt as he watched Jon cross the room.

Jon gazed in awe at his tall, handsome lover.

The captain had a way of making the act of dressing as sensual as the reverse; his agile fingers slipped the glass buttons through the slits in his vest in a way that made Jon feel like he was watching something terribly intimate. Walking up to Baltsaros, Jon pulled one of his hands away from their work and kissed the deeply lined palm.

Baltsaros reached up and caressed the side of Jon's face.

"Ready?" asked the captain, his expression unreadable. They were taking the first of the jolly boats across the harbour to start asking about Tom, and Jon had the impression that though Baltsaros was his usual stoic self, he was feeling nervous.

Jon swallowed hard and nodded.

The captain lowered his hand and started towards the door.

"Don't worry. We'll find him."

Awkwardly standing beside Baltsaros as he angrily questioned the figure wearing the long silks, Jon looked around.

The *Jewel* looked the same as it had so many months before, but this time he was seeing it with more experienced eyes. Not able to understand the language the captain was speaking nor the strange body language of the draped figure, Jon's talent was proving to be useless in this endeavour; he couldn't tell if there was information being kept from them.

However, as his eyes scanned the tiered tables, his gaze came to rest on a familiar figure: the brunette that had entertained him and Baltsaros the last time they were here.

She caught his eye and smiled; Jon blushed slightly and smiled back, thinking she remembered him.

A moment later, however, the pretty girl's eyes widened and she looked quickly away; Jon had the distinct feeling that she had just made some sort of connection and was nervous about it. When he recalled that she had previously seen Tom and him together as they were leaving, Jon felt the thrill of hope. Slipping away from the captain's side, Jon navigated the staggered platforms, making his way quickly towards the girl.

Looking at him in surprise when he deliberately placed a coin on the table in front of her, the girl's eyes darted to a door to one side of the bar before meeting his gaze again with a bland, lustful look on her face.

"Hello, pretty man," she said in her accented voice, leaning forward to run a finger down his chest. "I make you feel some love?"

Jon leaned forward and stared into her dark-blue eyes.

The girl looked down shyly, pulling her hand away from his chest to finger the watered silk at her cleavage.

"Where is he?" asked Jon softly.

The girl's full lips, dark like blood in her dusky face, pressed against each other as she swallowed. When she turned back to him, there was a worried look in her eyes.

Jon shook his head and pressed on.

"It's ok. I'm not going to tell anyone you told me. You know where Tom is, don't you?" he asked gently. "I need to find him."

The girl's gaze went pointedly to the door again and back to Jon.

He nodded and placed another gold coin on top of the first before walking swiftly to the door. No one was watching him as he opened it a crack and peered inside. On the other side was a long, dark corridor.

With a glance back at the captain who was still speaking with the host or hostess, Jon slipped through the door and walked quietly down the hallway. There were doors to the left and right, but when Jon tried the handles they were all locked. His heart high in his throat, he continued along the passageway, fearing that someone would come upon him trespassing.

I'll just say I got lost, thought Jon, trying yet another handle.

This one turned easily in his hand, and he started to open it, sunlight streaming into the dark hallway from beyond. However, Jon froze when he heard the familiar cadence of a mainlander accent coming from the other side. Though Jon couldn't hear what he was saying, the laugh that burst out of the man a moment later was unmistakably Tom's.

All thoughts of caution evaporated as Jon pushed the door open the rest of the way. He realized he was standing at the rear of the building in some kind of loading dock; stacked around him were rough-hewn, open crates of bottles and other supplies intended for the bar.

As he squinted against the light of the midday sun, Jon could see a group of men talking and laughing as they unloaded a cart full of fresh produce. Jon heard Tom's chuckle again, and his eyes snapped towards the man in the centre.

He felt a little faint.

The broad, muscular shoulders that tapered down to a narrow waist were heartbreakingly familiar. However, where before there had only been scars on the large expanse of tanned skin, now were intricate, black lines that curved and meandered down the left side of the burly man's torso, disappearing beneath the waistband of a pair of dark-green pants that were rolled up at the calf.

Jon took a step forward. He could see more tattoos peeking above the low-riding waistband on the right side too, curling around the defined lines of the man's hip. The matching scrolling, black designs on either side were exactly where Jon would put his hands if he were to—he swallowed.

As Jon watched, the massively built man shook his head and smacked the shoulder of the worker next to him with a large, scarred hand. Rooted to the spot and speechless, Jon felt his heart thrumming hard against his ribs. One of the workers, a case of wine high up on his shoulder, scowled at Jon and growled at him in passing.

"Ye could a' least help instead o' standin' there like a bloody post, son," he said, his voice rough.

The tattooed man's back went rigid, and he turned around slowly. The black lines that graced the man's back also curled around the left side of his chest, and Jon could see he had a metal ring through that nipple. The sight was alarming and terribly beguiling.

The thing that made Jon finally speak was the intense cascade of emotion that widened the man's beautiful sea-green eyes: shock, relief, and breathless elation.

"Tom," said Jon, his unsteady voice rendering that simple syllable into a near-croak. He took a step forward.

Tom's mouth was half-open as he stared across the space at Jon. A mere second later it was as if a metal door had closed in Tom's eyes, shearing off the emotions that had set them alight.

Jon heard the captain's soft step behind him.

"Well, well. What the fuck do we have here?" asked Tom, his face going taut with resentment.

"Hello, Tom," said the captain quietly, placing a hand on Jon's shoulder.

The muscles bulged in Tom's jaw, and he shot an accusing look at the dark-haired youth. When Jon shook his head gently, Tom's composure thawed slightly.

"What do ye want?" Tom asked, his eyebrows tilting up as he looked at them with suspicion on his rugged face.

"Just to talk," said Baltsaros. Though his voice was smooth and unhindered by the emotions running through Jon, the younger man thought he could feel a slight tremor in the captain's hand.

Tom stared at them for an uncomfortably long time, his face wavering between indignation and despair.

Finally, he nodded.

Tom turned to the men who were watching the strange spectacle and gave orders to square up with someone at the bar before motioning with his chin for Jon and Baltsaros to follow him.

Wordlessly, they went back down the corridor and up a set of spiralling stairs that Jon had missed. When they reached a flat panel in the wall, Tom looked back at Jon; he could have sworn he saw the tiniest hint of guarded emotion in Tom's otherwise grim face. The reason why was clear when they pushed through the hidden door to emerge into the same room where Tom had found Jon that fateful morning; the day Tom had been lost.

Jon's breath sounded loud to him as he stood, uncomfortable, watching the captain and his ex–first mate size each other up.

Tom began pacing back and forth across the thick red carpet, glancing up at Baltsaros with every pass, and Jon frowned.

The captain stood straight and tall, not a hint of emotion in his hooded eyes. Then, as if some decision had been reached in his mind, Baltsaros extended his arms to either side.

Tom stopped his pacing and let out a sharp bark of a laugh, shaking his head.

"Ye think it's that easy, *Captain?*" he spat, his hands balled at his sides.

Baltsaros made no move as he stared hard at Tom with his arms out.

The muscular young man looked down, bringing a hand up to rub the side of his thumb against the coarse, dark-blond stubble of his cheek. Tom laughed harshly again; however, when he looked back up, Jon was astounded to see that his blue-green eyes were wet and wide with anguish.

"Ye *promised*, Da," Tom said hoarsely. "And still ye whipped me like a bloody fuckin' cur." Unable to stand still, Tom renewed his pacing; it was a frantic motion, like an animal trapped in a cage.

There was a lump in Jon's throat, and he shifted on his feet, feeling like he was an interloper.

Baltsaros just nodded slowly and beckoned with his hands.

With a hitch in his breath, Tom surprised Jon by suddenly stepping forward into Baltsaros's embrace, trembling visibly.

Jon stared on in misery, unable to look away.

As he wrapped his strong arms around Tom, Baltsaros leaned down and murmured something in the big man's ear, words that were not meant for anyone else to hear.

Tom nodded and whispered something back.

His face burning, Jon stared down at his feet. This was not how he had imagined their reunion would be; no, this was suddenly a horrible, gut-twisting mistake. Why in the blasted hells had he thought himself capable of... of... this. He ground his teeth and blinked hard to clear his eyes of the tears that were threatening to fall.

There was no competing with the relationship between Baltsaros and Tom.

Completely overwhelmed and forgotten, Jon was debating whether he should leave when he heard Baltsaros's voice.

"Jon?" said the captain softly. Jon looked up and saw that Baltsaros was staring at him over Tom's shoulder, his brown eyes warm and kind. "Come."

It wasn't a command. It was an invitation.

Jon saw that the tension that had held Tom so rigid had melted away; he literally sagged against the captain.

"Come," repeated Baltsaros, his face gentle.

With a deep breath, Jon walked a few steps forward.

Baltsaros held out his hand and took Jon's in his own, pulling him the rest of the way. He felt breathless and nervous, utterly confused by the situation... And then Baltsaros placed Jon's palm flat against Tom's back. He felt Tom stiffen with a gasp under his hand, the hard muscles sliding under his touch.

Baltsaros stroked the back of Tom's neck with his long fingers, watching Jon with what his innate talent read as gratitude. The captain slid Jon's hand up Tom's warm side, and he felt the big man exhale with a small vibration against Jon's palm. Strong, unexpected desire began burning its way through his misgivings, and he brought his other hand up to grasp Tom's waist; this time the soft moan that came from Tom was audible.

Under Baltsaros's curious and inviting gaze, Jon traced the edges of Tom's tattoos with his fingertips, his heart beating swiftly in his chest as he watched his touch raise goosebumps on the bigger man's skin. Then, Jon leaned forward and did the unthinkable; he pressed his lips against Tom's broad shoulder, opening his mouth to touch his tongue to the man's salty skin.

The big man smelled of sunshine, whiskey, and tobacco, a familiar scent that made Jon warm with longing.

Tom's breath hissed out of him, and Jon looked up to see that Baltsaros had sunk his teeth hard into the other side of big man's neck. With a groan, Jon pressed his chest against Tom's broad back and slid his hands down over the other man's hips to press Tom back against him, kissing the hard muscles of his shoulder. Tom moved his pelvis to grind against Jon, and he nearly cried out at the hard surge of lust that shook him.

Breathless, Jon knew he had to step back, had to let go. His heart was careening in his chest, and he was growing uncomfortably hard in the front of his pants.

Tom turned at Jon's sudden departure, and he registered confusion and dismay on the handsome brute's rugged face.

"I... don't know what I'm doing," was all that Jon could say. His chest was tight, and he felt lightheaded; Jon wanted this more than anything in the world, but he couldn't wrap his head around it. It was too staggering.

Baltsaros pulled away from Tom and stepped back, a thoughtful expression on his face. He then turned and took the few steps to the bed, climbing up and leaning back against the pillows, his hands folded in his lap with his legs stretched out, ankles crossed. With a small smile, he pointed at Jon.

"Tomcat," he said. "Help Jon out of his clothing."

Jon's heart hit a new peak rate as he watched Tom turn around and look at him intently.

He was absolutely gorgeous, and terribly intimidating; the tattoos on his bronze skin outlined and enhanced Tom's musculature, making him seem even more brawny than he was, while his green-blue eyes recalled the warm waters of the tropics. Though Tom was staring at him with open desire, there was also the hint of how completely astounded and still somewhat skeptical of the situation he was.

Jon wanted to recapture those stolen moments during the storm, but with the captain present, how were they supposed to...

"Tom?" repeated Baltsaros from the bed.

Tom stepped forward as if pushed, and he grinned despite the tension in the room. Ducking his head, he reached for the front of Jon's grey shirt and undid the laces holding the neck closed. When he saw the terrible scar on Jon's chest, Tom's eyes flicked up to his in concern; Jon just shook his head and smiled grimly.

Later.

Tom's brows came down, and he suddenly leaned forward to capture Jon's mouth with his own, urgent and protective. The bigger man's hands came around him as he savaged Jon's lips and yanked his shirt free of his pants; Tom released him only long enough to pull it over his head before pressing himself hard against Jon again.

Jon was flooded with relief.

He had not been wrong about Tom's feelings for him.

He opened his eyes and saw that Baltsaros was staring intently at them, unmoving. What was the captain feeling about all of this?

Tom's hands had snaked down to the front of Jon's pants, and all thought left his head as he felt the buttons come loose. After a moment, Tom dropped to his knees in front of Jon; he then gently, almost reverently, peeled Jon's pants down, looking up at him with naked hunger as he did so.

"Good boy," said Baltsaros. The captain's eyes were dark and unreadable, but the hand curled over the front of his pants betrayed the desire he was feeling.

Jon's breath heaved in his chest, and he stepped out of his boots as Tom tugged at them. He was now stark naked in front of Tom who remained on his knees, gazing up at him. Jon could see the bigger man's pulse jumping in the veins at his neck, but he frowned in confusion when Tom made no other move. He realized with a start that Tom was waiting for Baltsaros's next command.

Jon reached out and touched the top of Tom's head, running his fingers softly through the short, sandy-blond strands.

"Do you want him to suck your cock?" asked Baltsaros, almost conversationally.

The question made Jon feel like he had just stepped off a cliff. He gulped and closed his eyes, nodding quickly.

"Tom, please use that talented mouth on Jon. However, let's not let him peak too soon, shall we?" said Baltsaros.

Despite the light tone Baltsaros was using, Jon could hear that the captain was breathing heavily, and it sharpened his arousal.

When Tom's hot mouth slid over the sensitive head of his cock, Jon let out a full-throated moan. He was so turned on that he didn't think he would last very long. His cock slid slowly down the back of Tom's tongue, impossibly far, the muscles of the kneeling man's throat enveloping him as his lips tightened to reverse the thrust.

With a gasp, he pushed on the back of Tom's head, wanting to feel the long, smooth plunge again once more before he had to pull away, lest he climax.

When he heard the creak of the bed, he opened his eyes and saw that Baltsaros was coming towards him. There was a familiar smell in the air, and when the captain pressed his mouth to his, Jon breathed in a lungful of the drug *char*.

Tom had stopped moving, realizing how far Jon had already come in his pleasure.

As the drug started swirling through his veins, Baltsaros nodded, and Tom resumed gorging himself on Jon's cock.

Baltsaros and Tom. Tom and Baltsaros.

They worked effortlessly as a team, even in this. The drug would work to offset Jon's climax while enhancing his pleasure; this time, however, Jon didn't feel as dazed as the first time, and he was glad for it.

Experimentally, he pushed on the back of Tom's head when his cock was in the bigger man's throat and held him there. Tom obediently stayed put, unable to breathe and shuddering slightly as Jon rocked his hips minutely to feel the head of his cock sliding down the back of the bigger man's throat. He threw his head back and Baltsaros put his arms around him, pinching his nipples and slowly kissing the side of his neck.

When Jon finally released Tom, the other man collapsed back on the carpet, coughing and wiping his mouth; however, there was a smile on the big man's face, and his eyes were wide with desire as he came back up onto his knees.

"You weren't kidding," Jon said to Baltsaros, amazed at Tom's eagerness.

The captain chuckled and slid his hands down to Jon's stiff, wet cock to stroke him.

"I don't 'kid' about much, my love," said the captain in his ear. "You know what I would really like to see? I want to watch you fuck him."

Jon closed his eyes and gave himself over to Baltsaros's hands for a moment. Tom had come forward again and licked softly at the cock in Baltsaros's grasp.

"You're really ok with this?" Jon asked softly.

"Yes," said Baltsaros.

Jon thought he could hear some hesitation in the captain's response, but it didn't worry him. The realization that this was not about competing with Tom and Baltsaros's relationship was beginning to hit him.

Something to think about later, he thought.

For the moment, Baltsaros's last suggestion was ricocheting through his mind. As if reading his thoughts, the captain released Jon and went to Tom.

"Up," he said, and Tom lurched to his feet. Baltsaros's hands stroked down the sculpted muscles of Tom's chest, lingering at the small silver ring in his nipple. The captain's brows went up as he tugged at it lightly, obviously pleased with the addition. Sliding his fingers over Tom's taut stomach, he eased his fingers under the waistband of the first mate's green pants and tugged forward. Baltsaros kissed Tom roughly as he undid the front of his pants and pushed them down when they were loose enough.

Jon watched as Baltsaros grabbed Tom hard by the throat and pushed his gracefully curved lips against the big man's jaw, just beside his ear.

"On your stomach on the bed," hissed Baltsaros loud enough that Jon could hear. Tom's cock bobbed in response to the words; its thick length was already a hard curve pointing up toward his stomach.

Jon watched in fascination as the muscular young man obediently lay down on his chest on the bed and closed his eyes. Baltsaros knelt beside him and slid two pillows under Tom's hips and then spat into his hand. Roughly pushing Tom's legs apart, he smeared the saliva over his puckered opening; Jon watched in a hot daze as Baltsaros slid two fingers inside Tom, readying him, and he realized he was breathing hard from the sight.

When Jon finally, impatiently, took his place between Tom's legs, he felt like a wanton beast. His hands closed exactly over the tattoos that curled over Tom's hips, like they were guides. He groaned and slid his whole length smoothly in one motion inside Tom.

Under him, Tom moaned and shuddered, pushing back on Jon.

Unlike the last time he shared a lover with Baltsaros, this body was the right one beneath him.

When he turned to look at the captain, Jon saw that the man's eyes were half-lidded with lust, his top lip curled on one side in a wicked sneer of desire as he stroked himself while watching Jon and Tom. Bolstered by the captain's reaction, Jon started thrusting hard into Tom, his breath heaving and groaning out of him from the glorious sensation of the man's slick muscles enveloping and sliding over his cock.

Tom met every plunge with a low moan, one hand frantically twisting the coverlet in his fist while the other worked his own hard shaft beneath him. The sound of Jon's pelvis slamming hard against Tom's muscular ass competed with the bestial sounds coming from the two men's throats.

Wanting to see Tom's face as he fucked him, Jon tugged at his thigh; the perfectly submissive brute below him obliged immediately when the man fucking him simply murmured: "On your back."

Tom looked up at Jon, his eyes narrow and forehead creasing in a look of almost agonized desire with every thrust, his lips parted to moan out his passion.

"Fuck… Jon, oh gods," Tom repeated over and over, his fist moving fast over his cock as Jon pounded into him.

Suddenly the mattress sank on either side of Jon's knees, and he felt the captain grab his hips and slow him. With a grunt of surprise, Jon stopped moving and gasped with shock as he felt the captain's fingers, slick with oil, slide into him. Almost dizzy with lust, Jon realized what Baltsaros aimed to do.

As he stroked deep inside him, the captain pressed and rubbed against the spot within him that triggered the waves of intensity that sent shocks through his body, enhancing all his sensations. Whimpering when Baltsaros's fingers left him, Jon moved forward when the captain brought Tom's legs up, almost losing his balance.

Low down over Tom's chest, Jon saw that the muscular rogue was smiling up at him.

"Breathe, Jon," said Tom, and Jon almost burst out laughing.

However, when Baltsaros's thick cock pushed slow and hard into his body, Jon captured Tom's mouth with his own, forcing himself to relax into the sensation of being stretched wide. He groaned loud, and Tom twisted his fingers into Jon's dark curls, kissing him with frantic, rough passion.

Baltsaros began fucking Jon with long strokes that drove him hard into Tom's body. It was perfect and exquisite, this feeling of fucking and being fucked.

Soon Jon was crying out loud with every thrust, the tempo becoming brutal and fast until it finally sent him toppling over into the throes of his ecstasy, a long low moan of pure pleasure bursting out of his open throat as he rode the staggering peaks of his orgasm, cumming hard and thick into Tom. With the last pulse, Jon pushed himself up onto his hands, elbows locked and head bowed as he panted hard over Tom.

He saw that the man beneath him was flushed, nearing his own culmination.

Baltsaros pulled out of Jon with a groan and crawled to Tom, his dark hand pumping the thick cock in its grasp, the purple head of it swelling with every hard stroke.

In a daze, Jon watched as a clear drop fell from its tip onto Tom's collarbone a second before the captain growled low in his chest, sending jets of pearly white cum over Tom's chest and stomach. Jon felt Tom's ass clench over his cock, and the man beneath him arched his back up suddenly, letting out a hard yell and sending hot jets of his own seed to mingle with Baltsaros's.

Jon collapsed onto Tom, heedless of the mess, completely spent. His thighs were shaking and his heart felt like it was going to crash through his ribs.

After a moment, Tom wrapped his arms around Jon, turning them onto their sides facing each other, and Baltsaros stretched out behind Jon.

. . .

The older man brought up a hand to start stroking Jon's side, gliding his fingers up over the hard muscles of Tom's arm and back down again to Jon's hip. Now that their passions were slaked, the room felt cool, and Jon was glad for Tom's constant heat. He nuzzled up under the big man's jaw.

I missed you, he wanted to say, among other things, but he didn't want to push his luck with the captain here.

Sex was one thing, emotions were another, and Jon was curious to see how things would settle in the end. He couldn't tell if it was the effects of the drug or the mind-blowing sex, but he thought he could sense strands pulling the three of them together. It was as if their talents, strengths, desires, and weaknesses were woven into a three-sided tapestry.

His fingers traced the rounded muscles that covered Tom's sides, and thought of the analogy. Meanwhile, Baltsaros's hand had slowed its motion and finally stopped, twitching once.

Tom lifted his head to look over at the captain and then put his finger to his lips, grinning: Baltsaros had fallen asleep.

After pulling away from Jon and sliding off the bed, Tom twitched the side of the duvet up and over the captain before walking to the closet to take out another thick, white blanket and a towel. Draping the blanket around his shoulders and wiping his chest with the towel before throwing it on the floor, he cocked his head at Jon and motioned with his chin for the dark-haired man to follow him.

Intrigued, Jon gently pried himself out of Baltsaros's grasp and padded after the big man to the far side of the room where there was a low, wide couch.

Tom turned around and sat down, the blanket spread out behind him and up over his arms.

When Jon saw that Tom meant for him to sit next to him, he stifled a laugh. It seemed silly at first, but when he sat down tight against Tom's side, the bigger man lowered his arms, wrapping them in the soft blanket, making Jon feel wonderfully safe. He leaned comfortably back on Tom's broad shoulder and saw that the man was looking at him with affectionate blue-green eyes; he felt warm, happy, and protected.

Tom leaned in to kiss Jon, deep and gentle and tasting like the ghost of tears shed.

"I've been wantin' to do that for a long time, lad," he said gruffly when he broke away.

Jon nodded. There were so many things he wanted to say but couldn't think of a single thing to start with.

The silence was finally broken when Tom started laughing to himself.

"Talk, my ass," he said, chuckling.

Jon looked up, confused, but Tom shook his head in amusement.

"When I asked Da what ye wanted. He said 'just to talk' didn't he?" asked Tom, grinning. "Aye... Fuck talk, I guess."

Jon shrugged with a small sigh. He desperately wanted to know what Baltsaros had said to Tom, but he knew it wasn't his place to ask; but, whatever it was, it had made things better between the two men.

Tom made a low, pleased sound in his chest and tightened his arms around Jon before leaning down to kiss him again. This time when Tom pulled away, Jon was smiling wide. The big man was so warm and effortlessly cheerful; it was soothing, reassuring, and incredibly addictive.

While they sat huddled in their comfortable embrace wrapped in the warm blanket, Jon then told Tom everything that had happened since they had parted ways.

Tom stared at Jon as he spoke, shaking his head at the news of Katherine's arm and the death of the others. When it came to his mother, Tom pressed his lips together and looked dismayed, though he honestly looked happy to hear of Eloise and Brutus.

Jon assured him that things would be different with Abetha

should he decide to go "home", and Tom's eyes darted to his at the use of the word, but he didn't say anything.

When Jon told Tom about the final fight with Reginald and how he had nearly died, he saw Tom's eyes go glassy with tears. Tom pulled back the blanket and leaned forward to kiss the tight scar on Jon's chest.

After a moment, the big man settled back to tell his own tale.

Tom had latched onto a floating barrel after having fallen off (*Of course I fell, don't be daft, boy. Who would'a pushed me?*) and was carried back towards the peninsula where he was picked up by a fishing boat by pure luck. (*You should stop calling me 'lad' and 'boy', Tom. As it turns out I'm over a year older than you, said Jon. Tom laughed. All right, old man, he replied with a kiss. Now, hush... I'm telling my story.*)

It was about six weeks later that Reginald and the fleet arrived. Tom had done everything in his power to dissuade them, including telling Reginald that the whole crew had died in the storm, but the crazed ex-soldier wasn't satisfied with Tom's answers.

Instead, he had put poor Fresia in irons and tortured her for a day and a half before she caved. She had since recovered but had chosen to leave town with a wealthy man who offered to put her up in a house of her own, and Tom didn't blame her.

Tom had sent the letter as soon as he could, hoping that it would reach Jon in time. (*Why didn't you come? asked Jon with a frown. How? With my own boat? Ye think I got rich floatin' in the ocean? Listen, love... I would have come. I would have. I prayed for ye every night, replied Tom.*)

When Jon saw the pain in Tom's eyes, he believed his words. Tom had also wanted to distance himself from Jon and the captain so as to remove temptation that would earn him some more stripes. (*Are you still afraid of the whip, Tom? asked Jon. Aye, love. Now and always, answered the big man.*)

Tom had taken up work at the *Jewel* doing maintenance and repairs and had recently been promoted to warehouse manager, a position that Tom thought suited him well. (*Well... mostly liftin' boxes and yellin' at folks, answered Tom truthfully to Jon's question. Same as on board, really.*)

Tom had given strict instructions to everyone he knew not to let Baltsaros know of his whereabouts.

"Because I was so angry, lad. So bloody fuckin' angry," said Tom, his face deadly serious.

"Because you love him," said Jon to Tom, his words plain.

"Aye, I love the shite out of that asshole, ducky. He's strong, smart, and fucks like a bloody madman. What's not to love?" responded Tom with a rueful twist to his lips.

"The fact that he had no heart," said Jon, looking curiously at Tom. "That's what you said to me that last night. Before you disappeared."

The big man nodded slowly to himself. Tom then frowned and looked sidelong at Jon.

"He been good to you, love?" asked Tom. "Da seems... different."

Jon nodded.

"I think whatever it was that was broken inside him has finally started to mend," he said softly. It was a hope not yet made fact, but it was something he liked to think was truth.

"All's it took was thinkin' ye died?" said Tom, his eyes suddenly bland in an attempt to hide his jealousy.

"Thinking that *we* died, Tom. Don't be such a fucking martyr. Your 'death' was the catalyst," said Jon, smiling. "Let's stop talking about death... I liked the subject of love." He still felt loose limbed and sentimental from the combination of *char* and fucking.

Tom grinned wide.

"Aye... love," said Tom. "Ye know, the difference between ye both is ye do have a heart. Ye might make my cock hard, but ye soften this." Tom tapped two rough fingers against the spot over his heart.

Jon had to laugh.

"Gods, Tom... That was almost poetic," he said, stroking his hand down Tom's chest and tugging playfully at the big man's chest hair. "Listen... The captain can beat the fuck out of you, and when you're done, you can come to me, and I will kiss you better," said Jon.

Tom's lips parted in response, and he stared at Jon with eyes suddenly darkened by desire and turbulent emotion. Tom's arms tightened around Jon again, and when he licked his lips, his breathing had a shaky quality to it.

"Gods, love," was all the big man said, and Jon had to laugh.

"You'd like that?" he asked, realizing the strange mastery over the powerful creature that held him.

"Aye," responded Tom, his voice barely a whisper.

Jon's heart beat double. They kissed again, only coming up for air when Jon had to beg off to relieve his bladder. When he came back and Tom lifted his arm again, Jon frowned, noticing something he hadn't before.

He sat down on Tom's left and peered curiously at the black lines that curled and swooped along his thickly muscled side. Tom watched curiously as Jon traced his fingers along the path they took over the bigger man's ribs.

"Ye like it?" asked Tom. Jon's fingers tapped a spot right under Tom's pectoral. There... That looked like something he recognized.

"Jon?"

As he looked up into Tom's eyes, he smiled.

"Sorry... Yes, they are extremely fucking sexy if you must know," he said, scarcely believing the words coming out of his mouth. It was simply the truth; somehow the markings enhanced the muscular young man's beauty in a way that made Jon feel hot inside. "But… What do they mean? Do you know?" he asked.

Tom looked down at himself and shrugged.

"The lot of it could be pure fancy, love. But… the man who did it, he told me that this here"—Tom put his fingers over Jon's—"is a map of the Devil's Isles and beyond. Somethin' about lost knowledge."

Jon's breath caught in his throat and he looked at Tom, alarmed.

"Gods, Tom. Now you won't believe me when I tell you what we're planning," he said in a hush.

Tom was quiet for a long time after Jon told him of their plans and of the captain's intention to ask him to be first mate again.

Jon rested against Tom's wide shoulder, waiting for the big man to say something. When Tom finally spoke, it was a rumble against Jon's ear.

"If ye don't mind, love, I'd like a day to think about it before I give ye my answer. Can ye grant me that, lad?" asked Tom, his rough hand coming up to rest against Jon's bare chest.

Jon nodded his head and closed his eyes.

"You're going to wear a groove in the boards and make Calum throw you overboard if you don't stop your pacing, Jon," said Baltsaros, looking down at Jon.

Jon laughed, but he felt completely frantic with worry. Tom had said that he would come give them their answer early this morning, but it was now noon, and there was no sign of him.

"It's not like we have to leave immediately, Jon," said the captain. "If Tom's not ready today, maybe he'll be ready tomorrow. He can be extremely proud, like his mother. I did him wrong, Jon… And an afternoon spent playing on bedsheets won't make it all better. We can afford to wait a day or two."

Jon nodded. He hoped it was the case. He'd already made two trips back to the mainland to see if he could find Tom on his own, with no avail. They could also put off the trip for this season if Tom was unwilling to join them. Jon was sure he could convince—

"Bloody fuckin' hells, Da! What in gods have ye done to my fuckin' boat?"

Jon started and looked over his shoulder.

The ocean-eyed, burly youth swung himself up over the edge of the raised gunwale like nothing was amiss and landed on silent feet on the deck next to Jon. After dropping his bag with a thump and ruffling Jon's hair affectionately as he passed by him, Tom swaggered to the stairs of the quarterdeck and looked up, feet splayed and hands on his hips.

The captain, his relief and amusement obvious for a mere second, brought his stark brows down in a fierce scowl.

"*Your* boat?" the captain repeated loudly. "She'll be yours over my dead body." Baltsaros allowed himself a small smile, and Tom grinned wide. "Whip these boys into shape, if you remember how," said Baltsaros as he lifted his head to look over the gathering crowd.

"First mate on deck!" shouted the captain.

Some of the old-timers reached out to pat Tom's shoulder as he made his way down the deck while the newer shipmates just peered curiously at the tattooed sailor that was built like an ox. However, when Tom started bellowing, everyone jumped quickly to obey.

"All right ye lot o' bleedin' twats, move yer asses. Shore up that fuckin' clutter and tighten those lines, ye bilge rat. Aye! I'll drown ye meself if ye don't heed, boy..."

Jon grinned, listening to the first mate yell out orders in his nonstop, rolling mainland accent that was thickly peppered with cursing and laughter.

He looked out over the calm water and took a deep breath. Jon knew there would be trying times in the coming months, both from inside the ship and from without, but at this precise moment in time, he felt he could face anything.

Jon picked up the bag that Tom had dumped unceremoniously beside him and trotted to the captain's quarters to throw it inside. With a glance up at the tall, dark man above him on the quarter-deck, Jon smiled.

There was nowhere he would rather be.

END OF BOOK I

EPILOGUE

While it was bitterly cold outside, the two men in the stateroom glistened with sweat. Tom, his arms bound behind him and his ankles tied to the legs of the table, grunted and hissed as another stream of hot wax landed on his bare skin. Jon groaned in response; he loved the way Tom's muscles tightened over his cock with the sudden pain. He thrust himself into Tom's body a few times, his hands sliding over the tattooed skin of the bound man's side.

The candlelight made Tom's skin pure gold, and Jon thought it was beautiful.

The door banged open behind them, and Jon turned his head. The captain stepped in amidst a swirl of snowflakes and quickly shut the door against the wind.

His cheeks were red with the cold, and the collar of his greatcoat was pulled high over his ears. He yanked his gloves off, sighing happily from the heat in the room, and nodded at Jon to continue.

Jon turned back to Tom and spilled some more burning wax on him, moving within his body. With the captain's eyes on him, Jon felt his pleasure mount quickly, and soon he was pounding into Tom, a harsh growl bursting out of his chest as he pulled his cock out to rain his seed down on the bound man's back.

Breath heaving fast in his chest, Jon began untwisting the hempen ropes that were binding Tom. He looked curiously at the captain. Baltsaros's face had darkened with lust at the display; he loved to watch the boys "play", as he put it. However, he made no move to join them as he usually did.

Tom straightened and flexed his wrists, his head cocked curiously at Baltsaros.

"What is it, Da?" he asked, still using the ridiculous title though the two were no longer related through marriage.

Baltsaros smiled wide.

"I thought you boys would like to know that we've arrived within sight of the Devil's Isles," he said.

Jon and Tom looked at each other in excitement. It had taken nearly two months to reach them; finally it was the time to see what it was they were up against.

WANT TO KNOW MORE?

See maps, a pirate glossary, diagrams and details of *Baal's Heart* at
http://geni.us/baalsheart.

—Bey

CAGED AUDIOBOOK - NARRATED BY MICHAEL FERRAIUOLO

Caged is available in audiobook format (*whispersync* ready). Relive the adventures of Jon, Tom, and Baltsaros, now exquisitely narrated by the very talented Michael Ferraiuolo.

Find it here: http://geni.us/pageCaged

BOOKS BY BEY DECKARD

For an up-to-date list of titles, visit:

https://beydeckard.com/blog/buy-my-books/

Max, the Series

Max

Max, the Sequel

Baal's Heart Series

Caged: Love and Treachery on the High Seas

Sacrificed: Heart Beyond the Spires

Fated: Blood and Redemption

Careened: Winter Solstice in Madierus

F.I.S.T.S

Sarge

Murphy

F.I.S.T.S. Handbook For Individual Survival in Hostile Environments

The Actor's Circle

The Complications of T

The Last Nights of The Frangipani Hotel

The Stonewatchers

Kestrel's Talon

Standalone Books

Better the Devil You Know

Exposed

Beauty and His Beast

The Blacksmith's Apprentice

Uncle Zach

Toxic AF

SHORT STORIES

Don't Touch Me (UnCommon Bodies Anthology)

Rakka Surprise (UnCommon Lands Anthology)

ABOUT THE AUTHOR

Artist, Writer, Dog Lover

Bey Deckard is the author of a number of novels including the *Baal's Heart books, Max, Beauty and His Beast,* and *Better the Devil You Know.*

Bey lives in Montréal, Canada where he spends most of his time writing, doing graphic work, painting portraits, speaking French, cooking tasty vegetarian eats, or watching more movies than is good for him. If you're the curious type, www.beydeckard.com is where you'll find art and free stories by Bey as well as information on his published works.

bey.deckard@gmail.com
Look for Deckard's Diablerie on Facebook

facebook.com/authorbeydeckard
x.com/BeyDeckard
instagram.com/beydeckard
goodreads.com/beydeckard
bookbub.com/authors/bey-deckard
pettingzoo.co/@Beybey

www.ingramcontent.com/pod-product-compliance
Lightning Source LLC
Chambersburg PA
CBHW021122260626
47169CB00005B/1409